NIGHT
IN
EDEN

NIGHT
IN
EDEN

Candice Proctor

IVY BOOKS • NEW YORK

For my sister Penny, with thanks

NIGHT
IN
EDEN

CHAPTER ONE

New South Wales, September 1808

Captain Hayden St. John stood beneath the over-hanging eaves of the ugly Parramatta prison block and watched the matron and a male guard drag the woman toward him through the teeming rain.

The howling spring storm was quickly churning the unpaved prison yard into a treacherous expanse of slick yellow mud. Rain pounded on the shingled roof behind him and slapped into the waterlogged ground, filling the air with the fetid smell of sodden earth and decay.

Mud caked the convict woman's ragged red cloak and ugly, old-fashioned dress of cheap brown stuff clear up to her knees. Her head was bowed, her dark hair hanging in stringy clumps over a pale, hollow-cheeked face. She looked like something picked up out of the gutter—which was undoubtedly where she'd come from.

Suddenly she bucked and pulled back against the grip of her keepers and screamed at the matron, "Let me go, you filthy, lice-ridden, drunken old hag!"

Hayden leaned his shoulders against the crumbling brick wall and pulled a cheroot from his waistcoat pocket. For such a skinny thing, the woman was putting up quite a fight. Somehow she'd managed to wrench her wrist away from the matron's hold and use her free hand to claw at the arm of the guard. The man howled in surprise and pain, and let her go.

She whirled and took off at a run toward the open gates.

Hayden rested the cigar against his lower lip and made a soft sound deep in his chest that was somewhere between an exhalation of breath and a chuckle.

Matron Sarah Gooding had taken two steps after the girl, but at the sound of Hayden's low laugh she turned to glare at him. The driving rain dripped off her bulbous red nose and crooked mobcap. "I tell ye, that girl's crazy," she hollered, waving one of her ham-like arms through the air. "A body'd think no woman'd never buried a babe 'afore, the way she's carryin' on. Ye want her, Captain? Ye go get her."

The woman was halfway across the unpaved courtyard of the Factory by now. Hayden wondered where the hell she thought she was going. Even if she escaped the yard, she couldn't escape the colony. The entire colony was a prison.

Officially the Parramatta Female Factory was both the colony's workhouse and the assignment point for all the women transported from Britain to New South Wales. But for the men who came here to select a woman, it functioned more like a cross between a whorehouse and a slave market.

Except that these women were free for the taking.

A gust of wind tugged at Hayden's open greatcoat and tried to snatch the broad-brimmed hat from his dark head. He pushed away from the wall, his unlit cheroot clamped between his teeth, his long-legged stride carrying him easily through the ankle-deep muck of the yard.

The woman had almost reached the gate when her ill-shod feet shot out from under her. She went down hard, landing with her arms flung out beside her, her face in the mud. . . .

Bryony Wentworth lay stunned, sucking in air. When she struggled up onto all fours, her hands and knees sank deep into the cold, stinking mud. Rain ran into her eyes, and she swiped at her face with the back of one arm. Only one thought raced through her head—to get back to her baby. She tried to push herself up onto her feet, but her skirts must have caught on something because she couldn't seem to move.

She twisted around, pulling at her dress with one desperate, cold-chapped hand. Then she froze. Someone had planted his black boot on the bedraggled hem between her legs.

They were tall black boots, she noticed, polished to a high sheen beneath the splattered mud. A gentleman's boots. At their heels jangled silver spurs of a type typically worn by officers of a hussar unit.

Above the gleaming black Hessians stretched heavily muscled thighs encased in buff buckskin riding breeches. Bryony had to twist her head around farther to see more. A gentleman's greatcoat hung open, revealing a frightfully large and most ungentlemanly knife strapped to a lean hip. She swallowed hard, her gaze traveling slowly upward, past a silk waistcoat to enormously broad shoulders and a linen shirt worn open at the neck with a knotted handkerchief in place of a more formal cravat.

The man was so tall she was getting a crick in her neck, just trying to look up at him. Above the white collar of his fine shirt, his throat was tanned to a tawny gold that gave him a savage look. His hair was dark, too, and he wore it long, so long it curled over his collar at the back. He had a face that seemed to be all harsh planes and sharp angles. It was a hard face, with a hint of cruelty about the uncompromising line of the mouth.

But it was his eyes that scared her the most. They were as bleak and cold as a winter sky. She thought he must be the coldest, meanest man she'd ever seen.

Then he smiled, and she was sure of it.

"Going someplace?" he asked, his lips curling back around the unlit cigar he held clamped between his teeth.

Bryony drew a shuddering breath. Her gaze fell to the muck beneath her. The rain pummeled her bare head and back. She bit her lower lip, tasting rain, salty tears, and acrid mud.

She heard a tinderbox strike and twisted around to find the man calmly lighting his cigar—no mean feat in this weather. His lean cheeks hollowed as he sucked in the smoke. He wasn't even looking at her.

He tucked the flint box back into his pocket, puffed on his cigar for a moment, then said, "My name is Hayden St. John, and you have just been assigned to me as my servant. I'm going to take my boot off your skirt now." He exhaled a stream of blue smoke. "Be wise and don't try to run away."

Bryony gathered her strength. His boot heel was still in the air when she bolted.

She barely made it up on her feet before his hand snaked out to wrap around her arm just above the elbow and yank her back so hard she slammed against him. She gasped with pain as her breasts, swollen and hard with milk for a baby that would never suckle again, crushed against his chest.

He brought his face to within a handsbreadth of hers, his mean eyes capturing her frightened ones and holding them for the length of five unsteady, pounding heartbeats. The rain poured down on them. "You listen to me, and you better listen carefully, because I don't like to repeat myself," the man said, his teeth still clutching the cigar. "You belong to me now. And if you ever try to run away from me again, I'll have you flogged. Is that understood?"

Fear, anger, hatred, and a bitter sense of defeat all burned within her, but Bryony was no fool and twelve months of prison had taught her a lot about swallowing pride and hiding hate. She clenched her jaw and nodded.

His dark brows drew together. His lean, strong fingers tightened around her arm until she could feel them digging into the thin flesh. "You'll say *yes, sir* when you answer me."

Bryony was a tall woman. So tall she was accustomed to looking most men in the eye—if she didn't look down on them. She didn't look down on this man. The top of her head barely cleared his shoulder. She had to tilt her head back to look up into his dark, forbidding face. She swallowed hard, hating him, hating herself.

"Yes . . . sir."

His cold, penetrating stare held hers a moment longer, as if he could see the hate and defiance she felt burning in her chest reflected in her eyes, as if he were challenging her to give tongue to it. But fear—or perhaps it was just common sense—clogged her throat and kept her silent.

She saw something flare in the icy blue depths of his eyes. Then he turned back toward the huddle of prison buildings, his iron fist gripping her arm mercilessly as he dragged her behind him.

Matron Gooding sat on a section of a log upended in the mud outside the open door of a small, crude hut and dabbed in an ineffectual way with a dirty cloth at the bloody, nail-raked arm of the guard.

Bryony hated that guard. He was a wasted wreck of a man with narrow, stooped shoulders and a face so dirty not even the rain had managed to wash it clean. But more than the way he looked, it was the gleam she saw in his eyes when they rested on her that made Bryony's skin crawl. She'd seen that gleam before. She knew what it meant.

The tall man with the black boots came to a sudden halt that had Bryony's feet sliding in the mud. She grabbed hold of his hard arm with her free hand to keep from falling again. But she dropped it quickly, as if she'd suddenly discovered herself grasping a deadly snake.

The guard looked up and saw her. "You!" he screamed, spittle spraying over his unkempt, faded-yellow whiskers. "You goddamn filthy whore. Look what she done to me." He held out his bleeding arm. "I want 'er taken before the magistrates. I want 'er flogged. Let's see 'ow full o' fight she is after a cat-o'-nine-tails 'as decorated her back."

The guard made a grab for her. Bryony instinctively shrank back, but before the guard could reach her, Hayden St. John's hand closed over the man's wrist in a grip that made him wince.

"Eow!" he hollered, cringing beneath that ruthless hold. "What the 'ell did ye do that fer?"

"This woman is mine now." Slowly St. John opened his fingers to release the man's filthy wrist. "And I'm not taking her out of here damaged."

Matron Gooding chuckled in a way that sent her grossly distended belly bouncing up and down beneath her dirty apron. "Aye. Not much good to ye, is she, Captain, if she cain't even lay flat on 'er back under ye. Ha! Ha!"

Bryony's stomach turned over as fear and horror slammed into her. She cast a quick glance up at the harsh, uncompromising profile of the man beside her, then glanced away again, because looking at him somehow made it all seem more real.

But it is real, Bryony, she told herself unmercifully.

She'd known this moment was coming for months, ever since she'd first learned what being transported to Botany Bay meant for the women convicts who were sent here. Even before the ship sailed from England, Bryony had heard the stories. About how the men took the female prisoners as their concubines. They said that in the old days, they used to line the women up on deck as soon as the ships anchored in the cove. The officers were allowed on board first to make their selection. Then the common soldiers. Then the rest.

Nowadays the women were usually sent to the Factory first. But that was about all that had changed. She'd heard some of the men kept the same women for years—even had children by them. But most traded their women around. Or sold them, for rum.

She'd known it all for months. But knowing didn't seem to have prepared her for the reality when she came smack up against it. Panic still coiled around her, squeezing her like a live thing. Her mind still screamed, *This can't be happening.* The same way it had screamed when they'd first thrown her into that dark, crowded, stinking prison cell in Penzance. The way it had screamed the day the jailer put his beefy hands on her breasts.

Bryony heard the matron laugh again, smelled her fetid breath and the stink of stale rum and rotten teeth. It mingled with the other odors of the prison—the stench of damp and decay, of urine and unwashed bodies and fear.

Bryony thought she might be sick.

She saw Hayden St. John's lip curl, although whether it was in disgust or disdain, Bryony couldn't be sure. "If she has anything worth taking away with her, get it," he told the matron. "And you," he added, his gaze shifting to the guard, "Fetch my horse. And bring me a length of rope while you're at it."

Bryony pressed her back against the dirty whitewashed wall of the hut and watched Hayden St. John relight his cigar. He exhaled a long stream of smoke into the cold air and looked her over appraisingly. She tilted her head back against the wall and closed her eyes.

The sound of mud squishing beneath hooves brought her head around. The guard was back, leading a big, raw-boned gray gelding. Hayden St. John took the gelding's reins and was tightening the saddle cinch when the matron reappeared, carrying Bryony's small bundle of rags. He tied it loosely behind the saddle, then reached for the length of rope and turned to Bryony.

"Hold out your hands."

She stared at the rope and swallowed hard. "Please. I won't try to run again. I . . . I was only trying to get back to Philip's grave. You see, they . . . they didn't give me time to say good-bye."

His eyes narrowed. "Philip was your baby?"

"Yes."

He stared at her for a long moment, then fastened the rope to his saddle. "All right." His long, callused fingers cupped her chin, none-too-gently, and he forced her to look up at him. "But just remember, I'm faster and stronger and a hell of a lot meaner than you are. Don't try anything."

She didn't say *yes, sir*, because she wasn't capable of saying anything at the moment. He didn't press the point. He held her gaze long enough to be certain she understood, then he released her and swung up into the saddle.

He was halfway across the yard before Bryony realized he expected her to follow him on foot. She had to hurry, slipping and sliding, to catch up with him before he turned out the gate.

The road outside the prison was no more than a muddy track ribbed with deep, water-filled ruts. It oozed downhill, running roughly parallel to the rain-swollen river, until river and road finally converged at a dockside inn a mile or so away.

The wind was stronger out here, away from the high walls of the prison. It flung the rain in her face and grabbed at her open cloak, billowing it out about her as she slogged through the mud.

Around her, low, slate-green hills thinly covered with strange, gaunt trees rolled away in every direction to be swallowed up by the gray clouds that hung heavily on the horizon. It was a vast, empty land—harsh and wild and unforgiving.

A row of bedraggled wattle and daub huts, inexpertly thatched, straggled away to the right. Near it, on the other side of the road, lay a crude burial ground. It was a wretched place, undignified by any markers and surrounded by a makeshift fence of brush and scrap timber. In another twenty years, most people would probably have forgotten it had ever existed. Only convicts were buried there, after all.

And their children.

Bryony stumbled to a halt, her eyes fixed on one tiny, newly filled grave.

Ahead of her, Hayden St. John reined in his horse and followed her gaze. "Is that where they buried your baby?"

She nodded.

He took one last pull on his cigar and dropped it into the mud of the road. "We have a few minutes . . . if you want to say good-bye."

Her head fell back, and she looked up at him through the driving rain. His eyes were a startling, brittle blue. She saw no mercy there, no compassion, and she found it difficult to believe she'd heard him right.

His gaze still locked with hers, he nodded.

She jerked away, walking stiffly toward the mound of ugly yellow mud they had piled on top of her Philip. He was down there in the cold and the dark. They hadn't even given him a decent coffin. Just wrapped him up in a strip of bark and laid him in that unloving cradle of earth and covered him up with dirt.

He was beyond her reach now. She would never hold him again. Never rest her cheek against his silky brown hair or breathe in the milky-sweet fragrance that was all his own. She would never see his quick, toothless grin, never hear the gurgle of his delighted laughter. Never watch him grow up to run and skip and holler. Never know the man he could have been.

She sank to her knees in the long, rank wet grass. She wanted to throw herself across the cold, bitter earth and shriek and howl and wail and let out some of the savage pain that was tearing her apart from the inside. But she was too afraid. Afraid that once the screams started, they'd never stop.

So she kept her spine rigidly erect, and clenched her fists at her sides to keep from shouting up into the gray, uncaring sky above her. *How much more? How much more must I suffer for what I've done? Hasn't it been enough? Must my children suffer, too? First Madeline, and now Philip. Why? Why did you have to kill my baby?*

Tears stung her eyes and burned the back of her nose and welled up to clog her throat. She closed them off, refusing to let them fall, because she knew that once they started, she wouldn't be able to stop them. And then everyone would see that somewhere, inside, where it mattered, she'd gone mad.

Behind her on his ugly gray horse was the man to whom she had been given. When he tired of waiting for her, she was going to have to get up and turn around and follow him. Not even the searing agony of Philip's death could numb her to what that meant. She was going to be expected to cook his meals and wash his clothes and clean his house and satisfy the urgings of his hard man's body. It was, after all, why women like her were sent out to this godforsaken corner of the world.

Bryony rose shakily to her feet. If she didn't leave soon, he might come and drag her away, and she didn't think she could bear that.

Walking away from Philip's grave was one of the hardest things she'd ever had to force herself to do. She had no idea where this man was taking her, or if she would ever be back here again. In time, the rain would flatten that sad mound and grass would cover the raw earth, and it would be as if Philip had never existed.

Bryony stopped and glanced wildly about, from the mist-shrouded hills, to the muddy, swollen river, to a nearby tree drooping gray in the downpour. In a cemetery without markers, how could she remember the location of one very small grave?

Her chest rose and fell with her labored breaths. She whirled and stared helplessly at Hayden St. John. He sat at his ease on his big horse, one hand resting on his hip. His hat brim was pulled low against the rain so that she couldn't see his eyes.

He sat there, unmoving, watching her. Then he swung out of the saddle and tied the big gray to the bottlebrush that grew beside the opening in the cemetery's fence. It was a crude fence, woven of brush and branches and odd bits of wood. There were even a few palings from someone's old picket fence stuck in there, and he pulled a couple of these out and brought them with him as he walked through the weeds and the mud toward her.

He didn't say anything, just slipped his hunting knife from its sheath at his hip and used the butt of it to drive the stakes deep into the earth, one at the head of the grave, the other at the foot.

She stood silent, watching him.

"Thank you," she whispered softly as he was putting his knife away.

But he didn't even look at her. He turned toward his horse. "Come on," he said, his voice hard and cold. "I want to make it back to Sydney before nightfall."

Then he pulled a linen handkerchief from his pocket and wiped the mud of her baby's grave from his hands.

CHAPTER
TWO

The inn at the base of the hill was a crude structure. Built of gray wood roughly hewn into long, vertical slabs, it was so low and squat it looked as if it were hunkered down in a forlorn attempt to endure the misery of the weather. Rain sloughed in steady sheets off the shingled roof of the wide veranda that completely surrounded it. The yard was a mudflat. Beyond it, at the base of a slight embankment, ran the Parramatta River. Bryony saw a wharf and a flat-bottomed boat bobbing up and down beside it in the rain-pocked, gray-brown waters.

Hayden St. John turned his horse into the muddy yard and reined in beside the veranda. "We've got about an hour before the boat heads downriver for Sydney," he said, tossing her small bundle at her the way one might flick a coin to a street urchin. "Come with me."

Bryony dragged herself up onto the stone-flagged veranda and followed him into a cold, dark hall. The floor inside was of the same rough stone as the veranda, the walls unplastered and blackened with wood smoke and grime. Warm, welcoming firelight flickered in the public room off to the left. She heard the sound of loud, male laughter and smelled the sweet, malty tang of ale wafting through the open door. But they didn't go in there.

Instead she followed St. John down a short, narrow hall, toward the private rooms at the rear. Rain dripped onto his collar from the dark wet curls at the base of his neck. She watched the tails of his greatcoat sway and slap against his thighs as he walked, and a sharp stab of fear sliced through her fatigue and twisted into her belly. The distant, muffled crying of a baby caused her to shudder. Her breath soughed in and out, and the scratchy wool ties of her cloak suddenly seemed too tight about her throat, as if they might strangle her. She tugged at them, trying to loosen them, but they were wet and knotted and her fingers were too stiff and unsteady.

He stopped before a crude plank door at the end of the hall and pushed it open. Rusty hinges creaked.

They entered a small room almost as dark as the passage, for the veranda outside the narrow, double-hung window blocked most of what little light there was on such a gloomy day. A fire had been kindled on the small stone hearth, but it burned sluggishly and hissed.

A great four-poster bed stood square in the middle of the room, virtually filling it. A straight-backed chair sat before the fire, and there was an old washstand with a plain white bowl and pitcher to one side of the bed. But what immediately drew and held Bryony's attention was the slight, sandy-haired young man she saw standing beside the window. He'd been peering out at the rain, but at their entrance he turned and gave her a friendly grin.

"Top o' the mornin' to you," he exclaimed in a lilting Irish accent so thick it took her a moment to decipher what he'd said.

He wore a blue, coarse wool waistcoat and coat with shapeless canvas trousers and a roughly woven shirt that marked him as an assigned servant. A convict. He was probably in his early twenties, although a light dusting of freckles across his upturned nose and the big ears that stuck out from his head gave him the look of an overgrown schoolboy.

But what made Bryony stare was the squirming bundle he held in his arms. A baby. *He's holding a baby,* she thought almost stupidly. Whatever she'd been expecting to happen in this room, it didn't involve a red-faced, squalling baby.

"I'm Gideon," said the young man. "Gideon Shanaghan, from County Kerry. And this here wee lad is young master Simon St. John." He held the crying baby up for her inspection.

Simon *St. John*?

"I . . . I'm Bryony Wentworth." She tried to return the Irishman's smile, but her face felt stiff, as if she'd forgotten how. "From Cornwall," she added. It seemed to be important here where people were from. When the *Indispensable* had dropped anchor in Sydney Cove, hundreds of small boats had descended upon them, with people hanging over the sides and shouting: "Anyone from Cork?" "Anyone from Chester?" "Anyone from Aberdeen?" Everyone was anxious for news from home. It was often the only way they heard about things. Things like parents or wives that had died. Or babies that had been born.

Her gaze dropped back to the baby. He was small and shriveled, with the pinched look of a child that wasn't thriving. In that sense he reminded her of Philip, although Philip had been dark, whereas this little boy was strikingly fair.

Like Madeline.

As always, the thought of the daughter she'd been forced to leave behind tore at something inside of her, something that bled and hurt. Oh God, how it hurt.

Hayden St. John shrugged out of his dripping greatcoat and tossed it over the rail at the foot of the bed. His gaze lingered on the baby in Gideon Shanaghan's arms, and the hard, cruel lines of his face softened. As she watched, he smiled tenderly at his small son in a way that tugged strangely at her heart.

"How is he, Gideon?" he asked quietly.

"He's that hungry." The Irishman grinned over at Bryony. "I hope you got supplies."

"Supplies?" Bryony clawed impatiently at the choking

ties of her cloak. There was a shredding sound as the worn material gave way completely, and the wet, hateful thing slipped from her shoulders and fell in a sodden heap on the floor.

St. John glanced from his baby to her, his face so hard and emotionless that she thought she must have imagined that earlier gentling. His narrowed blue eyes slowly traveled the length of her in a way that made her feel hot and uncomfortable. "God Almighty. You're a mess."

Bryony glanced down. Her dress was as wet as the cloak and caked with mud from the hem to the collar.

"The first thing you'll need to do is take that dress off," he said.

Her stomach rose and fell with a swift, sickening lurch, and her throat was so tight, her voice came out as a hoarse croak. "Wh-what?"

"You heard me. Get that dress off." He nodded toward the washstand by the bed. "There's water in the pitcher. You'll need to wash your hands and face, too, before you feed him. But be quick about it. He's hungry."

And then the meaning of the young Irishman's statement about "supplies" suddenly became clear to her. "You mean, you want me to be a *wet nurse* for your baby?"

Hayden St. John stood in the middle of the floor, his hips cocked forward, his legs braced wide in a stance she found decidedly threatening. Something flashed in his eyes. Something dangerous.

"That will be your main duty, yes."

Bryony felt her insides tightening up, tighter and tighter. She had expected to suffer rape at this man's hands; she still might, if the mother of that squalling baby didn't satisfy him enough in bed. But for some reason, the thought of having this man use her body to suckle his son seemed only marginally better than having him use her body to slacken his lust. It was still a violation, an abuse of something that for Bryony had always been private—tenderly intimate and very, very personal.

Her entire being rose in revolt. Her milk was *Philip's*, not his! This baby's mother, whether she was the man's wife or his concubine, could just keep feeding her child herself. She took a deep, hitching breath and said, "I won't do it."

She heard a kind of strangled exclamation from the Irishman, but she didn't have time to look at him. She was too busy looking at Hayden St. John.

And she thought that she indeed must have gone mad to have challenged the man in this way.

In the tense silence she heard a log on the hearth fall. A flame caught and burned brighter, throwing up a tongue of light that glazed the flaring bones of his cheeks. His eyes were slitted in a stare so cold and deadly she fancied it might pierce right through her. Without saying a word or even shifting his gaze, he jerked his head from Gideon to the door.

Gideon put the baby down in a nest of pillows on the bed and left the room, quietly shutting the door behind him. The silence stretched out between them, taut and deadly. Then he said, "I don't advise trying to challenge me. Take off your dress."

Fear clogged her throat, but she refused to back down. She knew he undoubtedly would triumph in the end. But pride—or maybe something as fundamental as her sense of self—demanded this show of resistance. She shook her head mutely.

He walked over to the washstand, picked up the pitcher, and poured some water into the bowl. He moved quietly, with a lean, lithe grace. She watched him warily.

"I'm telling you for the last time," he said calmly. "Take it off."

"I'm not going to feed that baby with my milk. I'm not a—a cow."

Without warning, he set down the pitcher and whirled around, closing the distance between them with two long strides. Before she realized what he was about, his hand closed over the collar of her dress and jerked it down.

She gasped and tried to turn away, but the dress was as old and worn as the cloak, and the bodice ripped easily, gaping open clear to her waist.

She wore only a thin shift beneath it. Her arms flew up in an instinctive movement to cover her breasts. But he wasn't through yet. His hand dropped to the waistband of her skirt. One more tug, and the dress shredded completely. He threw the ragged remnant away from him so hard, it landed with a thud against the far wall. She was left standing before him in nothing but her shift and petticoats.

His long, lean fingers gripped her bare shoulders, and he jerked her to him, so close she could see the creases in his tanned cheeks, so close she could smell his anger, feel his raw, masculine power. "When I tell you to do something, you do it. You have been assigned to me, woman. Do you understand what that means here? It means I can make you my cow, or my mistress, or even make you whore for me, if I want to. And if you think you can complain to the magistrates, just try it. They'll likely flog you for your impudence. Before they send you right back to me."

She stared up into his face. Something frightening whipped itself around her belly and squeezed tight.

"Have you ever seen a woman flogged?" he demanded harshly.

Bryony opened her lips, but no sound came out.

"Have you?"

She drew in a deep, hitching breath. "Y-Yes."

The captain of the *Indispensable* had had one of the women on the ship flogged for insolence, on what he delicately called her "bared breech." He'd made all the other convicts watch. Bryony would never forget it. The woman had been sentenced to fifteen lashes, but the woman fainted after the tenth. And all the while the metal-tipped rawhide thongs of the cat-o'-nine-tails were ripping apart her naked flesh she'd screamed, cries of agony mixed with

obscenities so vile the captain had ordered someone to stuff
a gag in her mouth.

They said it was a matter of pride among men to
take the lash without a sound, but after that experience
Bryony had decided that maybe if the men screamed
more, they'd be flogged less. The captain never ordered
a woman whipped again. Not even when one of them
said she bet he had a prick that would shame a scrawny
farmyard rooster. He'd just kept walking, pretending he
hadn't heard her. They said it was because the flogged
woman's screams had unnerved him. Or maybe it was
because the sight of the woman being stripped had made
the sailors so horny that some of them had broken into
the women's deck that night and had to be flogged themselves the next day.

They'd heard the cat often on the ship. Bryony had
come to fear it more than she did almost anything else.

"The lash is used a lot in this colony," he was saying.
He was so close, she felt the hot rush of his breath against
her cheek. "I can have you flogged for impertinence if
you simply use the wrong bloody tone of voice when you
talk to me. And if I ever, *ever* have reason to suspect that
you're neglecting my baby in any way, I will have it done,
and make no mistake about it. Do you understand?"

God, how she hated him. Her breath backed up thick
and hot in her throat. "Yes . . . sir."

Letting her go, he reached for the cloth from the washstand and held it out to her in one tanned fist. Her gaze
fell to that lean, strong hand because she didn't think
she could endure looking at the dark cruelty of his face
any more.

"Now, are you going to wash yourself? Or shall I do it
for you?"

She washed herself. She did it quickly, using a corner
of the cloth to scrub her face and shivering when she
splashed the cold water over her dirt-encrusted arms.

Hayden propped his shoulders against one of the massive bedposts and watched her as she bent over the bowl, her hips swaying back and forth with her movements.

Christ, she was thin. He could see the bones of her back and ribs sticking out through the cheap cloth of her shift. She had nice lines, though, he thought. A long back that tapered down to a tiny waist before swelling out into the angle of her hips. If she were better fed, he suspected she'd be strong and hale. She was a tall woman—much larger than Laura. Laura had been exquisitely petite and delicate, almost childlike, even when she was a woman grown. Laura had been the kind of woman that made a man ache to protect her and take care of her.

Bryony Wentworth was not that kind of woman. Her dark, mysterious eyes flashed pride and strength. She wasn't going to be an easy woman to master, but master her he was determined to do.

She straightened up, drying her face and arms with the other end of the cloth. Then she set the cloth beside the bowl and turned around. "If I have to feed him, I'd like some privacy," she said. Her head was held high, but she kept her eyes carefully downcast, hiding the hate he knew lurked there.

This woman is a survivor, he thought with reluctant admiration. She must have gone through the worst kind of hell in the last year or so. Yet not even all the horrors she'd suffered—and he knew they must have been considerable—had managed to break her.

In his experience there were three kinds of people in this world, and the wretched system that was the penal colony of New South Wales could be counted on to grind down and destroy two of them.

The ones who were weak, who gave up and let themselves be crushed, usually died quickly. And then there were their opposites, the rebels, the ones who felt compelled to butt their heads against authority. They were doomed, too. Penal colonies seemed to attract more than their fair share of sadists to positions of authority; they could always be counted on to flog and starve the rebels of this world until they either broke them, or killed them.

It was the ones in the middle, the ones like this woman here, the ones who could hold onto their pride and self-respect but had the sense to know when to hug it quietly to themselves; they were the ones who survived.

"Will you leave us, please?" she asked again.

Hayden shook his head. "No. I have no intention of leaving you alone with Simon yet."

He watched as a tide of hot color rushed up her neck to her cheeks. He couldn't tell if it was caused by anger or embarrassment, but he suspected it was a bit of both. Her chest heaved on a quickly indrawn breath, drawing his eyes to her breasts.

She might be skinny, but she had fine, ripe breasts. They were so full of milk they were leaking. He could see the dampness spreading across her shift. The thin, wet material clung to her, clearly revealing the dark shapes of her nipples.

Her gaze followed his downward. She brought her palms up to press them, flat, against her breasts, trying to stop the flow. The color in her cheeks deepened.

Standing tall and painfully self-possessed, she walked past him to lift the baby from the bed and take him to the chair before the fire. Hayden watched her carefully as she cradled Simon in the crook of her arm and untied the frayed ribbon that held her shift at the neck. She lifted her head, and her gaze captured his, never wavering as she peeled back the thin material of her shift to expose her breast.

The breast she revealed was so engorged with milk that he thought it must hurt. And he wondered at the kind of pride that would lead her to refuse to wet-nurse his son when her own body must have been aching for the kind of relief only a baby could bring it.

Simon smelled the milk on her and turned his head, rooting. But the breast was so full and hard he kept losing the nipple. He screwed up his little face and turned red, squalling more furiously than Hayden had ever heard him. It took several tries before she was able to guide the nipple with its streaming milk back into the baby's mouth and keep it there.

The crying ceased abruptly. In the sudden quiet Hayden could hear the plop-plop of rainwater dripping off the veranda roof outside the window, the slurping sound of his son nursing, and the crackling of the fire on the hearth. The woman was no longer looking at either him or Simon. She was staring into the fire, as if she wanted no part of either him or the baby she'd been forced to put to her breast.

Hayden stood there for a long time, watching his son guzzle greedily at the rich flow of life-giving milk. The skin of her breasts was fine, he noticed, almost translucent; he could clearly see the blue tracery of the veins that ran beneath where one of Simon's tiny hands rested against the pearly fullness beside his cheek.

Then he realized the convict woman was no longer looking into the fire. She was watching him eyeing her breast. His gaze rose to meet hers. He expected her to look away again, embarrassed by her nakedness, but she didn't.

"He seems very hungry," she said unexpectedly. "How long has it been since he's had anything to eat?"

Hayden straightened up. "Three days. Maybe four—since he had a woman's milk, that is. We tried giving him cow's milk and goat's milk, but he couldn't seem to keep it down."

She paused in the act of shifting the baby to her left breast, an inexplicable expression shadowing her pale face. "His mother's milk dried up?"

"His mother died in childbirth." Uncrossing his arms, he walked over to stand and gaze unseeingly out the window.

"Childbirth?" said the woman in a queer voice. "He's small, but he doesn't look newborn."

"He's not." Even to his own ears, Hayden's voice sounded dead, wooden. "He was born four months ago." He rested his hands on the windowsill and leaned into them, pressing down until the flesh showed white. "I had hired a woman from Green Hills. A settler's wife who had a young girl. But she's increasing again. It dried up her milk."

"Green Hills?" she repeated, questioning.

There was apprehension in her voice that Hayden put down to fear of the bush. Most women were afraid of the bush. "Green Hills is a settlement two or three days' drive north of here, on the Hawkesbury River." He turned around to rest his hips on the windowsill. "It's downriver from Jindabyne, my property. We'll be going back there as soon as I'm finished buying supplies in Sydney."

She didn't say anything, but swiveled her head to stare at the fire again. Then, with her face still turned away from him, she said quietly, "You should have told me his mother is dead. I never would have refused to feed him if I had known."

"Would it have made such a difference?" he demanded harshly.

"Of course." Her head swung back around, and he saw that her face was pale and tight with some emotion he couldn't name. "What do you think I am?"

Hayden rested his hands on the windowsill behind him, his legs stretched out in front, and studied her thoughtfully.

He wasn't sure what she was. She puzzled him. Her voice might hold a soft Cornish burr, but it was a refined voice and undeniably educated. There was a pride and quiet dignity there, too, beneath her stubborn, headstrong nature, that spoke of birth and breeding.

He wondered what she'd been transported for. She obviously hadn't started out in the gutter, even if she had ended up there. He felt an unexpected stirring within him, a stirring that was part interest, part admiration, and part something else.

And it occurred to him that it would probably have been better for both of them if she *had* been the simple twopenny trollop he'd first assumed her to be.

CHAPTER
THREE

The trip down the river to Sydney Town seemed as unending as the rain.

Slumped on a bench beneath the makeshift shelter at the rear of the boat, Bryony held Hayden St. John's baby in her cramped arms.

The rain fell in a continuous curtain, virtually obscuring the gray-green hills that rose up from either bank. Even the occasional stands of trees seemed but ghostly things. They appeared for a moment out of the mist to trail their silvery leaves over the water's edge, then vanish again into the gloom. The country around her seemed so wild, so alien. And as vast and empty as the soul within her.

She swallowed the knot in her throat and looked down at the sleeping infant. He was making sucking motions in his sleep, the way Philip used to do. It was a memory that brought with it an anguish so piercing she almost gasped.

This baby might fill her arms, but he could never fill her empty heart. And holding him was a constant, almost unbearable reminder of the other two babies she'd held. And had lost.

Her gaze lifted from the baby to his father, and the ache within her twisted itself into something sharper, something more frightening. He seemed unconcerned with the driving rain that beat down on his wide-brimmed hat and broad shoulders. He stood at the bow of the boat, his spurred boots spread wide, his arms folded across his chest in that aggressively masculine stance of his. As she watched, the sailor beside him said something, and a quick, wicked smile flashed across St. John's face. Then he tipped back his dark head and laughed. The deep, throaty sound of it reached her across the length of the boat.

She glanced quickly away, conscious of a tumult of feelings, deep down in her belly. God help her, she knew nothing about this man except that he was hard and mean and dangerous, and that he frightened her terribly. Yet she *belonged* to him.

I can make you my mistress. . . .

Bryony remembered the weight of his hands on her bare shoulders, and she felt her insides quiver. As if drawn by some kind of awful fascination, her gaze returned to settle on Hayden St. John.

He had the clothes and speech of a gentleman, but for all that, she decided, he was an adventurer. A man who acknowledged no laws but his own, who took what he wanted. A man as wild and untamed as this rugged land he had chosen to make his home.

" 'Tes hot, if'n you'd like some."

Bryony turned to find Gideon Shanaghan holding a steaming tin mug of tea out to her. "Oh, yes, thank you." She gratefully relinquished the sleeping baby's weight into his arms as he handed her the cup.

Gideon settled himself beside her. He held Simon with such easy confidence that she smiled and said, "Either you had a lot of younger brothers and sisters, or you've had babies of your own."

He grinned at her. "Sure, 'tes both. I was the oldest of seven, and Mary and me, we had ourselves two lusty boys . . ." His smile slipped slightly. "Before I went and got myself transported."

Bryony stared down into the murky depths of the tea. It looked like a vile brew, but at least it was hot. "I left a three-year-old girl in Cornwall."

She glanced up to meet his gentle gray eyes, and for a moment they shared the dark, unspeakable torment of each other's loss. Then he said quietly, "To be sure, her father'll be takin' good care of her."

Bryony shook her head. "My uncle has her. Her—her father's dead."

A familiar, aching weight of guilt pressed down upon her. Bryony had carried her guilt over Oliver's death with her, like a burden, for so long now. It had grown no lighter; she had simply learned to live with it. Yet, in a way, it seemed strange to be mentioning Oliver, here now. It was as if he'd been a part of someone else's life, someone who had died with him.

She looked over to where Hayden St. John still stood at the prow of the boat, the wind whipping his greatcoat about his thighs. He had one hand resting on his hip, his fingers curling around the hilt of that frightful knife. "Gideon?" she said, leaning forward. "Does he always wear that knife?"

Gideon turned toward his master. "Aye, most times. Unless he's wearing a pistol. Although I've known him to carry both."

"But . . . why?"

Gideon laughed. "And why do you think, then, livin' in a colony that's been mostly populated with nothin' but thieves and murderers? Just last week three bushrangers jumped him when he was riding 'tween Green Hills and Jindabyne. He killed two of them straight out, and the third didn't live long enough to hang."

"He shot them?"

"Lord, no. There weren't time for that."

She turned her face away from the sight of that hideous knife and the hard, unforgiving man who wore it. The thought of being touched by a man like that, of being forced to lie beneath him and take his body into hers, sent a chill through her that had nothing to do with the weather, and went far deeper than the marrow of her bones.

Her gaze dropped to the baby sleeping peacefully in

Gideon's arms, and she wondered how the other woman, the one who'd died giving his child life, had borne it. "Was Simon's mother his servant, too?" she asked in a queer voice. "An assigned convict?"

"Mrs. St. John? Lord, no. 'Tes a real lady, she was. A viscount's daughter." An odd, rapt expression crept into Gideon's face. "Sure, she was like an angel, she was that beautiful. The daintiest, sweetest thing a man ever did see. The Cap'n, he fair worshiped her—cherished her like, if you know what I mean?"

Bryony shook her head. She could imagine Hayden St. John ravishing a woman, but worshiping her? Cherishing her?

"He ain't been the same since she died," Gideon was saying. "Took it real hard, he did. Blames himself, I reckon, for bringing her out here. Heard him say once, he never shoulda done it. 'Tes no place for a lady, that's sure."

No place for a lady, Bryony thought. No, this wild, hard land was no place for a mere woman, either.

She didn't want to look at St. John again, but she couldn't seem to help it. He stood gazing out over the cloud-shrouded hills, his feet braced against the movement of the boat, his long, dark hair tousled by the wind. He looked as frightening and hard as the land he surveyed.

Yet he had taken to wife a lady, a viscount's daughter with a face like an angel and a temperament to match. She wondered what he would think of a woman like her—a felon. How would he treat her?

But she already knew the answer to that. In the space of a few hours, he'd stripped her half naked and threatened to have her flogged. Twice. Bryony drained the bitter dregs of her tea, and sighed.

"You look that tired, you do," said Gideon, stretching to his feet. "Why don't you try and get some sleep? I'll keep Simon here for a while."

She would have argued about it, but Gideon just laughed and told her not to be daft, and walked away, the baby still in his arms.

Bryony leaned back against a crate and gratefully let her eyes slide shut. She was so tired. She'd spent—how many days and nights? two? three?—fighting for Philip's life after the sickness took hold of him, clutching his wracked little body to her, too afraid to sleep even when he slept, lest she wake and find him dead.

But in the cold light of early morning, Philip had died anyway as she watched. One moment he'd been there, alive and breathing. The next moment he'd been gone, and she'd been left holding nothing but his empty body. All her care, all her watchfulness hadn't made any difference.

Bryony eased herself into the warm, sweetly scented bathwater, and sighed with rare contentment.

She had expected to be put in the servants' attics. Or to be forced to share her master's bedchamber, as well as his bed. Instead St. John had ordered a pallet put up for her in the private parlor of the Sydney inn, where he was staying.

In contrast to the crude, rustic inn where they'd rested beside the river in Parramatta, the Three Jolly Fishermen was a fine, two-story building of cut sandstone set high on the western rim of the cove. The private parlor was large and finely furnished, with a wide casement window overlooking the winding, rutted streets of the town and the choppy, mist-shrouded bay below.

Bryony's eyes drifted closed as the warm water enfolded her, soothing her soul as well as her body. It was the first bath she'd had in a year. She didn't count the time at Gravesend when they'd made them all strip and then dunked them before giving them the government-issued clothing, which was to last them on their voyage and beyond. That had been an exercise in humiliation rather than cleanliness. She tried to forget it . . . although she doubted she ever would.

When she opened her eyes, her gaze fell on Simon St. John, playing with his feet on the blanket she'd spread out on the floor beside her. He was already looking better, she decided, even after just a couple of feedings. That pinched, wizened look he'd worn when she'd first seen him was fading, and she realized he was actually quite a pretty baby, with big green eyes, pale blond hair, and delicate features. He looked nothing like Hayden St. John. She could only assume he took after his dead mother.

She must have been a beautiful woman, indeed.

As Bryony worked the landlady's gentle, rose-scented soap all over her, she remembered the rigid set of Hayden St. John's shoulders and the way his hands had gripped the windowsill when he told her of his wife's death. Had he loved his wife so much? Worshiped her, as Gideon said?

Bryony slipped farther beneath the water. What would it be like, she wondered wistfully, to be loved like that by a man? She thought of Oliver, and experienced a moment of such intense envy for Simon St. John's beautiful, well-cherished mother that it took her by surprise and she had to remind herself guiltily that the woman was dead. Sitting up, she dunked her head under the water and began to soap her hair, rinsing it over and over until it was squeaky clean.

The bath felt so wonderful, she had to force herself to get out. She dried off with one of the landlady's soft towels, then slipped on a worn but clean shift and petticoat. But she couldn't quite bring herself to put on her only remaining dress again. It was wet and stained from the ride down the river, and she felt too gloriously clean.

She settled on the rug beside the baby and pulled a broken comb through her tangled wet hair, letting the fire dry it. Simon abandoned his toes to stare in wide-eyed wonder at the slow, rhythmic motion of her hands, running the comb up and down.

"Getting sleepy, young man?" she said softly, smiling down at him.

Simon kicked his feet, chortled, and gave her a big, toothless grin.

The smile faded from her lips as she gazed down into his happy little face.

No, she told herself. *You are not going to care for this baby.* They'd torn out half of her heart when they'd taken Madeline from her, and she'd just buried what was left of it in a muddy grave in Botany Bay. She wasn't sure she could even go on living, let alone allow herself to love again. Especially not a baby. Especially not a baby that belonged to a man like Hayden St. John.

But she couldn't quite stop herself from reaching out and ruffling the golden curls that tumbled over his forehead.

Just once.

CHAPTER FOUR

It never occurred to Hayden to knock before entering his own private parlor. He simply pushed open the paneled door and walked in.

The convict woman was sitting in a chair beside the fire, one cheek resting against the chair's high back, her eyes closed. She was dressed in nothing but a thin shift and a tattered old petticoat. The shift was open at the front, revealing one white, rounded breast at which Simon suckled drowsily.

She definitely had nice breasts, Hayden thought, closing the door gently behind him. The kind of breasts a man liked to hold in his hands. Now that she was cleaned up, the rest of her wasn't bad to look at, either. She wasn't a classic beauty, like Laura. Her chin was too strong for a woman, and her nose tilted up a bit at the end, making her look somewhat like a willful child. But there was nothing childlike about her mouth; it was all woman, full and sensual.

His eyes settled on her hair, and he wondered how he ever could have thought her hair nondescript. It was the color of fine port wine, warmed by the fire. It curled around her head in reckless abandon, making her look as if she'd just gotten out of bed.

It was a thought that surprised him.

As if she sensed him watching her, her eyelids fluttered. They closed again for a moment, then flew open wide.

* * *

Bryony sat up with a start, staring at the man who stood just inside the parlor door, his hand still resting on the handle behind him.

The booted and spurred adventurer with the murderous knife slung at his hip had been transformed into a gentleman, dressed to go out for the evening. He wore an elegant, dark coat with a double-breasted front panel that curved toward the back. His waistcoat was of white silk, as were the stockings that showed beneath his formal breeches. He had an evening cape casually flung over one arm. From his hand dangled a *chapeau bras* and a pair of white gloves.

But for all his finery, there was still an aura of wildness about him, she noticed—an indefinable air of untamed danger that seemed at odd variance with the clothes he wore.

Painfully conscious of her naked breast, Bryony eased the sleepy baby off her nipple and pulled together her shift. She wished she'd had the sense to put her dirty old dress back on right after her bath.

She quickly tied the ribbon at the neck of her shift. When she looked up, she discovered his dark, somewhat disturbing gaze focused on her hair. His flaring brows were drawn harshly together, as if he didn't like what he saw.

Bryony's hair had been cropped short before she was put on the ship, but in the last six months it had grown to an awkward length. Now that it was clean, it curled wildly about her head in an untidy riot.

"What have you done to your hair?"

She blinked at him in surprise. "I—I washed it."

He walked over to the humidor that stood on a side table and extracted a cigar. Even in evening clothes, he had a lithe, coiled way of moving. "From now on," he said over his shoulder, "keep it pulled back. You look like a whore with it all over your face like that."

She felt her cheeks grow hot. "I don't have anything to hold it back with. Someone stole my caps on the ship."

He turned, the cheroot resting against his lower lip. "I was planning to have Gideon take you down into the town tomorrow to pick up some things for Simon. You can get yourself a new dress and cloak while you're there. And some caps."

"Yes . . . sir."

She rose to lay Simon in the cradle that stood near the fireplace, self-consciously aware of his disturbing eyes, watching her.

"We might not make it into town again for some months," he said, striking his tinderbox. "So be sure to buy whatever Simon is likely to need in the immediate future. I assume you know what will be necessary?"

She glanced up at him from where she bent over the cradle. He sat with his hip resting against the edge of the oak table near the window, carelessly swinging one silk-clad leg back and forth. His tinderbox flared. The flame cast harsh shadows across the sharp bones of his face. She thought of those wild, desolate hills, rolling endlessly into the distance, and swallowed hard. "Is your property so far?"

He shrugged and tipped back his dark head to exhale a long stream of blue smoke. "If the roads were decent, it could be done easily in a day. But the roads in New South Wales are never decent."

He flipped the ash from the tip of his cigar with one movement of his lean hands. He had nice hands, she thought; strong, yet well-formed, and tapered, like an artist's. Or a musician's. She wondered, idly, if he played an instrument.

He lifted the cigar to his lips again. "I hadn't meant to leave you alone with Simon yet, but I've received an invitation from Government House for tonight that can't be refused." He paused to inhale deeply, his gaze never leaving her. "I've already told you what will happen if I find you have mistreated or neglected my son in any way. Do you need me to repeat it?"

She stared at his harsh, arrogant face, and unconsciously

clutched her shift to her breast as if some flogger were
already about to rip it off her. "No . . . sir," she forced herself to say, thinking that she'd never hated anyone more
than she hated this man.

"There's one other thing I forgot to mention." He
stubbed out his cigar with a quick motion. There was an
edginess, a restlessness about him tonight that she could
sense even if she couldn't quite explain it. He glanced
back up at her, and she could feel his gaze on her body. It
made her skin feel hot, as if she were standing too close
to a roaring fire. She wished he would go away.

"If you've a taste for drink," he said curtly, "lose it.
Don't ever let me smell alcohol on your breath."

"I don't drink . . . sir," she said in a strangled whisper.

His nostrils flared. "I've never met a thieving whore
yet who didn't like to hit the bottle."

She felt an angry flush stain her cheeks. "I'm not a
whore. And I'm not a thief, either."

"No?" He pushed away from the table. "Then, what
are you?" he demanded, advancing on her slowly. "What
does a woman like you do to get herself deported?"

She didn't answer him.

"Well," he prompted, still coming at her. "What was
it? Forgery? Receiving? Uttering?"

"No," she said finally, goaded, her voice trembling
with fury. *"Manslaughter."*

In the suddenly silent room, the word hung in the air
between them. Bryony stared up into his deadly blue
eyes and wished she could call it back.

He planted himself in front of her. He was so close she
could feel the tension radiating from him, see the muscle
that jumped beneath his hard, tanned jaw. He towered
over her, six feet plus of raw, angry power.

"For *what*?" he demanded, his voice low and dangerous.

She swallowed convulsively, but she didn't cower and
she didn't back away. "Manslaughter," she repeated.

"Good God." He tossed his evening cape and hat on a
nearby chair and walked away from her, as if he didn't

trust himself to stand too near. Reaching the table, he leaned over it, bracing his hands against its edge. She could see the smooth line of his evening coat bulge over the bunched muscles of his arms and back, a kind of feral strength gloved in black silk. "They've given me a *murderer* to nurse my son?"

"I'm not a murderer," she said faintly, her earlier bravado gone. "It was an accident."

He twisted his head and looked at her over his shoulder. "Was it, by God?"

"Yes."

"And just who was it you *accidentally* killed?"

Bryony hesitated. "My husband."

His eyes narrowed. "I thought they still burned husband-killers in England."

Her breath left her in a whoosh. It had been one of her worst terrors—that they might burn her. The fear of it still haunted her. "It . . . it was an accident," she somehow managed to say again.

He straightened up and walked back to her with the slow stalk of a hunter advancing on his prey. She held her ground as he came right up to her again, only closer this time. Close enough that she could see the fine pattern of the silk of his waistcoat, the intricate folds of his cravat, the smooth tan of his lean cheek, the hard slant of his lips. Close enough for him to put his strong, beautiful hands around her slender throat.

She forced herself to stand still beneath his grip, barely breathing. "If you ever—*ever*—do anything to harm my son," he said quietly, increasing the pressure of his fingers slightly, "you won't live to hang. I'll break your neck myself."

CHAPTER
FIVE

Cornwall, twelve months earlier

"When is Papa coming home, Mama?"

Bryony forced herself to smile as she smoothed the tangled curls away from her two-year-old daughter's forehead. "Soon, sweetheart." She glanced to where the warm, golden light of the fine September evening slanted in through the nursery's mullioned window, and added, "It's time for you to go to sleep now."

"But he promised he'd be home in time to read me a story," Madeline insisted.

"I know." Bryony fussed with the cutwork trim on the child's sheet and noticed absently that the lace needed mending again. "Something must have come up to delay him."

Madeline's lower lip trembled, but she was too stubborn to let the tears that swam in her big brown eyes fall. "He only said he'd read to me because he didn't want to take me down to the village with him. He never really meant to do it."

"Oh, no, Maddy." But of course it was true, which was why Bryony didn't hold out any hope of the promised story being delivered tomorrow. Oliver disappointed the little girl enough on his own without Bryony adding to it.

She rose quickly and reached to close the curtains against the setting sun. Outside, seagulls wheeled high above the windswept cliffs behind the house, their mewling cries mingling with the crash of the surf against the rocks at the base of Cadgwith Cove, far below. Bryony paused with her hand on the faded chintz and watched the dying sun glint off the water and cast long purple shadows over the gorse and boulder-strewn cliffs.

The wild and desolate beauty of the familiar scene filled her with a poignant, aching sense of joy. But it was followed too swiftly by an unexpected surge of loneliness, and an uneasiness that was close to fear.

She jerked the curtains shut and turned back toward her daughter with determined cheerfulness. "Shall I sing you a song? What would you like?"

" 'Six White Horses.' "

Bryony smiled and settled on the edge of the miniature sleigh bed. Madeline always asked for 'Six White Horses.'

" 'Six white clouds, flying o'er the sea,' " Bryony sang softly. " 'Be six white horses, that will carry me . . .' "

Madeline's long lashes fluttered against cheeks rosy from a day spent with sun and sand and sparkling sea. Slowly the child's breathing eased, and she slept.

The song ended, but Bryony lingered at the side of the bed, gazing down at her daughter's sweetly parted lips, at the silky golden hair spread out over the worn linen. Her heart filled with fierce, desperate love for this child . . . and a deep, festering anger toward the careless man who had hurt her. Who was always hurting them both.

She kissed Madeline's forehead and stood up, her hands moving restlessly over the barely perceptible swell of her belly. By spring she would have another child. It was a thought which brought her, once again, that disturbing sense of trouble. She pushed it away.

The big old house settled quietly into dusty shadows as Bryony descended the single flight of bare wooden steps. The thump of her unfashionably sturdy shoes echoed in the stillness. When Bryony was a little girl, a Persian runner with vivid blue and red and gold swirls had carpeted the grand staircase that rose proudly from the slate-floored hall of Cadgwith Cove House to the half dozen or so bedrooms above. In those days, her sea captain father had still been alive, and her mother's gay, musical laughter had filled the house with sunshine and love. But Captain Peyton and his vibrant wife were dead six years now, lost together in a boating accident in the treacherous waters off the cove. This past June, Bryony had decided that the tattered, threadbare stair runner had become dangerous, and she'd had it taken up.

A rattle of crockery from the kitchen told her Mrs. Pencarrow would be putting dinner on the table soon. Mrs. Pencarrow was expecting Oliver home, too. He'd flattered and teased the old cook-housekeeper into making roast chicken with bread sauce, his favorite. Bryony sighed, foreseeing more wounded feelings that would need soothing tonight.

She pushed open the swinging door that led to the ancient, sandstone-flagged kitchen. The kitchen was the oldest part of Cadgwith Cove House, thick-walled and low-ceilinged and dark with the smoke of ages. It smelled wonderfully of roasting chicken and the fresh apple pie set to cool on the stone sill of the open casement window.

"Madeline's asleep, Mrs. Pencarrow," she said to the stocky, gray-haired woman who stood at the stove and stirred her bread sauce. "I'm just going out for a quick walk along the cliffs before dinner." She lifted the latch on the stout kitchen door and tugged it open. "I won't be long."

"The cliffs?" Mrs. Pencarrow swung around to shake her wooden spoon at Bryony. "The cliffs, is it? When you know you should be upstairs dressing for dinner like the lady your da woulda wanted you to be, rather than scrambling around on the sea cliffs like a hoyden?"

But Bryony only laughed and pulled the heavy, weathered door shut behind her.

A warm breeze laden with moist, salty air caressed her face as she clattered down the two cracked stone steps that led to the yard. A gull screeched. Bryony flung back

her head to watch as it floated above the house's weathered gray slate roof, then dipped toward the sea.

She hurried across the cobbled yard, past low-walled
beds of struggling, pathetic-looking herbs and vegetables,
and followed the weed-choked path of crushed seashells
that led up a small rise.

She crested the hill and stopped. The great blue sweep
of the sea opened up below her.

Bryony loved the sea. She loved its restless, primitive
pull, and the way the sea winds buffeted her ears and
whipped at her skirts. She breathed deeply, filling her
lungs with the essence of sweet heather and tangy brine
and the mysterious scents of faraway, wondrous and unknown places.

Once Bryony had assumed that Cadgwith Cove House
would always be her home. Then had come the unbearably gray, misty morning when they'd buried her mother
and father. The day her uncle, Sir Edward Peyton, had
come for her. He'd taken her away from the sea, to live in
his dark, joyless house in the middle of the moors. At the
time it had seemed to Bryony that all the sunshine and
laughter had gone out of her life forever. She'd endured
three miserable years of endless disapproval and lectures
and beatings.

And then she'd met Oliver Wentworth.

He'd been twenty-one at the time, handsome and
charming and always laughing. Late one night, she'd
crept out of that dark, miserable house and married him.

Under the terms of Captain Peyton's will, control of
Cadgwith Cove House had passed upon her marriage to
Bryony—or rather, to Bryony's new husband. But Oliver
saw the property as a source of income rather than as a
livelihood. And now he was talking about selling the
house and its adjoining land. He said it was because he'd
rather live in London, but Bryony suspected the real
reason was because he needed the money for his endless
gambling debts. She was desperately afraid that one of
these days he would go ahead and sell it, whether she

wanted him to or not. It was a thought that tore at her insides and suffocated her with panic and fury and a deep, abiding sense of failure.

The ominous loneliness she'd felt earlier returned, tinged now with despair. She turned and walked along the cliffside path, watching the first stars wink at her from out of the purpling sky.

She loved Oliver still, but it was in a different, diminished way. There was little in it of trust or respect, or even of passion. Sometimes she thought her love for Oliver was like the indulgent love of a woman for a spoiled but engaging and affectionate child. It was not the kind of love a woman wanted to feel for her husband.

Yet Oliver was her husband, and he always would be.

In the cove some hundred feet below her, dark green waves swelled and rolled, then dashed themselves to foam against the rocks at the base of the cliff. The air was heavy with salty spray and the endless, rhythmic boom and hiss of the sea.

Then she heard another sound, the high-pitched trill of a woman's laughter, coming from behind the mass of boulders that lay off the path ahead, to her right.

"Lawdy, Mr. Oliver," giggled the woman. "Do that again."

Oliver's familiar voice answered, pitched low and husky. "You like that, do you?"

Bryony's heart raced fast and painfully hard, sending the blood drumming in her ears and narrowing her vision with a red haze of sickened fury. She paused for a moment, her hand to her thudding chest, then left the path and circled around the rocks.

She saw the woman first, and recognized her as Flory Dickens, the wife of one of the village cottagers. Flory had an unmistakable mass of flame-red curls that tumbled from beneath her mobcap, and a plump, heaving bosom barely restrained by the low-cut bodice of her tawdry gown. She sat with her dirty skirts hiked up to her waist, her knees spread wide, straddling Oliver as he lay flat on his back in the long grass that grew between the rocks near the cliff face. Bryony could see the woman's white, naked buttocks undulating in rhythm with the rise and thrust of Oliver's hips. He had one hand beneath her bunched skirts, playing with her, while with the other hand he tugged at the lace-trimmed edge of her bodice, pulling it down until her generous breast spilled out into his palm.

"Ah, you do know how to touch a girl, Mr. Oliver," Flory moaned. Licking her lips, she tipped her head back . . .

And screamed.

"Get away from him!" Bryony grabbed a handful of red curls and yanked hard. "How dare you? How *dare* you?"

Yowling like a cat with a singed tail, Flory Dickens scooted back against one of the boulders and cowered with her arms wrapped protectively about her head.

Oliver rose to his knees in the grass and quickly hitched his pants up over his bare hips. "Bryony." He scrambled to his feet with his flap only half done up. "I can explain."

"Explain?" Bryony stared at him, her breath coming in short, angry huffs. For a moment she thought she might be sick.

He brushed an errant guinea-gold curl off his forehead and grinned at her sheepishly. It was a look that had melted the heart of every female Oliver Wentworth had ever encountered, from the doting nurse that rocked his cradle, to the old cook-housekeeper Bryony wouldn't let him replace. "Bryony," he said again, his voice low as he stepped forward to gaze down at her with sparkling gray eyes that always held just the right mix of sincerity and devilment. "Flory means nothing to me. You know that. You know how much I love you. But a man has needs, Bryony, and since you've been increasing—"

Bryony felt something break inside her, something that hurt. "I have never turned you away, Oliver," she said, her voice an agonized whisper. "Never."

He laid his palm, gently, against her cheek. "Bryony, you know how it was when you were carrying Madeline. When there's a baby in there, it just doesn't seem . . . decent."

"Are you saying the fact I'm with child again justifies this?" Her voice broke as she swept her hand toward Flory Dickens, who still crouched against the boulder and wailed.

He moved as if to take her in his arms. "Bryony—"

"Stay away from me." She whipped around and went to stand on the cliff's edge and gaze out over the rolling sea. The waves were running high and rough, as if a storm were blowing up. The water churned and thundered around the rocks below, restless and dark and dangerous. It called to something deep within her, something ancient and wild and sad. She choked back a sob until she thought it might strangle her.

The wailing from the cottager's wife ceased, and Bryony thought with relief that Flory Dickens must have finally taken herself off. She dashed an escaped tear from her cheek with the heel of her hand and turned back to confront her husband.

And found him helping Flory Dickens to her feet.

Rage, hot and bright and all-consuming, flamed within her. "Stay away from that woman!" Bryony threw herself at Oliver. "How dare you touch her?"

Bryony's fists pounded his chest as he swung around to face her. For a moment he looked startled. Then he caught her flailing fists and laughed. *Laughed.*

She jerked her hands from his grip and backed away, stumbling over a ring of stones that surrounded the remnants of a nearby, long-dead fire. She lost her balance and fell, landing with a jarring thump in the middle of the cold gray ashes. As she floundered about, trying to regain her footing, her hand knocked against a blackened length of wood. She seized it and brought it with her when she scrambled back up to her feet.

Oliver was still grinning. She put all her weight behind the wood and swung it at him.

The first blow hit him in the ribs. "Ow." He doubled over, holding his midriff. "Bloody hell, Bryony. That hurt!"

"Does it, Oliver? I don't hear you laughing now." She swung again, catching him this time on the arm.

"Bryony, don't." He jumped back, eluding the next blow. "This is not amusing, Bryony. Stop it."

"Amusing!" Bryony gripped the wood with both hands now. "Is it not *amusing* that I sit at home, trying to comfort your heartbroken little girl and growing big with your child, while you're out gambling away what's left of our money and satisfying your *needs* with the villagers' wives?"

She let loose with another swing. He sidestepped it nimbly. "Enough, Bryony."

"Enough, Oliver?" She swung again. "Enough?"

She was aiming for his shoulder. But when he tried to duck the blow, somehow his head got in the way. The stick caught him just above the ear with a sickening clunk. He reeled back, dizzy. It was only then that Bryony realized how dangerously close they'd come to the edge of the cliff.

"Oliver!" she screamed, throwing away the stick and reaching out to grab him. But he jerked away, unwilling to let her touch him.

And toppled backward into space, toward the crashing waves and dark, treacherous rocks far below.

"You are fortunate the authorities have decided to try you on the lesser charge of manslaughter," said Felix Fraser, brushing absently at some grains of snuff on his bulging waistcoat. "If they were to find you guilty of murdering your husband, they would burn you alive."

Beneath his watchful gaze, the woman seated on the

hard-backed chair before him maintained an unflinching, awful composure. But she couldn't hide the terror that flickered in the depths of her dark brown eyes.

They were in the small, stone-walled room the prison reserved for the use of lawyers and their clients. It was relatively clean, and the fire burning on the open hearth was enough to chase away the worst of the cold and damp. But nothing could keep out the stench of the prison around them. The air was foul with the smell of filth and rot and despair.

After three months in this hellhole, Bryony Wentworth looked more like a Billingsgate doxy than the niece of Sir Edward Peyton of Peyton Hall. Her dark hair was dull and unkempt, her dress stained and ragged and pulling tightly over a stomach swelled big with child. From behind her skirts peeped another child, a big-eyed girl with dirty blond hair and a finger that never left her solemn little mouth. It was something Felix could never approve of, this business of throwing a woman's children into prison with her. But the child looked healthier than her mother, and Felix suspected the woman was going without food herself to feed her daughter.

"The penalty for manslaughter is only hanging," Felix said, wishing the little girl would stop staring at him like that. "Because of your . . . ah . . . delicate condition, the Crown will need to put off the execution until after the baby is born, which means that the sentence will likely be transmuted to an order for transportation."

"Transportation?"

"Aye. To Botany Bay. It might be for fourteen years, but seven is more likely."

For a moment she looked relieved. But then a new fear must have struck her. "They—they will let me take Madeline, won't they?" she asked, clutching the little girl to her tightly, as if someone had already appeared to snatch the child from her arms.

"We can apply." Felix debated with himself, then decided it would be best not to raise the woman's hopes.

"Although I must warn you that they do not often allow it."

"But you're talking as if I've already been convicted."

Felix shrugged. "Not much doubt of that. There is this female who was a witness . . ." He frowned and picked up a paper from the litter he had spread out on the battered old table before him. "Flory Dickens, that's her name. And then there's the men from the village who spent the night looking for your husband. Why you went and announced what you'd done is more than I will ever understand." He gathered the papers together and thrust them into his worn leather satchel. "Still, I suppose if people were not foolish, I would be out of business."

"Oliver was always a strong swimmer," she said quietly, staring down at the hands she held clenched in her lap. "I was hoping they might find him alive. Or at least find his body."

She raised her head. Her face was white with a pallor that had little to do with her months in prison, and in her eyes was naked, soul-wrenching grief and an all-consuming guilt that was terrible to see. She looked smashed, destroyed.

Felix cleared his throat and glanced away. "Never much chance of finding him alive, no. Not along that stretch of coast. Especially with a storm rising." His chair scraped across the stone floor as he pushed it back and stood up. "So," he said with forced heartiness. "I will see you next week, at the assizes."

Somewhere in the gloomy depths of the prison cell, water dripped against stone. The constant, hollow, echoing sound went on and on, always there, behind the rustle of the rats in the straw and the wail of someone's newborn baby and the moans of the sick and the dying and the mad. Sometimes Bryony thought that if anything about this place finally drove her insane, it would be that monotonous *drip, drip, drip.*

She shivered in the fierce, biting cold and drew the

filthy rag of a blanket up around Madeline's thin shoulders. Hunger gnawed at her pregnant belly. Hunger and despair and raw, endless fear. There was so much, so very much to fear here.

There were other sounds, but she was careful not to turn toward them. She heard a woman's whimper and a man's labored breathing, and then Bryony shut her ears to the animallike grunts of the coupling going on beside her. It was impossible to tell whether or not the woman lay willingly beneath the man who was taking her so fiercely; even if she were not willing, she was likely too weak or too afraid to resist.

There was so much here to fear.

It was ever present, the fear. The fear and the hunger, the grinding, dehumanizing treatment, and the appalling filth. Once the stench of unwashed bodies and excrement and untreated disease that hung so thick in the air here would have made her retch. Once the rats, the lice, the creeping, scuttling creatures would have made her shudder. But eventually one grew accustomed to living under even the worst of conditions . . . or, at least, one almost ceased to notice it. There were few alternatives. One grew accustomed, one went mad, or one died.

Madeline stirred beside her. Bryony laid her hand on her daughter's hot forehead, and her own body trembled with fear and twisting, knifelike dread. The child was burning up with fever.

Dear God, don't hurt my Maddy. Not my little Madeline.

She prayed more out of habit than conviction. God hadn't been listening to her much lately.

No, that's not true, she told herself quickly, suddenly fearful lest He indeed be listening now and decide to wreak His vengeance on her for her lack of faith. After all, she hadn't been burned as a husband-killer. And although she'd been sentenced to hang for manslaughter, at the end of the assizes the sentence had been transmuted to transportation for seven years.

There'd been another woman—a girl, really, only fifteen—who'd been tried at the same assizes as Bryony. She'd stolen five yards of ribbon. They'd sentenced her to hang, with her body to be delivered up afterward to the surgeons for public dissection.

Sometimes, when Bryony lay shivering in her straw at night, she could still hear that poor girl screaming as they dragged her away.

Madeline coughed, a harsh, body-racking cough that cut through Bryony's thoughts. Dear God, it was always so cold. The children in the prison had been dying regularly throughout the winter. Lately just keeping Madeline alive had become a bigger worry to Bryony than gaining permission from the Crown to take the little girl with her on the transport ship. Felix Fraser had put a petition through for her after the assizes, but so far they'd heard nothing back. It was already the end of February, and rumor had it a ship—the *Indispensable*—was being readied to sail soon.

She heard the key grating in the lock of the heavy metal door, but there were dozens of other prisoners in the cell, and it wasn't until her name was called that she looked around.

"Bryony Wentworth," said the bullet-headed jailer, tapping his ring of keys against his greasy leather apron. "Somebody 'ere to see ye. And bring that brat o' yers with ye."

Madeline was too weak to walk. Bryony lifted the child's frail body in her arms and carried her out into the dim, stone-flagged passage. She followed the jailer down the corridor, up a short flight of steps, down another hall, and into the room where she had once met with Felix Fraser.

There were three people already in the room. A middle-aged servant woman named Potter, whom Bryony remembered from Peyton Hall, sat on a straight-backed chair near the window. She held her hands primly folded in the lap of her starched uniform, her mouth sour and disapproving.

Near the woman stood two men, their backs turned, talking. At the sight of Felix Fraser, Bryony's hopes soared. He must have heard back on her petition. Oh, surely—

Then the man beside the lawyer turned, and in the instant before he raised his scented handkerchief to cover his mouth and delicately pinched nose, Bryony recognized the thin, severe face of her uncle, Sir Edward Peyton.

She hadn't seen him in four years, not since the day she'd eloped with Oliver when she was sixteen. Other than for instructing his solicitors to release Cadgwith Cove House to Oliver's control and sending Felix Fraser to consult with her after her arrest, he'd refused to have anything to do with Bryony since the day of her marriage.

"Uncle Edward." She looked from him to the lawyer. "Mr. Fraser."

Madeline began to cough again. Bryony hugged her daughter to her. "It's all right, darling. It's nice and warm in here, isn't it? Everything will be all right," she said. But her uncle had turned away from her again, and with growing dread Bryony raised her eyes from Madeline's head to the lawyer's solemn face. "You've heard back on my petition?"

"Yes." Felix Fraser fiddled with his watch fob.

Bryony shifted the little girl's weight, so that Madeline's legs were wrapped around her mother's bulging waist and her head rested on Bryony's shoulder. "And?"

"It's been refused."

For a long moment Bryony could only stare at him. Horror and utter disbelief mushroomed within her, welling up and up, squeezing her heart, pressing against her lungs until she thought it might suffocate her. It seemed to spread like terror throughout her body, to her arms and legs, numbing her, bringing a ringing to her ears and a dimming of her vision.

"I have discussed the situation with your uncle, and he has agreed to assume the child's guardianship," said Felix Fraser, his voice brisk, his watery gray eyes sad and worried. "He is here to take her home with him."

"But—" Bryony looked wildly from the lawyer to her uncle's thin, stiff back. "But, surely . . . something. We must be able to do something? Could we not appeal? You will authorize it, will you not, Uncle Edward? Perhaps if—"

The lawyer shook his head. "There simply is no time, my dear. The *Indispensable* sails from Gravesend next week. You are to be transferred by coach to London tomorrow."

"Tomorrow!" Bryony's grip on her daughter tightened so hard, Madeline lifted her head and murmured in protest.

Sir Edward Peyton turned and spoke to her for the first time since she'd entered the room. "Give the child to Potter," he said, his voice devoid of all expression.

Bryony stepped back. "No." She shook her head slowly, once, from side to side. "I won't let you take her."

Uncle Edward's breath fluttered the handkerchief he still held fastidiously protecting his nose. "You have no choice." He nodded to the woman with the stiffly starched cap and dour expression. "Potter—"

"No." Bryony backed against the wall, hugging Madeline to her as if by sheer force of will she could make the child a part of her body again and keep her there, as safe as the unborn baby in her womb. "You can't take her from me. You can't. Oh God, no. *No.*"

Madeline clung to Bryony and began to whimper. "Mama," she wailed as they pried her clutching, white fingers from around Bryony's neck. "I want my mama. Let me go! Mama?"

"Madeline!" Bryony lunged against Felix Fraser's restraining hold, but her uncle and the servant woman were already carrying the screaming, frantic child from the room. Heavy, retreating footsteps echoed ominously down the length of the corridor.

"Mama! Don't let them take me. Mama, please. I'll be good. I promise I'll be good. *Mama.*"

Bryony had a final, heartbreaking glimpse of Madeline's tearstained cheeks and desperate, wildly thrashing little arms. Then the door at the end of the hall closed with a hollow thud. Long after Madeline was lost to her sight, Bryony could still hear her, crying, and calling her name. *Mama. Mama!*

It felt as if they had reached into Bryony's body and wrenched out her heart. Her breath came in great, tearing gasps. She would have collapsed had it not been for Felix Fraser. He turned her in his arms and held her while the anguished, tortured sobs racked her body. "Go ahead and cry, my dear," he said, stroking her hair as if she were a child herself. "Go ahead and cry."

She didn't know how long he held her like that. When he thought she was able to listen, he began to talk. At first it was just words, washing over her. But slowly some of what he was saying began to penetrate her shivering agony.

"I know it's hard to believe, my dear, but it is best this way. The child is already ill. She might not have survived the voyage if we had secured permission for her to go with you. I know you will miss her, but you must comfort yourself with the knowledge that she is alive, and that your uncle will look after her."

"*Uncle Edward look after her?*" wailed Bryony. "Oh, God. When I think of her growing up in that dark, miserable house, with all that disapproval, and no love or kindness or—"

Felix Fraser's hands slipped down to grip her arms. He held her away from him and gently shook her. "At least she'll have a chance to grow up, Bryony. At least Sir Edward finally agreed to take her, however reluctantly. I've seen children her age—younger—torn from their mother's arms and left on the docks with no one to care for them. No one."

Then he hugged her to him again, this lawyer who wasn't related to her and who hadn't seen her more than a few times in his life; this funny little man who was willing to hold her and comfort her despite the filth and the stench and the fear of jail fever that had kept her uncle from even approaching her. "Oh, don't listen to this foolish old man. Go ahead and cry, my dear. It's an obscene, brutal system, and it's the innocent who suffer the most."

"It's just that I . . ." Her voice quavered, and she swallowed hard. "I don't think I can go on without her. Missing her, wondering always how she is. If she's happy. If she's well."

"You must, my dear. You have another child, remember? And this one they cannot take from you. Not if the ship does sail next week, as scheduled."

Bryony put her hands on her swollen belly and felt the child within her kick, as if to remind her of its existence. She shook her head. "But it's not Madeline," she sobbed, feeling more helpless and desperately alone than at any time in these last, terrible six months. "It can't replace Madeline."

"No, but it needs you, too, my dear," said the old lawyer, taking her hands in his and squeezing them. "You'll still have someone you love with you—a child who will give you its love. For its sake, Bryony, you must not give up. You still have a reason to live. Whatever happens, you mustn't forget that."

A howling wind swooped around the inn and threw rain against the panes of the casement window overlooking Sydney Cove.

From her pallet before the fire in the private parlor, Bryony watched the dancing golden flames flicker up the chimney. For the first time in twelve months she was warm, well-fed, and clean. It felt strange, as if physical comfort belonged to the past and should have no part in the life of fear and despair she now knew.

She had lain awake for hours, listening tensely for Captain St. John's return, steeling herself to endure the rape she knew she must suffer. But as the minutes slipped past and he did not come, that expectant, watchful fear temporarily receded. In its place came a surge of desolation and loss so intense she almost cried out with the pain.

She had waited all day to be alone with her grief for Philip. It had been barely dawn when she had stood painfully dry-eyed in the gray light and listened to the scrape of shovels, the sodden thud of mud hitting bark as they'd buried him. She hadn't cried. She'd forced herself to hold it all back, waiting, waiting to be alone.

Only, now that she finally had the uninterrupted solitude she had craved, she found she couldn't cry after all. It was as if she sensed, somehow, that she wasn't capable of dealing with Philip's loss yet. Whenever she tried to let herself mourn, her thoughts just slid away. It was like peering into a great, fathomless abyss. She knew that if she fell in, she would never have the strength to pull herself out again. So she was careful to stay away from the edge.

She let her mind drift away to Madeline, then regretted it. In the past, whenever the agony of her longing for her golden-haired daughter threatened to overwhelm her, Bryony would pick up Philip and hug him to her for comfort. Except now she'd lost Philip, as well. She was utterly, frighteningly alone in this vast, wild, unknown land.

A part of her wanted to give up. Cease struggling, cease fighting to survive. But she knew that, for Madeline's sake if nothing else, she had to go on. She would live with loneliness and hunger. She would bear rape and the lash. She would endure whatever torment Hayden St. John subjected her to. And at the end of six and a half years, she would find some way to get herself back to Cornwall. Back to Madeline.

She tried to focus on the future, but Hayden St. John's dark, harsh face kept intruding.

Hayden St. John. Her master.

It was an idea so hard to accept that she actually forced herself to say the word aloud to the empty room. Her *master*. It tasted odd on her lips. The loss of freedom and control over her life that she'd experienced in prison had been difficult enough to deal with. But at least it had been impersonal—she had been part of a system, one of many, controlled by many. Nothing she had experienced in the past twelve months had prepared her for this final degradation, for being so totally subservient to one man. For being *owned* by him.

She rolled over and hugged her pillow to her chest. She found she couldn't even enjoy her solitude tonight, because she was convinced it was only temporary.

Her mind kept resurrecting the image of the way he'd looked earlier that night, leaning back against the table, one long, well-muscled leg swinging idly, his face taut. He'd been watching her then, she knew, the way a man watches a woman he wants. She'd seen it in the way he was looking at her. Felt it. Even after she'd lost her temper and told him why she'd been transported, even when he'd had his hands around her throat, she'd felt it still.

How long would it take him to act on it? she wondered. How long?

She was still awake, several hours later, when Simon began to stir. Sighing, she picked him up and put him to her breast. And, somehow, in the warmth of his sweet-smelling body and in the gentle tug of his eager mouth, she found the peace she needed to get to sleep.

She awoke with a start.

She sat up and glanced over at Simon's cradle, but he slept soundly, his position unaltered from when she'd put him down. Puzzled, she was about to lie down and go back to sleep herself when she heard the stamping of horses' hooves and the rattle and jingle of harnesses.

Not quite knowing why she did so, Bryony slipped from her pallet and crossed the room to the casement window that faced the front of the inn. The fire on the hearth had died down, and the room was cold. She slid quickly onto the window seat and drew her bare legs up under her thin shift. Wrapping her arms about her knees for warmth, she peered down at the street below.

It had stopped raining, although low-hanging clouds still obscured the stars and moon. But in the pool of lantern light in front of the inn she could see quite clearly the elegant town carriage drawn by a team of four blood bays that was just pulling up to a stop.

As she watched, a liveried servant jumped forward to open the near door and let down the steps. She heard a murmur of voices. A man's tall figure, enveloped in an elegant evening cape and wearing a *chapeau bras* set at a rakish angle, appeared in the open door of the carriage.

Ignoring the steps, he jumped down lightly. Behind him, a pretty young woman in evening dress and pearls leaned out the open door to say something to him. He turned back to her and laughed. The light from the lantern fell full on his face, but Bryony had already recognized Hayden St. John.

The young woman laughed, too, and laid a hand on St. John's arm. She was a fair young woman, probably no more than eighteen. She looked flushed and excited, flown on masculine compliments and the headiness of what had probably been one of her first grown-up dinner parties. Bryony tried to remember what it felt like to be so young and innocent and carefree . . .

And failed utterly.

Looking down at the other woman's shining smile, she suddenly felt old. Old and worn-out and utterly desolate and alone. So very, very alone.

The woman laughed again. Perched above them on her cold window seat, Bryony unconsciously reached out

to press her fingertips against the wavy glass of the
windowpane, as if by so doing she could reach out and
touch the scene below. It was like glimpsing a tableau
from another world. A world she'd once moved through
and taken for granted, but from which she'd now been
banned. Forever.

Then the scene below shifted. Hayden St. John stepped
back to allow the footman to put up the steps and close
the door. The driver started his horses, and the carriage
moved slowly off into the darkness. But long after the
last rattle of wheels had been lost among the other night
sounds, Bryony sat where she was, on the window seat,
her feet drawn up beside her, her arms wrapped around
her legs, and her cheek pressed against her knees.

CHAPTER SIX

Bryony stepped out the front door of the Three Jolly Fishermen to find that last night's wind had swept away the clouds. Above her arced a clear sky, a vast blue dome that reflected off the sparkling waters of the most beautiful bay she had ever seen. It was as if they intensified each other, sky and bay, blue on blue, deeper and deeper, until the color was so vivid it almost hurt.

A fresh, golden light drenched everything around her—not just the sky and the far-flung inlets and coves of the bay, but the whitewashed houses and the grass-covered slopes and the seemingly endless forest that stretched to the west. The very air vibrated with a bright, clear light more intense than anything she'd ever experienced.

It was a sight that couldn't help but lift even the most oppressed of spirits. She stopped and gasped in delight. "It's beautiful."

Gideon glanced back at her and laughed. "Aye, that 'tes. You act like you've never seen it before."

Bryony shifted Simon to her hip and followed Gideon down the still-muddy street. "I haven't—at least, not really. It's been raining ever since we sailed through the Heads."

Not that she would have noticed even if it hadn't been raining, she thought. Not with Philip sickening.

They crossed the long street that ran along the top of the ridge. It was wide and lined with fairly impressive stone and brick buildings, but the street itself was rutted and piled with garbage. There were even tree stumps in the middle of the street, Bryony noticed—three feet high. The traffic just went around them.

Then they turned off the Row into a narrow side street that sloped downhill toward the waterfront. The buildings here were crude, more like huts really. Built of wood and mud and thatch, they clung precariously to the side of a hill so steep the lane eventually degenerated into a series of steps, cut right into the rock. Goats and pigs ranged freely among the scattered garbage and scraggly gardens. Bryony saw one goat eating a petticoat off a line of tattered washing. There was a sudden, loud curse, and a slatternly woman with a short pipe hanging out of her mouth stood up and threw an empty rum bottle at it. The goat jumped and bucked away, bleating. The woman sat down again, but her stare followed Bryony on down the hill.

There was a time when the people Bryony saw here would have made her nervous. But after a year spent in the company of thieves, whores, and murderers, she barely noticed them. Rather, it was the birds that fascinated her. Almost every shack had a cage beside its door, with one or more large, vivid-colored birds that screeched at them as they passed. One, a particularly large, snowy-white bird with a yellow crest, opened its curved beak and cawed, "Five hundred lashes! Five hundred lashes! Lay them on! Lay them on!" The cry followed them all the way down the hill.

Eventually they turned onto a lane that curved along the waterfront until it reached a muddy little rivulet, spanned by a stone bridge. Readjusting the weight of the sleeping baby, Bryony leaned against the bridge's stone wall to rest for a minute and look up at the hill in front of them.

Here there were only a few, neat brick houses. They stood in an official-looking row near a white, two-story Georgian mansion set in splendid isolation in the midst of extensive, well-tended gardens stretching all the way down to the water's edge.

"What's that?" she asked Gideon, nodding toward the big white house.

Gideon followed the direction of her gaze. "That's Government House," he said, an odd expression on his freckled face. "Where the acting governor, Foveaux, lives."

Bryony had heard of Lieutenant Colonel Foveaux. They said that when he was commandant of Norfolk Island, he used to have the new women prisoners stripped naked and paraded around in a circle while he auctioned them off, for rum.

"Over there—" Gideon pointed to a row of massive warehouses built of carefully dressed stone that stood at the base of the slope. "That's the Government store, where we're headed."

Inside the store's thick stone walls, it was cool. The exotic scents of sandalwood and cinnamon and spices from India and the Islands overlaid the more familiar odors of new hemp, coffee beans, turpentine, and rum. Everything from tea to saucepans to sails could be had here, although there wasn't much in the way of baby clothes. Bryony ended up with bolts of material, spools of thread, and a selection of ribbons and trims. She was going to have to make almost everything that Simon needed.

She did manage to find a wool cloak and plain gray dress for herself. The dress was hopelessly old-fashioned, with a fitted bodice and an almost natural waistline. But it had been so long since she'd worn anything new— even if it was shoddily made and ugly—that she couldn't help but be pleased with it. She also found a couple of caps, and obediently tucked her hair up under one of them.

While Gideon arranged to have their purchases delivered to the Three Jolly Fishermen, Bryony went to stare out the open doorway. A new ship had come in during the night: a merchantman, lying low in the water. Balancing Simon on her hip, Bryony ventured out onto the flag way to see it better.

A white cloud of seagulls rose, screeching, from the nearby shingle and filled the air with their heartbreakingly familiar cry. The sun sparkled brightly on the bay, and for a moment, she might almost have imagined herself back on the waterfront of the village of Cadgwith Cove.

Then she heard the rattling chink of chains, and turned to see a chain gang stumble toward the wharf. The men were half-naked and filthy, their bare backs crisscrossed with the scars of repeated floggings, their eyes sunken and despairing. The illusion of comfortable familiarity was shattered.

Gideon came up beside her. She glanced at him, and saw a frown line appear between his brows as he watched the chain gang shuffle past.

Abruptly she said, "What is Captain St. John doing here, Gideon? He's not with the New South Wales Corps, is he?"

Gideon's nostrils flared with contempt. "The New South Wales Corps? No, he was never a part of that riffraff. He fought the French, in Europe. And then he was in India, with Wellesley's regiment. But he was wounded at Assaye. It was when he was recuperating in England that he married Mrs. St. John."

"So what's he doing here?" asked Bryony, turning to walk slowly along the waterfront.

"Sold out," said Gideon, falling into step beside her. "He tried going back to India with the army for a while, but the climate didn't agree with his wife's health."

"No?" Bryony tipped her head back. From here she could see two windmills on the top of the ridge behind the Governor's house. She watched their sails whirling around and around, flashing white against the crisp blue sky. And she thought, idly, that the sky was the same color blue as Hayden St. John's eyes. "I would have thought he'd take her back to England, if she wasn't strong."

Gideon laughed. "Do you, now? And what would a man like the Cap'n do in England?"

Bryony tried to picture Hayden St. John in the role of a sedate English gentleman, riding about his carefully tended green fields, going to church every Sunday with his dutiful wife and children, and dispensing alms to the poor at Christmas like her Uncle Edward. Only she couldn't do it.

In her arms, Simon yawned and rested his head on her shoulder. Bryony looked down at his flaxen head and felt a curious sadness well up within her. "Perhaps," she said softly. "But New South Wales must not have agreed with the Captain's wife any more than India."

"No," Gideon admitted, following her gaze. "No, it didn't."

Bryony pushed open the door of the parlor, then stopped short on the threshold.

She'd expected the room to be empty. Instead Captain St. John and another man were sitting at the oak table near the window, drinking wine. St. John had his head tipped back, draining his glass. When he lowered it, she noticed the wine had wet his lips.

"I'm sorry," she said hastily. "I didn't mean to intrude. I'll just go down to the kitchen and—"

She would have backed out of the room, but St. John had already risen. He stepped over and pulled the door open wider. "No, come in, Bryony. This is Dr. William Redfern. I've asked him to take a look at you and Simon before we leave Sydney."

Bryony looked from St. John to the pleasant-faced man of about thirty, then back at St. John again.

In the warm light of the afternoon sun, his face looked surprisingly relaxed. He was actually smiling at her, but Bryony recognized that smile. It was the same smile she used herself when she was trying to coax a child or a particularly slow-witted servant to do something they didn't want to do. To have that look bent on her was both humiliating and infuriating.

"I'll wait for you in the coffee room downstairs." He nodded to the doctor, and before she had a chance to say anything, he closed the door behind him.

Bryony glanced back at the doctor, who by now had risen also and was standing beside the table.

"Well," he said. "Let's start with Simon, shall we?"

Simon was awake. He suffered the exchange of arms quietly enough, but when the doctor unwrapped him and laid him on the hard table, he began to whimper.

"Hush, now, little one," said the doctor with a soft Irish lilt. "You remember me, don't you?" He kept talking in that same low, soothing voice as he loosened the baby's clothes, his exploring hands gentle, until Simon quieted and lay staring up at the doctor with wide, guileless green eyes.

Bryony stood back from the table, her arms crossed at her chest, watching the doctor in silence. But as her respect for him grew, she stepped closer. "Is he all right?" she asked. "He seems so small for four months."

"He was born early." Dr. Redfern glanced up at her. "That accounts for part of it. But then his mother was an unusually tiny woman. Simon here may well take after Laura."

Laura. For the first time, Hayden St. John's golden-haired wife had a name.

"Were you there when . . . when Simon was born?" She'd almost said, *when Laura St. John died.*

"No." He rolled the baby gently over onto his stomach. "The Captain had intended to bring her into Sydney, but there wasn't time." He paused a moment as if considering something, then said, "Laura St. John was an unusually beautiful, gentle woman. A true lady, in every sense of the word. I think her death affected all of us who knew her. But the Captain, he . . . well, it changed him somehow." He looked up and met her eyes. "I'm telling you this for a reason, you see. Hayden St. John has always been a hard man, but since Laura died . . . Let's just say it wouldn't do to cross him. Especially not where Simon is concerned."

Bryony remembered the feel of Hayden St. John's hands around her neck, threatening to throttle her.

Dr. Redfern straightened up and smiled. "Sure Simon's looking much better. When I saw him a few days ago, I wouldn't have given much for his chances of surviving another forty-eight hours. You've obviously taken good care of him."

"He was just hungry."

"Yes. But I can tell you also keep him clean. It makes a difference." He began to refasten the baby's wrappings.

"It's easy to keep a baby clean when you have fresh clothes for him. And water to wash him with," she added bitterly.

The doctor's hands stilled for a moment. He glanced up at her, his gray eyes gentle and caring. "I'm sorry about your own babe," he said softly. She knew he meant it, and it touched her so much that sudden tears stung her eyes and she had to blink them away.

Picking Simon up, Dr. Redfern carried him over to the cradle and laid him down. Then he turned. "Now, let's have a look at you, shall we?"

He peered in her eyes and her ears, and then had her open her mouth so that he could look at her teeth.

"No sign of scurvy," he said approvingly. "You must have had an honest ship's captain. When I was sent out, half the men on my ship were shark bait before we'd even rounded the Cape. But sure the captain made a good profit when he got to Sydney and was able to sell all those leftover supplies we were never allowed to eat."

Bryony stared at him. "You were transported?"

He gave her an odd smile. "When you're a doctor, and you're Irish, you need to be very selective about whose broken bodies you try to mend."

"But . . . you're not still a convict, are you?"

"Oh, no. I'm a free man now." He turned away to reach for something in his bag.

"Then, why . . . why are you still here?" For Bryony, obsessed as she was with the idea of making it back to Cornwall and Madeline, the thought of someone willingly choosing to stay here was incomprehensible. "Is your pardon conditional?"

"No, I could go back if I wanted to. But I like it here. It's . . ." He searched for the word, then grinned. "Freer. Besides, I'm needed here. And now," he said, his voice becoming professional again, "I'll have to ask you to take off your dress. You can keep on your shift."

He turned his back politely so she wouldn't have to disrobe with him watching her, although she didn't know what difference it made since he was going to see her when he turned around anyway.

She suffered his examination of her breasts. But when he asked her to lie down, she balked.

"I'm not a prostitute!"

"I'm not suggesting you are," he said gently. "But you have recently birthed a child under rather unfavorable conditions. And you were a guest of His Majesty for—how long? One year? More? Things happen to women."

Bryony felt her cheeks grow hot and looked away.

"There's no shame in it," he said gently. "Or, at any rate, not for the women who are the victims. The shame lies with the people in charge of the system. But it would still be best if you let me examine you."

So she let him, and studied the stubby candles in the wall sconce above her head until he was finished.

He left almost immediately afterward—going downstairs to report the results of his examinations to St. John, she supposed.

It was while she was refastening her bodice that the most likely reason Captain St. John had asked the doctor to examine her suddenly occurred to Bryony, and her fists clenched so violently she almost ripped the cheap material of her dress.

Oliver had once told her military officers were unusually careful about making sure that the women they bedded were disease free. He'd told her some joke about Mercury and Venus, but she'd been so young at the time she hadn't really understood it, and he'd laughed at her for her innocence.

She wasn't innocent now.

She was standing beside the window, Simon in her arms, when Captain St. John walked back into the parlor.

He carelessly tossed his broad-brimmed hat onto a side table near the door, then picked up the decanter and poured himself a new glass of wine before going to stretch out in one of the wing chairs near the empty fireplace.

She'd noticed that today he had bowed to convention and was wearing a cravat. It should have made him look more civilized, but it didn't.

He tipped his dark head back against the rear cushion, took a sip of wine, and sat regarding her over the rim of his glass for a moment before saying, "Dr. Redfern tells me you're taking good care of my son."

Not even twelve months in prison had quite taught Bryony to guard her tongue. "I don't believe in visiting the sins of the fathers on their children."

His eyes narrowed, but only for a moment. Then to her surprise, he laughed. The harsh lines of his face eased, and his normally cold eyes sparkled with amusement. He had such blue, blue eyes—startling blue, she thought, the color of the bay outside. Then he stopped laughing, and his gaze settled on her hair. She fancied she could feel the warmth of his gaze there, as surely as if he'd touched her.

"I see you found a cap."

"Yes . . . sir."

He stretched his buckskin-clad legs out in front of him in a careless sprawl and took another sip of his drink. "Why do you always say it that way?"

She shook her head in confusion. "What way?"

"As if the *sir* is an afterthought—and a grudging one, at that."

She stared at him, nonplussed. He tilted up his glass again, and she watched the smooth play of muscles in his tanned throat as he took another swallow of his wine.

She turned quickly away. "I bought everything you told me to today," she said, carrying a sleepy Simon to his cradle. "Including a new cloak and dress."

"Only one? You should have bought two."

She glanced back at him from where she knelt by the cradle. He had his glass resting negligently against one hard thigh. His pose looked relaxed, but she could feel the tension in him, the restlessness.

She stood up. "I ordered material to make some things for Simon. If I have to, I can make a dress for myself." She picked up one of Simon's blankets and began to fold it. "I was never particularly clever at it, but I—"

"Bryony," he said softly.

Her hands stilled at their task. She looked up slowly, feeling a strange heat warm her cheeks.

He regarded her in silence. She tried to swallow, but she couldn't. It was as if every muscle in her body had tightened, closing off her throat. There was something about the light in his eyes as they rested on her that made her aware of the fact that he was a man and she was a woman, and they were alone in this room with an entire night stretching ahead of them.

And that he owned her.

He jerked his head toward the door. "Go on and get yourself something to eat. I'll watch Simon for a while."

She let her breath out in a long sigh. "Yes, sir. Thank you . . . sir."

She fled the room.

Behind her, Hayden sat holding his empty glass, staring at it without really seeing it.

He knew he'd been aware of her in the way a man was aware of a woman, and it both surprised and annoyed him.

But he still wished he hadn't told her to buy that damn cap.

CHAPTER
SEVEN

In the cool, sunless light of false dawn, the bay below lay as flat and colorless as a tin plate.

Bryony wrapped a second blanket around the baby and took up a perch on the mounting block outside the inn door. In the harbor below a small boat shipped oars and began to row out toward a sloop anchored in the cove. She was too far away to hear the splash of its oars, but she could see the low, V-shaped wake that slowly spread out over the smooth silver surface of the water behind it.

The early-morning calm of the distant waterfront formed a sharp contrast to the scene immediately before her. Men swore. Restless animals stomped and shook their harnesses and filled the cold air with the steam of their breath.

Captain St. John had assembled some dozen men, four wagons, and a variety of stock in the street in front of the inn. There was one dray pulled by a team of horses, and two more pulled by bullocks, plus the small cart drawn by a pair of bullocks in which she and Simon were to ride. Gideon called it a "tilted cart." It had two wheels and a hard plank seat, and a canvas shelter rigged over the back.

Bryony wasn't sure how she felt about leaving Sydney. It wasn't simply a matter of leaving the vaguely familiar for the totally unknown. It was . . . it was as if the harbor and the ships within it were somehow her last link with home. To leave was to sever one more tie to her past, to put more miles and more obstacles between her and Madeline.

Somewhere up the street, a bullock bellowed. Bryony turned toward the sound and saw Hayden St. John walking down the line of his wagons. He ran his eye over the harnesses, checked the lashings of the loads, gave last-minute instructions to his men.

To see him among other men was to realize just how tall and broad-shouldered he was, Bryony thought. There was only one other man who was anywhere near his size: a big, red-bearded Scotsman in charge of the three graceful greyhounds that cavorted playfully around the wagons. But whereas the Scotsman was a hulking bear of a man, St. John was well-proportioned, lean, and lethal-looking.

He wore his black, broad-brimmed hat pulled low over a face set in forbidding lines. He seemed more distant this morning than ever before, and Bryony thought she might almost have imagined that strange and rather frightening moment of intimacy last night.

Then, as if he sensed her watching him, he turned, his cold gaze meeting hers and holding it across the street full of stomping horses and shouting men. Only there was something in his expression that wasn't cold at all. Something that brought a heat to her insides and a flush to her face.

She looked away quickly, panicked as much by her own reaction to him as by what she had seen in his face.

For it was no use trying to pretend he didn't have an effect on her, because he did. And although she disliked and feared him, what she felt when she was around him went beyond simple fear or dislike. It was . . .

Awareness. That's what it was. An intense, physical awareness of his masculinity, of his power. His power as her master. His power as a man. Because the fact was, he could take her anytime he wanted to. And they both knew it.

He walked up to her. "I told Gideon to have you wait inside where it's warm until we're ready to leave."

She tilted back her head to look up into his dark, shadowed face. "I didn't know it was an order."

For a moment, the taut lines of his features eased with what might have been amusement. "Do you *ever* do what you're told?"

"I . . ." She licked her suddenly dry lips, then regretted it when his gaze dropped to her mouth. "I am trying."

He propped one foot up on the block beside her, leaning forward as if about to say something. But at that moment Gideon came out of the inn, carrying the baby's red trunk. St. John straightened up and turned back to his men.

She didn't see Hayden St. John again until she'd taken her place beside Gideon on the wooden seat of the cart, with the baby settled in her lap.

He was mounted on a high-stepping bay gelding that looked as restless and edgy as the man who rode it. It was a big animal; it needed to be big to carry a man his size comfortably. But St. John controlled the spirited horse with the inimitable ease and grace of a born horseman.

As she watched, he lifted his arm and shouted something, something that was lost amid the cursing of the men and the snap of whips and the creak of the slowly turning wagon wheels as the whole line began to move. The cart jerked forward, bouncing and rattling over the rutted street.

They wound down the ridge, toward the outskirts of town. At first it seemed to Bryony as if they traveled almost southward. Then the road curved around until it headed west. Ahead of them, a jagged, wild-looking range of mountains loomed blue and menacing in the distance.

Soon the town gave way to open country. Magpies sang. The golden light of the rising sun spilled across stump-filled pastures and fields planted with scraggly

rows of corn and wheat. There were only a few scattered
houses, most of them pitiful, slab buildings that reminded
Bryony of the huts in the Rocks. Then, with an abrupt-
ness that was almost startling, the cleared ground ended,
and they were in untouched bushland.

Bryony was struck as never before by the untamed
wildness of this place. Strange, gaunt trees and grassy
slopes that looked as if they'd never known the touch of
man rolled on and on until swallowed up by the same
blue haze that shimmered around the rugged mountains
on the horizon.

The land seemed so lonely, so empty. It frightened and
excited her at the same time. Everywhere she looked she
saw something strange, something startling. Rock lilies
seemed to grow out of the very stones. Gray wallabies
and kangaroos grazed on the hillsides like deer, loping
about with their peculiar, thumping hops. Even the trees
were unfamiliar, with odd, silver-green leaves. Some had
incredibly smooth trunks, but there were others with bark
so ragged it hung down in tattered strips.

"What kind of trees are those?" she asked Gideon,
pointing to a stand with almost white bark.

"Eucalypts. The Cap'n says they're almost all eucalypts. Those there are called white gums. And that one
there—see it?—it's a red gum. Even those bushes on the
side of the track, they're all some kind of eucalypt." He
stared at the oxen's rumps for a minute, resting his
elbows on his knees, then said, "Mrs. St. John, she hated
the gums. Said they were eerie."

Bryony tilted back her head, staring thoughtfully up at
the pale, drooping leaves of the overhead canopy, trying
to imagine what it must have been like for the beautiful,
gently reared daughter of a viscount to suddenly find herself in the middle of this harsh, unforgiving landscape. "I
guess they are, in a way." She caught a flash of bright red
and yellow and blue flitting through the upper branches
of one of the trees and realized it was a bird. "Look at
that," she cried, pointing. "What's that?"

Gideon squinted. "That? That's just a Rose Hill parrot—rosellas, some people call them." He said it as if it were no great thing. But Bryony knew it wouldn't matter how many times she saw such a glorious bird flying free; it would always give her a thrill.

The day had dawned clear and sunny, with just a few high, scattered clouds. But as the morning wore on, the clouds steadily thickened until eventually it looked as if it might rain again.

Even from his place at the front of the line, Hayden could hear Simon fussing constantly. The convict woman had her hands full trying to hold him, as he refused to settle down because of the bumpy, rattling motion of the cart. She finally disappeared under the tilt with him. The squalling ceased abruptly, and Hayden knew she had put the child to her breast.

A sudden, loud crack of thunder rumbled through the surrounding trees. A great gust of wind came up, hurtling dry leaves and small branches before it. At the front of the line, a horse whinnied its apprehension. The sky opened up and poured.

Hayden pushed his broad-brimmed hat down on his head and hunched his shoulders against the rain. The deluge was savage but short. Within ten minutes the rain ended. Breaks in the clouds showed deep blue sky waiting above.

But as brief as it was, the storm had done its damage. The washboard, half-dried-out road became a slippery quagmire. All up and down the line, whips cracked, cattle bellowed, men swore. First one wagon, then another bogged down. Bullocks, horses, men, all slipped and fell repeatedly in the mud, until men and animals alike were covered with the stuff.

Gideon in particular seemed to be having a hard time with his bullocks. First one, then the other would lie down and refuse to budge. He'd crack his whip and shout, but it usually didn't do any good. Twice Hayden

sent McDuff and his greyhounds back to help. The dogs
barked at the beasts and bit their noses. The bullocks
stretched out their necks and bellowed, then heaved back
up onto their feet and started off again.

After he'd dispatched McDuff the third time, Hayden
rode back himself. He reined his bay in beside the tilted
cart and looked down at Bryony Wentworth. Simon was
still asleep in his cradle in the back of the cart. She cast
him one quick, nervous glance, then looked pointedly
away, her back ramrod straight on the hard plank seat.

"We need to lighten the load on the cart," he said. Her
head snapped back around. "You'll have to get off and
walk."

He expected her to complain, perhaps even try to argue
with him about it. What he hadn't expected was for her to
smile.

It was a slow smile, one that lifted the corners of her
lips, chased the shadows from her pretty brown eyes, and
lit up her whole face. It was the first time he'd seen her
smile, and he didn't like the effect it had on him. He felt
as if the blood in his veins had been heated, and there
was a definite stirring in his loins. He waited only long
enough to see her climb down out of the cart, then he
wheeled his horse around and cantered back up the line.

But he couldn't seem to banish the image of her from
his mind, no matter how hard he worked to keep the
wagons moving.

It wasn't long before the sun was out again, strong
enough to raise a sweat. Steam rose from the wet road-
way and the animals' soaked hides. Then the flies came
out. If there was one thing Hayden hated about Australia,
it was the flies. They landed on the men's mouths and
hovered about their eyes and drove the animals crazy.
One of the horses pulling the front dray was so maddened
by the swarming black things that it did a little half buck
and managed to get itself tangled in its harness. The
whole line had to stop while the horse was unharnessed,
then reharnessed again.

Hayden was just swinging back into the saddle after getting the wagons moving again, when he saw her. She walked along the verge of the road, staying out of the mud as best she could, although the grass and shrubs were still wet from the rain and the skirt of her new gray dress was already soaked to the knees. She had left Simon in his cradle in the cart and was striding along with the leggy, easy gait of a woman born and bred in the country.

It was obvious she was glad to be off the jolting cart. She seemed fascinated by everything she saw, whether it was the glorious sight of a banksia in bloom or something as simple as a lizard, scuttling off a sunbaked rock at her approach. As he watched her, a flock of galahs swept overhead, billowing up and wheeling like a great pink and gray cloud scuttling before the wind. She stopped, her hand coming up to shade her eyes from the sun as she followed their flight. For a moment a slow smile of pleasure once more lifted the sadness from her face, and it touched him again, in a way he hadn't expected.

He started to ride toward her, then wheeled and spurred the bay away instead, up and over the hill. He intended to check on the creek crossing at the base of the slope. But as he stopped his horse beneath an ironbark and sat for a moment watching the sunlight filter through its leaves and dapple over the surface of the clear water of the stream, he found himself thinking about the convict woman instead.

He liked the way the woman's chin jutted up and her eyes flashed when she had to say *yes, sir*. He liked the way her flame-licked, dusky hair curled around her face, making her look as if she'd just gotten out of bed. And when he saw his son at her breast, he found himself wondering what that breast would feel like under his hand. He wanted to put his hands on her.

He wanted his new servant woman.

He dismounted and loosened his saddle girth, letting the horse have a drink while he stepped a few yards upstream and hunkered down to splash the cold, fresh water over his face, as if it might somehow cool the heat in his loins, too.

Laura's death had left a painful ache, deep within him. But he was a healthy young man, with all of a man's physical needs. He supposed it was inevitable that those needs would become increasingly insistent as time went on. He just hadn't expected it to happen this soon.

Or to find that he could be so aroused by the resilient spirit and ripe body of a convict woman whose wary, hate-filled eyes seemed to follow him wherever he went.

CHAPTER
EIGHT

By mid-afternoon, Bryony was tired.

She barely noticed the pungent wattles, the bluebells and belly buttons, or the brightly colored cockatoos that flickered through the drooping branches of the overhead gums. She walked with her head bowed, all her concentration trained on the simple effort of putting one foot in front of the other.

She had lifted her head to brush the hair out of her sweaty face when she saw Captain St. John trotting his horse down the line toward her. He had taken off his coat and waistcoat, and had the sleeves of his white shirt rolled back, revealing tanned, muscular forearms. The slight breeze raised by the motion of his horse molded the fine cambric of the shirt to his powerful chest and shoulders, making him look more than ever like an untamed adventurer.

He drew abreast of her and wheeled the bay about to bring the horse to a walk beside her. He watched her for a moment, his face closed and unreadable. Then he reined in and said abruptly: "You're too tired to walk any farther, and the road hasn't dried out enough yet to risk your weight on the cart again. You'd better climb up behind me."

She whirled around to stare up at him in dismay. "I— I'm all right."

His eyes flashed danger. "Goddamn it, woman, when are you going to learn to say *yes, sir*, and just do what you're told?"

Her chin jutted forward and she took a deep breath, but then reason overruled instinct and she swallowed the angry retort that had sprung to her lips.

"Very wise," he said, moving the bay forward a few steps until he was once more beside her. He slid his boot from the stirrup and reached down his left hand for her. "Get up."

It was a big horse. She lifted her skirt and petticoats and had to reach up high with her foot before she was able to thrust it into his stirrup. She didn't even want to think about what kind of a view she was giving him of her legs, or the fact that the government budget for prisoners' clothing didn't stretch to include any under-garments beyond the traditional petticoats and old-fashioned shift. Without looking at him, she put her pale, thin hand into his strong, brown one. He grasped her wrist and hauled her up.

She settled behind him, acutely conscious of the way her thighs wrapped around his hips, the way her stomach pressed against the small of his back. She tried to hold herself erect and distant from him, but once he touched his heels to the horse's side and they moved forward, it was impossible to keep her breasts from occasionally brushing his broad back. She was determined not to hold on to him. But then the bay did a little standing hop over a log in its path, and she found herself clutching at his waist.

She let go of him almost immediately, but he said, "You'd better hold on." So she did. . . .

And tried not to think about his lean hips, his hard, flat stomach, and his broad, well-muscled back beneath the fine cloth of his shirt. With every breath she was aware of his scent, a scent of leather and horse and warm, hard-working man that was not at all unpleasant.

The afternoon wore on, and the sun grew progressively hotter. Her heavy petticoats stuck to her skin. Drops of sweat rolled down between her shoulder blades and soaked the rough, scratchy material of her dress. It didn't help to realize that beneath her hands, the man in front of her seemed cool and completely unaffected by either the heat or the long hours in the saddle.

"Don't you ever get hot?" she finally demanded.

He chuckled softly. "This isn't hot. Wait until it's January, when we haven't had any rain for a month and the wind swings around until it's coming from the north. Now, that's hot."

"This is hot," she said stubbornly.

He laughed again. "You'll get used to it."

"How long did it take . . . you to get used to it?" She had wanted to say *your wife*, but found she couldn't quite bring herself to do it.

"I didn't need to. I grew up in the West Indies. My father's regiment was transferred there before I was born, so until I was sent back to England for school, it was all I knew. And if you can't take the heat, you don't survive long in that part of the world."

The West Indies. It was one of the wondrous, faraway places she'd dreamed of when she was a little girl. *When I grow up, I'm going to sail across the oceans, like Papa,* she'd announced at the age of five. *Be careful what you wish for, infant,* her mother had told her with a gentle smile. *You might get it.*

They were crossing a marshy stretch, where the mud sucked at the bullocks' hooves and sprayed up behind the wagons' wheels. A small scrabbling noise made Bryony turn her head to see a green frog leap flying into the air and hit the water of a nearby pond with a splash.

"Did you ever go back?" she asked suddenly.

She thought he wasn't going to answer her. Then he said, "My parents and two younger sisters all died in a typhoid epidemic that swept the islands the year after I left."

"I . . . I'm sorry."

He shrugged. "I barely remember them."

She studied his closed, averted profile, and thought, *he may not remember them, but he remembers what it felt like to lose them.*

He brought his horse to a stand. "Look." He pointed to two large coal-black birds floating serenely in the open water. "See them? They're swans."

"Swans?" Bryony watched the two elegant birds take fright at the sound of the approaching wagons and lift awkwardly into flight. "But they're black."

He turned his head slightly, and she saw that his lips were smiling. "In New South Wales, the swans are black. And the trees lose their bark instead of their leaves and Christmas is one of the hottest days of the year."

Unconsciously she returned his smile. "Everything's so different here. It's . . ." She searched for the right word. "Exciting."

A peculiar expression shaded his eyes. "You think it's exciting?"

"Yes. Don't you?"

"Yes." He urged the big bay forward. "But in my experience, most people don't like things that are different."

After that, he withdrew from her in some way, although she couldn't quite figure out why.

It was late afternoon. Hayden urged the bay into an easy trot that soon outdistanced the wagons toiling behind them up a long, steep slope. When they crested the top of the hill, he reined the horse in.

Ahead of them stretched a broad valley through which a river wound its way slowly to the sea. It was a fertile valley, with well-tended fields and acre after acre of open pasture. There were a number of homesteads scattered here and there, up and down the river, and one particularly large estate on the near side of the river at the base of the hill.

A long, private drive lined with Norfolk pines wound through extensive pastures and fields and gardens, to sweep up before a stately, two-story brick mansion with a cluster of outbuildings grouped around its rear courtyard.

It had been nothing short of agony for Hayden to have her so close to him all afternoon. Her full, ripe breasts pressed against his back, her thighs lay intimately nestled around him, her breath tickled the nape of his neck. He'd been cursing the damn mud and Gideon's inferior driving skills and his own seemingly uncontrollable lust for miles now.

"Goodness." Bryony said suddenly, her hand moving against his side. "Is that your property?" That unexpected brush of her hand against his hip was almost more than he could bear.

"No," he said tersely. "Jindabyne is still a good day and a half away from here. And I'm afraid it's nothing near as grand as this. This is Priscilla Pines. It belongs to a man named Sir D'Arcy Baxter, who asked me to stop and stay with him on my way back up to the Hawkesbury. He and I share an interest in sheep breeding."

She gazed beyond the house to the river that flowed slowly past it. He noticed she was being careful not to let any more of her body touch his than was absolutely necessary. "That's not the Hawkesbury?"

"No, that's the Parramatta. See that town up there?" He pointed to the large settlement, just visible on the far side of the river. "That's where the Female Factory is," he added.

He heard her draw her breath in a quick, indignant gasp. "You mean it took us all day, just to get back to Parramatta!"

Hayden turned his horse with a low chuckle. "I told you the roads here are bad."

The dining table at Priscilla Pines was a massive thing, ordered especially from England and made of the finest mahogany available. Idly estimating chairs and distances, Hayden decided it would probably seat more people than there were free men in the colony. And only

those untarnished by convict status would ever be welcome at Priscilla Pines.

"Why, Captain St. John," exclaimed Miss Amanda
Baxter, smiling up at him provocatively. "I do believe
you haven't heard a word I said."

Hayden glanced down at the vision in white muslin
seated beside him. At just eighteen his host's daughter
was a decidedly attractive young woman. She had captured his attention at Government House two nights ago,
largely because her dainty, fair-haired good looks reminded him of his beautiful, dead wife. A fact her mother
had, unfortunately, picked up on very quickly.

Miss Amanda Baxter only recently had returned to the
colony from school in England. She was now ready for
a husband, and Hayden had a growing suspicion that
he had been selected as a suitable candidate. His estates
might still be fledgling, but his lineage was impeccable.
Not only had his grandfather distinguished himself as a
general in the French wars of the last century, but his
dead wife had been the daughter of a viscount.

The fact that his wife was only some four months dead
didn't seem to deter the ambitious Lady Priscilla Baxter.
Eligible husbands were scarce in the colony. She was
probably anxious to secure him for her daughter before
he took up with some convict mistress, the way most of
the men here did. It was a thought that, unfortunately,
brought the flashing brown eyes and strong chin of
Bryony Wentworth to mind, making it oddly difficult for
him to smile down at his dinner-table companion and
say, "You wrong me, Miss Baxter. Mrs. Marsden here
was giving us her opinion of Elizabeth Fry's recommen-
dations for prison reform, and you said you'd actually
attended one of her lectures in London. Are you interested in reform work?"

"Good gracious, no," exclaimed Miss Baxter with a
tinkling little laugh. "I went there with my mother's
sister, who *would* take me. *She* thinks the woman's ideas

are all nonsense, of course, but she says it's important to keep abreast of current trends."

Hayden eyed her over the rim of his glass. "And do you think her suggestions are nonsense? That women prisoners should be separated from the men, and supervised by female jailers?"

"Well, as to that, I don't know. But she went on ad nauseam as to how the wretches' crimes are a result of their poverty—as if everyone were not already aware of that."

Hayden slowly swallowed a mouthful of wine. "Is everyone aware of it?"

"But of course." She laughed again. "What I fail to see, however, is why I should feel sorry for the degraded creatures, simply because their indolence has made them poor."

"Ah. But then I believe Mrs. Fry argues that their poverty is the result, not of indolence, but of lack of opportunity."

"Preposterous." This came from the Reverend Samuel Marsden, on the opposite side of the table. Reverend Marsden was a stout, bald-headed man with beady eyes and a sour mouth, who managed to be both a man of God and a magistrate without any apparent sense of incongruity. "Everyone knows that the criminal classes are a race apart. Irreclaimably and genetically predisposed toward indolence and violence."

Hayden leaned back in his chair and smiled. "Is that why you do your best to rid the world of them, Reverend?"

From the head of the table, their host grunted his approval. Sir D'Arcy Baxter was a powerfully built, handsome man with silvered black hair and a dark, sharp-featured face. "How many was it you hanged last week in your magistrate's court, Samuel?" Sir D'Arcy asked. "Seven?"

"Five." The reverend helped himself to another serving

of roast beef. "The other two I let off with five hundred lashes each."

"They've started calling dear Samuel the Hanging Parson now, you know, rather than the Flogging Parson," said the reverend's short, homely faced wife. She smiled at her husband with obvious pride.

"Should have hanged all seven of them," said Marsden, motioning to a servant to bring him a platter displaying a glazed goose. "They were all obviously incorrigibles. The authorities should have hanged them in England and saved the taxpayers the expense of transporting them out here."

"But, then, where would you get the laborers to clear your farm for you, Reverend?" interposed Hayden.

"True," agreed Sir D'Arcy Baxter, draining his wineglass. "It's a sad quandary. Where I believe the authorities make their mistake is in transporting so many of the scoundrels for only seven years—or even fourteen. It ought to be for life. There's getting to be a sight too many emancipists around these days."

"And the pretensions they give themselves," agreed Lady Priscilla Baxter, from her end of the table. She was a fair-haired woman, in her early forties but still slim and handsome. She frowned, drawing down the corners of her mouth in a way that accentuated the length of her face and made her look considerably less attractive. "Why, the last time I saw Dr. William Redfern, I swear he behaved as if he had never been transported, and were in some way my equal. I felt compelled to remind him that my father was a Devonshire squire."

Hayden raised his hand and coughed. Lady Priscilla Baxter always found some way to remind people that she was the daughter of a Devonshire squire.

The ladies soon withdrew, leaving the men to their port. They talked for a while about the price of wheat and the conditions of their herds, then Sir D'Arcy Baxter said, "Before we rejoin the ladies, Samuel, I'd like to bring in one of my servants and have you sentence him.

It'll save me the trouble of sending him into Parramatta tomorrow."

"Of course," said the Reverend Marsden. "Always happy to oblige a friend. Bring him in."

Sir D'Arcy beckoned to a servant, who was sent running.

"Bit irregular, isn't it?" said Hayden, raising one eyebrow.

The reverend puckered his mouth until it looked like a squeezed-up old lemon. "How so? I'm the magistrate. If I should choose to hold a session here rather than in Parramatta tomorrow, what difference can it make? Frankly I think this business of not allowing masters to order their own servants flogged is nonsense. That's not the way we did it in the old days, I can tell you."

Privately Hayden thought things hadn't changed so much since the old days after all, but he kept it to himself.

At that moment a bullheaded man with a mean expression came into the dining room, dragging behind him a frightened-looking lad of about eighteen.

Marsden looked the convict over and puckered his sour lips. "What man is that?" he demanded in a booming, legalistic voice.

The bullheaded man, whom Hayden took to be Baxter's overseer, replied: "A man of Sir D'Arcy Baxter's, your worship."

"His name and offense?"

"Paddy O'Neal, your worship. Charged with neglect of duty."

The Reverend Magistrate Samuel Marsden paused to pour himself another glass of port. "Will you have the goodness to give your deposition?"

The overseer cleared his throat and clutched the tattered black book handed to him. "I, John Flood, now of Priscilla Pines, in the county of—"

The reverend waved one plump white hand. "Never mind all that. Just state why the prisoner is brought here before me."

"Yes, your worship. Paddy O'Neal here, he's a swineherd for Sir D'Arcy Baxter, you see. And he lost one of his master's pigs last week, and another pig this week. We looked for them, your worship, but we never did find them."

Reverend Marsden stared at the hapless Irishman in a way that made his beady eyes practically disappear into the folds of his fat face. "And what have you to say in your defense?"

The young man gulped. "I'm sorry, sir—your worship. I—I ain't never kept pigs before, sir—your worship. They sent me out in the bush with a herd of them, and they just ran in all directions. I—I—" His voice cracked and broke.

"Then, you do not deny the charges? Through your own negligence, you lost two of the pigs Sir D'Arcy Baxter entrusted to your care?"

"I didn't mean to! I tried. I really did try—" The lad broke off as the reverend's awful frown was bent on him again.

"Then, perhaps," said the reverend slowly, "a taste of the cat-o'-nine-tails will help you try harder next time." He sighed. "Two hundred lashes."

Paddy O'Neal went pale and started shaking so badly Hayden thought the lad might faint. Sir D'Arcy jerked his head toward the door. "Get him out of here, Flood." He turned toward his guests and smiled. "And now that that little bit of unpleasantness is over, shall we rejoin the ladies?"

The drawing room was a large, elegant room decorated in fashionable Chinese blues and greens. Like most of the other apartments on the ground floor, it had a double set of French doors that opened onto the veranda. A cool breeze blowing up from the river brought with it the sweet scent of flowering fruit trees from the garden.

The gentlemen entered the room to find the three ladies seated in a semicircle, sewing. At the sight of Hayden, Miss Baxter cast aside her frame and smiled charmingly up at him. "Whatever kept you gentlemen for so long?"

"Just a slight problem with one of the new servants," said her father. "The reverend took care of it for me."

Mrs. Marsden nodded approvingly. "Samuel allows that no new assigned servant is worth anything until he has been flogged three times, isn't that right, Samuel?"

"In my experience," said the reverend, puffing out his fat chest. "And if that doesn't work, you might as well hang them, because they're obviously incorrigible."

Hayden glanced toward the open doors to the veranda. The breeze from the river now carried with it a growing murmur of voices. Someone called out an order, and then he heard a sound no one who'd spent eight years in the army—or any time at all in New South Wales—could fail to recognize. It was the snap of a cat-o'-nine-tails whipping through the air to slash a man's back.

It was followed by the collective sigh of all those who had been assembled to watch.

Lady Priscilla Baxter obviously heard it, too. "Amanda, dear; do play us something on the pianoforte," she said. "And Captain St. John, if you would be so good as to close the doors?"

Miss Baxter obediently moved to seat herself at the instrument that was the symbol of every young lady's claim to gentility, and launched into a minuet without any hesitation. She played competently—and loudly. But not loudly enough to prevent Hayden, walking over to close first one door, then the other, from hearing the distressed cry of a baby.

His baby.

He excused himself and stepped out onto the veranda, closing the French doors behind him. The moon was only just up, spilling a silver path across the dark waters of the slow-moving river. From a stand of gums near the bank came the lonely, haunting cry of a curlew that formed a bizarre counterpoint to the sickening crack of the whip.

He heard a groan, but there were no screams yet. Paddy O'Neal was obviously taking the lash like a man.

Hayden followed the veranda through a covered archway that led to the large courtyard at the rear of the house. The courtyard was paved with sandstone slabs and surrounded by stables and carriage houses and various workrooms and servants' quarters. Near the center a triangle had been set up on a raised platform of stone blocks so that the unfortunate victim could be seen clearly by all who had assembled to watch his punishment.

Young Paddy O'Neal, stripped to the waist, was tied with his arms pulled around the triangle and his chest pressed so tightly against the post that it was impossible for him to move in any way to resist the lash. The blows rained down unceasingly on the poor lad's thin back, one after the other, tearing at skin and muscle until the bones themselves showed through the pulverized bloody mess.

Hayden scanned the courtyard full of people. It looked as if Baxter had ordered all of his servants assembled to watch the flogging, for it was intended to serve not only as a punishment for Paddy O'Neal, but as a warning to the other convicts as well. Hayden's servants, because they were here, had been ordered to be present as well.

He finally located Gideon, standing on the far edge of the crowd, his face pale, his normally placid eyes narrowed in outrage. It looked as if he were trying to shield someone from the worst of the spectacle. Someone who held a baby.

If Gideon was pale, Bryony was white. Though Gideon was doing his best to spare her, she stared at the mangled, writhing mess on the platform with wide, horrified eyes. Held tightly in her arms, Simon howled with all his newfound strength, but whether it was because she was communicating her anxiety to him, or because she was clutching him so tightly, Hayden wasn't sure.

He wove his way through the gaping crowd, his gaze on his baby and the woman who held him.

"Bryony," he said quietly.

She was beyond hearing him.

"Bryony!" He closed his fingers around her upper arms and pulled her around until she looked at him rather than at the calculated horror in the center of the courtyard.

He was shocked by the sight of her. The fine bones of her face were sharp, gaunt, her beautiful brown eyes two dark smudges against pale, pale skin. She stared at him for a moment as if she didn't even recognize him. The pain and fear in her eyes was so raw he could have winced at it. Then she gave a small, hoarse cry and collapsed against him.

Somehow he managed to disentangle the kicking, screaming baby from her arms. "Here," he said, handing the baby to Gideon. "Get Simon out of this."

Then he drew her through the covered archway and out into the darkness of the garden beyond.

CHAPTER
NINE

Great, gasping, gut-wrenching sobs tore through Bryony's body. She was out of control, clinging helplessly to a hard, massive chest, barely conscious of the fact those solid shoulders and the warm, comforting arms that held her belonged to Hayden St. John. She cried for Paddy O'Neal, she cried for Philip, she cried for Madeline, she cried for herself. She cried for a world in which so much agony and despair had to be endured.

And she cried because she wasn't sure she could bear any of it any longer.

She had no idea how long she stood in Hayden St. John's arms, crying. Then Paddy O'Neal's control broke, and he started to scream.

It was a terrible sound, a high-pitched, animallike scream of indescribable agony that cut through the sweetly scented evening air and brought her sobs to a shuddering halt.

Against her cheek, she could feel the steady beat of Hayden St. John's heart. His evening jacket was smooth and cool. But the arms that held her to him were hard and capable of violence. She sucked in a deep breath, and her senses swam with the scent of him. The scent of starched linen and fine tobacco and restless, deadly maleness.

He was a part of this system, a part of the establishment that perpetuated the barbaric ritual she'd just witnessed. He'd even threatened to have the same thing done to her.

Bryony backed away from him, revulsion, horror, and

fear welling up within her anew. Then she tipped back her head and saw his face.

There was a tense, heated look about him that sharpened the angles of his cheeks, flared his nostrils, narrowed his eyes. She knew that look, knew what it meant.

"I'm sorry," she whispered, horrified by the realization of what she'd done. "I don't know what came over me."

"I've seen something similar happen before," he said simply, his voice unexpectedly gentle. That frighteningly intense look faded. "In India."

He took her arm and led her farther away from the house, toward the base of the garden where a vine-twisted arbor stood overlooking the silver slash of the distant river, barely visible through the dark mass of gums along its bank. A light breeze stirred the night air, bringing with it the sweet, heady scent of roses and clematis. In the distance an unseen fountain could be heard, bubbling and splashing away beneath the louder, whistling snap of the cat.

"There was this one young officer who came out while I was there," Captain St. John said. "He went through two particularly bloody, brutal battles shortly after he arrived, but it didn't seem to have bothered him at all. Then one day we saw a dead dog on the road, and he completely fell apart."

Bryony glanced sideways at the man beside her, conscious of seeing him in an entirely new light. "That boy back there isn't a dog."

"No." He paused in the arched entrance to the arbor. "Although he's being treated worse than one."

She sank down on a bench and gazed out at the moon-glazed river framed by lacy lattice, unaware of the silent tears still streaming down her cheeks. To her surprise, he propped his foot up on the bench beside her and leaned forward, resting the palms of his hands against the sides of her face to wipe away her tears with his thumbs.

"You'll survive, Bryony," he said softly. "And so will he."

The awful sound of the cat stopped. Paddy O'Neal gave one final, pitiful scream. In the ensuing silence the hum of the cicadas seemed unnaturally loud.

"Will he?" She suddenly realized how close Hayden St. John was. And that one of his hands still rested, hard and warm, against her cheek. It sent a surprisingly pleasant tremor rippling through her. She tried to resurrect some vestige of her earlier anger, but found she couldn't.

"He'll survive this time at least," Hayden said, dropping his hand and turning away from her. "It could have been worse. The boy's lucky Marsden had some wine in him. He usually orders at least three hundred."

"His back was a mess."

"Aye." Bryony watched him go to stand with his arms braced against the sides of the arbor. He was gazing down at the river sliding past at the base of the slope, but Bryony had a feeling he was looking inward. "I saw a man given eight hundred lashes once."

"Good Lord," breathed Bryony. "What had he done?"

St. John shook his head, something that was not a smile twisting his lips. "He was just a soldier. It was at the end of a long, forced march, and he fell asleep on sentry duty. I guess Wellesley wanted to make an example of him. When his back couldn't take any more, they laid the whip on his backside, and when that was reduced to jelly, they started on his legs. It crippled him for life."

She stared up at the dark profile of the man gazing out over the river and remembered something Gideon had told her earlier, while they were watching Paddy O'Neal being tied to the triangle.

"Gideon told me tonight you don't usually flog your men," she said.

He turned at that and looked down at her. In the shadow of the arbor, his face was dark and unreadable. "No. I think there are more effective ways of controlling men."

"Such as?"

He shrugged and leaned back against a corner post of the arbor, his hips cocked forward, arms crossed at his chest. "In my experience a man's stomach is far more sensitive than his back."

Something twisted inside her. Something bitter and disappointed. "You *starve* them?"

"Hardly," he said dryly. He tipped his head back against the post and gazed down at her with hooded eyes. "I always make it a practice to give my men more than the basic ration. I find I get better work out of them that way. And the harder and better they work for me, the more sugar and tea and flour I give them." He took a cheroot from his waistcoat pocket and pulled it idly between his fingers. "Which means I have something to take away if they give me problems."

"Yet you threatened to flog me," she said quietly.

His tinderbox flared, throwing tongues of golden light and harsh shadows across his face. He sucked on his cigar, his eyes lowered. "I'll do whatever it takes to keep my son alive and well."

She made an inarticulate noise in her throat.

"Listen, Bryony," he said, looking down at her. "When I was a child in the West Indies, we were all basically raised by black servants. Slaves. I know only too well that most slaves are only as good at what they're set to do as they have to be, and the women who get shipped out here aren't any different. I've heard of toddlers falling down wells because the women who were supposed to be watching them had slipped off to the sly-grog shops instead." He jerked his head in the direction of the big house. "The Reverend Marsden's wife in there has lost two of her children to *accidents*—two of them! Half the babies in this colony are regularly dosed with rum to keep them from fussing and making too much trouble for their nurses."

"I would never do anything like that!" She dug her fists into the bench on either side of her and leaned forward. The motion caused her dress to pull taut over her milk-swollen breasts. She saw his attention lower, and quickly folded her arms across her chest.

"No," he said. He lifted one foot and braced it against the wall behind him, still studying her. "You're nothing like what I thought you were at first."

"You mean, a thieving whore." Her chin jutted up defiantly. To her surprise, she thought she saw him smile.

"Yes."

She caught his gaze and held it. "I've come to know a lot of thieving whores in the last twelve months. They're not all as bad as you might think."

He exhaled a thin stream of smoke. "Is that when you were arrested? A year ago?" His gaze grew intent, probing.

She looked away. "Yes. It—it was in September."

She was afraid he was going to ask her more. But just then, the distant sound of a door being thrown open drifted down the hill.

Bryony glanced up at the big house. Lady Priscilla Baxter stood silhouetted against one of the French doors opening from the drawing room onto the veranda. She peered out into the night, as if searching for her missing guest.

He pushed away from the post and dropped his cigar. "It's late."

Bryony stood up and moved to the arched entrance of the arbor. With the moon behind him, she couldn't read his expression. But the tension that had hummed between them all night was still there, quickening her breath, tightening the muscles way down low in her belly. She was suddenly, acutely aware that they were not just a master and his servant, but a man and a woman, standing beneath a rose-covered arbor.

And that she had spent the last fifteen minutes watching the way the moonlight and shadows played over the features of his face.

* * *

The next day dawned clear but balmy. The sun quickly dried the worst of the mud, but a blustery breeze kept away the unseasonable heat of the previous day.

This was more Bryony's idea of spring. After feeding Simon, she laid him in his bed in the back of the tilted cart and hopped down for a walk.

On a day like this she could almost—almost—forget about the constant ache in her heart. For a while, at least, she closed her ears to her inner scream of pain and grief. She forced herself not to think about what had happened to Oliver, or about Philip, lying in his muddy grave. Or about Madeline, alone and bewildered in that miserable dark house in the middle of the moors.

She walked along and listened instead to the high grass swish about her skirts. She found joy in the glory of the fresh air filling her lungs, the warmth of the sun on her face, the rustle of the breeze moving the leaves in the trees overhead . . . simple pleasures all now doubly precious for having been lost to her for a year. She threw back her head and experienced anew the exhilaration that comes from watching fluffy white clouds scuttle across a deep blue sky.

And wished she could be as free and lighthearted as those clouds.

She saw Hayden St. John only intermittently throughout the morning, and then only from a distance. He seemed to be avoiding her. She told herself she was glad of it. She found his presence and his dark, intense looks disturbing. But she couldn't seem to keep herself from remembering the way his arms had felt around her the night before, so warm and strong and comforting. Or the tense, restless way his eyes had moved over her when they'd sat in the arbor by the river. And she couldn't seem to keep her gaze from scanning the line for a stolen glimpse of his lean, hard body.

They crossed the river and left Parramatta behind. The road swung away to the northwest, drawing slowly closer to the hazy blue mass of mountains before them. At the top of a hill, Bryony stopped to shade her eyes with her hand and study the distant range.

She'd never seen mountains like this before, so high and rugged. Their jagged outline was like a tear in the sky. They seemed to loom over the plains and low hills at their feet, wild and restless, exciting and threatening at the same time. Even in the bright light of midday, they looked blue. Blue, mysterious, and otherworldly.

She was still gazing at the mountains when Hayden St. John rode up and reined his big bay in before her. He'd discarded his coat and waistcoat again not long after leaving Priscilla Pines. His cravat was gone, too, she noticed; she could see the triangle of bronzed throat and chest where he'd opened several buttons of his shirt at the top.

"Here." He leaned down to hand her a wide-brimmed straw hat similar to the one Gideon and most of the other men wore. "You'd better put this on. Your nose is turning red."

She took the hat from his outstretched hand, surprisingly touched that he'd thought of her. When she settled it on her head, she discovered it was a bit big, but at least it kept the sun off her face.

She tilted back her head and looked up at him from beneath the broad brim. He smiled, a slow smile that brought a crease to his cheek and warmed his eyes in a way she found disconcerting. "It'll do until we can get something more appropriate," he said.

There was something about his smile that made Bryony feel suddenly breathless. She glanced quickly away, toward the distant mountains and, feeling in need of something to say, asked, "What are they called? Those mountains, I mean?"

He turned his head to follow her gaze. "Someone gave them an official name once, but I've forgotten now what it was. Most people just call them the Blue Mountains."

"They look very near."

"They are. About twenty miles from here." He brought his horse to walk along beside her.

"What's on the other side?"

"The Aborigines say that on the far side of the highest ridges lie great valleys filled with sweet, lush grass ... enough to feed the biggest sheep herds the world has ever seen. But then again, there are others who claim it's nothing but desert."

She glanced up at him in surprise. "You mean, no one really *knows*?"

He shrugged. "No. No one's found a way to get through them yet. Every time someone follows a river up a likely looking valley, he finds himself staring at a waterfall tumbling over a cliff four or five hundred feet high. The Aborigines know how to get over them, I suppose. But so far they haven't shown anyone."

She gazed at the jagged peaks of the mountains in awe. "You mean, thousands of people live in a narrow stretch of coast along the edge of this great continent, and they don't even know what's on the other side of those mountains? Why, it could be anything!"

There was an arrested expression on his face. "Some ... some women hate the mystery of those mountains, the idea of something completely unknown and mysterious lying so close to where they live. Doesn't it frighten you?"

Bryony shook her head and smiled up at him. "No. But it does make me want to see what's on the other side."

He stared down at her for a long moment, his eyes narrow, his lips pressed into a thin line.

Then he wheeled his horse abruptly and rode away.

She didn't see him again until mid-afternoon.

She was sitting beside Gideon in the cart, waiting for their turn to cross a creek, when the dray in front of them sank unexpectedly into deep, loose sand and couldn't be budged.

The bullock driver shouted to the men up ahead, and

the whole line halted. Captain St. John sent the horses from the lead dray back to add their strength to that of the bullocks pulling the mired wagon. And still the wheels refused to turn.

Bryony climbed down from the tilted cart and spread one of Simon's blankets out on the grassy bank of the creek. Settling beside the baby, she drew her knees up to her chest and wrapped her arms around them, enjoying the way the sun warmed her back and sparkled along the dancing surface of the creek.

There was now quite a crowd of men, all standing around the dray, arguing about how best to deal with the problem. Then St. John himself rode up and sent one of the men running toward the forward dray. Five or six of the men sat down on the bank and began to take off their shoes and shirts.

Hayden St. John was one of them.

She watched him pull off his gleaming Hessians and stockings, then toss his hat aside and unbutton and strip off his shirt. He was twisted away from her, so that all she could see was his back. But she couldn't help noticing how hard and well-defined his muscles were, how smooth and tan his skin was, how broad he was at the shoulders, how sinuously his back tapered down to narrow hips. Then he turned to shout something to one of the men, and she saw how strong his chest was, saw the dark hair that curled across it and plunged down the hard, flat slab of his stomach to disappear beneath the waist of his breeches.

She hugged her knees tighter, watching him wade into the water, telling herself she shouldn't be looking at him like this. But she was too fascinated to turn away.

The man who'd been sent running came back carrying some long boards and laid them in front of the sunken wheels of the dray. The rest of the men waded into the creek to take up positions at the wheels and behind the wagon and add their own strength to that of the beasts.

Whips cracked. Horses and bullocks leaned into their collars. Men pushed. Hayden stood beside the near rear of the dray and leaned into the wheel. Bryony could see his shoulders and arms cord and bunch with the strain. The bright sun glazed his naked, sweat-sheened back with a golden light and glinted off his dark hair as he bowed his head.

There was a sucking sound. The wagon shuddered free and bounced, rattling, up the far bank.

The men cheered and laughed. Someone bent to retrieve the boards from the creek bed, while Hayden slapped the man nearest him on the shoulder and said something she didn't hear.

She watched him turn back toward the center of the creek. His breeches were wet clear up to his thighs. She could see the dark line, just below his crotch, where the water had reached. Sweat beaded his forehead, ran down into his eyes. He swiped at it absently with the back of one arm as he waded farther out into the creek and bent down to splash the cold water over his face and shoulders.

When he straightened, he still had his eyes closed. With his head tilted back, he reached up and ran his strong fingers through his dark hair, combing it back off his forehead. He had his arms lifted high, his elbows spread wide. His wet, bare skin stretched taut over his corded muscles, glistening in the sun. Dark, wet hair curled around his nipples. Tiny rivulets of water trickled down the ridges of his stomach to darken the waistband of his breeches. She saw the hair under his arms. Saw the drops of water that gathered and ran down his hard cheeks. Then he opened his eyes and caught her watching him.

Their gazes locked while he used one hand to slowly wipe the water off his lower face. Something flared hot and bright in his eyes. Something that ignited a slow fire that licked at her insides. She felt the heat of the sun on her skin. Felt the swell of her full breasts against the bodice of her dress, felt something squeeze the air from her lungs until she was breathless.

She knew she should look away, but she thought if she did, it would make it seem as if there was something to the way she'd been looking at him. And then she realized there *was* something to it, because of all the half-naked men who'd been in the stream, she'd seen only him, watched only him.

CHAPTER
TEN

Bryony sat with the baby nestled in her lap and watched Gideon ram the bases of skewers topped with kangaroo meat into the earth beside the campfire.

While the rest of the men were still setting up camp, Hayden St. John had shouldered his gun and walked off into the brush. Hunting, Gideon said. She'd heard the *boom* of his gun several times in the distance.

The air was heavy with the scent of burning eucalyptus and the rich aroma of roasting meat. Bryony had never spent a night in the open before. She was acutely conscious of the newness, the strangeness of it all. Exotic birds flitted through the shadows of the trees at the edge of the clearing and filled the evening sky with their songs, some high and tuneful, others low and almost coarse, but all unfamiliar. In the fading light, the surrounding gums seemed more ghostly than ever, holding up the dark, spreading umbrellas of their foliage against the dusk-reddened sky.

It would be dark soon.

She glanced at the second campfire, some fifty or so feet away, around which the rest of the men were gathered. As soon as the Captain returned and dinner was over, Gideon would be going there, too. Leaving her here, alone, with Simon and St. John. In the solitary tent that had been pitched behind her.

"Tell me about Captain St. John's property," she said suddenly to Gideon.

"Jindabyne?" He glanced up from mixing a kind of

unleavened bread he'd told her was called damper. " 'Tes . . ." He paused to consider his answer. " 'Tes rare country. Most of the Cap'n's fields are down in the valley, of course, but Jindabyne itself sits on the side of a hill that rises right up from the Hawkesbury. You can see for miles."

"Is it this wild?"

"Aye."

A twig snapped behind her. Bryony whirled around to see Hayden St. John appear out of the rapidly darkening fringe of the trees, the gun slung over his shoulder, a string of wild ducks dangling beside his thigh.

His white shirt glowed in the firelight, making his skin appear darker than it was. She thought he looked savage, primitive. Conscious of a warm, earthy sensation in the pit of her stomach, she watched him walk toward them with that rolling-hipped grace of his.

Gideon stood up to take the birds. The two men exchanged a few words, then Hayden St. John turned, and his gaze met and held Bryony's across the campfire. The evening had been steadily growing colder, but she suddenly felt hot. She ducked her head and fussed with the baby until she heard him go into the tent.

He reappeared a moment later and sat down on the opposite side of the fire from her. She was careful not to look at him. Shifting Simon around so that he lay on her lap with his head against her knees, she occupied herself making nonsense noises at him. The baby chuckled in delight, his mouth breaking into his toothless grin so that she couldn't help smiling back at him. Then she unconsciously glanced up at the baby's father, and the smile faded from her lips.

He was sitting cross-legged on the ground cleaning his gun. The dancing flames of the fire cast mysterious shadows across the harsh lines of his face and bronzed his naked forearms with golden light as his lean, sure hands moved over the gun in a way that reminded her of a lover's caress.

It was a manly pose, and a manly occupation. She couldn't begin to imagine Oliver, stripped down to his shirt, breeches, and boots, sitting cross-legged beside a fire in the middle of a primeval forest.

Oliver had never liked the country, not even the tame, settled countryside of Britain. He hadn't had much use for provincial towns like Penzance, either. Oliver had always prided himself on being a Man of the Town. London Town. A man comfortable in clubs and drawing rooms . . . and boudoirs, she thought wryly.

His body had been slim, not broad and well muscled. White instead of bronzed.

And thinking of Oliver's body had never made her blood heat as it did now, when she thought of the way Hayden St. John's body had looked this afternoon with the creek waters lapping at his darkened loins and glistening like dew drops across his hard, naked chest.

She jerked her mind away from the memory just as Gideon swept the ashes away from the damper he'd set to bake right in the coals. "Ready," he said with satisfaction.

The bread was surprisingly good—crusty, and lighter than she'd expected it to be. She wasn't so sure about the meat, but after a year of prison food, she'd eat anything.

After dinner they drank tea out of tin mugs, the water boiled in a big tin bucket Gideon called a billy can. She sipped her tea slowly, watching Gideon pack away the ducks he'd roasted into airtight crocks for tomorrow. Then he put the dishes and mugs he'd washed back in the tucker box, wished them a jaunty good night, and left to join the men around the other campfire.

Bryony watched him walk away, and shivered. With the sun finally down, the heat had suddenly gone out of the air and the night had become surprisingly cold. She glanced down at Simon. He'd fallen asleep.

"Give him to me, and I'll lay him in his cradle in the tent."

She looked up to find a pair of black boots planted

beside her. Her eyes traveled up the long line of his thighs, then quickly jumped to his face.

But his expression was unreadable.

"Yes . . . sir."

He reached for the baby as she handed Simon up to him, and her hand brushed his bare arm. It was only a simple, accidental touch, but it made her breath hitch.

She stood up quickly and reached to pour herself some more tea while he disappeared into the tent. To her chagrin, her hands were shaking so badly she spilt some of the dark, bitter liquid onto the fire. It hissed at her, sending up a plume of smoke.

She heard him come out of the tent. "Here," he said, dropping her cloak around her shoulders.

"Thank you."

He went to stand on the far side of the fire. He'd put on his greatcoat, but left it open. She looked into his taut face and felt something tremble deep within her. The campfire flared up between them, and for an instant their gazes met and held. Then a burst of laughter from the men's camp jerked Bryony's head around.

Someone had produced a fiddle, and Gideon and the redheaded man called McDuff were dancing around the fire. Against the dark background of the bush, the orange glow of the flames flickered on their white shirts and faces as they twirled around and around, their arms raised high, their feet kicking, their heads thrown back, laughing.

She glanced back at St. John. He lifted a flaming branch from the fire and touched it to the end of the cigar he held between his lips. The flame on the end of the branch flared, casting a reddish, almost sinister light across his handsome face.

There might be a dozen men only fifty feet away, but Bryony realized suddenly how alone with him she really was.

He threw the piece of wood back into the fire in a shower of sparks and glanced up to find her watching him. His eyes narrowed. He exhaled a cloud of smoke that looked white against the night sky.

She stood with the elbow of her right arm cupped with her left hand, watching the smoke from his cheroot mingle with the smoke of the fire. Cicadas hummed. Somewhere beyond the firelight a horse snorted, moving awkwardly in its hobbles. The fiddle wailed, the men laughed, but the night around them seemed so silent and empty, it ached.

She tilted back her head and looked up at the clear dark sky above. An infinity of unfamiliar stars sparkled down at her, and she felt a wave of loneliness spread over her.

All her life she had looked up at the same stars moving above her in predictable patterns across the night sky. But here, all was strange, all unknown, all alien. There was nothing that brought home to her how far she was from everything and everyone she knew and loved, more than looking up at the Southern sky.

Tears burned her eyes, and she had to swallow to keep from letting them spill over.

"It's different all right," came his harsh, almost cruel voice, cutting into her thoughts. "But you don't look excited anymore. You look . . ." He paused, as if searching for the right word. "Scared."

She met his eyes and found them filled with a challenge. A challenge, and something else she didn't want to think about.

She shook her head, conscious of a thickness in her throat that made it difficult to speak. "No. Not scared."

It was only partially a lie. She was scared, all right, but not of the Australian sky. She was scared of him.

He drew deeply on his cheroot, his disturbing gaze still fixed on her face. "What, then?"

She made a depreciating gesture with her hand. "I feel . . . disconnected. From my home. My little girl. From myself—the person I was before."

"I thought your baby was a boy."

"I have another child—a daughter. I had to leave her behind when the ship sailed." She took a sip of her tea, but it was cold, and she threw away the rest of it with a quick, violent gesture.

"Bryony."

She didn't want to look at him, but she couldn't help it. The red glow from the flames of the fire seemed to accentuate the sharp bone structure of his face. He drew on his cheroot, staring at her through the smoke that rose from it.

Her breath caught in her throat, causing her breasts to rise. His gaze lowered for a moment before flickering to her face. There was a hunger there, a hunger that frightened her even as it called to an answering need deep within her.

Then he closed it off. His face was flat, emotionless, and she thought it must have been a trick of the firelight.

He tossed his cheroot into the dying fire. "Go to bed."

A wind had come up. Bryony lay in her narrow bed of heather covered with canvas, listening to the wind sigh through the leaves of the surrounding trees. The moon was high enough now to shine brightly through the tent, clearly illuminating Simon asleep in his cradle, and the empty bed beyond him.

In the distance a night bird gave a low, mournful cry. She heard what sounded like a dog howling and thought there must be a homestead nearby. She could see the distant glow of the men's campfire, hear the low drone of their voices, the occasional outbreak of laughter. But the men were quieter now. It was getting late.

She shifted slightly, glancing toward the door of the tent. The flap hadn't been secured, and it flipped back and forth in the growing breeze.

He still stood before the fire. She could see the inverted V-shape of his legs, the boots widely spread. As she watched, he dropped his cigar and ground it beneath his heel.

For a moment she thought he was coming. She could barely breathe, her heart pounded so hard. Then she heard his voice from the direction of the other campfire, and she realized he must have gone to talk to the men.

More minutes passed. She was aware of an almost incredible stillness all around, broken only occasionally by the murmur of voices from the distant fire, and the croaking of some unseen frog. Her limbs started to feel very heavy. Her eyelids fluttered.

Even after almost a week away from the ship, when she closed her eyes she could still feel the incessant pitching and rolling that she'd known for some six months.

And it rocked her to sleep.

Jindabyne.

The hill the Aborigines called Jindabyne thrust up from the fertile floor of the valley, forcing the Hawkesbury to curve around it on its way to the sea. A gentle spring breeze ruffled the mass of red gums growing thickly at the base of the hill. Slate-green leaves swayed back and forth against the vivid sky. From here, the river was only a flash of sun-sparkled silver, glimpsed through a mass of foliage.

Hayden reined in his horse and let the wagons roll past him as he sat surveying his land with the fierce joy that never failed to fill him at the sight of it. Stands of ironbark and blackbutt covered its grassy slopes, along with pungent wattles and a dozen different kinds of gums. River gums and red gums, stringy barks, and the pale-trunked, ghostly white gums.

There were mounds of banksia, glorious now in their bloom, and stretches of deep grass sprinkled with native pansies and wild geranium and candytuft. He'd had to clear parts of it, of course, to make way for his fields of wheat and corn and the pastures for his growing herds of cattle and sheep and horses. But he would never clear it all, for it was the very wildness of this land that called to him. He might need to work it, but he never wanted to see it completely tamed.

If he had his way, fifty years from now there would still be wallabies here, hopping down to the creek in the late afternoon. Curlews would still wail at dusk, and dingoes howl in the night. His grandchildren would still be able to look up and thrill to the flight of an egret, or watch a flock of sulfur-crested cockatoos wheel like a sun-streaked cloud across the blue Australian sky.

He rested his hand on his thigh and allowed his eyes to roam proudly over his land, seeing all that it was, all that it would be. And he felt an unexpected and unaccountable ache deep within him, an emptiness, that not even the rich beauty of his land could fill.

A whip cracked beside him, startling a crowd of blue wrens from a sheltered place beside the road. They rose suddenly into flight, looking like a gossamer of jewel-toned silk lifting in the breeze. He raised his hand to push back the brim of his hat, watching them . . .

And knew she was there.

He glanced over his shoulder to find that the tilted cart had stopped beside him. Gideon cracked his whip again, shouting at the balking bullocks. But Bryony sat still. She had her head thrown back, following the sun-sparkled ribbon of blue with her eyes, a smile curling her beautiful lips. Then, slowly, as if becoming aware of the heat of his gaze upon her, she turned her head.

They looked at each other. Her deep brown eyes took on a dusky, smoldering look. He felt the ache within him grow until, for a moment, it became something almost desperate. Her lips parted. She breathed in sharply.

And he wanted her.

He wanted to pull her off that cart seat and lay her down in the sweet, clover-scented grass and take her, right now, beneath the wide, sun-drenched Australian sky. He wanted to smother her smiling lips with his hungry mouth. He wanted to cover her pale woman's flesh with his hard man's body. He wanted to possess her, to make her his, to master her in every sense of the word. He wanted to hear her moan, to feel her wrap her long, naked legs around his hips and have her beg him to fill her.

And maybe, just maybe, have her fill the desperate emptiness within him.

CHAPTER
ELEVEN

Jindabyne's yard was crowded. McDuff's greyhounds barked and chased one another in a frenzy of excitement, weaving between the legs of lowing bullocks, sweating horses, and swearing, shouting men. But Bryony stood alone, hugging Simon to her, feeling lost and out of place.

The yard was basically a long, slightly uneven rectangle, half cobbled, half mud. Large sandstone brick barns and stables ranged along one end. She could see a string of stockyards and paddocks stretching beyond them, and a smithy and a carpenter's workshop built to one side of the largest barn. At the far end of the rectangle, opposite the stables and barn, rose the house.

Hayden St. John's house was built of the same sandstone brick as his farm buildings. A wide, stone-flagged veranda held up by trimmed posts ran around all four sides of the house, protecting it from the harsh Australian sun. The house was well built but unpretentious. The barns and stables were considerably larger.

Bryony glanced from the house to the man who had built it. He had dismounted near a stone, prisonlike building with barred windows that lay on the northern side of the yard. Beside him stood a rough-looking man with graying brown hair and a receding hairline who kept casting speculative glances in Bryony's direction.

He was big, although he wasn't as tall as the Captain, and much of his weight was beginning to run to fat. A week's growth of whiskers shadowed his cheeks, accentuating rather than concealing the livid scar that ran down one side of his face from temple to chin.

But it was something about the way he kept looking at her that made Bryony feel ill at ease. The other men in the yard had taken one quick glance, then studiously avoided letting their eyes drift toward her again. Not this man. He looked her over as freely as if she were a filly about to come up for auction.

Turning away with burning cheeks, Bryony scanned the crowded yard. She was searching for other women among this throng of milling animals and shouting men. There were none.

"Why don't you take Simon into the house?"

Bryony whirled around. Hayden St. John had left the man with the scar and walked up behind her.

His face was so closed and hard, it frightened her. It reminded her of the way he'd looked when she'd first seen him at the Factory in Parramatta, and she knew it was this place—his home—that had changed him. No, not changed him, she realized suddenly. Reminded him. Reminded him of Laura.

"When I can spare Gideon, I'll send him up and he can help you fix something to eat."

"Fix something to eat?" she echoed in dismay.

"You do know how to cook, don't you?"

Bryony thought of all the hours Mrs. Pencarrow had spent with her when she was a child, trying to teach her how to cook. She'd paid very little attention to those patient lessons. She had a feeling she was now going to regret it.

"Well?" The tone demanded a response.

She cast an almost wild look around the yard filled with men. "You expect me to cook for all these people?"

He laughed, momentarily dispelling the harshness of his face. "No. The men live in groups of four or six in those huts there." He nodded to the row of bark-roofed, rough slab cottages on the south side of the rectangle.

"They each have their own hut keeper. You'll only be expected to cook for me."

He would have turned away, but she stopped him. "Don't you have any other female servants here?"

He glanced back at her over his shoulder. "No. I brought several out from Sydney with me at first, but after . . ." It seemed to Bryony that as she watched, all expression died in his face, and he took on that sculptured cold look she hated. "After Simon went to the wet nurse in Green Hills, I sent them back to the Factory."

No women? Something clenched at Bryony's stomach as she turned in a slow arc, taking in the yard full of rough, dirty men. The miles of gently undulating fields and pastures dotted with the unfamiliar shapes of gum trees stretched as far as she could see into the distance. For the first time she realized just how isolated she was here. The ragged, jutting crags of the Blue Mountains seemed to loom over her, looking hard and mysterious and intoxicatingly frightening.

Hayden St. John's house contained only five rooms, but they were large rooms, well proportioned and exquisitely decorated. Balancing Simon on her hip, Bryony wandered through the dining room and parlor, noting the silk-covered settees and lace curtains, the long mahogany table and massive, glass-fronted cabinets filled with heirloom china and crystal and silver.

On the opposite side of the hall stood two bedrooms, separated by a large dressing room. Shifting Simon's sleepy weight to her shoulder, Bryony paused to peek through the open door of the first bedroom.

This was a masculine room, the furniture heavy and dark, and much of it Oriental in origin. Two very good watercolors hung on the wall above the desk. One showed Port Jackson, all its heart-stopping beauty skillfully captured with sure lines and gentle nuances of color, while the other was of Jindabyne itself, set high on the side of its hill. Subtle traces of tobacco and leather scented the air, stamping the room as Hayden's. And Bryony knew, instinctively, that Laura St. John had never shared this space with her husband.

A wide, polished floorboard squeaked as Bryony wandered farther down the hall, past the darkened dressing room, to the final door, the door to Laura St. John's bedroom. A strange tumult of feelings confused her. She had been curious about the rest of the house, but *this* room—this room fascinated her. It was as if she were in some way becoming obsessed with Hayden St. John's dead wife. As if she were driven by a need to understand her, almost to get to know her. As if she needed to apologize to Laura.

But that was ridiculous, she told herself. What would she need to apologize to Laura for? For taking care of the woman's baby son? For letting herself care for Simon, in the hope that it might in some small way ease the permanent ache left within her by the loss of her own two children?

Pushing the thought aside, Bryony stood in the open doorway of Laura's room, holding Laura's sleepy, tousle-haired baby in her arms, and breathed in the faint, musty smell of rose water, which was all that was left of the essence of Laura St. John. Here again was the same, familiar English mahogany and rosewood furniture that Bryony had seen in the dining room and parlor across the hall. No watercolors of Australia hung on Laura St. John's walls. Instead Laura had surrounded herself with pictures of half-timbered, thatched English cottages draped in a riot of roses and honeysuckle, and quaint country churches captured on rainy mornings, their stones glistening with the wet.

There were pictures of India here, too, and Bryony moved closer to study them in the dim light. She saw gallant English officers, their wives dressed in filmy, high-waisted white muslins, sitting in delicate cane chairs on a carefully manicured lawn, all laughing together and being waited upon by dark-skinned servants. In another frame a young officer perched atop the gaily-colored trappings of an elephant and laughed down at the artist.

Sucking in a deep breath, Bryony looked closer at the officer's handsome, laughing face. It was Hayden St. John. Younger, more carefree, perhaps, but unmistakably him. As comprehension dawned, she stared down at the signature on the painting.

Laura St. John.

Bryony hadn't realized she'd been holding her breath until she let it out in a long sigh. She glanced around the room at the carefully hung rows of pictures, seeing them with new eyes. In an age when all young ladies were taught to paint as a matter of course, Laura St. John had been an artist of incredible talent. All these watercolors—and the ones in Hayden St. John's room as well, Bryony now realized—were her work. Hayden had kept and framed the pictures she had done of Australia, but Laura . . .

Laura had covered the walls of her room with pictures of the world she had loved. And left behind.

As if feeling Bryony had neglected him too long, Simon let out a little grunt. She looked down and saw he had his face schooled in an intense look of concentration that could mean only one thing.

Bryony wrinkled her nose and half laughed, half groaned. "Did you have to do that *now*, Simon?" She walked over to the set of French doors that overlooked the yard, pulled open the curtains, and threw back the shutters.

The men were still at the other end of the quadrangle, unloading the supplies from the wagons and carrying them into the stone building that Bryony now realized must be Hayden St. John's version of the government store in Sydney. Flour, salt, tea, tobacco, kegs of nails, even stacks of work clothes were being taken inside. And when she remembered that his men were all felons, and most of them thieves at that, she supposed it made sense to build the place like a prison. Only in this case, the intention was to keep the criminals out instead of in.

She scanned the milling men for Gideon, but he was nowhere to be seen. She lingered at the window, torn. Simon needed to be changed, but his trunk was still on the tilted cart, and she felt oddly loath to venture back out into the yard, locate Gideon among all those rough, strange men, and ask him to haul Simon's things up to the house for her.

She glanced around the bedroom. Laura's room did not appear to have been touched since her death. Even the canopy bed with its elegant pink silk hangings had been stripped and never remade. Surely during the long months of her pregnancy, Laura had prepared clothes and stacked them away in one of these drawers, so they'd be ready for the day her child was born? There might still be some here.

Folding Simon's blanket into a kind of a pad that she tucked beneath his dirty rump, Bryony laid him on the thick, flower-strewn rug beside the bed and carefully eased open the top drawer of the tall mahogany bureau.

It was filled with underclothes of the finest batiste and lawn, trimmed with satin ribbons and—

"What are you doing?"

Bryony jumped and whirled around, an embarrassed flush staining her cheeks. Hayden St. John stood in the doorway. His face was set in cold, angry lines, but it didn't prevent her from seeing the pain there. It was as if she had stolen a forbidden glimpse of his private hell.

"I—I'm sorry. Simon needed to be changed, and I didn't have his trunk. I thought some of his things might be in here, since . . ."

"There is nothing of his here." She expected him to walk over, slam the drawer shut, and order her from the room. Instead he turned on his heel and walked out onto the veranda, where she heard him send someone running for Gideon, with instructions to bring the baby's trunk and cradle up to the house.

He appeared again in the doorway, his broad-brimmed hat pulled so low over his eyes, she couldn't see his face. "This will be Simon's room now." His voice was utterly expressionless, but Bryony knew what it must have cost him to say that. "Until he's older, you will share it with him. Gideon can show you where the bedding is kept. I'll have him bring up a trunk in the morning for you to pack away my . . . the things Simon won't be needing."

He turned around and left her standing there, holding his son, in his dead wife's bedroom.

CHAPTER
TWELVE

Between the stone store and the house lay a brick building with a slab lean-to attached. It turned out to be the kitchen.

Bryony stood in its darkened doorway, her nostrils filling with stale wood smoke and the smell of damp clay from the packed earth floor. Shelves took up most of one wall above a crooked cupboard, and a rough bench ran across the opposite wall. A crude table stood in the middle of the room, while most of the rear of the building was taken up by the primitive, open fireplace where Bryony was expected to prepare St. John's meals.

She glanced back at Gideon. "Where's the oven?"

"There." He pointed to a Dutch oven sitting on the shelf.

"No, I mean the *real* oven."

Gideon frowned. "Well, there used to be one out the back, but it ain't been used much lately." He led her around the side of the hut to a weed-grown tumble of bricks. "Looks as if it needs to be rebuilt."

"Outside?" she said, aghast.

"Aye. Sure then, you wouldn't want it inside, not as hot as it gets around here in the summer. On really hot days, we build a fire and roast the meat out here, too."

"And if you want to bake bread when it's raining?" It had been enough of a shock to discover that the kitchen was located in a building separate from the house. But an outside oven?

Gideon shrugged. "Like I said, 'tes not much used." He led the way back into the kitchen.

Hayden St. John had sent Gideon to help Bryony fix dinner. But it was Gideon who built up the fire on the hearth, Gideon who put the salt pork on to fry, Gideon who mixed up the damper and set it to bake in the Dutch oven.

"What kind of vegetables are available?" Bryony asked, standing at his side, watching, and trying desperately to remember what he was doing and how.

Gideon looked up, puzzled. "Vegetables?"

She laughed. "Surely you don't eat just meat and damper?"

"Aye. That we do."

She thought it was a joke . . . until she saw the serious expression on his freckled, boyish face. She stopped laughing and turned toward the door. "Tell me where the dairy is, and I'll go get some butter and some milk for the tea."

"Oh, we don't have a dairy," he said, flipping the meat.

Bryony paused, her hand resting on the doorjamb, and stared back at him. "No dairy? But I saw lots of cows when we drove up."

"Aye, there's lots of cows. But no dairy." He thought about it a moment. "We did used to have a goat and her kid. One of the girls from the Factory would milk her for Mrs. St. John's tea."

"Goat's milk? In *tea*?"

"Aye. Mrs. St. John didn't care too much for it, either," said Gideon, checking his damper. "But then one day the goats up and disappeared. The Cap'n always figured some of the men must have taken and ate 'em, but nothin' was ever proved."

Bryony came back into the kitchen and sank down upon the bench, conscious of an absurd desire to cry. After all she'd been through, what did it matter if there were no vegetables and no milk for tea—or butter for bread, or even any real bread, for that matter? So what if the kitchen was unbelievably primitive and she had only the vaguest idea of how to go about preparing meals on a stove, let alone over an open fire? She glanced out the open door, where the golden light of evening drenched the yard and its surrounding buildings. She had survived six months expecting to be hanged and another six months of hell battened down in a stinking hull awash with bilge water, urine, vomit, and worse. She could surely survive this.

Bryony sighed. She could survive it. She was beginning to realize people could survive most things. Not because they were brave or strong, but because there wasn't any choice.

While Gideon finished fixing dinner, Bryony went to set the mahogany table in the dining room. She found a linen cloth in the bottom drawer of the giant cabinet, then laid out Laura's silver and Laura's china and Laura's crystal.

She stepped back to admire the effect. Laura St. John had set a beautiful table. But it was now a table set for one, and as the evening sun slanted through the open French windows, spilling its golden light across the white cloth and making the facets of the crystal sparkle like diamonds, Bryony thought it looked a bit sad and lonely.

And she thought Hayden St. John must sit here every night, staring at the empty seat across from him, haunted by Laura's absence if not by her actual ghost.

Bryony ate her own dinner in the kitchen, perched tailor fashion on the bench, with Simon nestled in an old packing crate lined with a blanket on the floor beside her.

After dinner Gideon hauled out two half barrels, which he set up on a table on the veranda. Then he showed her the spring near the creek behind the house from which they drew water to drink, and the places where the creek was deep and it was easiest to fill buckets for the washing. The water needed to be heated in big cauldrons over the fire. Only then could the dishes be washed.

She was standing over one of the steaming barrels when she heard the scrape of boot heels on stone and looked up to see St. John.

"You can come up and help Bryony with breakfast and dinner again tomorrow," he told Gideon. "But after that she's on her own. You'll be working with the stock from now on."

An errant lock of hair fell in front of Bryony's eyes. She lifted her wet hands from the dishwater and tried to swipe it back with her dry forearm, but it only fell forward again. St. John propped one shoulder against the nearest timber veranda post, crossed his long legs at the ankles, and stood watching them. The dark, forbidding look she'd seen on his face this afternoon was still there.

He made her nervous, standing there like that. She wished he would go away. Then she realized he wasn't looking at her anymore. He was staring down at the unlit cheroot he kept drawing between his fingers, over and over again.

Perhaps it was because she'd gone through so much pain lately herself that she recognized the pain she saw in him, and it suddenly clutched oddly at her heart. She felt a ridiculous urge to go to him and soothe the frown from his brow.

Instead she picked up the skillet and plunged it into the dishwater.

"I've already been learnin' about growin' wheat and oats and corn out here," Gideon told her cheerfully. Taking the pan after she rinsed it, he dried it with a linen tea towel. "But the Cap'n, he says the future of this colony lies in sheep, so I want to learn about 'em for when I get my own land grant."

Her hands thrust back in the dishwater, Bryony twisted

around to stare at the little Irishman. "Oh, surely—surely you're not thinking of *staying* here?"

"Why not?" It was Hayden St. John who asked the question. She glanced up into those blue eyes. "In Ireland, he isn't allowed to own a horse worth more than five pounds. But here, once his sentence has expired, he can apply for a grant of forty acres. And if he works hard and makes a go of that, then he can keep right on expanding. One day soon, a lot of people like him are going to pay money to come out here. Why would he think of going back?"

"But Mary," she gasped. "And the boys . . ."

"Sure I'm plannin' to get them out here real soon," said Gideon, drying the last of the pots. "I been savin' all my money . . ." He picked up the pan of dirty dishwater and flung it over the side of the veranda. Watching him, it didn't occur to Bryony to wonder until later how an assigned servant could even get his hands on money, let alone save it. "And the Cap'n says we can have one of the huts for ourselves."

Bryony slowly dried her hands on the tea towel, but she couldn't stop her gaze from drifting back to the man who now stood with his back to the post, his hips thrown forward in that pose she found so intimidating.

"Is it so inconceivable to you that anyone would stay here?" he asked.

She thought of the boat ride up the Parramatta River to the Factory, when the boatmen and guards had whiled away the boredom of the long trip by systematically raping the women prisoners until the men were so sated they could barely stand.

She met his gaze squarely. "If they've been transported here, then yes, I do find it inconceivable. How could they ever think of this place as anything other than a prison? And the scene of their ultimate degradation and subjugation?"

He grunted. "Are you trying to say you weren't subjugated and degraded in the prisons of Britain?

She felt the flush steal into her cheeks, but she didn't drop her gaze from his. "Yes. But I will know nothing else here, whereas when I think of Cornwall, I don't remember the prison. I think of the gulls wheeling free over Cadgwith Cove, and . . ." She stopped for a moment, aware of the dangerous prickle of tears at the back of her eyes, and added more quietly, "And I think of my little girl. Not the way I last saw her, when they took her from me in prison, but laughing on the beach, with the sea foaming around her ankles and—"

But at that point, Bryony's voice caught in her throat, and she had to turn away, toward the house.

She heard Gideon empty the second bucket, then pick them both up to carry them back to the kitchen, but she was too close to tears to turn around.

"Bryony?"

Hayden came up behind her and put one hand on her shoulder. He felt her tremble beneath his touch. "Bryony," he said again, softly, moving his hand in a comforting gesture that came perilously close to being a caress. "Tell me about your little girl."

She shook her head, sending her flame-shot hair whisking around her shoulders. "I can't. I'll cry."

"There's no shame in crying."

"Isn't there?"

"You cried for Paddy O'Neal."

"No." Beneath his fingers, he felt her back stiffen. He realized he was still touching her, and although he didn't want to, he dropped his hand. "I think I was really crying for myself."

He knew it was true, so he didn't argue. Instead he said, "How old is your little girl?"

"Three." He heard her voice break, and it was all he could do to keep from taking her in his arms and holding her close. It was an impulse as tender as it was sexual, and it disturbed him. "She's only three," Bryony said.

"By the time I get back to Cornwall—if I ever do—she'll be almost grown. She won't even remember me."

She turned around and looked up at him, and he realized how near he was to her. He gazed down into her beautiful brown eyes, as deep and enduring as the earth itself, and at her lips, as soft and dewy as rose petals at dawn. He didn't step back.

A warm evening breeze blew up from the river, flattening the shirt against his back. The sun slipped toward the mountains, the light leached fast from the sky. A curlew called once, twice, from the river gums that grew down by the creek, and she turned toward the sound.

"What is that bird?" she asked, her lips trembling slightly. "I've heard it before, at night. It makes such a mournful sound."

"It's a curlew," he said, only he wasn't looking at the trees by the creek; he was still watching her. "The Aborigines say the curlew was once a woman. She had eight beautiful children—four tall, strong sons and four nubile daughters.

"One day while she was off gathering food for their dinner, some men from a tribe with whom her people were at war came into the camp. They killed her strong sons and carried off her nubile young daughters. The woman came home to find half of her children dead, the rest gone, and in an agony of grief she threw herself on the cold cinders of the campfire and smeared herself with ashes until she was all streaked brown and white. Then she stood up and set out to search for her daughters. She wandered through the bush for days, not eating or drinking, until at last she was too weak to walk any farther and all she could do was call for them, over and over again, *kerlee, kerlee.* It was then that she was changed into a bird, so she could fly over the earth, still calling for them, until one day they say she will find them."

Bryony's chest rose on a quick intake of breath. "It's a very sad story."

His eyes lingered on the long, delicate arch of her neck. He could see her pulse beating, rapidly, at the base of her throat. He wanted to reach out his hand and rub the backs of his fingers, gently, against her smooth skin. "The Aborigines don't think it's just a story," he said.

Her lips parted, as if she were going to say something. He could see the trace of moisture left on her lower lip by her tongue. He lifted his gaze to hers and stared into her dark eyes, and felt a hungry yearning slam into him. It engulfed him, until he thought he might drown in his desire. He sucked in a steadying breath of air, and his nostrils filled with the scent of her. She smelled clean and earthy, like a newly turned field lying in the sun. He pictured laying her down in that field, peeling back her clothes to let the warmth of the sun shine on her pale, pale skin, then spreading her legs and burying himself inside her.

The image was so enticing that he almost shuddered.

And it was so damned near overwhelming that he had to turn on his heel and walk off into the night. Before he took her, right there under the sunset-streaked sky.

Whether she wanted him to or not.

Bryony sat before Laura's dressing table, watching her own reflection in the mahogany-surrounded mirror as she drew her broken comb through her hair.

On the marble-topped surface before her, Laura's silver-handled brush and comb still lay, but Bryony wouldn't have dreamed of using them.

She laid down her own old comb, and cautiously reached out to touch the tarnished back of the silver brush. She could see one or two long, blond hairs still caught in the bristles, hair so pale it was almost white.

She must have had beautiful hair, Bryony thought, letting her hand fall.

She would be glad when Gideon brought up a trunk from the store tomorrow so she could pack all of Laura's things away. Perhaps then she would feel less an intruder, and more as if she belonged here.

She turned away from the mirror and cursed herself for a fool. She would never *belong* here. This wasn't even her room now, it was Simon's, and she would be sleeping here only until he was old enough to be left on his own. Then she would probably be moved into the slab lean-to beside the kitchen, where she'd been told the two female servants St. John had brought from the Factory to wait on his wife used to sleep.

That is, if she wasn't sent back to the Factory herself.

The thought filled her with a horrible feeling of dread. She remembered her first night in Parramatta, when a man came into the Factory to pick out a woman. He wanted a blond woman, he said; he liked blond women. And when Matron Sarah Gooding produced Susan, a thin, golden-haired girl from Brighton, he made the girl open her dress and shift so that he could see her tits, as he called them. But Susan had been lucky; the man turned up his nose at her small, gently rounded breasts.

So Sarah Gooding gave him Polly, a buxom milkmaid who'd been caught stealing butter from her mistress's dairy. The man had been happy with Polly. So happy, in fact, he'd taken her right there in the yard, up against the brick wall. Bryony thought she'd never forget the sight of the man's filthy hand, its back covered with coarse, dark hair, pawing at Polly's full breasts as he shoved up her skirts.

No, she had no desire to be sent back to the Factory.

And then she remembered the way Hayden St. John had looked at her tonight, on the veranda. She had watched his face grow taut, his eyes hard with arousal. There'd been no mistaking that look. For one heart-stopping moment she'd thought he was going to thrust her back against the rough wall of the house and take her right there, the way that man had taken Polly.

She knew he had thought about it. And though he

might not have done it tonight, the nights stretched out ahead of her. Night after night, to be spent with him in this house, alone except for Simon lying asleep in his cradle by the hearth.

And for how long would he hold himself back? Her pulse did strange, forbidden things, just at the thought.

She picked up her candle and carried it over to gaze down at the sleeping baby. He lay on his back, his tiny fists thrown up on either side of his head. His cheeks looked rosy, almost plump now. His mouth puckered, and he made slow sucking motions, as he often did while he slept. Smiling, she smoothed the tangled blond fluff at his forehead, gently, so as not to awaken him.

And then she admitted to herself there was another reason she couldn't bear the thought of being sent back to the Factory. Simon might not be hers, but, God help her, she didn't want to lose this baby, too.

Turning away, she cupped her hand behind the candle flame and blew it out. As she climbed the steps into Laura's grand canopy bed, she heard someone outside her room, on the veranda.

She threw back the covers and slid out of bed. There were two sets of French doors in the room; the ones that looked out over the yard, and another set, on the adjoining wall, that opened onto the hill at the side of the house. It was to this window that she crept, drawing back one edge of the heavy silk curtains and lace panel, just enough so that she could peer out through a chink in the shutters.

A man paced up and down the veranda. She knew it was St. John by his long-legged stride, by the way his spurs jangled and his boots clicked on the stone flagging. She could see the red glow of his cheroot, held clenched between this teeth as he walked back and forth, back and forth.

He stopped, his back to her, his gaze seemingly fixed on something far up the hill. She saw his hand go up, saw the muscles of his shoulders bunch as he flung the cigar onto the stones at his feet and ground it beneath the sole of his boot. In the still of the night, the slow, almost agonized release of his breath as he exhaled a stream of smoke looked white against the night sky before it was blown away by the restless wind.

CHAPTER
THIRTEEN

The batiste of Laura's night rail was so fine, Bryony was afraid her own rough, chapped hands would snag the delicate material.

She lifted it carefully from the drawer and laid it beside the dainty chemises, petticoats, tuckers, and handkerchiefs that already filled the bottom of the trunk.

It was only mid-morning, but she was already tired. She'd been startled from a deep sleep at five o'clock by the loud clanging of a bell being rung right outside her bedroom window. They rang the bell like that every morning, Gideon had told her with a grin as he helped her fix breakfast.

The early spring sun streamed in from beneath the veranda roof and threw bands of golden warmth across the polished floor. She had the shutters and curtains thrown back and the French doors overlooking both the yard and the hill at the side of the house open, letting in fresh air scented with the smell of sun-warmed grass. With most of the men out in the fields, a peaceful quiet had settled over the homestead. She could hear the distant sound of a hammer striking iron in the smithy near the barn. A new lamb bawled in one of the pens, and a kookaburra laughed from the stand of gums up the hill, but she was alone. Simon napped contentedly in his cradle beside the empty hearth.

She reached for the second night rail in the neat stack in Laura's drawer. This time she was unable to resist the temptation to unfurl the fine folds and raise it up against her own cheap, rough work dress.

Never, not even in her old life at Cadgwith Cove, had Bryony owned anything so exquisite. Holding it against her for a moment, she closed her eyes and breathed deeply of the faint sent of rose water as she smoothed the expensive material down over her breasts and stomach.

But although Bryony might admire Laura's beautiful clothes, she could not covet them—the gown barely reached her knees. Sighing, she laid Laura's night rail on the bed and refolded it.

She must have been an incredibly tiny woman, Bryony thought. An unbelievably small, delicate woman, barely larger than a child. Folding the exquisite little clothes made Bryony feel like a rough, uncouth giant.

She put the night rail in the trunk and emptied the rest of the drawer quickly, lifting the entire stack of night rails together. She pulled open the next drawer, then paused in surprise. A variety of shawls, cashmires and other fine wools in rich reds and blues and elegant creams, filled half the drawer. But the other half was taken up by sketchbooks.

She lifted the top one and saw Laura St. John's name, written in a neat, controlled script in the upper-right-hand corner. There was nothing bold or aggressive about Laura's signature; it was quiet, genteel. Like the woman herself, Bryony thought.

Beneath the signature was the date January 1808. She looked at the other books; they were all dated, with the first one beginning in August 1804, the year Bryony knew Laura had married.

Bryony picked up the entire stack and carried them over to the chair. Setting the rest aside, she opened the first book and found herself staring at an English harbor. Laura's neat copperplate had labeled the picture: Portsmouth. Laura had obviously decided to begin her new life with a new sketchbook.

Bryony turned the pages. There were views of the

coast, views of the ship. Masts cutting dark against a pale, cloudy sky. A seaman rolling a barrel across a plank deck. A handsome young man in a hussar uniform leaning against the rail, laughing. Hayden.

Laura drew her young husband often. On deck, in their small cabin, in ports of call. It seemed he was always laughing, his eyes so full of love for his beautiful, dainty, talented bride that it made Bryony's chest ache to look at him.

She set aside the first sketchbook and reached for the second. Here was their life together in India. She stared at pictures of lush, exotic gardens. Neat little bungalows tucked beneath tall, waving palm trees. Picnics beside a quiet lagoon, the ladies gay and serene beneath their lace-covered parasols, the gentlemen dashing and handsome in their uniforms. Bryony knew she was intruding on something she wasn't meant to see, but she couldn't help it. It was like finding herself outside, alone and friendless on a cold winter's night, and peeking through an unshuttered window to see a room bathed in the warm, golden glow of a fire. A room where people laughed and smiled and loved.

And loved. Ah, how they must have loved.

She thumbed through more books of India. Then there was another ship, another voyage, this time carrying Laura to New South Wales.

Bryony flipped through the book. There were the famous Heads. More views of Port Jackson and Sydney Cove. Sydney Town, with its muddy, stump-filled streets, its grand stone buildings, and its tumbledown shacks. But this was the last notebook save one, and she had almost reached its end. Laura had filled book after book with her life in India; in New South Wales, she must have gone months without picking up her pencils or brushes. Why?

Bryony turned to the last page and found herself staring at a watercolor of the Australian bush. The grass was yellow, dry, dead-looking. The gray-green leaves of the gums hung listless and still in a heat that was almost palpable. In the background loomed the Blue Mountains, mysterious, menacing. It was a disturbing picture, and Bryony laid it quickly aside.

She reached for the last sketchbook, the one Laura had begun in January of 1808, and never finished.

She opened it to find herself staring at an English garden. A riot of sedate, gentle pinks and greens and blues spilled across the page. Stately hollyhocks and Canterbury bells pushed up against a soft English sky beside rambling roses scrambling over a drywall. Frowning, Bryony checked the date on the front cover again to make sure she'd read it right, then turned the page.

It was a picture of Hayden, mounted upon his big bay gelding. The Blue Mountains brooded in the distance behind him. He wasn't smiling.

But the next picture was another sketch of England. It was as if, unable to bring herself to draw the Australian countryside, Laura had taken to painting her memories of home.

Had she disliked Australia so much? Bryony wondered.

Then she turned the next page, and her hand stilled, for she was gazing at what could only be a picture of Laura herself.

It was a self-portrait, exquisitely done. Bryony's breath caught in her throat, and she felt a squeezing inside her, somewhere in the region of her heart. She'd been told that Laura was beautiful, but she could never have imagined her as being this lovely.

Hair the color of sunshine. Large, almond-shaped eyes of a clear, sparkling emerald green, the same green Bryony saw every day in Simon's wide, guileless gaze. Skin of the smoothest alabaster. A fine, delicately shaped nose. High cheekbones, a high, noble forehead, gently flaring brows. And an exquisitely shaped mouth that seemed almost to tremble with innocence.

It wasn't simply a beautiful face. It was a kind face, a gentle face, a—

Bryony heard the faint tinkling of bells, followed by a heavy tread on the stone flagging of the veranda. She sat up with a start, the sketchbook clutched to her, looking about wildly, as if she could find someplace to hide it. But the front door to the hall had already been thrown open with a bang, and she heard a woman's voice—loud and husky, but still undeniably a *woman's* voice—shouting.

"Helloooo. You there? We've come acallin'."

Bryony dropped the sketchbook on top of the others and stood up, just as the large figure of a woman filled the doorway from the hall to Laura's room.

"Well, will you look at that," said the woman, pausing on the threshold, a gap-toothed grin splitting her homely face. "William told me the master'd brung a woman back with him, but I was afeard to believe it till I seed it with me own eyes."

She was big and she was broad, with a wart on her dimpled chin and gray hair that stuck out in every direction from beneath her cap. But in that moment Bryony thought she was the most beautiful sight she'd ever seen. *Another woman!*

Bryony wiped her hands on her apron and extended the right one to the woman. "How do you do? I'm Bryony Wentworth. From Cornwall."

The woman's fat hand engulfed hers. "Lord bless me, it's good to see you. I'm Louisa Carver, from Dublin, and this here little tyke is me Sarah. Make your curtsy, Sarey."

It was only then that Bryony noticed the little slip of a girl hiding behind her mother's skirts. She was a tiny thing, probably no more than three or four, with a riot of fair curls and pale blue eyes. It seemed hard to believe such a mammoth woman could have produced this elf-like child.

Bryony's heart felt as if someone had reached out and twisted it, for the little girl wasn't much older than Madeline had been the last time she'd seen her. She forced herself to smile and squatted to bring herself down to the child's level. "Well, how do you do, Sarah? I didn't even see you there at first."

The girl stared at her with wide blue eyes, a slow smile curling up the corners of her mouth. She was wearing a dress that looked as if it might have started life as a flour sack, although Louisa had done her best to shape it to the little girl's tiny body. Around her waist was a wide sash to which were sewn half a dozen small bells. It was these Bryony had heard tinkling when they arrived.

"I like your bells," Bryony said. "Do you always wear them?"

The little girl nodded her head up and down, but she still didn't say anything.

"Aye, I put bells on all me children, ever since Nathan, me firstborn, wandered off when I was doing the washin' and tumbled into the river and drowned himself afore I could find him."

Bryony straightened up. "I'm sorry. How—how many children do you have?"

"I birthed five, but Sarah here is the only one I got left."

Four children. This woman had buried four children. Bryony wondered how she could possibly have survived it.

They ended up in the kitchen, where Louisa planted her large bulk on the bench while Bryony made tea and Sarah used an old spoon to trace patterns in the packed earth floor.

"From something Captain St. John said, I had the impression there weren't any other women at Jindabyne," said Bryony, filling the kettle from the supply of water Gideon had left her with that morning.

"There ain't, 'cept me. And I don't work for the Cap'n meself, 'cept for the occasional odd bits. It's me man, Will Carver, what's the Cap'n's overseer. We had us a small farm here on the side of the hill once, ourselves, you see. But when the Cap'n took up his big land grant, he bought us out. Wanted this hill to build a fine house for his lady, he did. He said this were the best spot in the valley."

Will Carver, Bryony soon realized, was the big man with the scarred face she'd seen talking to St. John while the wagons were being unloaded. He'd been a sergeant in the New South Wales Corps, Louisa said, before he'd decided to try his hand at farming. But Bryony got the impression he wasn't much of a farmer, and Louisa had been relieved when Captain St. John had bought them out and given him a job handling men again.

Louisa herself had been transported in '95, for stealing a tankard from an inn. "I guess I must 'ave taken two or three dozen of 'em in my time," she said without any apparent sign of contrition. "We used to sell 'em to this Israelite who'd melt 'em down for the pewter." As she said it, her Irish accent grew even thicker than Gideon's. "Sure then, 'tes a risky dive. I was bound to get caught."

Bryony swallowed a mouthful of tea too quickly, and choked.

"What was you sent out for?" Louisa asked, thumping Bryony helpfully on the back.

"M-manslaughter," she managed to gasp.

Louisa was very impressed.

After Louisa left, Bryony closed Laura's last sketchbook without looking at the rest of it. She couldn't bring herself to pack it away, though, or the others, either. Once she finished emptying the chest of drawers, she put the stack of sketchbooks back in the bottom drawer, along with the materials and other things for making Simon's clothes.

She cleaned the remainder of the room quickly, smiling every once and a while when she remembered something Louisa Carver had said. The woman was a wonder. A nimble-fingered Dublin thief grown into a fat, middle-aged colonial farmer's wife. In its own way, her life had been as strange and full of twists as Bryony's.

After lunch, Bryony fed Simon, then put him down for a nap while she threw open all the doors and curtains in the dining room and set to work in there.

She scrubbed the walls and floor and waxed the furniture, and took all of Laura's things out of the cabinet and washed them, too. This house was not hers, would never be hers, yet somehow by cleaning every surface she felt as if she were bringing it under her control.

But she couldn't keep her hands from shaking as she replaced Laura's delicate, beautifully made silver and crystal and china on the shelves.

She closed the glass-fronted door of the cabinet and went to throw open the French doors of the parlor and let the warm sunlight flood into the room.

That's when she saw the harp.

It sat in a corner, covered, which was probably why she hadn't noticed it the day before when she first walked through the darkened room. Excited, Bryony pulled off the cover and gasped with delight.

It was a beautiful harp, made by a master and painted by an artist of rare skill. Bryony had played the harp since she was five, but she'd never played a harp like this one. This was a harp worthy of a princess. Or a viscount's daughter.

She reached out her hand and ran it across the strings. It was badly out of tune. She plucked a note and was just reaching up to adjust it when hard, cruel fingers closed over her arm and jerked her around so roughly she stumbled. She would have fallen if he hadn't grasped her other arm and yanked her upright with so much force her neck snapped back.

"How dare you?" St. John snarled. "How dare you touch that harp?"

She drew in a deep, shuddering breath. "I was going to—"

"Don't." His voice shook. "Don't ever touch it again." He thrust her away from him, then picked up the cover and threw it over the harp.

* * *

The next morning Bryony slammed the breakfast plate on the tablecloth in front of him so hard, Hayden was surprised it didn't shatter.

"I should have been out in the fields half an hour ago," he said, reaching for his knife. "Didn't you hear the bell being rung?"

She planted her hands on the far side of the table and leaned into them. "Of course I heard the bell. How could I help but hear the bloody thing, when it's hanging right outside my room? Unfortunately, Simon also heard it. Which meant that before I could fix your breakfast, I had to give your son his. And then I had to get the firewood, and the water, and chase around the yard looking for eggs. Why you don't build a bloody henhouse for your chickens, rather than letting them lay wherever they—"

"I like my steak well-done and my eggs runny." He laid down his knife and fork and glared right back at her. "Not the other way around." The way she was standing made her dress pull tight across her ripe breasts. He had lain awake half the night thinking about those breasts. He didn't need to be confronted with them at the breakfast table. He almost growled. "Where is the damper?"

"I didn't make it."

"You—"

"I didn't have time."

She didn't sound the least bit apologetic about it. In fact, if anything, she sounded as if *she* were angry at *him*. Damned if he'd ever had a servant like her before. She wasn't even afraid of his disapproval.

And it occurred to him that the only time he'd seen her frightened of him was when the sun was going down, or she found herself around him without all her clothes on.

It was an unfortunate thought, since it reminded him all too clearly of what lay beneath that ugly work dress she was wearing.

"God Almighty." He flung down his napkin and stood up, thrusting his chair back so hard it scraped across the floor. "When I come in tonight, I'm going to be bloody hungry. You'd better have something decent for me to eat, or be prepared to suffer the consequences."

He crushed his hat down on his head and strode from the room. Behind him, he was surprised to hear her breath break on a sob.

It should have pleased him.

But it didn't.

She waited until she saw his big bay cantering out of the yard, toward a distant sheep station. Then she went into the parlor and took the cover off Laura's harp.

It was a beautiful instrument, she thought as she carefully tuned it. An instrument that should be played, not covered up and preserved as some kind of a monument to the dead woman who had once sat where Bryony now sat, plucking the strings.

She closed her eyes and let herself drift away on her own music. It had been so long, so very long since she had played. She felt the music well up within her and flow out of her, soothing her. It was like a gift, this harp. A gift from one woman to another.

If Laura had played the pianoforte, it would have been useless to Bryony. But the harp . . . ah, she had played the harp for almost as long as she could remember. It seemed somehow right that Laura had played the harp, too, and that she had left her harp here, for Bryony.

She played Laura's harp until her fingers were raw. And still she sat and played, and played, and played.

CHAPTER
FOURTEEN

Midway through the morning, Bryony finished her cleaning. She stood before the open French doors of the parlor, gazing down at the swift-flowing river at the base of the hill. A desire for fresh air and the warmth of the sun on her face pulled her. She tied Simon to her with a shawl, and went for a walk.

The grass beneath her feet was fresh and green, the grass of spring. Bryony shaded her eyes with her hand and looked up at the awesome blue sky above her. The day was still clean and cool with the newness of the morning, but she suspected that by the middle of the afternoon it would be warm. She thought of the dead, dry grass in Laura's picture, and wondered how long the fresh green grass of spring would last.

She explored the yard, then turned to the garden. Only there was no real garden. The area around the three sides of the house that didn't face the yard had been cleared, and it looked as if someone might have tried to lay out a garden once, but their efforts had not been crowned by success. She saw some scraggly, half-dead lavenders and some thyme and rosemary and wormwood in what looked as if it had once been an herb garden. She saw some blackened sticks which might once have been roses standing in a forlorn circle, while over by the creek she found some carrots that had been left in the ground and allowed to go to seed.

Crossing the cleared area, she climbed to the trees above the house and looked down on Jindabyne. She

could see why St. John had bought this hill from the
Carvers and chosen it as the site of his house. It domi-
nated this entire stretch of the Hawkesbury valley. She
could see for miles up and down the river. The wild,
jagged crests of the Blue Mountains looked so close she
fancied she could reach out and touch them.

A parrot flew by, a bright flash of blue and red and
yellow that made her smile. She turned and walked along
the side of the hill, studying the plants, some of which
looked familiar but most of which were unknown to her.
She did find wild sorrel and chickweed and dandelion,
and she thought she might pick some for a salad before
she went back to the house to cook dinner.

The thought of setting another meal before Hayden St.
John brought the sting of tears to her eyes, but she wiped
them away with the back of a balled-up fist. She would
not allow him to defeat her. She had cheated the hang-
man's noose and the sharks; she wasn't going to be done
in by something as paltry as kangaroo steaks and uncoop-
erative hens.

She spotted what looked as if it might be wild cabbage,
growing near some bushes. She leaned over to have a
better look at it, and found herself staring at a human foot.

A black human foot. Attached to a black leg, above
which dangled a male appendage, above which stretched
a naked torso. This was surmounted by a short neck and a
black face, painted with white wavy lines. Its nose was
hideously flattened, its lips puffy and pulled back into an
awful grin.

Bryony screamed, picked up her skirts, and ran.

She ran in the opposite direction from the naked black
man, which meant she was running uphill, and she got
winded fast. She had a stitch in her side, her breath came
in ragged, tearing gasps, but still she ran. Simon woke up
and began to whimper. She clutched him to her and ran
on. A branch dealt her a stinging slap across her cheek,
but she barely felt it. She didn't even know if that savage
was still behind her. She simply ran.

Abruptly she stumbled out of the trees into a cleared patch of ground and staggered to a stop. An old slab hut squatted in the center of the clearing, the ground around it completely bare even of grass. But nearer to her some stumps still stood, three feet high, showing where once great eucalypti had been felled.

She leaned against one of the old stumps and held Simon to her, gasping for breath.

"Bryony?"

She heard the tinkling of little bells and looked up to see Louisa, trailed by her Sarah, hurrying across the clearing toward her.

"Bryony, what's wrong?"

"A man . . . a black man," she gasped. "Back there, in the trees." In spite of herself, she shuddered. "He was completely naked, even his . . ." Her voice trailed off as she waved her hand vaguely back and forth in front of her thighs. "His nose looked like someone had broken it, and he had paint—"

"Paint?" Louisa asked, frowning.

"White paint, on his face, and in wavy lines down his arms. It made him look like a skeleton."

"Well, if it was white paint, you don't got nothin' to worry about," said Louisa, taking her by the arm and leading her toward the house. "It's when they put on red paint you know they mean trouble."

"But he was a savage!"

"Aye. Sounds like you done had your first up-close look at an Aborigine."

She drew Bryony through the door of the hut and pushed her down onto a bench fashioned from a split log with stout sticks hammered into it for legs. A rough-hewn plank formed the table. All the furniture in the hut was homemade, Bryony realized. The two beds were simply hide stretched over four posts driven into the ground and piled with sheepskins.

"Drink this." Louisa poured Bryony a tin mug full of something that smelled suspiciously like rum.

Bryony took a sip. It was rum.

"I admit they're a fright to look at, especially at first, but in general you don't got much to worry about with the Aborigines you see around here. Every once in a while, some settler'll do 'em dirty, and they'll bash his head in or burn his homestead, but the Cap'n, he's always had a pretty good understandin' with 'em. Why, you'll even see 'em come into the yard sometimes to sharpen their knives. You better get used to 'em."

Sharpen their knives? Bryony shuddered again.

"Here." Louisa pushed the tin mug toward her. "Have some more rum."

"I can't. Captain St. John said if he ever smelled rum on my breath, he'd have me flogged."

Louisa looked at her hard. "Well, then, I guess you'd better not drink it." She emptied the mug herself in one long gulp, then got up to pour Bryony some water.

She was on the veranda, washing dishes, when Hayden strolled outside to enjoy an after-dinner smoke in the cool evening air. The sun was just slipping below the red gums down by the creek and painting the horizon a brilliant vermilion that brought out the highlights of her hair. She wasn't looking at him.

She hadn't looked at him all the while she was serving him dinner, either. He knew from the proud lift of her chin and the pained way she avoided him that she was still angry with him. Angry over the way he'd yanked her from Laura's harp, and over the things he'd said about her cooking, too.

This was a side of her he'd only glimpsed before. A side she'd always been careful to quickly hide, and he found it intrigued him. But it also annoyed him. They'd developed a wary but unmistakable affinity over the past week; an affinity that was almost a peculiar sort of friendship. He found he missed it.

And he wanted it back.

He walked up to her and said, his tone light, almost teasing, "So you made your first damper."

Her hands stilled at their task, but she didn't look up. "Yes . . . sir."

"Bit doughy in the middle," he observed casually, sucking on his cigar.

She didn't say anything.

"The kangaroo steak, now, that was well-done." He paused to exhale. "So well-done, in fact, I couldn't quite chew my way through it all. But it's not a complete loss. I figure we can save what's left and use it to shoe one of the bullocks."

She still had her head bowed, but he heard her chuckle. It was a nice laugh—low and husky. The kind of sound a woman might make when a man touched her in just the right spot.

Bloody hell.

He jerked his mind away from the thought and went to lean against a veranda post, looking out over his fields, toward the river. He'd come out here looking to reestablish harmony and goodwill between them, he reminded himself. Not to seduce her.

She was his *servant*. His bloody servant. And yet . . .

And yet all he could seem to think about every time he looked at her was laying her down and tearing the clothes off her and easing himself inside her.

He ground his half-smoked cigar beneath his boot heel, ground it long and hard. Any other man in the colony would have taken her by now without a second thought, and considered it his right. And for one unguarded moment Hayden found he almost wished he was one of those men. He wished he was the kind of man who could satisfy his own sexual hunger without any regard for the wishes or suffering of the woman he took.

But rape was still rape in Hayden's way of thinking, even if it was condoned by the society in which he lived. Even if the woman he took was a felon transported to Botany Bay for killing her husband.

"I saw an Aborigine today," she said.

He swiveled around to look at her. "Did you?"

She'd been studying him, but when his eyes fell on her, her gaze skittered away, as if she knew, just by looking at him, what he'd been thinking. "Louisa Carver says they sometimes come into the yard."

"Yes." He remembered the first time Laura had seen an Aborigine at close quarters. She'd collapsed in a dead faint, and then had hysterics when she came around. He'd had to dose her with laudanum to get her to calm down enough to sleep. "They often use the grinding wheel."

She was staring at him now, with that quiet, intense way of hers. "Is that wise?"

He shrugged. "They don't think the way we do about property. If something is here, they think it's here to be used by everyone. I've found it wisest not to try to change that attitude any more than I have to."

"Are they always . . . naked?"

He grinned. "Always."

She stared at him with an arrested expression, her dark brown eyes wide and startled, her lips parted almost as if in wonder.

He couldn't begin to fathom what it meant.

He reached out his hand and very gently touched her cheek. "You have a bruise," he said, frowning. "Did someone hit you?"

"A branch." He felt her tremble beneath his touch, watched the muscles in her slender throat work as she swallowed hard, and knew a tightening in his chest. A throbbing. A wanting. "I . . . I ran into a branch."

She turned her face away from him and picked up the washtub. It was heavy, and she staggered under the load. The water sloshed from side to side, wetting the swelling curve of her bodice and cascading in a stream down her apron and skirts. She couldn't fling it the way Gideon did, so the water splattered in the dirt off the veranda, splashing mud all over her hem.

Some of her hair fell over her brow. She swiped at it with the back of her forearm as she slammed the empty tub back on the table and reached for the rinse water.

Hayden reached it first. "I'll do it, damn it," he said hoarsely.

He wasn't sure whom he surprised the most. Her. Or himself.

There was a noise in the yard, just outside her window.

Bryony paused in the midst of getting ready for bed and listened. Something scraped over the stone flagging of the veranda floor. There was a clattering sound, and someone laughed. Another man swore.

Curious, she refastened her bodice and stepped over to part the heavy curtains she'd just closed against the night.

Through the slats of the shutters she could see two men on the veranda. They had a slush lamp, and a ladder, and they were taking down the bell.

Before she had quite managed to absorb the fact that St. John must have ordered the bell moved, someone knocked at her bedroom door.

She opened it to find a lithe, handsome, dark-haired, dark-eyed lad of about fourteen standing in the pool of light cast by the oil lamp on the hall table. Instead of taking off his cabbage palm hat, he simply pushed it back at a cocky angle and scowled at her.

"The Cap'n said I was to tell ye I been assigned to fetch yer water and wood every mornin' and night," he said, looking her over in an appraising way she might have expected if he'd been a few years older.

"Why, thank you, Mr. . . . ?"

"Quincy."

"Mr. Quincy."

"No, it's just Quincy." He met the question in her eyes and threw it right back at her, challenging her to make something of it. "Quincy's the only name I got."

"Very well, then, Quincy." She smiled at him. She

wasn't sure she knew how to treat this lad, who looked like a child but had doubtless seen more of life than most men twice his age. "I'll see you in the morning."

"I'll tell ye right out I don't like it," he said, his handsome eyes flashing. "It's nothin' against ye, mind. But I'd rather be out in the fields with the other men."

"I suppose you would," agreed Bryony, hiding a smile. "But I'll be very grateful for your help."

"Well, as long as we got that straight." He pulled his hat brim lower and turned to leave just as Hayden St. John walked in the front door of the house.

He brought with him the smell of horses and tobacco and a restless tension that made Bryony feel suddenly hot and slightly breathless.

Quincy's aggressively masculine swagger became decidedly less pronounced. "I was just tellin' her, like ye said, Cap'n."

Hayden held the door open for the boy. "Thank you, Quincy. Good night."

A ghost of a smile warmed St. John's eyes and tugged at the edges of his lips as he watched the boy dash away. He took off his broad-brimmed hat, brushed the dark hair from his forehead, and turned back into the house. His gaze fell on Bryony, and the smile faded.

"Thank you for assigning him to help me," she said, uncomfortably aware of the light in his eyes as he stared at her. "And for having the bell moved."

A beguiling smile tugged at his lips. A kind of smile she hadn't seen before. "Don't thank me. It's my breakfast that's at stake here, remember?"

A gust of cool wind rattled the open door behind him, bringing the fresh night air laden with the lemony smell of gums into the house. He shut the door and moved past her, on down the hall toward his room.

Bryony's voice stopped him. "How old is that boy?"

As soon as she said it, she regretted the question, regretted what could only be seen as invitation to him to linger beside her. He paused and slowly swung around to face her with a look in his eyes that managed to be both sleepy and heated at the same time. She became aware of her pulse, beating against the collar of her ugly work dress; of her breasts, rising and falling rapidly beneath her bodice.

"He's fourteen. But he's been on the streets picking pockets since he ran away from a foundling home at the age of six and hooked up with some mountebank who knew a good thing when he found it. He's quick and he's clever and he has the morals and instincts of an alley cat. He's no boy, and don't ever make the mistake of forgetting it."

Bryony swallowed hard and saw his gaze drop to her bare throat. She could feel it there, feel the heat of it, as surely as if he'd reached out and touched her. "He's a boy."

He walked back to her with a slow, rolling gait that seemed to emphasize his slim-hipped leanness, his broad-shouldered strength. The light from the lantern on the hall table flared over the sharp bones of his cheeks, and cast dark shadows over his eyes. "Six months ago I found him between the legs of one of my servant women. In every way that counts, he's a man."

A tense, tight feeling curled low in her belly, then spread outward, filling her chest and carrying with it a heat that coursed through her limbs. Hayden St. John was definitely a man. And there were only the two of them here, in this house, filled with the long shadows of night and the gentle breathing of a sleeping baby.

Was it fear that clenched at her belly? That made her heart pound so hard it seemed to be taking up all the space in her chest that should have been used by her lungs?

And what about you? she wanted to ask. *Did you crawl between the legs of your servant women?*

But he hadn't, of course, because Laura had been alive. And a man like this . . . ah, a man like this would be faithful to the woman he loved, even when she was great with his child.

No, he wouldn't have lain with those other servant women. Not when Laura was alive. But now . . .

Now Laura was dead.

Bryony felt a flush of heat stain her cheeks. He took another step that brought him right up to her. She saw the desire leap in his eyes, hot and desperate. Saw the muscle jump in his temple. Saw the determined slant of his mouth.

He's going to take me, she thought, her lips parting as the breath left her body in a long keening sigh. *He's going to thrust me back into my room and take me now, the way a man takes a woman he wants.*

She swallowed hard, and his fierce, hungry gaze dropped to her mouth. He leaned forward. She knew he was going to kiss her. She couldn't move.

He made a harsh, tearing sound, deep in his chest and straightened up. He pushed past her and headed toward the front door. The wind of his passing caused the lantern flame to flicker and almost go out. His hand twisted the door handle and yanked it toward him.

As if released from a trance, Bryony whisked herself into her room and slammed the door shut behind her. Panting, she pressed against it, her hands splayed at her sides.

She remembered the tumult of fear and want that had swept over her as he leaned into her. Long after she heard his footsteps disappear into the night, she stood there with her head tipped back against the door panel, her heart thudding wildly in her chest. But she could not decide which was the stronger. The fear.

Or the want.

CHAPTER
FIFTEEN

He would make her his mistress.

Hayden leaned against a veranda post and watched the moon-silvered river slide past through the darkened trees. He had spent too many nights out here, he decided. Too many nights smoking cigars and willing the frigid air to cool the heat in his blood and help ease the pressure in his loins.

He'd had a lot of reasons for holding himself back, but none of them seemed good enough anymore. Yes, she was his servant. Yes, he felt guilty about desiring another woman so soon after his wife's death. But his need for this dark-eyed convict woman with her full, ripe breasts and mysterious past was turning his life into an aching, howling hell. If it hadn't been for the fear he'd seen in her eyes tonight, he'd have taken her, right there on the floor of the hall. He'd have thrown up her skirts and spread her silken white thighs wide, and sank his hard man's body into her soft woman's flesh. Right there.

The problem was, she did fear him. It was obvious in the way she stiffened whenever he touched her, even when he touched her tenderly, in comfort. And it was obvious in the hunted look that sharpened her fine features every time he looked at her with desire blatant and hot in his eyes.

He swore crudely and reached in his pocket for a cigar. It wasn't going to be easy, convincing Bryony to become his mistress. But he was determined he was going to convince her. He wanted her willing. He wanted her to want him. He wanted her to enjoy him.

He bit the tip off his cigar and fumbled for his tinderbox. He struck the flint, his hands shaking as he remembered the smoldering fire he'd glimpsed in the dusky depths of her dark brown eyes tonight as he leaned into her.

She might be afraid of him, he thought—afraid of his sexuality, afraid of the power that his position as her master gave him over her. But there was more to her awareness of him as a man than fear, he was sure of it. He'd seen it in the telltale flush that stole across her high cheekbones whenever she let her gaze rove over his body. In the way her lips parted and her breathing grew rapid and shallow whenever he was near her.

Her woman's body wanted him. Even if she didn't know it yet. Even if her woman's caution made her fear where that wanting might lead her. She was skittish. Like a filly that had been badly handled by rough, clumsy men in the past and now needed to be gentled.

He would gentle her. He would give her time to get used to having him around. Time to get over her fear of him.

Then he would have her.

Bryony looked up from the table at which she sat, cleaning the glass chimneys of a half-dozen oil lamps, and watched as St. John tilted his chair back against the house wall. Simon lay along the length of his father's thighs, his head on Hayden's knees, and played with his father's watch. The soft, husky sound of the baby's laughter mingled with the rustling of the wind in the gum trees and the shouts of the men herding his bloodstock back toward the barn at the far end of the yard. At the base of the hill, the river rushed by deep and fast, swollen with rain from the dark clouds that hung over the Blue Mountains to the west.

It had been several days since the incident in the hall.

They had never spoken of it. But, then, what was there to speak of? He hadn't kissed her, hadn't even touched her. She had taken extra care to avoid him once the sun set and the yard quieted for the night, but she was beginning to feel foolish for her caution. His attitude toward her had been gentle, almost caring. Perhaps he really did not intend to force her to share his bed. After all, wouldn't he have taken her by now? Perhaps she could begin to let go of some of her earlier fear. To relax.

Sunlight flashed on the gold back of the watch as it slipped from Simon's fingers. His father just managed to catch it before it hit the stone flagging. The smile faded from the baby's toothless little mouth, and a lip quivered as the watch disappeared into a vest pocket.

"Now he's going to cry," said Bryony.

"No, he's not going to cry, are you me lad?" Hayden said, imitating Gideon's Irish lilt. Bryony watched him lift the baby up to his shoulder and hold him close, fair head to dark, and her chest tightened with a warm, elusive sweetness that held more than a touch of sadness in it.

There was something about the sight of an innocent, tiny baby being held so gently and lovingly by such a big, hard man that couldn't help but make her wish for one suspended moment that the baby and the man were both hers.

Annoyed with herself, she jerked her gaze away and reached for another lamp. She had worked so hard tonight trying to fix a decent dinner for that ungrateful bully, and he hadn't said one word, not one word.

"Your damper wasn't bad tonight," he said.

Bryony looked up into eyes that were narrowed with what might have been amusement. Her fist tightened around the lamp base. "What was wrong with it?"

He looked surprised. "Nothing. I said it wasn't bad."

"Exactly. You didn't say it was good."

His lips curled up into a slow, lazy smile that did

something funny to her insides. "All right, it was good. But the meat—"

She thrust the lamp away from her. "The meat wasn't that overdone."

"No," he agreed.

She waited for him to say more. He didn't. Finally she said, "What about the salad? Did you like it?"

He stood up from the chair and went to lean against the veranda post, cradling Simon in the crook of his arm and looking at her sideways. "I might have liked it more if I could have been sure of what was in it. Last time I checked, we didn't have a vegetable garden."

She laughed. "It was wild sorrel and dandelion and chickweed. I can't believe you've been eating nothing but meat and damper."

He shrugged and lifted Simon to his shoulder. "Most men in the bush do. It's only women who worry about things like vegetables and salads."

"Then, it's too bad there aren't more women in the bush."

"Most women don't like the bush."

That cold, forbidding look that she hated was back in his face . . . as if all the sharp planes and angles of cheek and jaw had been chipped from stone. She'd seen that look before, whenever something happened or she said something that reminded him of his dead wife. And Laura definitely had been a woman who didn't like the bush.

It wasn't very encouraging, but she pushed ahead anyway. "I—I would like to start a garden, if I could. Not much, just a few vegetables, and some herbs. I was thinking if you'd let me keep Quincy a couple of mornings a week, and let us have some shovels and maybe some seeds and cuttings—"

She realized he wasn't paying attention to her. He had turned away and was watching someone walk toward the house from the yard.

Bryony wiped her palms on her apron and looked around to see Will Carver wrap one of his big hands around a veranda post and climb up onto the flagging.

"Evenin', Cap'n," he said, touching the brim of his hat. He didn't say anything to Bryony, but she felt his gaze slide over her, like a snake through water.

"Will." St. John lifted the baby from his shoulder and held him out as Bryony walked forward to take him. "What's the matter?"

"This," said the foreman, unfurling something he held, rolled up, in one of his beefy fists.

It looked like a hide of some kind. It was fresh, with the hair still on it.

Hayden didn't move. "Where'd you get it?"

"McDuff brought it in just now. He was out with the dogs huntin' a roo when he come across one of yer calves layin' on its side, bawlin', with it's mama standin' over it, not knowin' what to do. When he went to take a look at it, he found out the calf 'ad stepped in a hole and broke one of its legs, so he slit its throat. Only then he realized that while the cow was wearin' yer SJ brand, someone had slapped a Q8J over the SJ on the calf."

St. John's eyes narrowed in a look that was cold and dangerous. "Take Simon and go inside," he told Bryony over his shoulder.

"Why? What does it mean?" She leaned forward to take a better look at the raw hide.

"Never mind," he said grimly. "Just go inside."

Bryony flushed. It was none of her business, of course, whatever it was. If she'd been Laura, he would have talked to her about it.

But she wasn't Laura.

Bryony lit the candle beside her bed and crawled between the covers. The house was still around her. Hayden St. John had ridden out with his overseer, and although darkness had fallen, he hadn't come back.

She opened the sketchbook and propped it up against her blanket-covered knees. This was Laura's last sketch-book, and Bryony had never finished looking at it. She turned the pages until she came to the portrait of the woman herself, then stopped for a moment, staring at it intently.

She decided that Laura had not been particularly kind to herself in this self-portrait. The face was undeniably, heart-stoppingly lovely. But the artist had hinted at something behind all that beauty, which was obviously something that Laura herself did not admire. There was an introspective, almost melancholy look to those limpid green eyes, and more than a hint of weakness to the bow-shaped lips and delicate chin. Feeling oddly disturbed, Bryony turned the page.

She was looking at a garden. Not a sketch of a garden, but a *plan* for a garden. Bryony turned the book side-ways, studying the plan more closely. There were the red gums, and there, at the base of the hill, was the river. The house with its verandas sat in the middle. There was the circular rose garden that was now nothing but black, dead stalks, and there, down by the creek, was where she'd found the carrots, gone to seed.

Bryony leaned back against the pillows and sighed. So Laura had tried to plant a garden, too. She had probably sat here, in this very bed, drawing out her plan, seeing it all in her artist's mind: the arches covered with roses and honeysuckle, the neat parterres of lavenders and thymes, the carefully laid out rows of melons and squashes, of feverfew and monkswort and valerian. She'd seen it, and designed it with a grace and skill Bryony could never hope to match.

But she hadn't had the knowledge or experience she needed to make it a reality. Not without the assistance of her father the viscount's army of well-trained gardeners.

Bryony sighed again and looked at the next plan, a detail of the herb garden, each area of planting carefully labeled. And for some reason she couldn't quite understand, she felt tears sting her eyes, for this gentle woman who had dreamed of planting a beautiful garden.

And reaped only death.

Sarah's tiny bells jingled as she ran, laughing and chasing the butterflies that danced through the flowers growing in the tall grass.

"Don't you go too far, Sarey," called Louisa, straightening up from the laundry tub to frown after her daughter.

But Sarah only laughed, her fair hair tumbling in sun-streaked curls down her back, her laughter joining the tinkling of her bells to be carried away by the breeze.

They were down by the river, doing the laundry. Bryony had discovered that here in the bush, it was much easier to take the laundry to the water than to haul the water up to the homestead to do the washing. So she and Louisa had hitched a mare to an old cart, loaded the cart's bed with clothes and pots and buckets and washboards and wooden dollies, and headed for the river.

Bryony reached for another of Hayden's shirts and began scrubbing it against the washboard. "She'll be all right. We're both watching her."

Louisa shook her head. "Things can happen so fast. Me Mary, she got bit by a king snake, she did, while I was only fixin' dinner. I told her to stay away from the woodpile, but she was always takin' the split logs and usin' 'em to make tiny houses—for the fairies, she used to say."

Bryony's eyes wandered over to where Simon lay, asleep in his packing crate beneath a big old river gum. How easy they were to lose. How hideously, heart-stoppingly easy.

She thought of Philip, racked with a cough that rattled the breath in his thin chest. She thought of Madeline in that cold house on the windswept moors, and a wild, helpless fear for her only living child tore at Bryony's stomach like something live and vicious. She would not, she could not, think about it.

"Now, me Joseph," said Louisa, stirring the sheets they were boiling over the fire. "He died of the measles. And little Thomas, it was the flux that got him. I'll have to take you and show you their graves some time. All sleepin' in a row, they are, right up there on the crest of the hill above the house, where I could be sure the floods wouldn't get them. You wouldn't think it to look at that river now, but I've seen it so high it reached halfway to the house."

Bryony looked down at the river and almost smiled. There was no way that river could ever reach anywhere near that high.

"I told the Captain he better be careful where he put that beautiful young lady wife of his, on account of the floods. So he laid her up there, too, right next to me wee ones."

Bryony's hand stilled at the washboard. "He—he was very much in love with her, wasn't he?"

"Lord, wasn't he," said Louisa with a sigh. "She was such a sweet, gentle thing. A real lady."

A warm, restless wind blew across the clearing, bringing with it the smell of sun-warmed earth and ripening fields. Bryony felt a shiver dance along her spine, and even before she looked up, she knew he was there.

He was sitting on his horse at the edge of the trees, his hand resting on his hip beside his knife. He had the brim of his dark hat pulled so low that all she could see was the hard slant of his mouth. He was just sitting there, watching her. She straightened up, pushing the hair off her damp brow and feeling herself grow hot from the inside out. He wheeled his horse and rode away.

Louisa cast her a knowing look. "Have you lain with him yet?"

"What?" gasped Bryony. She bent over her washboard, scrubbing furiously in an attempt to hide the hot color that flooded into her cheeks.

Louisa showed her missing teeth in a broad grin. "I seen the way he looks at you."

"He . . . he hasn't forced me," said Bryony, reaching for another shirt.

"I didn't think he had. Not the Cap'n." Louisa pushed her dollie through the boiling sheets. "But I seen you lookin' at him, too."

Bryony's hand clenched around the linen shirt she still held. It was his shirt. She breathed deeply, and her senses filled with the smell of horses and tobacco and . . . and him. She glanced up at Louisa. She wanted to deny it, but somehow she couldn't.

She *had* been looking at him.

It was that evening, after she'd laid Simon in his cradle and was sitting up in bed studying Laura's garden plans, that Bryony found the drawing of him.

She was flipping through the various garden plans in the sketchbook when a loose sheet that evidently had been pulled out and then stuck back in among the blank pages of the book fell out and fluttered to the floor. Bryony bent over to pick it up.

And almost gasped.

It was a picture of Hayden St. John. Laura had drawn him as if he stood, naked and threatening, beside a hot fire. Bryony could see the lean, taut muscles of his buttocks, the long, corded line of his thighs. Firelight gleamed over the sweat-slicked, bulging muscles of his broad back and strong arms. She knew the way his body would feel if she could touch him—the hard and unyielding strength of muscle beneath the softness of skin.

His back was turned to her, but he had his head swiveled around, as if he were looking at her over his shoulder. Dark hair curled at the nape of his neck. There was a hint of shadows on his half-hidden chest. His lips were set in a hard, almost cruel line. And his eyes . . .

His eyes glowed with a fierce, hungry, frightening heat.

It was an intense picture, a disturbing picture. And Bryony knew instinctively that the woman who had drawn it had been both intimidated and troubled by the raw masculinity of this man. By the potent masculinity that drew Bryony so inexorably.

She reached out, tentatively, and touched that hard mouth, and a low moan escaped her own lips.

Have you lain with him yet?

She felt something clench tight, deep within her, something that burned and spread its slow heat through her body. She rolled over, clutching her pillow to her chest, to her aching breasts, then brought it down until it was pressed between her legs.

She wanted him. He hadn't forced her and according to Louisa, he wasn't the kind of man who would. But she found she almost wished he would. She wanted to feel his man's body covering her. She wanted to run her hands over his hard, sweat-slicked shoulders. She wanted to thread her fingers through the dark curls at the base of his neck and draw his mouth down to hers. She wanted to see his eyes glow with a heat that was hungry for her.

Not for Laura.

For her.

Some time later she was still awake when he came back to the house. She heard his long-legged stride pass down the hall, heard his door open and close behind him.

She could imagine him standing beside the hearth in his room, peeling off his clothes. She knew he must sleep naked, because there were never any nightshirts with his washing. She could picture what his naked body must look like as he rolled, alone, across that big, exotic bed carved with entwined birds and flowers.

And as she stared up at the pink silk hangings of

Laura's bed, imagining it all, she found herself wondering about the woman who used to sleep in this bed.

The woman who had drawn such an aggressive, frighteningly sensual picture of her husband and insisted that she sleep every night in her own bed, in her own room.

With a dressing room separating her from the man who should have been lying beside her.

Two days later, he asked Bryony to become his mistress.

He came upon her in the middle of the afternoon. She had dragged one of the mahogany, balloon-backed chairs from the dining room into her bedroom and was standing on it, trying to take down the box of materials she had shoved up onto the top of the wardrobe. She was reaching over her head, the box half in her arms, when she felt a frisson of excitement, a heating of her blood, that told her he was there.

She glanced sideways and saw him standing in the doorway of her bedroom, one shoulder propped against the jamb as he watched her, just watched her. She gave a small mew of surprise and lost her balance.

The box of materials slipped sideways and crashed toward the floor. She tried to grab the top of the wardrobe, to steady herself, but she was already falling.

"Bloody hell," he swore, springing forward to catch her.

She came down on top of him, knocking him off his feet. He locked his arms around her, so that they fell together. He held her tight to his chest, twisting his body so that he took the brunt of the fall. She heard him grunt as his shoulder and hip slammed into the floor. She landed on top of him, but he rolled with her in his arms, and somehow she ended up sprawled beneath him.

She went utterly still. The breath left her body in a rush as she gazed up into his face, just inches above her own. She saw his pupils dilate, the blue of his irises disappearing beneath a sea of black that seemed to glow with a primitive, exotic heat. A sexual heat that sharpened the angles of his cheekbones and parted his lips.

She lay beneath him in the age-old position for penetration, and they were both intensely aware of it. He already had her pinned down. She could feel the long, iron-hard proof of his arousal wedged against the cleft of her legs. All he'd have to do was free himself from the confines of his breeches, shove up her skirts, and enter her.

Tension shimmied in the air between them as they stared at each other. She waited, not daring to move, scarcely breathing. She could feel every inch of him, pressing her down onto the wooden floor. Feel his heat, smell his musky, male scent. Her entire world seemed to have reduced itself to this man, to her awareness of his big, strong body, hard and ready to take her. . . . And to her awareness of her own body, beneath his.

Unbidden and unwanted, her desire for him uncurled from the depths of her being, swelling her breasts, making them ache, until it was an agony not to arch beneath him, not to rub her nipples against his broad chest, not to press the center of her need against the hardness above her. She had clutched his shoulders as they fell, and she realized she still held him, her fingers curling into the muscles of his back. She willed herself to let go, but she could not. It was all she could do to keep her hands still, when they wanted to explore, to caress. She was afraid of him; afraid of what he wanted of her, afraid of what he might do to her. And yet, still, her body reacted to his.

"Are you all right?" he asked, his warm breath washing intimately over her face.

"Yes." She sounded breathless. He shifted against her, raising himself up on his elbows to let her breathe easier. But as he raised his shoulders, he lowered his head, so that his lips still hovered over hers.

She saw him breathe in, felt his chest expand against

hers. A tremor ran through him. His head dipped lower. He speared his fingers through her hair, cradling her skull between his hands, holding her steady. Holding her steady for his kiss.

She saw his lashes droop, saw his head tilt, his lips part. Her entire being yearned for his kiss, yearned to join her mouth to his, to feel the texture of his lips, to taste him. Only she knew that if it happened now, with her already beneath him like this, it wouldn't end with a kiss. It wouldn't end until he buried himself, shuddering and satiated, between her legs.

Desperate, she shifted her hands until they lay flat against his chest, and pushed. "No."

It was only a whisper, but it was enough to stop him, or at least deflect him. Instead of descending on her mouth, his lips skimmed enticingly over her cheek, nuzzled her ear, laid a trail of fire down her throat.

"Hush," he murmured. "I'm not going to hurt you, Bryony. I won't do anything to hurt you. I won't do anything you don't want me to."

His lips moved against her neck, warm and soft, and suddenly her control broke. She made a low, keening sound in her throat, her fingers clutching at his chest, her back arching up off the floor, straining toward him. At her unwilled response, she heard him growl, an animal sound of triumph that rumbled in his chest. His hand slid down her neck, closed over her breast, just as his mouth closed over hers.

It was as if every nerve ending in her body exploded. She gasped into his mouth, twining her arms around his neck, pulling him down to her as she opened her mouth to him. He was hot and wet and demanding. His tongue curled around hers, penetrating her, taking her, while his hands coursed over her body, searing her with his heat, inflaming her desire for him. She squirmed beneath him, wanting him, burning for him.

"I want you," he whispered, his breath hot against her ear. "Tell me you want me."

She wanted him. She was aching and trembling with her want. But she felt his hand at her thigh, fisting in her skirt, bunching it up, and, somehow, in the grip of that intoxicating swirl of sensual innervation, she found the strength to lunge up against him, her hand closing over his, stopping him.

She tore her lips from his. "*No*. Oh, God. Please, no."

She felt him shudder, felt his fingers dig, cruelly, into the flesh of her thigh. And she thought, *he's not going to stop. Dear God, he's not going to stop.*

But he did stop. He let his breath out in a harsh, ragged sound, and bowed his head until his forehead pressed against hers. He didn't relax his hold on her leg; if anything, he gripped her harder, but she gritted her teeth against the pain because she knew it wasn't so much her that he was holding on to, as his own self-control.

She lay still beneath him, tense and frightened, while his raging savage male instincts warred against his gentleman's code. Gradually she felt the tension within him begin to ease. He lifted his head and stared down at her.

It was the moment she'd been dreading. She expected him to be angry, to pour out his rage and frustration on her, for encouraging him and then turning him down. Instead he brushed her lips with his, just once, gently, in a brief kiss.

"Listen to me," he said, his voice as gentle as his kiss. "You don't need to be afraid of me. I said I won't do anything you don't want me to, and I meant it. But that doesn't change what I want. I want you, Bryony. And I know that you want me."

She wanted to deny it. Yesterday she could have denied it. But not now. Not after the way her body had betrayed her when she found herself so unexpectedly in his arms. She stared up at him, too engulfed by shame and guilt and fear to say anything.

When the silence stretched out and she still didn't say anything, he lowered his head and nuzzled her neck, his warm breath teasing her ear. "I want you, Bryony. I want you to become my mistress."

She stiffened.

"I'll take good care of you, sweetheart." He flicked the sensitive skin at the base of her ear with his tongue, nipped at her earlobe with his teeth. "I'll get another woman from the Factory to help you with the work, so you won't have so much to do. I'll buy you nice clothes, and—"

"Don't!" With an angry sob, she pushed against him, catching him so unawares that he drew back, and she seized the opportunity to roll out from beneath him. "Don't!" She sat up and scooted backward on her hands and bottom until she felt her back slam against the smooth side of the wardrobe. "I told you I'm not a whore, but you didn't believe me, did you? You think that because I'm a convict, I'm any man's for the taking. Well, I'm *not*."

His eyes narrowed as he, too, sat up. "If I wanted to *take* you, damn it, I'd have taken you weeks ago, and you know it. But I don't want to just take you. I want you to come to me willingly, as my mistress."

"I'm not a whore."

She saw a muscle jump along the side of his jaw, and she knew he was fighting to keep his temper under control. "I know you're not a whore, Bryony."

"Do you?" She shook her head, angrily, from side to side. "I don't think so. Not when you think you can pay me for sharing your bed with pretty clothes and an easier work schedule."

He leaned forward, coming up into a kind of crouch. "I wasn't talking about doing those things as payment," he said, enunciating each word carefully. "I was telling you what I'd like to do for you."

"If I become your mistress."

He reached out and caught her chin in his hand. She didn't try to wrench away from his grasp. "You can't deny what happens between us every time we're around each other. I've tried fighting it, but it doesn't work. You're scared of it, but that doesn't seem to make any difference, either. So why don't we just acknowledge it and let it happen?"

"Because I'm not a whore," she said quietly.

"Bloody hell." He straightened up, towering over her. "I'm talking about making you my mistress, not turning you into a whore."

She scrambled to her feet and backed away from him. "And what exactly is a mistress except one man's private whore?"

"You're looking at this all wrong, Bryony." He took a step toward her. "I want you to think about it. Consider it."

She flung up one hand, to ward him off, and he stopped. "No. Don't you see? When they made me a convict, they took away from me everything they could. My freedom. My children. My home. But things like my pride and my principles, they're in here." She curled her hand into a fist and pressed it tight against her breast. "No one can take those away." She dropped her hand, still clenched, to her side. "And I'm not about to give them to you. You can force me. But I will never come to you willingly."

He let his breath out in a long, ragged, frustrated sigh. "I don't want to take your pride, Bryony. And I don't want to destroy your principles, either. I only want to give you pleasure. It can be good between us. Think about it."

"No."

She thought she saw a glitter of anger in his eyes. But he reached out his hand and ran the backs of his fingers lightly down the side of her neck. "Think about it," he said softly. And before she could say no again, he turned around and left.

She heard the front door of the house slam behind him, and sank down on her bed, hugging herself, almost quivering with reaction.

She had come so close. So close to giving herself to him. She still couldn't believe it had happened. How could she have allowed herself to react to him that way? To let him see how much she desired him?

It was because it had all happened so fast, she decided, rubbing her hands up and down her arms, as if she were suddenly cold. That was it. She had lost control because of the shock of finding herself in his arms. Because of the swift, unexpected intensity of her arousal. She hadn't been prepared. Next time she would be prepared.

Her hands stilled at the thought. *Next time.* He had decided he wanted her for his mistress, and Hayden St. John was not the type of man to give up easily. There would be a next time, and a time after that, and a time after that, she was sure of it. And each time she would be tempted. Each time she would have to fight not only him, but herself.

She didn't want to give herself to him. But that didn't mean she wouldn't.

He didn't come back for dinner.

Gideon walked up to the house a few hours later and told her the master had ridden into Green Hills and didn't expect to be back until sometime the following day. She hadn't realized how tense she was about seeing him again until she felt herself sag in relief.

The next morning, she decided it was time to introduce Simon to solid food.

She supposed in some way it was a result of her confrontation with his father. She didn't know how her refusal of Hayden was going to affect her future at Jindabyne, but if there was any chance that he might send her back to the Factory, then the sooner Simon became accustomed to solid food, the better.

She sat beside the dining-room table, Simon balanced in her lap, and dipped one of Laura's silver relish spoons in a bowl of fine, thin porridge. "Come on, Simon," she coaxed. "Open up."

Simon eyed the unfamiliar concoction with decided suspicion. She touched the spoon to his lips, and he sucked it inside . . .

Then opened his eyes wide and made a sound that sounded suspiciously like *"yuk."*

Bryony laughed. "It can't be that bad."

A long shadow fell across the polished surface of the dining-room table. "If you made it, it probably is."

Bryony looked up to find herself staring into Hayden St. John's startlingly blue eyes. They were narrowed, gleaming with the memory of everything that had passed between them the last time they were alone together. His words might have been light, his tone teasing. But his expression was intense. Tension twanged between them.

He walked forward, not stopping until his knees almost touched her skirt. He peered into the bowl and wrinkled his nose. "What is it, anyway?"

"Rice powder, mixed with milk." She wished he wouldn't stand so close to her. "I made it for Simon. I don't exactly expect him to eat it yet, but I thought it would be good to introduce him to the idea that nourishment comes in more than one form."

His gaze dropped to her breasts. "And what's wrong with the form it takes now?" he asked, his voice low and just a bit wicked.

"N-nothing." Her hand came up to her chest, as if to protect herself from the heat of his gaze, then fluttered away.

He looked at the small bowl of white paste. "Where did you get the milk?"

"Where do you think I got it from?"

He didn't understand at first. But she watched as comprehension slowly dawned. A dark flush spread across his sharp cheekbones, and she stared at him, conscious of an unwelcome softening, a tenderness that bloomed within her at the realization that a man as hard and aggressively masculine as Hayden St. John would actually blush at the thought of a woman expressing milk from her own breasts.

Disturbed by her own feelings, she pushed the bowl away and stood up, walking to the open French doors to look out toward the distant river curling around the base of the hill.

The late afternoon air was heavy with an approaching storm. Clouds piled up overhead, hanging low and threatening, and the breeze that sent dry leaves scuttling across the veranda was cool and pregnant with the smell of rain.

"It would be better if Simon had access to cow's milk," she said, being careful not to look at Simon's father. "So he could get used to it. I was surprised when we got here and Gideon told me you don't have a dairy."

"I'm trying to build up my herd." He strolled past her onto the veranda, and stood gazing out over the valley, squinting at the coming storm.

She walked to stand several feet away from him. She, too, looked at the storm. "It would only take a few cows. And then we'd have not only milk, but cheese, and butter, and—"

He swiveled his head around, and she felt as if his gaze had slammed into her. "No one here knows a damn thing about keeping a dairy."

"I do."

One dark, flaring eyebrow rose even higher. He leaned back against a veranda post and pulled a cheroot from his pocket. She was acutely, agonizingly aware of him as a man. Of the length of his lean legs, stretched out in front of him. Of the length of his tanned fingers, slowly stroking his cigar. She remembered the way those fingers had felt, stroking her flesh. A silence stretched between them that was taut with emotions that had nothing to do with cows or dairies.

"Well?" she said at last.

He stuck the cigar between his teeth but kept his hard, restless eyes leveled on her face. "Well, what?"

She sucked in a deep breath. "May I have a dairy?"

He lit his tinderbox and held it to the cigar. "I'll think about it."

She whirled away, conscious of a turmoil of feelings, but unsure what half of them meant.

"I came here to tell you I'm going to Sydney tomorrow." He exhaled his smoke long and slow. "I'll be gone awhile."

She spun back around as something tight squeezed her chest. She didn't want him around her. She worried about what would happen when they were together. But she found she didn't want him to go away, either. "Tomorrow?" she said, not quite able to keep the dismay out of her voice.

He nodded, eyeing her through the smoke. "A message came. There's some business I need to attend to. I thought I'd tell you in case you wanted to write a letter to . . . to someone. I can see that it gets sent on to England for you."

"Th-thank you," she stammered. "Yes, I would like to write."

He straightened up and turned away, stepping off the veranda, headed toward the stables. But he paused for a moment, and twisted around to look at her over his shoulder. "See that your letter is ready tonight," he said. "I leave first thing in the morning."

There was something about his pose that reminded her of Laura's sketch of him, now safely hidden in her bottom drawer. Just the thought of the raw, sexual drawing was enough to make Bryony go hot all over. Her breath seemed to catch in her throat, and all she could do was nod.

And think that it was probably a very good thing he was going away tomorrow, after all.

CHAPTER
SIXTEEN

The candle on Laura's marble-topped bedside table had gutted low in its socket by the time Bryony signed her letter and reached for the blotter.

Since leaving Britain, she'd written Uncle Edward only one other letter, which she'd managed to send from Cape Town. A sailor who couldn't write had dictated a letter for his mother to her, and in exchange he'd promised to see that her letter went out with his. But she'd never really been sure he'd kept his promise.

That first letter had been hard enough to write. To avoid dwelling on the miseries of life on the transport ship, she'd filled her page with talk of Philip, telling Madeline all about her new baby brother. Because it was really Madeline to whom she wrote, Madeline she was desperate to keep from forgetting about her, Madeline whose face she held in her mind now as she described the beauty of the harbor at Sydney, the vivid colors of the birds that flickered through the tops of the gums, the cuddly looking little animal that Hayden told her was called a koala, which she'd seen sleeping in a tree fork.

It was easier by far to tell Madeline about the clear blue Australian sky than to tell her about the muddy grave that held her baby brother now. Easier to tell Uncle Edward about the merino sheep being bred here than to tell him about the man to whom she'd been given to use in any way that a man could use a woman.

She sealed the letter and set it aside, then blew out her

candle to lie awake in the darkness thinking of all the things she couldn't write about to anyone.

Such as the way she felt, sometimes, that she didn't even know herself anymore. It wasn't only her world, her life that had changed, but she'd changed, too. Maybe if she could tell someone about the agony of guilt she carried with her, always, it might be more bearable. Or if she could tell someone about the weight of loneliness and sorrow she sometimes feared would smother her. If she could tell someone about the *fear*. There was so much, so very much she feared.

But she had no one. And so she curled herself up into a ball, and cried herself to sleep.

Oliver's face floated before her, ghastly white against a swirling background of gray.

He was falling away from her, falling down, down, into a sucking mist. Someone was laughing, laughing wildly, and she thought she was the one who was laughing. But that was all wrong, because she hadn't meant to make him fall.

She called out to him, and he looked up at her. And then she realized that he was the one who was laughing, and that he wasn't falling alone. He had her children. Dear God, he was taking her children with him, taking her children away from her.

She could see Madeline's tear-streaked face, see her thin, frail arms reaching up from the swirling gray mist. But Philip had his eyes closed and he looked . . .

He looked dead.

Bryony screamed and leaned into the abyss as Madeline began to struggle against her father's grip. She could hear her little girl calling to her, over and over again. *Mama! I'll be good Mama. Don't let him take me. Mama? Mama!*

"Bryony."

Rough hands seized her shoulders, holding her back, keeping her from reaching Madeline. She tried to fight—

"Bryony!"

She opened her eyes and stared into Hayden's harsh face as he jerked her up and shook her.

The curtains had been hastily pushed back from the French doors. The uncertain light of a cloud-tossed moon filled the room. He was sitting on the edge of her bed, his warm, strong hands still gripping her shoulders.

"It was only a dream, Bryony," he said softly.

She realized she was shaking so badly her teeth chattered. She shook her head. "No it wasn't. It was real."

He relaxed his grip on her shoulders and slid his palms down over her back, pulling her closer, holding her against the warmth of his body. "It was a dream."

Barely realizing what she was doing, Bryony brought her hands up and clung to him, digging her fingers into the muscles at the base of his neck. She must be crying, she thought, because his chest was wet against her cheek and she tasted salt. A great sob racked her body, and he brought one hand up. It hung in the air for a moment, as if he hesitated, then he brought it down on the back of her head and began to gently stroke her hair.

She relaxed against him completely, letting the tears come, holding his warmth and strength to her, listening to the steady beat of his heart beneath her cheek and luxuriating in the feel of his strong fingers stroking, stroking.

"Who is Madeline?"

Her head fell back, and she stared up into a face that was dark and shuttered—taut with tension, like every muscle in his body.

"Who's Madeline?" he said again.

She moistened her lips with the tip of her tongue. "Madeline . . . Madeline is my little girl." Her chest lifted with a ragged breath.

His gaze fell to her breasts. She didn't have a night rail, and since she hadn't bothered to tie her shift up properly after the last time she'd fed Simon, it gaped open, revealing most of her full, swollen breasts.

She thought for a moment he might have shuddered. He released her abruptly and went to stand by the window. He rested one hand against the frame and leaned into it.

"And Oliver?" He twisted around to look back at her over his bare shoulder.

He was half naked, she now realized. He'd pulled on his breeches, but they were only half fastened. He wasn't wearing a shirt.

"Oliver was my husband."

Seconds ticked by. In the distance a dog howled. No, not a dog. She knew by now it was a dingo. Still, he stared at her, his face tight, his eyes glittering bright in the darkness.

"Tell me how you killed him."

She blinked and looked away, bringing her knees up to her chin so she could hug herself. "Don't make me tell you," she whispered.

"I need to know, Bryony."

She could have asked why, but she didn't, because she knew why. She clutched her knees to her chest almost wildly, as if by doing so she could still the rapid thudding of her heart. In the cradle on the other side of the room, the baby stirred.

Hayden shoved away from the window and came to stand beside the bed. He looked down at her, his legs braced wide, his arms folded across his bare chest. She was painfully aware of the sheer, raw power of him, of the nearness of him, of her nakedness beneath the covers and her thin shift.

His lips narrowed into a thin line. "Tell me."

"I'll tell you," she said, feeling a pain in her chest that was almost unbearable. "But not here. Not now."

"Now."

"Then, not here."

* * *

The night was cold, dark. The moon had been hidden completely by clouds. The trees farther up the hill were only restless shadows. He watched Bryony pull her cloak closer to her as she let herself out onto the veranda. All was silent except for the hum of a cicada and the sighing of the wind in the branches of the gums. He drew hard on his cigar. The tip glowed, and his nostrils filled with the acrid smell of burning tobacco.

He pushed away from the veranda post and walked toward her. He'd put on his boots and shirt but not his coat. He felt the sleeves of his shirt flutter against his arms in the wind. He should have been cold, but he wasn't. He burned from within.

"Tell me."

She couldn't seem to look at him. She turned away and went to stand on the edge of the veranda, looking out at nothing. "I found him . . ." She stopped, drew a jagged breath, and started again. "I found Oliver with another woman." She passed her hand over her eyes, as if to wipe away the vision her words re-created. "We lived in a house on the cliffs above the sea, and I was going for a walk when I saw them. I was . . ." She paused. "I was very angry. I hit him. I hit him with a stick, and he fell over the cliff. I didn't mean for it to happen, but it did."

He came right up behind her. She trembled, but whether it was a reaction to his nearness, or from fear of his intentions, he had no way of knowing.

"Did you love him very much?"

He watched her head lift, watched the night wind catch at her dusky hair and flutter it against her cheek. She swallowed painfully, and he watched the muscles in her slim neck work as he waited for her answer.

"I loved him. I was sixteen when we first met. He seemed all lightness and gaiety and laughter . . . everything life in my uncle's house was not. I thought that with him I would be free. Happy. So I ran away and married him."

Free and happy, Hayden thought. *Free and happy.*

She reached up and tucked her hair behind her ear. He watched as her hand trailed slowly back down her cheek. "I was happy, for a while. Oh, he'd be moody, but there was always a reason. And then the sun would come out again, and he'd be gay and carefree. Sometimes he was so carefree I'd worry, but he'd only laugh at me—or get angry with me, and accuse me of not having faith in him.

"I tried to have faith in him. Really I did. But slowly I began to realize that he was like a child—a badly spoiled child who'd never grown up. What he wanted, he had to have—thought he could have. No matter how far in debt he was, he was always convinced he was going to come about soon." A sad little smile hovered around her soft lips. "And the amazing thing is, he usually did. He was always lucky." The smile faded. "I think that's why I couldn't believe he was really dead."

"It wasn't your fault."

She turned to look at him. Her face was white, drawn, her eyes dark with sorrow. And he thought he hated Oliver Wentworth for what he had done to this woman.

"Yes it was." Her voice was calm, strong. Like her. "It was fate. And it was his fault. But it was also my fault. I've accepted that. I can even bear it. What I can't bear is the way my children have had to suffer for what I did."

He stared at her for a long time, not moving, and something caught at his chest. Something tender and sweet and painful. He wanted to take her in his arms and smooth the sorrow and pain from her face and make her laugh again. Make her feel free again.

But the problem was, that wasn't all he wanted to do. He also wanted to crush her trembling lips beneath his. He wanted to run his hands over her slim, white body and feel her swelling breasts shiver beneath his palms. He wanted to lay her down across his bed and take her. And it wouldn't be a gentle taking, because while there was much that was tender in his feelings for her, he didn't love her, he just wanted her. And his wanting was hot and hungry and almost dangerously fierce.

He'd come damned close to taking her once already tonight, back there in her bedroom. Even though he knew she was afraid of him, afraid of what he wanted to do to her. Even though he knew she would not give herself to him willingly.

Not yet.

So he was careful not to touch her again. Careful not to hold her in comfort when he knew he'd end up wanting to do more than comfort her. Instead he drew deeply on his cheroot, but it tasted bitter, and it occurred to him he was smoking too damned many of the things lately.

He supposed it gave him something to do with his hands.

Something besides putting them on her.

"Captain St. John!"

She came running toward him across the yard. She had her skirt and flannel petticoats bunched up in one of her fists, holding them free of her feet while she ran. He could see her shoddy shoes and the coarse stockings that covered her ankles and calves as her legs pumped back and forth. The golden rays of the rising sun touched the dark hair that tumbled out from beneath her cap with a hint of fire. Her lips were parted, and she called again, "Captain St. John!"

He reined in his horse, and she skidded to a halt beside him, holding up something white in her hand. "My letter," she said, breathlessly. "You said you'd take my letter."

He gazed down into her flushed face, and something within him tore painfully at the thought of leaving her, at the thought of how long it would be until he saw her again. He took the letter from her outstretched hand and turned it over. "Sir Edward Peyton," he read. He looked at her again, hard. "Who is Sir Edward Peyton to you?"

She stepped back, as if afraid to stand too close to him. "My uncle. He's my uncle."

"The one who has your daughter?"

"Y-yes."

He tucked her letter into his pocket, touched his spurs to his horse, and rode away.

CHAPTER
SEVENTEEN

"Manure!" Quincy stared at the malodorous pile heaped up behind the stables, and his handsome black eyes flashed with indignation. "Ye want me to shovel manure?"

Bryony glared right back at him. "Captain St. John left orders you were to help me with the garden two days a week."

"He didn't say nothin' about manure."

"Gardens need manure." She handed him the pitchfork. "Now, load it into the cart so we can get it dug in before it starts raining again."

Quincy's chest rose and fell rapidly, and she knew he hovered on the brink of refusal.

The clatter of hooves on the cobbled yard brought both their heads around. Gideon appeared at the corner of the stables, leading a limping horse. He stopped and threw Quincy a long, searching look. Quincy mumbled something obscene that most fourteen-year-old boys had never even heard, let alone said, and grabbed the pitchfork.

Bryony blew on her numb fingers and hugged her cloak against the cold. It had been unbelievably wet and miserable for weeks now, reminding her more of an English winter than what she expected spring in New South Wales to be. She watched Quincy just long enough to make sure he knew she was serious, then she left the paddock and walked into the stable, where Gideon was unsaddling his gray mare.

"I'm glad you happened to show up when you did."

She stroked the mare's velvety soft nose. "I was afraid for a minute there he wasn't going to do it."

"Sure he'd have done it, even without me," said Gideon, stripping the saddle off the horse's back. "He was just wantin' to make it clear it was a touch beneath him, that's all."

She reached up to straighten the mare's forelock, hesitating. She didn't want to ask, but somehow she couldn't seem to help it. She tried to make the question sound as casual as possible. "No word yet on when Captain St. John is coming back?"

Gideon's eyes met hers over the horse's head. "No." She knew he wasn't fooled. He'd probably seen the way she looked up, anxious, every time someone rode into the yard, every time there was a step on the veranda. He knew she was watching, waiting.

Bryony felt herself blushing and turned away. She hadn't even been told what had taken St. John back to Sydney so unexpectedly. She thought Gideon probably knew, but she'd been too shy to ask.

As if sensing her thoughts, Gideon said, "It can take awhile to get a ship ready to sail."

Bryony whirled back around. "Ship? What ship?"

Gideon was busy working a currycomb over the mare's withers. "The *Lady Laura*. She was running a shipment of coal to India, and she come back earlier than expected. The Cap'n is planning to send her to England next, with a consignment of wool."

"You mean, he *owns* this ship?"

"Aye. The *Lady Laura*, and a couple of others. And when she sails for Britain this time, she's goin' to bring back my Mary and the boys."

"Oh, Gideon!" She threw her arms around him and hugged him, laughing. "I didn't think you'd saved enough for their passage yet."

She knew by now that there was a set amount of work that male assigned servants were required by the government to perform each week, and that honest masters like

Hayden St. John paid their men for any extra work they performed. Gideon worked every extra hour he could, doing everything from hoeing fields to weaving cabbage palm hats. But at something like one shilling for every ten extra hours' labor, it took a long time to save up enough to pay the fares of a woman and two small boys.

"I ain't. But the Cap'n, he's advancin' me the rest."

Bryony buried her face against the horse's warm, fragrant hide. No one had ever set the daily tasks expected of women servants, so there was no way Bryony could hope to earn any money. She'd have to wait until her sentence was expired before she'd be able to start saving for her own passage money back to Britain. "I'm happy for you, Gideon." She straightened up and gave him a tremulous smile. "Really I am."

"Aw, Bryony . . ." His funny, little-boy face was troubled. "Sure you'll find a way—"

He broke off as a mighty roar erupted from the paddock. Bryony ran to the stable door, then froze.

Will Carver stood beside the manure pile, his hat in the hoof-churned mud beside him. Manure clung to his hair, dropped off his whiskers, splattered his shirtfront. He was shaking his big, ugly head back and forth, like an angry bull, and spitting, as if some of it had gone in his mouth.

"Why, shit, Mr. Carver," came Quincy's gay voice. "I didn't see ye standin' there. Did I get some of this . . . *shit* on ye?"

Carver threw back his head and growled, his hands clenching into two fists at his side. He was a big man; beside the slim boy he looked massive. "Why, ye ruttin', struttin' little whore's whelp. Ye been a bloody pain in me ass ever since ye was assigned here. Ye know what I'm going to do to ye, boy? I'm going to take those balls yer so proud of and feed 'em to the pigs fer dinner."

The big man swung, his fist catching the boy below the ear and spinning him around to send him sprawling into the mud.

Bryony ran, slipping and sliding across the sodden paddock. She flung herself on the overseer just as he reached down to haul the boy to his feet.

"No!" she cried, hanging onto his arm. "No, don't. It was an accident."

The overseer's face swiveled around to her. She read murder in his eyes.

"Like hell," he panted, trying to shake her off. "Let go of me, ye interferin' little strumpet."

"No. He's just a boy. And you know you're not supposed to strike an assigned servant."

It was true. A master could beat his free apprentice and a husband could beat his wife. A master could work a convict to death or send him to a magistrate to be crippled by a flogging for the most trifling of offenses. But neither a master nor his overseer was allowed to *hit* a convict.

Will Carver's fist closed over Bryony's wrist and squeezed until she almost whimpered from the pain. She released her hold on his arm, and he shoved her back so hard she stumbled and landed with a teeth-rattling *thump* in the mud. He reached again for the boy.

"Don't do it," said Gideon. He stopped beside Bryony and helped her to her feet, but he never took his eyes off Carver. Beneath his freckles, his face was white.

"Ye going to stop me, Irish? Ye? Ha! Yer no bigger than he is." He cast one, derisive glance at Gideon, then turned his back on him to lean over and close his beefy fist around Quincy's shirt and haul him to his feet.

"Don't."

Carver turned around again, an ugly sneer on his face. But the sneer died when he saw Gideon standing there with the pitchfork in his hands, its sharp prongs pointed determinedly at the overseer's chest.

"Ye dare? Ye dare threaten me?" His ugly face was suffused with angry color. Only the old saber cut showed white against his livid cheek. "I'll see ye hanged for this, Irish."

"No, you won't." Bryony slipped her shoulder beneath Quincy's arm when the boy wavered and looked as if he might collapse. "None of you has done anything here you can be proud of. It is all best forgotten."

Carver's bloodshot eyes moved slowly from her to Gideon, then back again. He bent over to pick up his hat and whacked it hard against his thigh to get rid of the worst of the mud and manure.

"I won't forget," he said. "I won't forget." He smashed the hat back on his head and pushed past her toward the barn.

Quincy swayed on his feet, holding himself upright by a sheer effort of will. "It wasn't an accident," he said stubbornly.

"I know," said Bryony. "But it was a foolish thing to do." She hesitated a moment, then gave him one of her rare smiles. "A foolish, deliciously wicked thing to do."

Hayden saw her standing outside the kitchen door when he turned the tired bay into the yard.

She looked as if she'd been gathering something, something she still held in her bunched-up white apron. But at the sound of his horse's hooves squelching through the mud and clattering over the cobbles, she turned.

She wore her ragged old brown dress. Her head was bare, her rich, mahogany hair unbound and tumbling around her shoulders in a wanton riot of curls. Not even the dull light of the overcast day could diminish its brilliance.

He watched her beautiful eyes narrow with hope and expectation. Watched the recognition dawn, watched the joy spill across her face like sunlight across a field after a rain.

She dropped the edges of her apron, sending green leaves flying as she ran toward him across the yard. One of his men shouted, a greeting, perhaps, but Hayden didn't turn. He had eyes only for her.

He swung out of the saddle, aware of a lightness of heart he hadn't known for a long time. She was so beautiful, with her cheeks flushed and her lips parted, and he had missed her so very much. She came right up to him, skidding to a halt at the last minute, and it was only with an effort that he stopped himself from sweeping her up into his arms and twirling around and around with her.

"You're back." Her smile was still brilliant, but trembled slightly now with shyness, with wariness, perhaps, because of all that had happened between them before he left.

"I'm back," he said simply.

Later that evening he sat in a chair on the veranda while he smoked a cigar and watched Bryony beat a broom against a rug hanging over a line she'd stretched between two posts. Beside him, Simon lay on a blanket and chortled happily as he played with the brightly colored string of spools Hayden had brought back from Sydney.

The sky was still overcast, but a warm wind blew from the north, suggesting a change. Hayden tipped back his chair and exhaled a cloud of smoke, then watched it drift away. He'd missed these quiet times with his son.

And Bryony.

His gaze settled on her again. She still held the broom gripped between her hands, but she was just standing there, not moving, looking at him.

She jerked her gaze away and whacked the broom against the rug so hard it almost jumped off the line. "Simon likes those spools you brought him."

"Yes," he said, conscious of the way her hips swayed back and forth every time she swung the broom.

He was hoping she'd look at him again, but she didn't. So he said, "I brought you something, too."

Her head came around, her lips parted in surprise. "Did you? What?"

His gaze fastened on her sweet mouth, and desire slammed into him, hot and savage. He wanted her.

Christ, he ached, he throbbed with his want for her. He'd spent the better part of a month away from her, he'd tried to sate himself with other women, and it hadn't made any difference. He still wanted her.

And if she didn't let him have her soon, he thought he just might die.

"I'll show you," he said.

Bryony swung the broom against the rug again with all her strength, one last time. Behind her, she heard the click of Hayden's chair legs hitting the veranda as he brought it forward and stood up. She heard him go into the house, leaving the French doors open behind him, and she knew even without looking around when he was back. She was that aware of him. It was like an invisible charge that passed between them, powerful and dangerous.

She set aside the broom and turned. He had come right up behind her with a brown paper-wrapped parcel in his hands. A smile played at the corners of his mouth, deepening the creases in his cheeks and making him look almost boyish.

She put out her hands for the package, but he held it just out of her reach, his grin deepening. "You have to finish beating the rug first."

"I have finished the bloody rug." She snatched the parcel from his slack grasp. "What is it?" she demanded, sitting down on the edge of the veranda and tearing at the paper, excitement making her clumsy.

"It's a dress. I owe you one, remember?"

Her hands stilled beneath the onslaught of memories of that first day, when he'd torn her dress right off her. She remembered the sound of the rain, drumming on the roof, and the hiss of wet wood on the fire. She remembered the sight of his long, lean fingers closing over the bodice of her dress, ripping it away. The feel of his hands lying hot and threatening on her bare shoulders.

She remembered other things, too. Like what it felt

like to lay beneath his hard body, and the taste of his mouth, and the warm, insistent pressure of his lips, opening hers. A woman's need curled low and hot within her, and she shoved the memories away almost in a panic, forcing herself to concentrate on ripping away the last of the paper.

She held a dress. But this was no work dress, for a servant. It was a lady's dress, made of the finest fawn-colored muslin, with moss-green ribbons catching its puffed sleeves and high waist. There were shoes, too. Soft, moss-green kid half boots. Delicate, sheer stockings. And a petticoat and chemise of the finest batiste.

It had been so long, so very long since she'd had anything this fine, this beautiful. She hugged the clothes to her, overwhelmed. "I-I don't know what to—"

"Put them on."

She looked up. He wasn't smiling anymore. There was a tautness about his face, a restlessness in his half-hooded eyes. He looked fierce, dangerous. From the huts on the far side of the house, she heard the men calling to one another. Someone laughed, and a hut door closed. The light was fading rapidly from the day. The gum trees down by the river were only dark and mysterious shadows. They were alone, and soon it would be night. She glanced down at the clothes again, and felt chills of fear alternating with hot flashes of anger rush through her body.

"Why did you buy these for me?"

His eyes narrowed. "Masters are required to provide their assigned servants with clothing."

She shook her head once, slowly, from side to side. "Not this kind of clothing."

"What do you think?" he asked, his voice harsh. "That I bought it for you as a bribe? To tempt you into becoming my mistress?"

It was exactly what she thought. For a long moment her frightened eyes held his hard, hungry ones. She opened her mouth to say something, but nothing came out. The tension between them leapt and crackled almost unbearably.

He turned away and went to lean against the veranda post and stare out over the pale silver thread of the river that curled between the dark trees. She saw the flare of his tinderbox and realized he was lighting another cheroot. The silence was filled with the exhalation of his breath. They both watched the smoke curl away toward the evening sky.

"That's not why I bought it, Bryony," he said. He swiveled around to look at her, although in the growing darkness his eyes were mere shadows and she couldn't read the expression hidden there.

"Then, why? Because you felt sorry for me? I don't want your pity."

"It wasn't pity. It was . . ." He drew hard on his cigar. "Oh, bloody hell." He exhaled a thin stream of smoke. "You smile so seldom. I just wanted to give you something to smile about."

It was the last thing she expected him to say, and it touched her more deeply than she'd have imagined possible.

She kept the dress.

But she couldn't quite bring herself to put it on.

Two days later, he surprised her by offering to build a dairy for her.

She was in the kitchen, heating irons before the fire so she could press his shirts, when she heard him calling her. Hastily wiping her sweaty palms on her apron, she walked to the doorway and stopped short.

He stood in the golden, slanted sun of late afternoon, his shirtsleeves rolled up to reveal his strong, tanned forearms. His broad-brimmed hat was pushed back far on his head, revealing startlingly blue eyes that sparkled with amusement and something else. Something hungry and quietly speculating.

He held the end of a rope halter in one hand. The other

end was attached to a brown cow that stretched out its head and went *mooooo* when Bryony appeared.

"Before I go to the trouble of building you a dairy," he said, resting his hands on his hips, "I want to be sure you know what you're doing."

She met the challenge in his words and threw it right back at him. "Tie her up at the bail, and I'll get a bucket and a stool."

She'd seen a bucket and stool in the kitchen, but the bucket needed to be washed, so it was a few minutes before she came out again. He had tied the cow to the bail and secured her with a leg rope, and now stood with his back braced against the sun-warmed brick wall of the kitchen, his arms crossed at his chest, his hips shot forward in that way of his.

"Where's her calf?" Bryony asked, positioning her stool beside the cow's flank. The cow turned around and stared at her suspiciously.

"In a holding pen behind the barn."

She set the bucket on the ground between the cow's rear legs, and watched the cow kick it over. She picked up the bucket. "Has this cow ever been milked before?"

"As a matter of fact, yes." She turned to look up at him, and saw his lips curl in amusement. "I decided to be nice to you."

Bryony reached for the udders, and the cow laid back her ears.

The air filled with the *whirr* of milk hitting the bucket. Bryony knew what she was doing, but barely. It had been a long time since she'd milked a cow, and she'd never done it all that much. But she managed to carry it off, sighing with relief when the bucket was full and she could stand up.

She put her hands at the base of her spine and arched her back. Then she realized the movement thrust out her breasts, and she dropped her hands almost at once. But not before his heated gaze had fastened onto the bodice of her gray work dress.

"I noticed there are some settling pans and a skimmer in the store," she said, suddenly self-conscious. "If you could send someone to—"

"I'll get them," he said almost harshly, and turned away.

She was on the veranda, pouring the milk into the settling bowls and covering them with damp muslin when Hayden strolled back up from taking the cow to the barn. He leaned against the veranda post and watched her.

"Where did Sir Edward Peyton's niece learn to milk cows?"

"From my mother," she said simply, not looking up at him. "My grandfather was a local landowner, but my grandmother started life as a kitchen maid. My mother always said people go down as well as up in this world, and I'd better be prepared for whatever might happen to me. Prophetic, wasn't it?"

She paused for a moment, then went on. "My uncle didn't want my father to marry her, even though she'd inherited all of her father's property." He watched her smooth the muslin cover over one of the bowls with exaggerated care. "She wasn't considered good enough for a man who was a Peyton of Peyton Hall and an officer in the King's Navy."

Hayden stood gazing down at the proud angle of her head. "But he married her anyway?"

"Yes."

"He must have loved her very much."

Her hands stilled at their task. "Yes, he did. Their love for each other was . . . something beautiful to see. I don't think either of them could have lived without the other, so perhaps it was best . . ." She swallowed hard. "They drowned together, you see. When I was thirteen."

He studied the gentle tilt of her nose, the flaring of her cheekbones, the sensuous curve of her lips. "Did she look like you?"

"My mother?" She glanced up.

"Yes."

Her eyes met his briefly, and whatever she saw there made her turn away and blush. "I have her coloring. But as to looking like her . . . I don't know. She was very beautiful. And vibrant. I used to think she glowed with the joy of life." A sad smile played about her lips. "It was my mother who named me Bryony. She loved the white bryony and black bryony that grow wild along the hedgerows in Cornwall. She used to say she named me after it because I was born when they're in fruit, and because she wanted me to grow up to be as wild and free and beautiful as a wayside vine."

Her voice broke slightly, and she turned away from the settling bowls to go and stand at the edge of the veranda, looking up the valley toward the purpling ridge of mountains. "My uncle hated my name, just as he hated my mother. When she and my father died and I had to go live with him, he said I was like a wild filly that needed to be broken. He did his best to break me."

Hayden walked up behind her, resisting with difficulty the urge to pull her into his arms and soothe away the pain he sensed within her. "He didn't succeed," he said softly.

She turned around. "No." An evening breeze caught a strand of her flame-tinged, dusky hair and fluttered it across her pale face. "It took marriage and prison to do that."

He reached out and tucked the loose strand behind her ear. "No," he said, trailing the backs of his fingers down her cheek. "Your name still fits."

CHAPTER EIGHTEEN

The work on the dairy began early the next morning.

Before she'd even finished the breakfast dishes, the men were already digging the foundations. To keep out the fierce heat of New South Wales, half the dairy was being built underground, the log walls reinforced with mud some two feet thick.

Bryony watched the progress on the dairy off and on throughout the day. When she stepped outside after putting Simon down for his afternoon nap, she discovered that Hayden had joined the men working to lay down the three to four feet of stringy bark that would act as insulation beneath the roof.

He had stripped down to his shirt and breeches. His fine white shirt was dark with sweat and clung to him, clearly outlining every bulge and hollow of muscle as he worked. His hair curled damply at the nape of his neck. Even the dark hair on his bared forearms glistened with sweat.

As she watched, he paused for a moment to lift his hat from his brow and wipe the sweat from his forehead with the back of his arm. The sun glinted off his dark head, and sparkled on the bead of sweat that rolled down his cheek.

He was big and he was strong, and he was so much a man, and a slow, sweet yearning curled up within her as she stared at him. He made her acutely aware of her own body, of the fullness of her breasts and the flannel of her petticoat lying heavy against her thighs as she stood beneath the hot Australian sun, watching him. She felt, in that moment, wholly in tune with herself, with the world around her, with him, and she wanted him so badly that she almost wished she were a different kind of woman. The kind of woman who could become his mistress, gladly. The kind of woman who knew nothing of pride and principles, but only of desire, and the slow, delicious ecstasy of a man's body, driving deep within her.

Then he turned, his arm falling to his side, and stared back at her.

Their gazes met and locked while he slowly lifted his hat and put it back on his head. The brim shaded his eyes, and it was as if he'd hidden his thoughts, hidden himself from her.

"Ride a cock horse to Banbury Cross . . ." Bryony gave Simon a little jiggle, and he giggled his delight. ". . . to see a fine lady upon a white horse . . ." Another jiggle was rewarded with another giggle, and this time Bryony laughed, too. ". . . with rings on her fingers and bells—"

She broke off at the sound of a shout from the yard. She knew the rhythms and sounds of the homestead by now. Something was wrong.

Lifting the baby to her hip, she walked out the open French doors to the veranda.

Will Carver, mounted on a big gray, thundered into the yard and reined his horse in hard. He pulled behind him a bound man who half ran, half stumbled in the effort to keep from being dragged over the rough ground by the short length of rope that tied him to the overseer's saddle. When the overseer stopped and released the tension on the rope, the man collapsed.

Bryony heard the scrape of boots on the stone flagging of the veranda and turned to see St. John emerge from the house. He had washed and changed, but his clean shirt still hung open and his hair curled damply against his tanned neck.

"What is it, Will?" he asked, fastening his shirt as he stepped down into the yard.

"This." Carver reached behind him to untie something from his saddle and held out what looked like an iron rod with the letters Q8J on the end. "I caught him red-handed, Cap'n. He had the fire lit and one of yer calves hogtied when I rode up. There was another one with him what got away, but not before I seen who it was."

Hayden walked over to gaze down at the man on the ground. Bryony had seen the young man around a few times, usually with Quincy, although she didn't really know him.

"Jennings," he said, staring down at the man with an expression so cold it sent a shiver up Bryony's spine. "Do you have anything to say in your defense?"

The man rolled over. His chest heaved painfully. He was covered in so much blood and dirt Bryony couldn't even see where he was hurt. "I ain't got nothin' to say, Captain," he managed to gasp.

"You don't deny it?"

"I don't deny it."

There was a long pause, during which none of the many people assembled in the yard made a sound. Hayden turned back to his foreman. "Put him in the lockup room for now. It's too late to take him into Green Hills tonight." He glanced over at the crowd of men who had gathered outside the huts. "Gideon, take a couple of men to help carry him in there and get him cleaned up. McDuff and Butler, saddle up and ride out with Carver to find the other man."

"We'll get the little son of a bitch, Cap'n." Carver spat into the dust.

Hayden eyed his overseer hard. "Just get him, Will. Don't kill him."

The two men shared a look Bryony couldn't begin to

understand. Then the overseer reined his horse toward the stable. "Yes, sir."

A feeling of foreboding stole over Bryony as she hurried down the steps. "Who is it?" she asked. "Who is the other man?"

For a minute she thought Hayden wasn't going to answer her. Then he turned and looked down at her as if only becoming aware of her presence. "Quincy. The other man is Quincy."

"Will Carver hates Quincy. You know that. How can you believe him in this?" she demanded.

Hayden sat at his desk, mending a pen. The night was unusually warm and sultry, and he was stripped down to his breeches. Lamplight spilled across his cheek, throwing the other half of his face into hard shadows as he turned to stare at her. "It isn't just a matter of believing Carver," he said. "What do you want me to do, Bryony? Take you down to the store so you can hear it from Quincy himself? He doesn't deny it."

She hesitated, one hand on the frame of the door to his room. Simon was asleep, and the house around them was dark and still. They usually avoided each other after the sun went down. But the tension that thrummed between them tonight was angry and cold.

She twisted her fingers through her apron, but kept her gaze fixed firmly on his forbidding face. "What are you going to do with him?"

Carefully setting aside his pen, he stood up and came toward her. "I'm taking them both into Green Hills tomorrow, to the magistrate. Why?"

Bryony's stomach churned. "You told me you don't flog your assigned servants."

He came to a halt in front of her, his uncomfortable eyes staring down at her. "This isn't some lost pig, or even a lamb that ended up as someone's unauthorized dinner. Do you understand what was going on here? Jennings' sentence expires next year. He was planning to use my calves and lambs as the nucleus for his own herd. Those men—"

"Quincy isn't a *man*. He's a boy."

He was close enough for her to see the shadow of the day's growth of beard on his cheeks and the creases left by the years he'd spent laughing with Laura. Abruptly he turned away. "Quincy's old enough to get into a man's kind of trouble."

"But he—"

He whirled back around suddenly. His gaze slammed into her like a fist in her stomach. She could see his pulse beating, hard, beneath the dark skin of his bare throat as he controlled himself with visible effort. "Enough, Bryony."

"But—"

Something flashed in his eyes, something bright and dangerous. "Enough!"

Her breath caught in her throat, hot and burning. He was hard, he was cold, and he could be unbelievably cruel. She stared at him in the warm, golden light of the lamp, and thought how much she hated him.

Bryony couldn't watch them drive away in the morning. She waited until the sound of the cart wheels and horses' hooves had faded with the distance, then she went into the parlor and uncovered Laura's harp. But while the music soothed her, it offered no real solace, so in the end she turned to the earth. She worked in Laura's garden all day.

She was planting a hedge of lavender cuttings when they brought Jennings and Quincy back. She stood up and brushed the warm earth from her old skirt with a shaking hand. She tried not to hurry, but when she came within sight of the yard and saw only Hayden St. John, mounted astride his big bay, and Will Carver, driving what looked like an empty cart, she broke into a run.

She was halfway across the yard when Gideon caught

her in his arms and spun her around. "Don't look, Bryony."

"What do you mean, don't look?" She clutched at his shirtfront. "Oh God, Gideon! What has he done to them? Where are they?"

"They're lying in the cart."

"In the—"

She whirled back around. Some of the men were lifting two limp forms from the bed of the cart. At first she thought they'd been hanged, but hanging was neat and relatively quick. These men had suffered and bled. Their clothing was dark and stiff with their blood.

"Let me go, Gideon," she said, her voice low and calm.

He let her go. She walked slowly across the rest of the yard, her head held high, her hands pressed to her stomach in an effort to still the churning nausea.

Hayden had just handed his horse to one of the men. His face was remote, hard, his eyes forbidding. He was a stranger.

She walked right up to him. "You had them flogged."

A muscle tensed in his jaw. "Yes."

"How many? How many lashes?"

"Jennings was given three hundred."

She felt herself flinch, as if one of those lashes had landed on her. "And Quincy?"

He started to turn away, but she reached out and put a hand on his arm, stopping him. "How many did Quincy get?"

She could feel his steely strength through the fine cloth of his coat sleeve. It was as if she'd suddenly seized hold of the hot end of Jennings' branding iron. He swung slowly back around, his angry gaze colliding with hers. She let him go.

He took a step toward her and leaned into her, so close she wondered that the fury in those blue eyes didn't scorch her. "Go into the house. Now."

"How m—"

He laid his hands on her shoulders, his grip hard and a

little cruel. "You're not my wife, Bryony," he said, his voice low, his tone cutting through her in a way that hurt far more than the angry pressure on her shoulders. "You're not even my bloody mistress, although I doubt there's a man here who doesn't think you are. It's not your place to question me, let alone challenge me. *Now, get into the house.*"

His hands fell from her shoulders, and he swung abruptly away, dismissing her. Bryony went rigid. She turned and forced herself to walk slowly back toward the house, her head high.

She swallowed hard, trying to hold back the fiery well of anger and hurt that burned within her.

She made it as far as the veranda before the hot tears spilled over and ran down her cheeks.

Quincy had been given seventy-five lashes.

It was Gideon who finally told her, when he came up to the kitchen that evening to help her fetch the water and wood.

She was kneading the dough for St. John's damper when he told her. She stopped dead still, feeling as if a piece of her—an important piece—had just been torn out and thrown away.

Gideon eyed her dispassionately for a moment, then said, "Yer wrong, Bryony—what yer thinkin'."

Bryony pushed her fist into the dough the way she'd like to slam it into Hayden St. John's hard, handsome face. "How do you know what I'm thinking?"

"Yer thinkin' he's no different from the others—the ones like Sir D'Arcy Baxter."

"He is no different."

"Isn't he? Bryony, if Jennings and Quincy belonged to Baxter, they'd be dead now—or on their way to a penal colony like Norfolk Island, which is worse'n being dead, in most people's way of thinkin'."

"The magistrate hands down the sentence, not the master."

"Sure he does. And why do you think the Cap'n went into Green Hills yesterday with those men himself, instead of jist sendin' 'em in to the magistrate with Will Carver?"

Bryony shrugged.

"He went to make sure the magistrate didn't hang 'em, that's why he went. And he's the only reason those two men are over there in their hut nursin' bloody backs, 'stead of bein' rolled up in bark and lyin' at the bottom of some unmarked grave."

She threw the damper into the Dutch oven and thumped it down among the coals on the hearth. "He didn't have to send them to the magistrate at all," she said, shoveling more hot coals onto the lid.

"Oh? And what was he supposed to do? Let them and any other man who takes the fancy steal all his cows and sheep?"

"Quincy is only fourteen, damn it. He's not a man. And I don't care how many calves he brands or servant women he seduces," she added, picking up the basket she used to gather greens, "he is still only a boy."

Gideon had opened his mouth to say something, but at that he closed it and shook his head in the age-old gesture of a male hopelessly confused by the thought processes of a female.

Hayden sprawled in his chair at the end of the dining table, his legs thrown out before him, his waistcoat unbuttoned, a crystal glass cradled in the palm of the hand that rested against his crotch. A bottle of port stood open and nearly empty at his elbow.

The room was in semidarkness. He hadn't bothered to light the brace of candles Bryony had set on the table. The only light came from the mellow glow of the setting sun filtering in through the lace curtains at the French doors.

A soft mew of surprise from the doorway brought his head around. Bryony paused just inside the room. She had waited until it was almost dark before she ventured to come clear his place from the dinner table. He supposed she hadn't wanted to risk running into him.

She stood with her arms wrapped around her waist, and stared at him as if he were the greatest beast imaginable. Her eyes were dark and bruised-looking in a pale face.

He looked at her long and hard, then he raised the glass to his lips and drained it. "How ill-mannered of me," he said, rolling the empty glass between his fingers. "I should have vacated the room by now."

She didn't say anything. He sloshed the last of the port into his glass and let his gaze rove slowly over her. She was wearing her old brown work dress. The apron she had tied about her small waist was stained with water from the dishes she'd been washing, and she had a servant's mobcap perched on her head, hiding her beautiful hair.

He frowned at it. "Why do you always wear those ugly caps?"

"Because you told me to."

Had he? What a stupid thing to have done. "Well, stop wearing them."

"Yes . . . sir," she said. But she made no move to take the thing off.

He stretched slowly to his feet, his glass in his hand. She skittered backward, closer to the door. He let out a harsh laugh. "What in the hell do you think I'm going to do to you, anyway?"

She was breathing quick and heavy. He watched the rapid rise and fall of her breasts, and he wished . . . he wished he was the kind of man she obviously thought he was, so he could do to her what he wanted to do to her.

She shook her head slowly from side to side. "I don't know. I don't know what you're capable of."

He swore crudely and turned away from her to stand

beside the French doors. The yard below lay quiet and empty in the fading light.

He wasn't proud of what he'd had to do today, but he was damned if he was going to justify it to her or anyone else. However much he himself might hate the lash and what it did to a man, it was a part of the society in which he lived. If he was to keep control of his motley crew of thieves, footpads, and Irish rebels, then he couldn't be seen to shrink from using it when it was undeniably called for. He'd secured the lightest sentence he could for his men, and he'd made sure the lashes were laid on easy with the oldest cat available. And he'd stood there and watched every damned stroke fall.

He raised his glass and drank from it, letting the heady fumes of the wine wash away the metallic stench of blood that seemed to cling about him still. When he lowered his glass and glanced behind him, she was gone.

He took to leaving the homestead in the morning without breakfast, chewing on dried beef as he rode out to his fields. She made her first butter and her first cheese, but she was unable to take much pleasure in it, and if he enjoyed the new additions to his diet, she didn't know because they no longer spoke.

In the evenings he stood outside, smoking a cheroot and staring off down the valley, while she put his dinner on the table and quietly left the room. After dinner she washed the dishes on the veranda with only Simon for company. She tried to tell herself that the happy babble from the baby in his blanket-lined packing case was enough; she didn't miss the restless, disturbing presence of the baby's father.

But as she lay awake in her bed at night, listening to his boot heels scrape across the stone flagging of the veranda as he came back up from checking on the horses in his stables, she knew it was a lie.

She ran her hand over the space in the bed beside her, feeling its emptiness, feeling her loneliness. She'd known from the day she'd first seen him that he was a man who could be cruel when he had to be. And although she hated what he'd done, she was beginning to admit to herself that he'd had to do it.

She'd taken to sending a fresh pitcher of milk every morning over to the huts, for Jennings and Quincy. That afternoon, Quincy had brought the empty pitcher back himself.

He was still pale, and he walked with the studied care of one who knows he'll regret any quick or ill-judged movement. But she'd been stunned to discover that he bore Captain St. John no ill will for the flogging. On the contrary, he was profoundly grateful for having been saved from the hanging he'd been convinced he'd earned. And when she suggested it was wrong to flog one of his tender years, he'd actually gotten mad at *her*.

"What are ye saying, then? That I'm not a man? That I can't take the lash? What do ye think? That I cried out? Well, I didn't. I took it like a man, I did. The Cap'n knows what I am, even if ye don't." And with that he stomped off, leaving her with the absurd suspicion that he was actually proud of the healing wounds on his back.

It was a strange, male world in which she lived. She didn't understand it, and in many ways she didn't like it. She rolled over and stared at the door to the dressing room that separated her room from his.

It's not your place to question me.

His voice had been pitched low, so low that none of the men in the yard could have heard what he said. But there hadn't been a one who hadn't stopped what he was doing to watch. She felt a hot tide of mortification wash over her at the memory.

He would never have treated Laura in such a way, Bryony thought. But then, Laura was a true lady. Laura would never have allowed her anger to lead her to confront her husband in the yard, beneath the interested eyes of his men. In fact, Laura probably had never confronted him at all, about anything.

You're not my wife, you're not even my mistress. His words were like a dagger, piercing her heart. No, she wasn't his wife, and she had refused to become his mistress. She had no claim on him. She was, simply, his servant woman.

A servant who had made the foolish, dangerous mistake of falling in love with her master.

A sob slipped out from some lonely, hurting place deep within her, as she finally admitted the awful truth to herself. It was bad enough that she'd been lusting after the man, but how could she have allowed herself to start loving him? It was all wrong, and she knew it. Nothing could ever come of her love for this man. Men like Hayden St. John did not marry convict women.

And Bryony would never become any man's mistress.

The slab hut stood in the center of its clearing, baking beneath the afternoon sun. Insects hummed in the dusty heat. A pair of black cockatoos cawed at her from a big white gum on the edge of the nearby stand of trees.

"Louisa," Bryony called, shifting Simon's weight to her shoulder as she crossed the sunbaked clearing. "Are you there? Louisa? I thought I— Oh."

Will Carver appeared at the door of his hut. He wore only a dirty pair of canvas trousers stuffed into lace-up boots. His bare, sagging chest and protruding belly were a sickly white and thinly covered with graying dark hairs that glistened with grease from the rib he was chewing. He sucked the marrow from the bone, eyeing her all the while. Then he chucked the bone at a scrawny hen scratching about in the yard and wiped his hands on his pants.

Bryony knew by now that though Louisa carried Will Carver's name, the man had never actually married her. He'd first noticed Louisa when he'd struck the fetters off her wrists on the day she'd been brought on board the transport ship that was also carrying him to his new assignment. It hadn't been a week later that he'd caught her in a deserted companionway and raped her. But he'd bought her a pretty yellow hair ribbon at the next port, and after they reached Sydney, he'd had her assigned to him. They'd been together ever since.

"I'm sorry," Bryony said, coming to a halt some distance away from him. "I was looking for Louisa."

"She ain't here."

His eyes slid insolently over her. He had a way of looking at her, a way that was different from St. John's other men. Most men saw all transported convict women as whores. Even if they weren't whores when they were sent out here, it was hardly a system designed to protect a woman's virtue. And Bryony knew only too well that whether a woman fell from choice or from ill-usage, it made no difference in the eyes of her world. If a woman wasn't a virgin or a wife, then she was a whore.

But while the other men on Jindabyne might see her as a whore, most of them assumed she was Hayden St. John's whore, and therefore off-limits. With Will Carver, it was different. She didn't think she had anything to fear from him; he had too much respect for the Captain for that. But there was something about the way he looked at her . . . as if he knew she was off-limits for now, but he was waiting his turn.

She lowered Simon from her shoulder until she was holding him like a shield before her. "It wasn't important," she said, turning to leave. "If you could tell her I—"

"She's at the buryin' ground." His voice stopped her. "It's at the crest of the hill there, just a few hundred feet beyond those trees. Go on, if you like." He nodded toward a stand of ironbark.

"Thank you." She hesitated a moment, then headed toward the trees. He stood in the doorway of the hut, watching her, until she was out of sight.

She followed a well-worn path. Louisa must visit this cemetery every day, Bryony thought with a pang of sadness, to wear the path down like this.

She could hear the woman before she saw her. She was singing, which surprised Bryony because she had never heard Louisa sing before. It was only when she drew closer she realized Louisa was singing a lullaby.

" '. . . Lay thee down now and rest, may your slumber be blessed . . .' "

Bryony heard the tinkling of little bells and turned to see Sarah fluttering about beneath the trees, picking flowers. She waved to her, and the little girl smiled and waved back.

" '. . . Lay thee down now and rest, may your slumber be blessed.' "

Louisa looked up then and saw her, and her face broke into a wide grin. "Why, Bryony. You come to see me babes? I was just fixin' up their beds."

Bryony looked about her. The cemetery had been laid out in a large clearing. Someone, probably Hayden St. John, had recently fenced it in with neat white palings. In one corner stood a large marble monument. Bryony paused before it.

In loving memory of Laura Beaumont St. John, 28 August 1781 to 26 May 1808. Beloved wife of Hayden Seymour St. John. Daughter of—

But she didn't want to read Laura's tombstone. She didn't want to think about a Laura who couldn't hear the wind rustling the gum trees or smell the rich, earthy scent of the long, ripening grass, or feel the warmth of the baby who nestled sleepily against Bryony's neck.

And she couldn't bear to think of Hayden standing here, mourning his beautiful, gentle wife.

She jerked away. There were a few other graves in the cemetery, graves of assigned men who'd never lived to see their sentences expire. But what clutched at Bryony's heart and chilled her soul was the sight of the four tiny graves so carefully tended by Louisa Carver.

They lay in a row, Louisa's babes. There were no marble headstones for these children of a transported Dublin thief, but each had a slab marker with their names and ages burned deep by a hand that had cared. And each tiny grave was topped with a curious cover of bark and planks that made them look not unlike the crude beds Bryony had seen in Louisa's hut.

The earth around the graves was swept clean. Louisa had brought a broom with her and had been sweeping the graves when Bryony walked up. Bryony thought she must come here every day and sweep, for not a blade of grass grew near them. The ground was as bare and hard-packed as the floor of Louisa's hut.

"This here's me firstborn, Nathan," Louisa was saying. "And here's me Mary, and, beside her, Thomas. And this here is me wee one, me Joseph." There was something about the way she said it, as if she were introducing children who stood there, alive and well. It sent a small shiver up Bryony's spine.

"I had Will cover their beds like this. I didn't like the idea of them sleeping out in the rain. The sun's all right. The sun feels good on yer face. But I couldn't have 'em sleepin' in the rain."

Sarah danced up to them, a flutter of silver bells and sun-streaked hair, to lay a posy on Mary's grave. She'd already gathered flowers for Thomas and Joseph.

"I made sure they were laid out so there's room here for two more," said Louisa, watching her daughter skip off to gather flowers for Nathan. "If anythin' ever happens to me Sarey—"

"Oh, Louisa. You mustn't think of it." Which was a stupid thing to have said, thought Bryony to herself, because how could the woman help but think of it?

"If anything ever happens to me Sarey, I'm just going to walk into that old river down there, and make me bed here, next to me babes."

Bryony stared at the woman beside her in dismay.

She'd always thought of Louisa as being so strong. Louisa had taken the worst that life could throw at a woman, and she'd survived. She'd not only survived; in her own way she'd seemed to flourish.

But someplace, deep inside, where it mattered, Louisa Carver truly had gone quietly mad.

And Bryony was afraid, so terribly afraid, that if she didn't stop dwelling on her grief for Philip and her fears for Madeline, the same thing might happen to her.

CHAPTER
NINETEEN

The haunting strains of Bodin de Boismortier's Suite No. One in E Minor floated away on the late afternoon breeze. Hayden had arranged it himself, for flute and harp. Except there was no flute, only a harp. Laura's harp.

Hayden stopped with one hand clutching the veranda post, conscious of a tightening in his chest, an ache in the region of his heart. For the space of one, pounding heartbeat he thought it wasn't real, that his imagination had conjured up the sound to torment him.

Only he would never have imagined Laura playing like this. Laura had been a skilled, well-trained musician. But whoever was playing Laura's harp was drawing the music from the depths of her very soul.

He entered the house quietly, although the woman who sat at Laura's harp was so lost in her music he doubted she would have heard him had he ridden his bay at a charge right into the hall. He stood in the doorway of the parlor, watching her. Her hair was unbound and tumbled down her back in a cascade of dark, flame-shot curls that made him yearn to lift the heavy mass from her slim shoulders and let it fall again, just so he could feel it as it slipped through his fingers.

She played with her head thrown back, her eyes closed, her fingers moving nimbly over the strings. Her face was suffused with a curious mixture of earthly sadness and sublime joy. He thought she had never looked more beautiful.

He watched her a moment longer, then quietly crossed

the hall to his room, to take out the flute he hadn't touched for six long months.

She heard the flute in her mind, its notes high and clear and sweet. Her fingers faltered at the strings, and her eyes flew open.

His brilliant blue gaze met and held hers above the flashing silver of his instrument, but he never missed a note. He wove them around her, a delicate filigree of sound that enticed her, wooed her, seduced her.

Of their own accord, her fingers began once again to pluck the strings. Their gazes remained locked. They talked to each other with their eyes, with the gentle, swaying movements of their bodies, with their music.

At times the music was low and sensual, at other times high and clear and bright. They moved wordlessly from one piece to the next; sometimes one would start a piece, sometimes the other. Once they looked at each other and began the same piece simultaneously. There was no need for speech. They knew each other's pain, each other's fear, each other's sorrow, and they played it, they shared it, they eased it.

They played until the shadows in the room grew long and Quincy came pounding at the door. "Bryony? What the hell ye think yer doin'? I got yer fire started, but if ye don't hustle it, it's goin' to be dark before ye get the Cap'n's dinner ready. Bryony?"

Hayden lowered his flute, Bryony's arms dropped to her sides. They looked at each other and smiled.

Hayden stood with his shoulders against the frame of the French doors and smoked a cigar while he watched Bryony sew in a chair before the empty hearth.

"I thought you'd be angry with me," she said, keeping her gaze focused on the tiny stitches she was setting in a nightgown for Simon. "You told me not to touch it."

He lifted his cheroot, drew in deeply, then exhaled a stream of blue smoke. "I didn't think you knew a damn thing about harps. What have you been doing? Playing during the day, when I'm not around?"

She didn't say anything, but a telltale stain of color stole up her cheeks. "Ha," he said, shaking his cigar at her. "At least you have the grace to blush."

The blush deepened, and he thought how beautiful she looked, with the golden light of the setting sun streaming in to touch her cheeks with a warm glow. He thought about how much he'd missed their evenings together, talking to her, watching for the elusive smiles that sometimes flitted across her face. He thought about how much he'd hurt her, both by what he'd done to his two men and by what he'd said to her, and he wished he could explain it all to her. Explain how he, too, had been hurt by what he'd had to do. And how he wished he'd never said what he'd said to her that day, in the yard.

There was so much he wanted to tell her. But she was his servant, and he was her master, and although he wanted to subtly alter that relationship, she would have none of it. So he just stood there, listening to a couple of magpies chatter in the distance, and smoked his cigar.

They played together often, in the evenings after Bryony had finished the dishes and put the baby to sleep. When the weather was fine, Hayden would carry the harp and a chair out onto the veranda for her, and they'd play while the sun slipped behind the jagged blue tips of the mountains and the river turned into a streak of silver, gleaming beyond the shadows of the trees.

But it was a dangerous practice, because it meant they were spending time alone together as it grew dark, something she'd avoided doing in the past.

One particularly warm night, he'd been playing in his shirtsleeves as he usually did, but the shirt was damp with his sweat and dirty from a day spent riding the fields, getting ready for the harvest, for he'd ridden in late and there'd been no time to change before dinner. He finally set aside his flute with a soft oath and stripped the shirt off.

The warm evening breeze curled around his naked torso, cooling him. He lifted his flute again and started to play Purcell's Minuet when he realized Bryony was staring at him.

Her breath came shallow and rapid from between her lips, her beautiful brown eyes were dark with nameless yearnings as her gaze roved over the sweat-sheened muscles of his bare chest and his arms. She jerked her head away almost at once and gave her attention to the music, but he could tell she wasn't concentrating. Every once in a while he'd catch her eyeing him, covertly, from beneath her lowered lashes.

And the knowledge of it brought such a shuddering, aching need that he finally laid down his flute.

She stopped playing at once. "What's wrong?" she asked. Her face was blank with surprise, but her eyes . . . ah, her eyes burned with the same heat that threatened to consume him.

"Nothing." He turned away before she could bloody well *see* what was wrong with him. "We're starting the harvest tomorrow, and it's going to be a long day. I think I should carry the harp back inside now."

Alone in his bed that night, Hayden tossed and turned for endless hours until the covers were like a twisted rope wrapped around his hot, naked body. He finally swore and kicked them off the bottom of the bed.

He lay in the darkness, breathing heavily, remembering the curve of her wrists as she plucked the harp's strings, the lift of her breasts when she tossed her hair over her shoulder, the light in her eyes as they moved hungrily over his naked chest.

It was the look in her eyes that he kept coming back to. He had seen her watching him at other times over the course of the last few months. But in the past the eyes that followed him had always shone with a kind of wariness, as if she were aware of his sexuality, his power, but afraid of it.

He'd seen no fear in her tonight. Only an aching want.

He glanced toward the door to her room. If it were true, if she were no longer afraid of him, then he could go to her. He could go to her now. He knew what she would look like, lying in her bed, her breasts swelling above the neck of her night rail, her fire-kissed hair spread across the pillow. He pictured walking up to her and gently lifting the gown from her body and running his hands up her naked thighs, opening her for him. It was an image so vivid, so compelling that he shuddered.

But what if he were wrong? What if he went to her and she was still determined to hold him off in the name of pride and principles? If he went to her now, wanting her the way he did, he wouldn't be able to stop himself from taking her. Not even if she didn't want him. Not even if she fought him. He would have to have her.

With a groan, he rolled out of bed and went to throw open the French doors and the shutters. The night was clear and almost still. He stood listening to the cicadas hum, to the whisper of the wind in the branches of the river gums.

And he found he had to grip the edge of the door, hard, to keep himself there, where the night air washed cold over his hot body.

To keep himself from walking through that other door, the one that led to the room where she lay sleeping in his dead wife's bed.

The long, hot days that followed kept the men out in the fields until it was dark. Hayden St. John worked beside his men, harder than any laborer. Almost everyone on the station was drafted to work in the fields at harvest time, for the wheat not only had to be cut, it also had to be gathered and tied into sheaves in preparation for being picked up and carried to the threshing floor to be threshed with a flail. Then the fields would be burned and planted again, with corn this time.

With all the men out in the fields, Bryony and Simon were left alone at the homestead during the day. Even Quincy had had to give up the two mornings a week he usually stayed to help with Laura's garden. Normally Bryony didn't mind being alone. But on this particular day she was feeling oddly nervous.

She was down near the creek with Simon tied to her chest with a shawl, picking her first crop of beans for dinner. It was hot. A film of sweat, gritty with dust, glazed her face. The day was oddly still. No wind rustled the gum leaves. Even the birds were silent. She found she kept looking over her shoulder, kept straightening up to scan the nearby trees. She told herself she was being foolish. She told herself it was an effect of the weather, which was cloudy and close without a breath of fresh air moving. But it didn't seem to help. She finally picked up her basket and headed back toward the house.

It was when she came around the side of the kitchen that she saw them. A group of six Aborigines stood outside one of the huts at the bottom of the yard. Three or four of their mangy dogs lay panting in the shade beside them.

She eyed the black men warily. She'd seen Aboriginal people around often enough by now to feel slightly foolish every time she remembered the way she'd run from that first encounter. They regularly came into the yard to sharpen their tomahawks at the grinding stone, as one of them was doing now, or to talk Hayden out of a sack of corn.

But she'd never been entirely alone with such a large group of them, as she was now. She set her basket of beans on the kitchen table and went to lay Simon in his bed in the house. It was time to milk the cows. And although she didn't relish the idea of walking down to the bottom of the yard where those men were, it had to be done.

She felt their eyes follow her as she led the cows to the bail and secured their leg ropes. She was hoping by the time she was done with the milking they'd be gone, but they weren't. Sighing, she set the milk in the dairy and went to take the cows back to the barn.

It was when she was walking the two cows back toward the stockyards that one of the dogs, lying seemingly asleep by the huts, suddenly stood up. He lifted his head, as if sniffing the wind, and whatever it was he smelled, he didn't like. His lips curled back over his teeth, and he let out a deep, throaty growl.

Bryony eyed the dog nervously. He took a step toward her and growled again. It seemed to act as a kind of cue to the other dogs. They all stood up and growled together.

Bryony kept walking. She was almost past them when the dog suddenly lunged at her. She never knew if he was going for one of the cows or for her. She had a brief, terrifying vision of wild eyes and snarling teeth. She lashed out with the end of the lead ropes. They hit with a stinging snap across the dog's nose. He ran off howling across the yard.

The black man stopped grinding his tomahawk. They all stared at her. One particularly big man with an ugly scar on his shoulder strode up and cuffed her hard, on the side of the head. She went sprawling facedown into the dust, dropping the lead ropes. The two cows kicked up their heels and took off bawling.

She rolled over slowly, coming to a half-sitting position. Her ears were ringing so badly she didn't think she could stand up. She sat in the dust, holding her head and eyeing the man who stood over her.

Throughout the entire encounter, no one had said a word. Now the man who had hit her grunted as if in satisfaction. He said something she couldn't understand to the man with the tomahawk, then turned away from her. The man with the tomahawk took one step toward her . . .

And Bryony found her legs and her lungs at the same time.

"Hayden!"

She picked herself up out of the dust and bolted, screaming as loud as she could. She knew he probably couldn't hear her, but she kept screaming his name anyway, over and over again, as she dashed toward the house. She wasn't sure what she thought she was going to do when she got there. She only knew she couldn't run off in the other direction and leave Simon there alone.

She never made it to the house. She hadn't even reached the veranda when one of the men tackled her from behind. She rolled over, kicking and biting for all she was worth, until he finally sat on her and pinned her arms down in the dust.

He wasn't a particularly large man, and he wasn't very young, either. When he opened his mouth, she saw he'd already lost a good many of his teeth. "Ba-eel, ba-eel," he said. "No good you run for cooly. You cry to cooly, and cooly come here and kill everybody. No good."

Bryony gave one mighty, useless heave, then lay still. Slowly it began to dawn on her that nothing more was going to happen. The man who sat on her just kept saying, "Ba-eel, ba-eel. No good cry to cooly and get cooly to kill everybody." She glanced over at the huts, but the men who had been standing there were gone, melted into the afternoon shadows, the dogs with them.

The man who was sitting on her turned his head, as if he heard something. But he waited for several more minutes before he finally rolled off her and ran for the river.

It was only then that Bryony heard the pounding of hooves.

Hayden saw the black man running away from his homestead and knew a moment of pure terror. He'd always managed to have a pretty good relationship with the Aborigines in the area, largely because he respected the people and their culture in a way that few Europeans did. But he also knew that when hurt, both whites and blacks had a tendency to strike back at whatever member of the other race happened to be near at hand. More than one innocent settler in the area had had his head bashed in for some rape or other transgression committed by a neighbor up the river.

And Bryony and Simon were alone at the homestead.

He spurred his horse into the yard at a wild gallop, reining in hard when he saw Bryony picking herself up out of the dirt in front of the house.

"Where's Simon?" he demanded, still on his horse, ready to give chase if needed.

"He's in the house." She had her head bowed and was whacking her skirts in an effort to shake the dust off them.

"Thank God for that." Hayden slid to the ground beside her. "What the hell happened here? Why was that black man running away?"

"There were six of them, with their dogs," she said, still thumping her skirts. "One of the dogs tried to bite me, so I hit it. Then one of the men knocked me down. After that I thought they were going to kill me, but I think they were just scared I was going to run and tell you. What does *ba-eel* mean?"

She looked up then, and he saw her face for the first time. She was as white as one of her buckets of milk, except for the ugly bruise that was forming on her temple.

"Bloody hell." She swayed slightly, and he swept her up into his arms and carried her into the house. He kicked open the door to the parlor and laid her on one of the silk-covered settees. She tried to struggle up, saying something about her dirty dress, but he just shoved her back down again. "Lie still," he said. "I'll be right back."

For once she seemed content to do as she was told,

lying back and closing her eyes. She didn't open them again until he knelt beside her and laid a cool, damp cloth on her forehead.

"Thank you." She gave him a tremulous smile and raised her hand to her forehead, but what she touched was his hand, holding the cloth there.

It was the simplest of accidental touches, but it sent a frisson of fire jolting through him. He realized how close he was to her. He smelled her scent, a mixture of warm earth and warm woman, and it seemed as if it entered his very blood and went pounding through his body. Her lips were open, still trembling slightly from the shock. His gaze fastened on her mouth. It would be the easiest thing in the world to lean forward and taste that mouth.

Swallowing an oath, he stood up and moved to the far side of the room, putting distance between them. Christ, all he'd done was touch her, and his entire body had grown hard, taut with the urge to mate. "You shouldn't have hit their dog," he said, leaning against the doorjamb to stare through the glass at the leaden sky. "Aborigines don't like people touching their dogs."

Bryony struggled up on her elbow. "Well, I'm glad you told me that. Next time, of course, I'll let the mangy cur bite me."

He looked at her over his shoulder and regretted it. She was sitting up now. She looked dusty and disheveled and as sensual as hell. He remembered the way she'd felt in his arms when he carried her into the house, her head resting confidingly on his shoulder. It was all he could do to keep from crossing the room and sweeping her up into his arms again. Only he'd take her to his bed.

"There won't be a next time." His voice was harsher than he meant it to be. "I'll take care you're not left at the homestead alone again. It's not just the Aboriginals you need to worry about. You've probably more to fear from bushrangers than you do from the blacks." He studied her for a moment, frowning, then said, "Do you know how to handle a gun?"

"Yes," she said, eyeing him with surprise. "Why?"

He straightened up. "Get an old tin cup from the kitchen and meet me by the outcropping of rock on the hillside behind the house."

"But—why?"

"Just do it."

Bryony watched as he set the cup on a tree stump in front of a pile of boulders and pulled a small, elegant pistol from his waistband.

"I keep it loaded and primed in the chest beside my bed," he told her. "It doesn't have the range of a rifle, but it's easier to aim and fire, and it has the advantage of having two barrels, which means it'll give you two shots. If you're ever in trouble, all you need to know is how to aim it and how to pull the trigger."

She met his gaze squarely and took the pistol from his hand.

It was heavier than she'd expected. She lifted it with both hands and aimed it carefully at the cup. It wasn't far away—no more than fifteen paces. She took a deep breath, squeezed the trigger . . .

And missed.

Her eyes swiveled to Hayden. He stood off to one side, his arms crossed at his chest, his hips cocked forward, watching her. His eyes were narrowed to two blue slits, his mouth hard. She was still shaken and scared, and desperately in need of some comfort. But he had never seemed more cold or distant, and she couldn't understand why.

"Try again," he said.

She turned back to the cup and raised the pistol.

She missed the cup, but hit the tree stump.

"You missed again."

She thought she'd done pretty well. She turned to glare at him. "It's getting dark."

"Not that dark."

She put her hand on her hip. "A man is bigger than a tin cup."

"But a tin cup isn't moving, and it sure as hell isn't shooting back or throwing spears at you." He strolled forward and reached out to take the gun from her slack hold. His fingers just brushed the back of her hand, but she felt the impact of that touch all over, like a flash of fire.

His whole body seemed to stiffen, and she thought she heard him suck in his breath. Then she decided she must have imagined it, for he was turning away, his attention focused on the gun before returning it to his waistband. "You'll need to practice," he said, going to retrieve the tin cup. "I'll send Will Carver in from the fields early tomorrow to help you."

"No," she said without even thinking about it.

He swiveled back around and his smoldering gaze slammed into her. "What the hell do you mean, no?"

He looked so fierce, only her fear and dislike of Carver gave her the courage to say, "I mean I won't practice shooting with Will Carver. I don't like him."

He sauntered back toward her. "You will if I say so."

She sucked in a deep, shaky breath. "I won't."

He came right up to her. She could feel his heat, his anger, his raw, male power. "You forget yourself, Bryony."

Her heart was pounding so hard it seemed to be shaking her whole body, so that she could scarcely speak. "Couldn't you have one of the other men—"

"No." There was a kind of coiled tension about him, and he looked strained, as if the skin were pulled too taut across his high-boned face. "The other men are all convicts," he said. "It's a hanging offense for one of them to be caught with a gun."

"But *I'm* a convict."

One corner of his lips curled up. "Exactly. Which is why you'll do what you're told. You're going to come out here tomorrow afternoon and practice with Will Carver."

He had already started to turn toward the house when she quietly said, "I won't."

He swung slowly back around. "You will."

Her chest felt so tight it hurt, and her mouth had suddenly gone dry. She moistened her lips with the tip of her tongue, and felt his gaze settle there. "Why can't you come back and do it yourself?"

A restless wind blew between them, fluttering the fine linen shirt that covered his hard chest. Desire flared in his eyes, naked and aching. His voice was hoarse, tortured. "You know why I can't do it."

She felt her stomach clench with a kind of wild excitement. She knew she was pushing him, but she couldn't seem to make herself back off. "Why?"

He came right up to her. Her nostrils filled with the scent of him. The scent of ripe wheat and sun-warmed fields and hot, aroused male.

And then all the self-control he'd been practicing since he'd first ridden in tonight—no, longer, she realized. Since the first, charged encounter between them in the Factory's yard—now snapped. "This is why, damn you." He snagged his fist in her hair and pulled her head back until she was staring up into his face. She opened her mouth, but her exclamation—of fear, of want—was smothered by his kiss.

It was a savage kiss, hot, hungry. He slanted his mouth roughly back and forth across hers, the breath coming harsh and searing from between his lips. It was a fierce kiss, made deliberately cruel. A kiss full of angry need and denied desires. A kiss full of months of watching and wanting. A kiss intended to punish, to intimidate.

She opened her mouth to protest, and he plunged his tongue between her lips, filling her, warning her. *This,* he seemed to be telling her, *this is what I want to do to you.*

*I want to fill your body with mine, to join your body with
mine. I want to lay you down and take you, the way I'm
taking your mouth.*

And for one, wild, intoxicating moment, she lost herself in his kiss. She didn't—couldn't—pull away. Hot
blood thundered through her veins, surging out of control. She leaned into him, her hands curling up around his
waist to pull him closer to her aching, needing body.

A moan rumbled deep in his chest. He stroked her
tongue with his, sinuously, insistently. He threaded his
fingers through her hair, cradled her head in his palms
as the kiss gentled, grew almost wondrous. She felt his
warm breath against her face as he kissed her cheek, her
brow, her eyelids.

His mouth moved slowly down her throat, licking,
sucking, spreading fire. She shuddered as his hand closed
over one of her breasts, kneading its fullness. Then his
fingers fumbled impatiently with the fastenings of her
dress. He swore softly, his hand tightening on the worn
neckline, and she realized he meant to rip the thing
off her.

She whimpered in panic, her fist tightening around his
wrist, stopping him.

He lifted his head, his eyes narrow with lust, his
breathing harsh with frustration as he stared down at her.
She thought for a moment he meant to rip her dress and
take her anyway, right there on the side of the hill. He
shuddered. Then his lips curled into a snarl, and he let go
of her dress to reach down with both hands and cup her
buttocks, pulling her up against the long, throbbing heat
of his erection. "This is why I need to stay away from
you," he said, his breath coming ragged against her ear.
"Because this is what you do to me. Do you *feel* what
you do to me, Bryony?" He ground the hard ridge of his
erection against her belly, and she trembled in his arms.

"I want you, Bryony. You know I want you. I want to
feel you naked and beneath me. I want to fill my hands
with your bare breasts and feast my eyes upon your flesh.

I want to taste you, all of you. I want to lay you down in the grass and sink my body into yours, right here, beneath the open sky. Is that what you want, Bryony?"

She sucked in a deep, rasping breath and tried to answer him, but she couldn't.

"If that's what you want, Bryony, then tell me," he said against her ear, his voice low and suddenly gentle. "Tell me."

She stared up into the mesmerizing heat of his beloved blue eyes, and she almost said yes. She yearned for him. Her body throbbed with want of him, her heart ached with love for him. But it was her sense of who and what she was that had enabled her to survive this far, and the woman she was brought up to be would never consent to become a man's mistress. No matter how much she loved him.

"No," she whispered, her voice a raw agony.

She saw frustration rage in his eyes, his nostrils flaring with angry need. "Then, don't push me like this again, Bryony. Because if you're looking for me to overcome your pride and principles with force, I just might oblige."

Bryony stared at him in horror. Was that what she wanted? Is that what she'd tried to do here tonight? Hot with confusion and shame, she wrenched herself from his arms and ran blindly back toward the darkening homestead below.

She didn't stop running until she had slammed the door of her room behind her. And she didn't look back.

It was only later, when she lay empty and yearning in her lonely bed, that it occurred to her to wonder if the principles by which Sir Edward Peyton's niece had been raised had any real relevance to the life of a convict woman living in New South Wales.

CHAPTER
TWENTY

He never mentioned the shooting lessons again.

By silent, mutual consent they stayed away from each other, for to be physically near each other was an agony. To be alone together was to invite disaster.

The weather grew hot. The cooling breezes turned warm, then died completely as the Australian summer sank its teeth into the Hawkesbury and didn't let go. Hayden, busy with his harvest, welcomed the long hours of sweat-drenching, mind-numbing work that kept him away from the house. Bryony took off all her petticoats and still felt damp and listless in the sweltering heat. Even Simon fretted and grew troublesome.

It was one day when Bryony was having trouble getting Simon to settle for his morning nap that Hayden forgot something and came back to the house unexpectedly. She'd been singing a soft lullaby, the baby at her breast, when she heard Hayden's quick step in the hall and looked up to find him standing on the threshold.

He stared at her exposed breasts. His head reared back, and his nostrils flared like a stallion scenting a mare in heat. She could feel his gaze on her naked flesh as surely as if he had touched her there. Her gaze roamed over his lithe, hard body. She tried to swallow, but found she couldn't. The simple sight of him, standing there lean and beautiful, was enough to take away her breath and send shafts of desire darting through her body.

Their gazes caught and held as the silence stretched long and taut between them. The heat in the room was palpable. She felt a bead of sweat form and roll down between her shoulder blades. Then he spun around on his heel and left.

And she sat holding his sleeping baby and wondering how much longer they could go on like this.

It was two days later, when Bryony and Louisa were down by the river doing the laundry, that the weather suddenly turned.

The day had begun as hot as the ones before. By midmorning the sun was already so bright and fierce that it seemed to have bleached all the color from the sky. Bryony stood over a pot of boiling sheets. Heat roiled up from the fire until she thought she might be sick.

Then, as if from nowhere, a breeze licked across her sweat-streaked face, as cool and clean as if someone had just opened the door of an icehouse. She lifted her head in wonder.

"Well, Satan's whores," gasped Louisa, straightening up slowly, for the washing was always hard on Louisa's back. "Three bleedin' weeks without a bleedin' storm, and it has to bleedin' rain *today*?"

Bryony glanced up at the sky. Tiny puffs of clouds had appeared, scuttling across the deepening blue of the heavens as if pushed by an unseen hand. "It doesn't look like rain to me."

"No? Look behind you." She motioned to the south.

Bryony whirled around. Dark, heavy thunderheads loomed ominously up over the horizon, like some kind of evil, threatening presence. She glanced about in dismay at the pots of laundry at various stages of boiling, scrubbing, and rinsing. "Will we finish?"

"Aye. But gettin' it all dry is goin' to be another thing entirely."

They worked quickly, and within half an hour had the cart loaded up. By that time the sky was a solid wall of gray and the temperature had dropped a good twenty degrees, but the rain held off.

"Come on then, Sarey," Louisa called. "We gotta go."

Sarah came skipping up, her fists full of flowers, her fair hair fluttering behind her in the wind, her little bells tinkling. "Look, Mama," she said, proudly displaying her collection of native daisies and flannel flowers. "I picked some flowers for Nathan and Thomas and Joseph. Now I need to get some for Mary."

"We'll get Mary's flowers later, sugar. I want to get these clothes hung up and let 'em dry some in the wind before the rain hits."

"But I saw some pretty yellow flowers under the red gums down by the creek," said Sarah insistently. "Yellow was Mary's favorite color."

Bryony hid her smile. Bryony had no idea what Mary's favorite color had been, but she knew Sarah loved yellow. Bryony had planted a yellow rose in her garden, just for Sarah. Hayden had brought it back to her from one of his trips into Green Hills.

"Later, pet." Louisa lifted the protesting child into the cart.

Back at the homestead, Bryony dropped Simon in his bed and hurriedly strung a line between the posts on the veranda so she could hang up her clothes there. By now the wind was blowing fiercely, whipping the linens back and forth with a snap that was uncomfortably reminiscent of the crack of a cat-o'-nine-tails. It was hard work, struggling to keep the clean clothes from being carried away by the wind. When a sudden gust snatched one of Hayden's shirts from her fingers and sent it sailing into the dust, she swore and tore them all down. She hoped they didn't start smelling musty before the storm blew itself out, otherwise she'd have to wash them all over again.

She was rolling up the last of the sheets when she caught the faint tinkling of bells. She looked up, expecting to see Sarah and Louisa. Instead she saw only Louisa, coming down the hill at an ungainly lope. She had Sarah's sash of little silver bells gripped in one big fist, and a look of stark terror on her homely face.

"Bryony! Oh, for the love of God, Bryony," she gasped as she ran. "It's me Sarey! She was sittin' by the side of the hut playin' with some blocks of wood Will made once for Thomas, while I hung up me clothes. I was sure she was there, 'cause I never heard her bells. Only when I turned around, she was gone! She took off her bells, Bryony. She took them off, and I don't know where she's gone."

Bryony fought to swallow her own panic. "Sit down, Louisa, and catch your breath. We'll find her. She can't have gone far. Did you check the cemetery? She had those flowers—"

"I done looked there already. Oh, Bryony! You don't think she went back down by the river to pick flowers for Mary, do you? That bank's so steep, and it would be so easy . . ." But at this point Louisa's voice became suspended. She shoved one work-worn fist into her mouth, and just sat there, rocking back and forth on the chair.

Bryony squeezed the older woman's shoulder reassuringly. "She'll be all right, Louisa. You just sit here and get your breath back. I'll run down to the barn and find someone to send out to the fields for the men, and then we'll go look by the river ourselves. We'll find her, don't worry."

Bryony flew down the yard, thankful that ever since the incident with the Aborigines' dogs, Hayden had made sure that at least one man was always around the homestead. She found McDuff in an empty paddock, working with his greyhounds. She was afraid he'd scoff at her for her concern, but his ruddy face grew grim when she told him what had happened, and he took off at a lope toward the far field, where the men were working to bring in the last of the crops before the rain hit. For McDuff knew only too well that the Australian bush had a bad habit of swallowing children. Too many of those that wandered off were never found. Or found too late.

Bryony hurried back up to the house, snatched a sleepy

Simon from his nap, and went with Louisa back down to the river.

The wind ravaged the trees overhead, thrashing them wildly back and forth against the steadily darkening sky as the women searched frantically, up and down the river. They smashed through undergrowth, called Sarah's name, shouted until they were hoarse in an effort to be heard above the fury of the coming storm.

They found the yellow flowers that looked almost like buttercups growing under the red gums by the creek, but they didn't find Sarah. And then the rain came, slashing out of the unforgiving sky, and Bryony had to draw her shawl over Simon's head and hurry with him back to the house.

By that time the men had come in from the fields and were spread out over the surrounding area, beating their way through the bushes and trees and fanning across the grasslands.

Hayden finally brought Louisa back up to the house. She was half fainting with exhaustion and fear. But no sooner had Bryony succeeded in pressing her onto one of Laura's silk-covered settees with a cup of hot tea, then it suddenly occurred to Louisa that Sarah might somehow find her way home, and that if there were no one at the hut waiting for her, then she'd very likely wander off again.

Louisa shot up off the settee, determined to go back to the hut. Unable to dissuade her, Bryony finally went with her.

They waited together as the long afternoon wore on, listening to the rain pound on the bark roof and the wind howl around the pitiful hut. At one point Bryony went out and gathered up Louisa's forgotten laundry and brought it inside, but Louisa was past caring. She sat on a stool beside the hearth, rocking back and forth with Sarah's bell sash cradled in her arms. "Why'd you take it off, Sarey?" she kept saying. "Why? Why?"

Then Bryony became aware of another sound, audible only when there was a lessening in the roaring of the wind and the drumming of the rain. It was her cows, lowing to be milked. She walked over and threw open the hut's only door. She stared out at the driving rain and the churning mud, and she found herself cursing the cows and the dairy and New South Wales. But most of all she cursed the men, for it was the men who brought women out here so selfishly, to slake their male lusts and make their lives a bit more comfortable. They didn't seem to care—if they even thought about it at all—that by bringing women here they were condemning them to bear and try to rear their children in this harsh, unforgiving environment. It was difficult enough to keep children alive in England, where there were other women around to help and support and advise, where no one had ever heard of funnel web spiders or tiger snakes. Where it wasn't so hot that meat could turn putrid in a few hours. Where children didn't just wander off into the bush, never to be seen again.

"Go on, Bryony," said the onetime Dublin thief who'd already lost four children to this merciless land. "Go milk yer cows."

Bryony looked back at her friend. Louisa sat huddled on her stool, the only movement that of her hands, skimming back and forth across the little bells. She seemed to have shrunk, to have aged. Bryony wanted to go to her and put her arms around her and hold her and cry for her—and with her.

Instead she said, "Come with me."

Louisa shook her head. "No, I'll stay here, 'case Sarey comes back. You can leave Simon, if you want."

But Bryony took Simon with her. She wasn't sure Louisa was in any condition to watch him.

It was when she was coming out of the dairy, after filling and covering the settling bowls, that she saw Hayden's big bay turn into the yard. He came at a walk, but not from the direction of the river. He was coming from the Carvers' hut.

And she knew. She knew from the way he sat his horse, from the cold and forbidding harshness of his face. She knew.

She stood in front of the dairy, her hands pressed to her sides, watching him ride up to her. The rain lashed her, the wind swirled around her, but she was aware of none of it.

He swung off his horse and tossed the reins to one of the men who followed him.

"You found her," she said.

"Yes." He studied her through narrowed eyes, but she knew he could see nothing in her face because she wasn't feeling anything. Just a cold, numbing emptiness. "She was on the far side of the hill, at the bottom of a steep embankment. She must have lost her footing and slipped in the storm. Her head hit a rock. She . . ." He paused for a moment, and Bryony knew what he was seeing. Fair, baby-soft ringlets, darkened with blood. "She'd been picking some yellow flowers. She still had them in her hand when we found her."

Yellow flowers. Yellow flowers for Mary. She'd gone back to get the flowers for her sister's grave. *Dear God,* thought Bryony.

"You'd better go sit with Louisa," he said, turning away. "I don't think she should be left alone."

Bryony's head snapped around. "But Will—"

"He doesn't know yet. He's still searching the sandbars downriver. I sent one of the men to tell him."

She grabbed Hayden's arm, her fingers digging frantically into his warm, solid flesh. "You told Louisa? You took the dead child to her?"

"Yes. I—"

"Dear God." She picked up her skirts and ran. Not toward the hut but to the river.

"Louisa!" she called frantically, her feet slipping and

sliding through the rain-churned mud of the yard. "Louisa!" She ran down the long, grassy slope. She was gasping for breath, and her lungs felt as if they might explode, and still she ran on. The wind whipped her hair in front of her eyes, and the rain stung her shoulders and mingled with the tears that coursed unchecked down her cheeks. "Louisa," she screamed, over and over again. "Louisa, don't do it! Louisa! *No.*"

She never knew if Louisa heard her. For one instant Bryony saw her, poised on the edge of a great boulder that thrust out deep into the current. Then Louisa took a step forward and disappeared.

"Louisa, no!" Bryony plunged into the storm-swollen river. She was up to her knees in the swirling water when strong arms closed about her waist, lifting her high.

"No, let me go," she gasped, struggling against him. "I can reach her. I must—"

Hayden turned her around and swept her into his arms, wading back out of the treacherous waters. "No, Bryony. No. You can't save her."

With an agonized, gut-wrenching sob, she subsided against his warm, broad shoulder and let him carry her back to the land of the living.

CHAPTER
TWENTY-ONE

Rain dripped off the silver-green leaves of the gum trees to patter like thousands of little feet on the storm-flattened grass below.

The sky hung low and oppressive, obscuring the mountains, hiding everything but the little clearing with its white marble monument and sad row of bark-covered graves. But even though she couldn't see it, Bryony could still feel the vast, empty continent stretching out around her. For a moment she felt as if Australia were smothering her—swallowing her, the way it had swallowed Louisa and her children.

The damp earth thudded dully on the lids of the two roughly built coffins, one large, the other pitifully small. Gideon said an Our Father, but there was no priest to perform the ritual of the dead, for the Irish exiled here suffered as much from the deprivation of the comforts of their religion as from the deprivation of their freedom.

Louisa, at least, would suffer no more. For a moment Bryony almost envied her.

"Come, Bryony," said Hayden. "It's over."

Bryony put out her hand. "No, wait—please." For some reason she couldn't explain, she had to see the graves filled. She needed that sense of finality.

Only when the last shovelful of dirt was put back did she lean down to lay two roses on the fresh earth. A yellow one for Sarah, a white one for Louisa.

She looked up to see Will Carver staring down at the row of graves. She wondered not for the first time how this man really felt about the Dublin thief he'd once raped in the hull of a transport ship. Together they'd lived thirteen years of their lives, carved a home out of an alien wilderness, and brought five children into the world. Had he loved her? He'd never married her.

She paused beside him, wanting to say something in comfort, but their enmity ran too deep, even in grief. All she could think of to say was: "You will make those bark covers for their graves, won't you?"

His graying head swung around to her, the old saber scar standing out white against the beard stubble on his face. At first she didn't think he was going to answer her, then he said, "No. I always thought 'twas a daft thing to do." He pursed his lips to spit a stream of golden-brown tobacco juice into the dank grass at her feet, and strode off into the wet bush.

Bryony stared after him, conscious of a welling of dismay. How could he not cover their graves? How could he leave Louisa and her little Sarey to lie out here unprotected in this rain?

By nightfall the rain had stopped. A warm wind swinging out of the north blew away the remnants of the clouds. The temperature rose, the wind died, and the earth steamed.

She lay in bed with both sets of French doors and shutters thrown open to the darkness, but not a breath of air stirred. A koel in a tree somewhere up the hill had been emitting its tuneless cry for hours. It sounded precisely like a child trying to whistle, and Bryony thought if it didn't shut up soon, she was going to go mad. A dingo howled in the distance and a pair of crickets set up a monotonous *creek-creek, creek-creek,* until she finally flung her pillow across the room with a smothered oath and got up.

It was a dark night. The moon was no more than a pale sliver, but the storm seemed to have swept the sky so clean it sparkled. And the stars . . . Ah, the stars were a sight to behold. She ventured out onto the veranda at the side of the house and stood with her arms clasped around a post, just staring at the stars.

It's different all right.

It seemed so long ago, that night when she'd stood in the light of the campfire and gazed up at the stars arcing above her. She had felt so lost and lonely and afraid.

She was lost and lonely now, but for a different reason.

She loosened her hold on the post and walked along the veranda, watching the flashing dark shapes of the sugar-gliders hunting insects in her fledgling garden.

When had she stopped thinking of it as Laura's garden, she wondered, and started thinking of it as her own? The inspiration, the plan had been Laura's, but the reality was all hers.

A sudden ripple of heat passed over her, like a breath of restless wind. Only there was no wind. She jerked her head around and found herself confronting Laura's husband.

He stood in the shadows of his room. She knew he slept naked. Sometimes at night when she couldn't sleep, she'd lie in her own bed and think about him sprawling long, lean, and naked across his bed in the next room.

He was naked now.

A band of silvery starlight spilled through the open door and lay like a slash across his body, contouring every bulge and hollow of his work-honed muscles. He stood there, hard and blatantly virile, and the wonder of him stole her breath.

"What are you doing here?" he asked, his voice harsh, aching.

"I . . . I couldn't sleep." She sounded breathless. She was breathless. "I couldn't stop thinking about Louisa and Sarah and . . . And it's so hot."

He was hot. He took a step closer, and she saw that the dark hair that matted his chest was wet with sweat. It curled around his nipples, plunged like an arrow toward his groin. Her breath left her lungs in a *woosh*. She had imagined what he would look like. But she had never imagined him like this. He was magnificent.

Her head snapped up and she drew in a deep, shuddering breath that caused her breasts to rise. She was drenched in sweat herself. Her damp shift clung to her, hugging her breasts, revealing every swell of hip and thigh. She felt his relentless eyes upon her. She'd never been more aware of her own body.

A slow, sweet yearning bloomed within her, and she had to bite back a moan. He braced his palms against the door frame and leaned into them. She could see the veins stand out and the sinews tighten beneath the brown skin of his arms, see the shadows of hair in their hollows. She could see his face. See the taut, almost frightening look of arousal, the dark blaze of desire that shone in his eyes. He was fierce and he was beautiful and he was frightening, and she wanted him. She wanted him so very badly.

He squeezed his eyes shut, his fingers gripping the wood, and she thought he might have shuddered. She could see the pulse that beat, hard and fast, at the base of his throat. She had to clench her hands to keep from reaching out and touching him there.

Then she felt the seductive heat of his eyes flow over her, wrap itself around her, coax her to him.

"Let it happen, Bryony," he said, his voice low and tempting. "You know you want it. Stop fighting me. Stop fighting yourself. And come to me."

"No," she said, or wanted to say, but her voice was only a sigh. And when her mind willed her legs to move, all they did was tremble.

"Come." His hands dropped to his sides, and he took a step toward her.

"I won't be your mistress," she said in an agonized whisper. "I won't be any man's mistress."

She saw the yearning in his eyes. Saw the need in his soul. "Bryony . . ." He took another step toward her.

She whirled around and fled.

* * *

A few days later Will Carver asked for leave to go to Green Hills and catch a sloop for Sydney Town. When he came back, it was with a pale, redheaded girl from the Parramatta Female Factory.

Bryony was milking her cows when they rode into the yard. She stood up, stretching her back as she watched the girl slide wearily down from Will's roan. While Carver went to unsaddle his horse, the girl stayed where she was, slumped in the shadow of the barn.

She looked so lost and afraid, standing there by herself. Bryony finished her milking as quickly as she could. She set the pails in the dairy and hurried down the yard toward the girl.

"Hello," Bryony called, waving to her.

The girl glanced up, and Bryony was shocked to realize how young she was. She was fourteen, maybe fifteen at the most. Her gray eyes were wide with fear, and she had an ugly bruise discoloring the side of her face.

Bryony slowed to a halt a few feet from her. "Hello. I'm Bryony Wentworth. From Cornwall."

The girl cast a scared glance toward the barn behind her. "Ann McBride. From Glasgow." Her voice was a whisper. "Do you . . . do you belong to Mr. Carver, as well?"

Bryony shook her head. "No. I'm assigned to Captain St. John." She reached out and carefully turned the girl's marked face to the light. "That's a bad bruise," she said softly, frowning. "Did he give it to you?"

The girl cast another apprehensive glance toward the barn, and nodded. "When I . . . when he . . ." She put up her hands to cover her face, as if in so doing she could hide her shame.

Bryony pressed her lips together tightly, biting back her opinion of Will Carver. When she could trust herself, she said, "He's not allowed to hit you, you know. It's against the—"

There was an angry growl, and a big fist descended on

the girl's shoulder, swinging her around. "Ye stay away from her," Will Carver told the girl, pointing one fat, dirty finger at Bryony. "Stay clean away from her. And ye remember it, girl, because if I ever see ye talkin' to her again, ye'll regret it."

His hand slid down to wrap around the girl's slim arm as he turned toward Bryony. "Ye leave my woman alone, ye hear?"

He strode off toward his hut, dragging Ann McBride behind him.

"How can you let Will Carver do this?" Bryony demanded.

Hayden knew exactly what she was talking about. He paused in the yard with one hand on the veranda post and turned slowly to face her. She stood at the corner of the house, her intent, accusing gaze fixed on him. She must have been digging in her garden because she held a bunch of carrots in one hand and a shovel in the other. There was a smudge of dirt on her strong chin.

He was hot and tired and dirty. The harvest was in, but the threshing wasn't finished, and they were still burning off the stubble in the fields, a risky thing to do in this heat.

Against his will, his eyes wandered over her. He might be tired, but he wasn't too tired to notice the way the summer sun had touched her cheeks with a rosy glow and deepened the burgundy highlights in her hair. Nor was he too tired to remember how she'd looked in the moonlight, with her hair curling wildly about her bare shoulders and her chemise clinging damply to the curve of her hip. Desire rose within him, hot and insistent and unwelcome.

He swore softly under his breath and climbed the low step to the veranda. "You heard about Will Carver's new woman, did you?" he said over his shoulder, walking into the house.

She laid the shovel and carrots on a bench and followed him into the house and down the hall. "Ann McBride is not a woman. She's a child. And he raped her—and beat her."

Hayden pressed his lips together. He didn't like it, either, but there was nothing he could do about it. He shrugged with studied casualness. "It's not my affair, Bryony. Or yours."

"Will Carver works for you."

"Precisely. He works for me; I don't own him. He's a free man, and he has as much right to a woman from the Factory as any man in the colony."

She had followed him into his room by now. "I thought it was against the law to strike an assigned servant?"

He tossed his dusty hat on his desk. "It is. In Sydney, servants have been known to go to a magistrate and lay charges against their masters. But out here in the bush, it's different. A servant needs a pass from his master to get into town to see a magistrate. And if the master refuses to give him a pass and he decides to go anyway, then he can be picked up and flogged or hanged for absconding." He stripped off his dirty shirt and flexed his tired muscles.

"But he's raping her!"

"Then, in that case, she'd be considered his de facto wife, and men are allowed to beat and rape their wives." His hands dropped to the flap of his breeches, and he looked up at her and gave her a deliberately nasty grin. "And unless you want to suffer the same fate, I suggest you get the hell out of here."

Her eyes dropped to his breeches. He had them half open by now, and the effects of his thoughts about what she looked like in her damp chemise were more than evident. Her dark brown eyes opened wide, and the sunny glow on her cheeks deepened to a richer hue. "I . . . I'll put a can of hot water outside your door," she said hastily, and backed out of the room.

He stood watching her go, the smile fading slowly

from his lips. He'd have a talk with Will this evening, he
decided.

But he doubted it would do any good.

Bryony wasn't the only one upset by what Will Carver
was doing to Ann McBride in his hut on the far side of
the hill. Quincy, too, seemed to be taking a healthy interest in the young girl's plight.

Only in Quincy's case, Bryony was afraid the effects
of his interest could be decidedly *unhealthy*.

"She's sportin' a black eye today," he said one afternoon, when he brought Bryony some water from the
spring. "Did ye see it?"

Bryony shook her head. "I rarely see her. Every time I
come anywhere near her, she runs."

"Aye, he said he'd beat her if he ever caught her
talkin' to ye."

Bryony looked up from the stew she was stirring over
the fire. "How do you know that, Quincy?"

"She told me. I stop by there sometimes in the
mornin', when I finish here. Carver's always out then,
and the poor girl needs help—she hasn't got a notion of
how to do the simplest things."

There was something about the airy way in which this
was said that set alarm bells to ringing in Bryony's head.
"Quincy," she said levelly. "You be careful. You have
enough trouble with Carver. You don't need more."

Quincy pushed his hat back at a jaunty angle and gave
her a devil-be-damned smile. "Tosh, don't worry none
about me; I'll be right."

Simon lay on his stomach on the rug, a look of determination hardening the gentle features of his face.

Bryony set aside the shirt she was mending to watch
him. He'd been restless the last few days, as if he wanted
something but he wasn't quite sure what it was. His eyes
were fixed on the bright red wooden rattle that he'd just
dropped. He stretched his hand out toward it, but it had

rolled away from him, and he fussed angrily when his arm proved too short to reach it. He tried again, with the same result. Then, propping himself up on his elbows, he moved first one arm forward, then the other, giving a little half kick from behind with his feet so that he somehow managed to half drag, half push his fat little body forward.

He didn't move far, and it wasn't a very elegant motion, but it was enough to enable his plump little hand to close over the end of the rattle. He seized it in triumph and crowed his delight.

Bryony scooped him up into her arms and spun around with him, laughing in delight herself. "You did it! You really did it, Simon. You crept! Aren't you a clever little boy?"

She hugged him to her, wishing Hayden was here so she could tell him. But Hayden had gone to Parramatta to talk to Sir D'Arcy Baxter about sheep, and wasn't expected back until the end of the week.

She was still dancing around the room with Simon when she became aware of voices in the yard. Angry men's voices.

Shifting Simon to her hip, she walked out onto the veranda. What she saw there made her clutch the baby to her in swift, awful fear.

After the cool darkness of the house, the sunlit yard was hot and dazzlingly bright. A large crowd of men had gathered down by the barn. Bryony had seen this type of gathering enough times in the past year to recognize it for what it was.

It was a flogging.

The victim had been stripped and tied to a post. He was small and slim and dark, and his bared back already bore scars from the whip. Recent scars.

"Quincy," Bryony whispered.

Her horrified eyes focused on the big man with long, graying hair who was shaking out a cat with practiced ease. Will Carver.

"Ye cocky little son of a bitch," she heard him snarl. "Ye think you can mess with my woman? Ye been askin' fer this, boy, and now yer going to get it." He drew back his arm and sent the metal-tipped lashes whistling through the air to land with a sickening snap against Quincy's back.

The boy didn't flinch.

"I'm gonna peel yer hide right off ye, boy. By the time I'm through with ye, there's not a woman in this colony would take a second look at ye, 'cept maybe in pity."

The cat sang again.

He's going to kill him, Bryony thought. She looked at the cold, mad hatred twisting Will Carver's face and knew that he wouldn't stop swinging that cat until the boy tied to the post was reduced to nothing but a bloody hunk of dead meat. And there was no one to stop him.

The cat snapped a third time.

Her heart pounding so hard it hurt, Bryony whirled and ran into the house. She laid Simon in his bed and passed through the communicating doors to Hayden's room.

The pistol was in the drawer of the bedside table, loaded and primed as he'd said it would be. She lifted it in her right hand, feeling its weight, then tucked it under her apron. It felt cold and deadly through the thin cotton skirt covering her thigh as she walked out of the house and down the yard.

The sun blazed hot on her back. She felt her upper lip grow damp, felt her dress stick to her sweat-slicked back. No one noticed her; everyone's attention was focused on the scene before the barn.

She stopped just outside the group of watching men and lifted the pistol. Supporting it with both hands, she aimed at a point on the side of the barn some four feet directly above Will Carver's head. She hadn't touched the pistol since the day the Aboriginals' dog had attacked her, and her hands shook alarmingly. But she gritted her teeth, held her breath, and pulled the trigger as Carver drew the cat back over his shoulder.

Bryony's bullet shattered the whip just above Carver's fist.

It would have been a brilliant shot, if she'd been aiming for it. As it was, it was so far off the mark she'd sighted on that it scared the very devil out of her. But she resolutely pulled back the second hammer and leveled the pistol at the overseer's chest as he swung around to stare at her.

Shock and fear drained Carver's face white. He dropped the broken whip handle as if it, too, might explode in his hand. But when he saw who challenged him, his look of fear slid slowly into a sneer. "Ye goin' to shoot me with that, ye worthless little strumpet?" His jaws worked silently as he pursed his lips and sent a stream of tobacco juice in her direction.

The crowd of men had fallen abruptly silent and drawn back, leaving Bryony to face Will Carver across a cleared space of perhaps fifteen or twenty feet. "If I have to," she said.

His grin widened to reveal yellow, tobacco-stained teeth. "Ye'll hang just fer pointin' that gun at me."

"Then, it doesn't matter if I kill you, does it?"

He seemed to consider this. "Thing is, ye might miss. Then what'll ye do? Ye only got one shot left."

"I didn't miss the whip, and it was a considerably smaller target than you, Mr. Carver."

He spat again, but Bryony saw his eyes narrow. "A lucky shot."

"Are you prepared to take that chance?"

She wondered what in God's name she was supposed to do next. It had never occurred to her that the man might refuse to back down. She took a deep breath and willed her hands to stop shaking. "Get on your horse and ride out of here, Mr. Carver."

Carver threw back his head and laughed. "Ho! Ye goin' to make me, woman? And what if I decide to ride you, instead?" He took a menacing step toward her, his sneer turning into a leer. "I hear ye don't like what I been doin' to Ann McBride. Well, maybe ye'd like to take her place. Maybe yer gettin' tired of servicin' jist the Cap'n, huh?"

Bryony took an involuntary step back, then hated herself for it. A gleam of triumph flashed in the overseer's eyes. He thought he had her measure. He thought she wouldn't shoot him.

Only, she would. She'd rather hang for murder than let this man touch her, and she was probably going to hang anyway for what she'd already done. But she knew she had only one shot, and she couldn't afford to miss, so she let him come on. She held her ground, the pistol growing oddly steadier as he advanced on her.

"Leave her be."

Carver stopped and swung slowly around to face the barn.

Gideon Shanaghan stood in the open doorway, a look of grim determination on his face and a pitchfork in his hands. "Leave her be," he repeated. "And get out of here while you still can."

Will Carver's face hardened. "Ye threatened me with a pitchfork once before, ye little Irish shit. I let it go then, but not this time. This time yer both goin' to hang. I'll ride out of here, all right. Straight to Green Hills. Only I'll be back. With a magistrate."

He took one step toward the stables.

"No," said McDuff, coming forward to range his bulk alongside Gideon. "I'm thinkin' ye'll wait here where we can keep an eye on ye, 'til the Cap'n gets back."

"Aye," said a second man, then a third.

And Bryony knew the worst was over.

For now.

The door of her room flew open with such force that it hit the wall with a resounding thud.

Bryony jumped, pricking her finger with her needle and almost dropping the gown she was stitching. She carefully folded her sewing and set it on the table beside her chair, then raised her eyes to the man who stood, booted and spurred, on the threshold of her room.

"You're back," she said, unable to keep a slight quiver out of her voice.

"Obviously." He stood with his legs braced wide, his hands on his lean, knife-slung hips. "Do you care to tell me why my overseer is locked in the holding cell in my store?"

Her mouth felt suddenly dry, but she resisted the impulse to moisten her lips with her tongue. "Perhaps Gideon would be better able—"

"No. I want to hear it from you. After all, you seem to have been the key player in this little drama."

She rose shakily to her feet and smoothed her gray gown with a hand that was not quite steady. "Very well."

She walked past him, her head held high even though she was quaking inside. He followed her into the darkened dining room with a heavy, menacing tread. When she spun around to face him, he was so close he nearly ran into her.

He stood where he was, unmoving. She was the one who backed up.

"It started with Quincy," she said.

He walked away from her then, to where a decanter of brandy and some of Laura's crystal glasses stood on a table. "Somehow I thought it might," he said dryly, unstopping the decanter.

"He . . . he took an interest in Ann McBride."

He glanced up at her, one eyebrow cocked, a sardonic smile curving his lips. "You mean, he took her to bed."

"I don't know about that." She realized she was wringing her hands, and made herself stop. "He . . . he felt sorry for her."

He laughed softly. "I'm sure he did." Bryony watched him pour the brandy into a glass. "I take it Will Carver, however, was unappreciative of his sympathy?"

"He had Quincy tied to a post down by the barn and was flogging him. He would have killed him. There was no one to stop him."

He slowly eased the stopper back into the decanter and set it down. "So you stopped it. With my gun?"

"Yes."

He lifted the glass to his lips and drank from it, slowly. The heat of his gaze never left her face. "You realize you could be hanged for what you did?"

"Yes."

He drained the glass and reached for the decanter to refill it. "I've given Will Carver until tomorrow morning to clear out. After some persuasion, he agreed not to press charges against you and Gideon, in return for my agreement not to press charges for his assault on Quincy. And he'll be leaving Ann McBride here."

Bryony let her breath out in a soft sigh.

"It was a stupid thing to have done," he said. He refilled his glass and regarded it for a moment without making a move to pick it up. "I feel like beating you myself."

She stared at his dark, shadowed profile and noticed for the first time the traces of concern, even worry, that etched his forehead and deepened the lines about his lips. It was concern that fueled his anger, she realized; concern for her. He was angry because she'd put herself at risk by what she'd done. He was angry with her because he *cared*.

Cared about her. Cared *for* her.

The thought caused a warm happiness to surge within her. Her love for this man flooded through her like something that could not be denied. It overwhelmed her. Submerged her.

"Someone had to stop him," she said.

He twisted his head around, and his hard gaze slammed into her. "As far as I can figure, there were some two dozen men watching that flogging. But *you* felt you had to stop it?"

"Yes."

He advanced on her slowly, his eyes never leaving her face. She knew he wanted her. Knew it by the arousal on his face, by the fire that burned in his shockingly blue eyes. He came right up to her, until he was only a sigh away from her. Then he turned away abruptly.

"Get out of here, Bryony," he breathed, his voice harsh, tortured. "Get the hell out of here now."

"No."

He spun back around. "Goddamn it, woman! Don't you know what I want to do to you? I want to lay you back on that bloody table there and rip that ugly work dress off you so I can fill my hands with your bare breasts. I want to wrap those long white legs of yours around my hips and bury myself inside you and take you . . . hard and fast and *now*."

She felt the blood drain from her face as the heat of his words washed over her. But all she said was: "I know."

He stared at her with dark, intense eyes. "Then, why the hell are you still here?"

"Because I want you, too."

He snagged his fist in her hair, slamming her up against him. His breath beat hot and fast against her face. "You're playing with fire, Bryony. I won't be able to stop."

She placed her hands on his chest and curled her fingers into the fine linen of his shirt. "I don't want you to stop. I already burn."

A low moan tore from him as his mouth crushed down on hers. He kissed her fiercely, hungrily, slanting his mouth savagely back and forth against hers. She whimpered, bringing her hands up to drag his head down to hers as she strained against him. It was as if she couldn't get close enough to him, couldn't get enough of him. He thrust his tongue inside her mouth, and her own met it, mated with it, danced a timeless cotillion of seduction and surrender.

Fire burned within her, consumed her, drove her. His

hands were all over, coursing roughly down her back, her waist, her hips and buttocks, as if he would touch every inch of her, leave his imprint everywhere. And everywhere he touched, she burned.

He shoved her back against the table, pinning her there with his hips. He splayed his fingers through her hair, tilting her chin up with his thumbs as his mouth left hers to scorch a path down her throat to the hollow where her pulse beat so wildly. His hands closed over her breasts, kneading them roughly through the cheap cloth of her dress. Then his fingers were at the neckline of her dress, fumbling with the laces until he cursed with impatience and tore at them.

His hands closed over her breasts again, his fingers scorching her flesh through the fine linen of the chemise he'd given her. She felt him smile against the hollow of her throat.

"Why you little cheat," he said with a low, wicked laugh that clutched hotly at her belly. "You were too bloody proud to wear the dress I bought you, but you've been wearing this." She gasped as his thumbs swept back and forth across the points where her turgid nipples pressed up against the chemise.

"I couldn't . . . resist. Sometimes when it's warm and I feel the cloth against my skin, I pretend it's your hands touching me."

He loosened the ribbon at the neck and pushed the chemise down so that he could put his hands on her bare breasts. "Like this?"

"Yes." She groaned. "Like this."

His mouth closed over hers again, hungry and demanding. The edge of the table bit into her buttocks as he pressed her back harder, grinding his pelvis against her. His hands left her breasts to fumble with her skirt.

"Tell me you want this." His breath beat harshly against her ear as he pulled up her dress and petticoat. "Tell me you want it."

"I want it," she whispered obediently as his hands slid

around her bare thighs, shoving her legs apart. "I want you."

"That's good," he said as he pushed her petticoat up farther and ran his silken fingers up the insides of her thighs. "Because you're going to get me." She gasped as he found the center of her need, his suddenly gentle touch sending spasms of desire rippling through her body.

He loomed over her and gazed down at her with dark, tempestuous blue eyes. He slipped one finger inside her, and she thought he shuddered.

"Christ, Bryony . . ." He slipped a second finger inside her as his other hand fumbled with the flap of his breeches. "I've never wanted a woman the way I want you. Never."

She reached between them, her fingers closing over his erection as he freed it. He let out a rasping cry that sounded as if it had been torn from him against his will. His hands spanned her hips, settling her on top of the table. She wrapped her arms around his waist, pulling him close between her legs as he slipped his hands beneath her naked buttocks and positioned her for his entry. She felt him, velvety smooth and hard and hot, pressing against her. Then he was inside her, stretching her, filling her with his hardness, his maleness, and she was the one who cried out.

He pulled almost out of her, then drove in again, harder, deeper, again and again. His mouth captured hers, and he kissed her ruthlessly as he pounded into her. His lips traveled lower, to her throat, to her breasts, and he was pressing her back until she lay flat on the table before him, her chemise pushed down below her bare breasts, her petticoat rucked up to her waist. His hands, his eyes, his mouth were all over her. She threaded her fingers through his dark hair, holding his head down to her, arching her back to rise up and meet him. Her blood pounded through her body, her senses soared.

She was awash in pleasure, adrift in a world of sensations. She wrapped her legs around him, drawing him deeper inside her as each grinding thrust sent wave after wave of aching pleasure through her. She was thrashing beneath him now, writhing with her need, screaming with her need, until the waves finally peaked and rolled over into a gasping, shuddering fulfillment that swept over them both.

He raised up on his arms and looked down at her. In the half-light his expression was shadowed, hidden. Slowly he lifted a finger to trace a line from her chin down her neck, between her naked breasts, to the point where her clothes bunched about her waist.

"You're one hell of a woman, Bryony," he whispered.

She hugged him to her again, burying her face in his warm shoulder, feeling suddenly, desperately afraid.

God help her, she had given herself to this man: body, heart, and soul. But what did she have of him? A moment's passing passion? And then what?

His head lowered to her breast. He cupped its fullness with one lean, strong hand as his tongue traced a slow circle around her large areola before he sucked her nipple between his lips.

She jerked in surprise and delight, and he laughed softly against her naked flesh. "I've been wanting to do that for months. I've even found myself envying Simon for his ready access to what I've wanted so badly."

He lifted his head so he could watch his hands caressing her breasts, and she felt the heat begin to glow within her again. She moved slightly, arching against him, and he looked up at her face, his eyes heavy-lidded with his own desire.

"I want you again, Bryony," he said, his voice low and husky. Then a slow smile curved up the edges of his lips as he added, "And again and again and again . . ."

She laughed. And for the moment, she was happy.

CHAPTER TWENTY-TWO

She was Hayden St. John's convict mistress.

When she allowed her thoughts to dwell on the reality of what she'd become, Bryony knew a deep and abiding sense of shame. But at night, when his hot, hungry mouth closed over hers and his lean, hard body covered her, she knew only divine pleasure and an aching kind of happiness.

He was a tender, exquisitely skilled lover who pleasured her body in ways she'd never dreamed of. Her couplings with Oliver had always taken place in bed, in the dark, with her night rail quickly rucked up out of the way. Whatever he might have done with his whores, Oliver had had very traditional ideas about what he could do with his wife.

But she wasn't Hayden's wife; she was his mistress. They made love on the floor, against the wall, in the chairs—even, on one hot, memorable night, in a pool of the creek beneath a myriad of twinkling stars.

Now that she was his mistress, he bought her things; dresses and shoes and chemises and fine batiste night rails. But she told him laughingly the night rails were a waste of money because he was always taking them off her—either ripping them away in his haste, or easing them off with deliberate, sensuous slowness. He liked to sleep with one arm thrown possessively over her naked body, and he liked to wake up in the morning and find her beside him. So eventually Bryony made some space in one of his chests and moved her belongings out of Laura's room.

It was when she was going through the drawers, looking for anything she might have missed, that she found herself staring, once more, at Laura's sketchbooks. It had been some time now since she'd looked at them. She picked out the last one and flipped through it until she came to Laura's self-portrait.

Easing back into a sitting position, she laid the notebook open on her knees and gazed upon the dead wife of the man she was now sleeping with. God, but Laura had been a beautiful woman. So fair and delicate. It made Bryony ache just to look at her. Made her feel awkward, coarse, in comparison.

What a foolish thought, she chided herself bitterly. How could she compare herself with a woman like Laura St. John? Laura had been a viscount's daughter, Hayden's lady wife.

She was his mistress, a convicted killer.

She was sliding the notebook back into the drawer when she heard hasty footsteps slamming across the stone flagging of the veranda.

Ann McBride's pale, freckled face appeared around the door. Ann now slept in the lean-to beside the kitchen and helped Bryony with the cleaning and washing. But Quincy had been right when he'd said the girl hadn't a notion of how to do the simplest things.

"Lord amercy," panted Ann. "I'm that sorry, Bryony."

Bryony stood up, eyeing the redhead with an increasingly familiar sense of impending doom. Ann claimed to have been in service in Glasgow before she was convicted—wrongly, she insisted—of trying to pawn one of her mistress's sets of embroidered pillowcases. Maybe it was true; Bryony was beginning to suspect that Ann's long-suffering former mistress had succumbed to the temptation of having the girl transported, just to be rid of her. "What happened, Ann?" she asked now.

"I done left the door to the dairy open when I went to

fetch some butter this morning, and those dratted
chickens of yers are in there, peckin' at all yer lovely
cheeses!"

Hayden rode into the yard just as Bryony descended
upon the dairy, her broom swinging. When she wanted
to, she could swear as fluently as any convict ever transported to Botany Bay, and she was swearing now, in that
husky, almost hoarse voice of hers. He reined in, a slow
smile curling his lips as he watched her send her squeak-
ing, squawking chickens flying every which way.

Everyone called them Bryony's chickens, because she
was the one who fed them and gathered their eggs. But
he knew she hated them, and he wasn't surprised to see
her laying about her with the broom with an almost
savage delight, taking revenge for every malicious peck,
every rotten egg of the past months.

One of the hens, a particularly nasty but prolific layer
Bryony had named Eunice for reasons she'd never ex-
plained to him, was made of sterner stuff than her sisters.
Instead of squawking about with feathers flying, Eunice
turned in the doorway of the dairy and contemptuously
stuck out her head. Her long, skinny neck arched, her
beady eyes stared unblinkingly at Bryony. Then Eunice
flew right at her.

Bryony seized the attacking hen with both hands and
wrung her scrawny neck.

"Ha! Take that, you vainglorious little biddy," she
cried in triumph, stomping up the steps from the dairy
with the dead chicken dangling from her hand.

Ann gasped. "Bryony! Ye done killed yer best layer!"

Hayden laughed.

Bryony's head snapped around. The late summer sun
glinted off the flaming highlights in the hair that curled
about her face in typical wild abandon. Her cheeks were
flushed, her eyes sparkling with triumph, and she was
breathing heavily enough that her breasts rose and fell
noticeably. He stared at her, the smile dying on his lips,

and he wondered anew at the way the sight of her, even in her old work dress and with a dead chicken in her hand, could make him ache to sweep her up in his arms and carry her off to their bed.

At the sound of his laugh, her eyes flashed, and she descended upon him, the disreputable hen still clutched in one angry fist. "These bloody chickens! They've been in my dairy and pecked all my cheeses."

He swung slowly out of the saddle. She stopped before him and shook the dead chicken under his nose. "I need a henhouse! I am sick and tired of searching all over this bloody yard for eggs, and having the bloody hens under my feet in the kitchen every bloody time I turn around. And last week some bloody dingo came into the yard during the night and stole that white hen I raised from a chick myself. If he'd taken Eunice here"—she gave the hated hen another shake "—he'd have been welcome to her. But I need a henhouse!"

"Why did you call her Eunice?"

"What?" She slowly lowered the hen and stood stock-still.

"The hen. Who did you name her after, Bryony? Who is Eunice?"

As he watched, all the fight and fury seemed to drain out of her to be replaced by a sad, aching want. "My aunt. Eunice is my aunt . . . my Uncle Edward's wife. She's the one who . . . who has Madeline."

She would have turned away, but he reached out and laid his hand gently on her shoulder. "I'll have the men start on a henhouse right away," he said.

He wanted to say he'd give her anything she wanted, if only it would make her happy.

But he didn't.

Hayden sat in a chair in the garden, reading the *Sydney Gazette* and smoking a cheroot while Bryony worked among her herbs. His pose was relaxed, but in reality he wasn't relaxed at all, for he had to keep getting up to rescue Simon, who seemed bent on either falling off the veranda or eating whatever bugs he happened to come upon in the course of his exploration of the garden.

"I'm beginning to wish he'd never learned to crawl," Hayden said as he reached down to remove a slater from his fascinated son's clutches.

Bryony laughed. She laughed more often these days, he'd noticed. And not just in bed, when his hands were on her body and he made her sigh with pleasure. Sometimes he could almost believe she was happy . . . until he'd catch that sad, faraway look in her eyes, and he'd know she was thinking about Madeline.

"Just make sure he doesn't eat those, will you?" She smiled fondly at the little boy, who now sat in the middle of the gravel pathway, piling pebbles into the old tin cup she'd given him to play with.

Hayden grunted. He'd been trying to read the published names of those people with letters awaiting collection in Sydney, and he'd had to start the column over again three times. Suddenly a name leapt out at him from the print. He laid the paper aside and glanced over at her.

"Bryony."

"Yes?" She was on her knees, busy pulling weeds.

"Your name is listed here; there's a letter for you in Sydney."

She stopped pulling weeds, but she didn't look up. He watched the blood drain from her face and knew what she was thinking. It was only February. It was unlikely the letter she'd sent by the *Lady Laura* had even reached England yet, so there was no way this letter could have been written in response to it. Yet from the few things she'd said about him, Hayden doubted that Sir Edward Peyton would have written to his disgraced niece without a reason.

Hayden stood up and went to kneel behind her so he could wrap his arms about her waist and pull her back against his body, comforting her with his warmth. "Don't assume it's bad news, Bryony." He pressed his lips to her sun-streaked hair.

But there was nothing he could say or do to stop her trembling.

It was five days before Gideon made it back from Sydney Town. He rode by horseback to Green Hills and took a sloop from there. But he had other business to transact for Hayden, and so Bryony waited, day after anxious day.

She was in Simon's room, putting away clean clothes, when she looked up and saw Gideon ride into the yard. She stood before the open French doors and watched Hayden stroll out of the stables. Watched the two men stand, talking, in the shadows of the barn. Watched a small white packet change hands. Watched Hayden walk slowly across the sun-flooded yard.

Watching, watching, watching. It seemed as if she were standing outside of herself, watching her own life being played out before her.

She was in the hall to meet him when he walked through the door. She held out her hand for the letter and took it without a word, carrying it into the parlor. She couldn't sit down. She stood in the middle of the floor and broke the seal with trembling hands as she wondered if this letter were about to break what was left of her heart.

Her gaze raced down the page. Sir Edward Peyton's letter was brief and cruelly impersonal.

Dear Mrs. Wentworth,
Your letter postmarked Cape Town received this morning. I have instructed the servants that any future communications arriving from persons styling themselves Bryony Wentworth are to be destroyed unopened, as I no longer have a niece by that name. Madeline, of course, has been informed of her mother's

recent death, and I am convinced you will understand that any further attempts on your part to contact her would only be detrimental to all concerned.

Bryony felt as if all the blood had drained from her body, leaving her cold and dead. She read the letter through three times, as if she couldn't quite bring herself to believe what it said. Then she slowly and methodically crumpled the single, salt-stained sheet in both her hands.

"Bryony?"

She looked up, but though her lips parted and her throat worked, she was beyond speech.

Hayden lifted the crumpled paper from her unresisting fingers and carefully flattened it out while she went to stand by the window and stare unseeingly out at the sun glinting off the river below. This time it was Hayden who crushed Sir Edward's letter in his fist, and hurled it with a violent oath into the empty fireplace.

"Madeline's not dead," said Bryony in a queer voice. "I am."

She turned away from the window and faced him, her hands gripping her elbows tight against her.

"Bloody hell, Bryony." He came to her and put his arms around her and pulled her close, but she continued to hold herself rigid, her fingers clutching her elbows as if she'd fall apart if she let go.

He held her away from him, his hands on her shoulders, and gave her a small shake. "You're not dead, Bryony, just because that bastard says you're dead to him."

"I feel as if I were dead."

"We all feel dead inside sometimes. And God knows you've got more reasons than most. But you're not dead." He cradled her face in the palm of his hand and slid his thumb along her lower lip. "You're the most vibrantly alive woman I've ever known."

Her lip trembled beneath his touch, and when he drew her to him again, this time she didn't resist. *"Bryony,"* he breathed softly, his lips against her hair. "Oh, Christ, I know I can't make it any better, but I wish . . . I wish I could."

Her head tipped back and she stared up into his concerned, beloved face. "You can hold me," she whispered, reaching up to draw his head down to hers. "And make love to me," she said, her lips almost touching his. "Oh, please, Hayden . . . make love to me. Now."

He swept her up into his arms and carried her away to their bedroom.

Afterward, they lay together in the heat of the afternoon, the curtains drawn against the hot sun, their bodies naked and entwined.

She talked to him of things she'd never told him about before. About her life with her mother and father in the house at Cadgwith Cove. About the gray, unhappy years at Peyton Hall. About the day they'd taken Madeline from her when the *Indispensable* was being readied for sail.

"I remember there was this one woman on the ship," she told him as she lay curled in the protective circle of his arm, her head on his shoulder. "She was one of the last ones boarded, and when they brought her down to the docks, she still had her two children with her. One of them was a boy of maybe six, the other a girl of no more than two."

She had to stop and draw in a deep, ragged breath before she was able to continue. "I'd heard they would just leave a woman's children on the docks if she were away from her own parish so that the poorhouse wouldn't take them. But I never really believed it until I saw them tear that woman from her children and drag her, screaming, on board."

Bryony rested her hand on his chest, absently tracing a pattern along the hollows between his muscles. "Those children were still standing on that dock, holding each other and staring after us, when we sailed. I'll never forget the sight of them. Their mother of course was out of her mind. They kept her tied down below for days. When they finally let her up on deck, she ran right at the railing and jumped overboard."

Hayden stroked her hair lightly with his hand, wishing he didn't have to hear this, but knowing she needed to tell it, had needed to tell it for months. "I was on deck at the time." Bryony swallowed hard. "I'll never forget her face. When she went over the side, it was twisted with the most unbearable agony. They threw a lifeline to her, but she just ignored it. And then . . . and then she smiled. She was still smiling when her skirts dragged her under. I remember thinking in that moment how much, how very much I envied her. I was missing Madeline so badly, I didn't see how I could go on living with the pain I was feeling. I remember pressing my hands against my stomach, willing Philip to kick me, willing him to remind me that he still lived within me and that I had to go on living for his sake, if not for my own."

Hayden gathered her in his arms and hauled her up so that she lay full along the length of him. Hugging her close, he ran his hands up and down the swell of her hip, the curve of her waist, and marveled again at the strength and endurance of this woman he held in his arms.

When he'd first seen her on that wet, miserable morning in Parramatta, she had just lost what she considered her last reason for living, but she'd gone on living anyway. She'd suffered pain and degradation and humiliation, yet she'd borne it all and still found the strength to stand up to him when she felt she needed to. Somehow she had managed to build a new life for herself, here.

And in the process she'd also built a new life for him, and for Simon, too.

He wished he could tell her what he thought of her. How much he admired and respected her, how terribly much he'd come to need her in his life. But he knew he'd never find the right words. So he rolled her over, pinning her beneath his hardness.

And told her with his body.

Simon was ten months old when he took his first steps.

He'd been pulling himself up to a stand for weeks, getting a little steadier on his feet each time. And then one hot, late summer's evening when they were sitting out on the veranda, hoping for a faint breeze from the river, he finally made up his mind he was going to walk.

Bryony was sewing at the time. She had her head bent, cursing beneath her breath as she attempted to unravel a snarled thread. Hayden said softly, "Bryony."

She looked up. A gentle smile curled up the edges of his lips in a way that made her heart fill with her love for him. He nodded quietly toward Simon.

She turned her head to look at his son. Simon sat on the low step of the veranda. He was rocking back and forth, grinning up at both of them and making excited little noises in his throat, as if to say, *look at me.* Then he pushed himself up onto his little feet, and walked.

He took four, stiff-legged, tottering steps before tumbling backward onto his well-padded backside. By that time Bryony and Hayden were both there. Hayden lifted him up, high above his head, laughing, while Bryony clasped her hands together and said, "Oh, I wish Laura could have been here to see him!"

Hayden slowly lowered the baby, and the laughter died in his face.

He had never discussed Laura with her, never even mentioned his wife's name in her presence. At first, Laura's death had been so recent she'd assumed it was simply too painful for him to talk about. But lately she'd begun to suspect that his thoughts of Laura were now shadowed with guilt because of what he and Bryony did together every night in that big, carved bed of his.

"I-I'm sorry," she stammered. "I don't know why

I said it, except that it was such a beautiful moment, and . . . and I couldn't help thinking how sad it was that Laura . . . that his mother missed it."

Laura. Her name seemed to hang in the air between them, driving them apart. He didn't say anything. He just handed her Laura's son and walked off into the gathering dusk.

The moon was high and full, throwing a band of silver light across the shadowed floor. Bryony slipped from the bed and padded softly over to the open French doors.

He stood with one shoulder braced against a veranda post, his back to her, his eyes on the distant hillside. She saw the end of his cheroot glow fiery red as he inhaled, then brought the cigar down to dangle half forgotten by his thigh.

She hesitated just inside the door, her love for him an ache in her heart. Had he been her husband, she would have gone to him. But he wasn't her husband, he was her master. And although she was his mistress, she was also his servant. Their relationship was confused, indistinct. In bed they were lovers—profoundly, almost uncannily in tune with each other's needs and desires. But outside of bed she was sometimes so terribly unsure of where she stood with him.

She must have made some small sound because his head swung slowly around. He exhaled a long stream of smoke and regarded her through narrowed eyes. "You should be asleep."

She shook her head. "I can't sleep when you're not in bed."

He turned to stare up the hill again.

"Do you miss her terribly?"

He stiffened, but she went to him anyway. She wrapped her arms around his waist and pressed her cheek against his hard, broad back. "I found a painting of her, you know, among her things. She was very beautiful."

He lifted his cheroot and inhaled deeply. She thought

he wasn't going to answer her. Then he said, "I never should have brought her here. She didn't belong here. And she hated it so much."

"I think she was afraid of it," said Bryony, remembering those paintings of brooding mountains and haunting, drooping gums. "But surely she didn't *hate* it."

"She hated it. She hated it for what it was. For the mud and the flies and the heat. But she hated it even more for what it wasn't. It wasn't England." He took another drag on his cigar, one corner of his lips twisting up into a sad travesty of a smile. "It was the simple things she missed the most. The sight of brick chimneys, rising above parks full of oaks and chestnuts. The sound of church bells, ringing out the changes on a crisp Sunday morning. She always talked about how empty and quiet it was here. Everything was too new, too wild, too *different*."

"And yet she enjoyed India, didn't she?"

He shrugged. "India was . . . oh, full of pageantry and well-trained servants and a constant whirl of social activities attended by the kind of people she'd known all of her life."

Bryony remembered Laura's pictures. Paintings of officers in smart uniforms, ladies in fashionable dresses. Lawn parties. Picnics. And dark-skinned, obsequious servants.

"But New South Wales . . ." He paused. "New South Wales is raw, and so are the people. Even in Sydney. Most of the officers here could never have made it into a better regiment, and very few of them bring wives out. Most of them make do with convict mistresses. And they don't take them into society."

Convict mistresses. Women like her, Bryony thought, feeling the heat of shame stain her cheeks. Women who might share a man's bed, but could never aspire to share his table . . . at least not in the company of ladies such as Laura St. John.

"It wasn't as if she complained," he said, putting out his cigar. "She simply grew silent, nervous. Everything was too much for her; the weather, the lack of supplies, the servants who weren't really servants at all but thieves who didn't know how to wash clothes or plant a garden or cook a decent dinner. And she didn't have a clue how to teach them. Sometimes I'd come home and find her sitting in her room, quietly weeping with despair." He pivoted in Bryony's arms so that he could look down on her. "She wasn't like you, you see. She gave way to despair."

"I despair," said Bryony quietly.

"Yes. But you don't give way to it."

She stared over his shoulder at the top of the hill, trying to reconcile his words with the image she'd built up in her mind. She'd always thought of Laura St. John as having come to this alien land willingly. And yet how much say had Laura really had in her husband's decision to settle here? In her own way she had been as much a prisoner of New South Wales as Bryony. Thinking always of home, missing the places and people she'd left behind. And finally dying here.

"She didn't give way to it, Hayden. She just . . . died."

He turned away from her, and she heard him expel his breath in a long sigh. "She didn't just die, Bryony. I killed her. I spilled my seed inside her, even though I knew she never really enjoyed it, even though she'd already miscarried one child, even though I knew she was afraid of having another. I stayed away from her as much as I could, but . . ." He flung back his head and squeezed his eyes shut. "Oh God, Bryony . . . In my own way, I killed her, as surely as you killed Oliver."

"No," she whispered, her voice as hoarse and agonized as his.

"Yes. If I hadn't married her, she'd still be alive and happy in England."

"You can't know that, Hayden. Besides, she chose to marry you. She chose to leave England with you."

She went to him again, and he drew her close against his chest and buried his face in her hair. "She begged me to take her home. We hadn't been here six months when she was desperate to go back to England. But I asked her to give it another year. I hoped that in another year everything wouldn't seem so strange to her. Jindabyne would be more established. I planned to add on to the house, make it something more like what she was accustomed to. But by the end of the year she was dead."

"Would you have gone back to England at the end of that year, if she had still wanted to?"

"Yes. But I'd have hated it." He snagged his fingers in her hair and tipped her head back so he could look into her face. A breeze kicked up, scuttling the dry leaves on the veranda and bringing with it the smell of gum trees and kangaroo grass and wide-open spaces. The smell of Australia.

A light she could only have described as visionary appeared in his eyes, shining through all the pain and the guilt. "This is where I belong," he said quietly. "I never really felt as if I belonged in England. Maybe it was because I wasn't born there, because when my parents sent me away to school there, I didn't want to go. I grew up dreaming about the day I'd leave it again. At first I thought I'd go back to the West Indies, or maybe Canada, but the more I learned about New South Wales . . ."

He ran his hands up and down her back. "There's something exciting, something wonderful being built here, Bryony, even if the colony hasn't gotten off to the best of starts. I want to be a part of it. I wanted to be here to help make it as good as it can be." The light in his eyes dimmed suddenly. "But not at the cost of Laura's life."

She laid the palms of her hands against his cheeks. "What do you think? That because you were able to stay here when Laura died, that her death was somehow your fault?" His fist tightened in her hair so hard it almost hurt, but she went on. "She must have wanted children, too, Hayden. She must have wanted Simon, even if she was afraid of what she had to go through to have him. I wanted Philip, but I was so terribly afraid of having him.

A week before I was brought to bed with him, another woman on the ship had a child, only she didn't make it." Bryony stopped. She would never forget the deep and hollow plunge of that woman's dead body hitting the water. "I was so afraid. And I felt so terribly alone."

He drew her head against his chest, and the movement of his fingers in her hair became gentler, more of a caress. "Sometimes I think we men are such a selfish, uncaring lot, I wonder why you women put up with us." His hands trailed slowly down her neck. "We take our pleasures of your bodies, and we take joy and pride in the children you present us with, yet how little thought most of us give to the pain and danger you must suffer for it all."

His hand slid down between her breasts to rest on her stomach. "I could have planted my child in your belly already," he said, his breath soft and warm against her ear. "Does that thought frighten you?"

Bryony laid her hand over his, pressing it to her. "No." And it was only partially a lie. To have another child, Hayden's child . . . Just the thought of it was enough to send a ripple of desire through her body.

She was fairly certain his child was there already. She thought that maybe now was the time to tell him. But his lips were warm against her neck, his hands soft and moving exquisitely, expertly to arouse her body. "God, Bryony . . ." he said, his voice hoarse. "I can't seem to get enough of you."

She pressed herself against the hardness of his dark, strong body. "Don't," she said, with more desperation than she'd intended as she reached up to drag his mouth down to hers. "Don't ever get enough of me."

CHAPTER
TWENTY-THREE

It was April, and cold enough at night for Bryony to be grateful for the warm fire Hayden kindled in their room every evening before they went to bed. But by mid-afternoon the sun could still be surprisingly warm, and the grass on the hillsides was still a golden brown, waiting for the refreshing rains of winter.

Despite the cold nights, Bryony watched in vain for a blaze of autumn color in the surrounding bush. As the days shortened and wood smoke drifted on a freshening breeze and birds filled the sky, no deep reds and oranges and yellows appeared to splash their vivid hues across this strange, gray-green countryside. She didn't realize how much she was missing them until one day when Hayden surprised her with a cart full of familiar saplings—ashes and chestnuts and oaks and elms.

She fell laughing upon his neck, and he kissed her with swift, surprising tenderness. "They're only trees, Bryony. You act as if I've just handed you a chest of jewels."

"You have," she said, her voice muffled against his chest. "You have."

She was kneeling in her garden later that day, firming the earth around one of the young chestnuts, when she looked up and found him watching her from the veranda. She eased back on her heels and lifted her hand to shade her eyes so she could see him better. She knew him well now. Knew by the closed look on his face and the un-compromising line of his shoulders that he had some-thing to tell her she wasn't going to like.

"What is it?" she asked as he stepped off the veranda and strolled down the graveled path toward her. The autumn sun was warm on her back. The smell of freshly turned earth filled her senses.

He stopped before her. She saw he had a cigar in his hand, and he lit it before he answered her. "A messenger just rode in. We're going to have company."

"Company?" She was annoyed at the way her voice squeaked.

"Sir D'Arcy Baxter. He wants to see for himself how my sheep-breeding is progressing."

"Oh." It could have been worse, she decided. The man could have been bringing his wife and daughter with him. She watched Hayden frown down at his cheroot, and she knew there was more. "He's bringing his wife and daughter with him, isn't he?"

He nodded. "And I don't think they're coming to talk about sheep." He drew hard on his cigar, then expelled a long stream of smoke. "From one or two not-so-subtle hints dropped by Lady Priscilla last spring, I suspect she's more interested in bridals. Her daughter's bridals."

Bryony felt the earth rise and sink beneath her in a movement oddly reminiscent of one of the *Indispensable*'s most sickening, foul-weather lurches. "You mean Amanda?"

He nodded again. "And unfortunately, since they're already on their way here, I don't see how I can forestall them."

A wallaby loped slowly toward the edge of the gum trees, heading for the creek. Bryony stared at it in silence, feeling the blood drain from her face. She couldn't think of anything more calculated than this to remind her of what her true position was.

She rose to her feet and carefully wiped her dirt-stained hands on her apron. "Well, do tell me, what is the normal procedure in circumstances such as this? There surely must be no shortage of precedents, given the proliferation of convict mistresses among the officers of the

New South Wales Corps. What a pity I've never met Hetty Abrahams, so that I could ask her advice. I understand she's been living as Major Johnston's concubine for . . . what? Fifteen? Twenty years now? Tell me, what does Hetty—and her eight children—do when you come calling on the major? Wait on you at dinner? Or quietly disappear?"

"Bryony, I am not interested in Amanda Baxter."

He would have taken her in his arms, but when she jerked away from him, he let her go. She stared at him from across a space of perhaps five feet. "Where the hell are they even going to sleep?" she demanded.

"Sir D'Arcy and his wife can sleep in Simon's room. We can put up a bed in the dressing room for Amanda, and Simon can sleep with us."

"*Us?* I can't sleep with you with the Baxters in this house! There's another bed in the kitchen lean-to. I'll make it up and sleep there."

"You will not." He closed the distance between them with two long strides. "Damn it, Bryony, I'm not ashamed of having you in my bed."

"Oh, Hayden," she sobbed, collapsing suddenly against his shoulder. "Don't you understand? I'm ashamed of myself."

"I will not sit down to dinner with those people," Bryony said, scooting around to the far side of the bed.

She was wearing a delicate white muslin dress embroidered all over with a tiny yellow and green flower motif, with a matching spencer and yellow and white satin shoes. Bryony had had nothing to blush for in her dress when she'd stood on the veranda beside Hayden earlier that afternoon to greet Sir D'Arcy, the exquisitely arrayed Lady Priscilla, and their beautiful daughter Amanda. But as she'd watched the ladies' knowing gazes slide over her finery, Bryony had found herself wishing for her old brown or gray work dress. For nothing marked her as Hayden's mistress more clearly than the expensive clothes she wore.

"Yes," he hissed, "you will." He regarded her stonily across some four feet of counterpane. "What do you think I'm going to do? Make you eat in the kitchen? This is my house, damn it. I wouldn't take you to her house and expect her to sit down at the table with you, but she's the one who decided to come here."

He hadn't said it to hurt her, she knew. But, God, it hurt. It hurt like hell.

"They wouldn't have come here if they'd known you had me living with you openly as your mistress," she said quietly. "I heard Lady Priscilla say so to Sir D'Arcy. She said it's one thing if a man tumbles his servants *occasionally*, or even regularly, as long as he still treats them like the servants they are. But it's something else entirely if he singles out one of them and actually begins *consorting* with her outside of bed."

One corner of his lips twitched, as if he were trying hard not to smile. "She couldn't have said that."

At any other time Bryony might have found it funny, too, but at the moment she was in no state to be amused. "She did. She reminded him that her father was a Devonshire squire—"

"She would."

"—and that whatever might be the custom among the officers of this colony, she was a lady born and bred, and even if it was *your* father who had been the viscount, she would rather die than utter one syllable to some degraded creature who had not only been shipped out to this colony as a convict, but who was obviously willing to spread her legs for any man who offered to buy her a pretty dress or hair ribbon."

"Would she, by God?" The amusement died out of his face, to be replaced by something cold and decidedly lethal. "That can be arranged."

He spun about on his heel and had almost reached the

door when Bryony, moving around the edge of the bed, got there first.

"Hayden, no." She laid her hand on his arm. "I can understand how she feels, and you should be able to, too. How would Laura have reacted if she had been expected to sit down to dinner with some thieving whore? How would *you* have reacted if someone had asked her to?"

He fastened his hands about her waist and hoisted her up against the door, leaning hard against her, the heat of his anger flowing over her since she'd balked him of his original target. "You're not a thieving whore, damn it."

"She doesn't know what I am. She doesn't know anything about me—"

"Then, she shouldn't judge you."

"—except that I'm a convict, and that I've allowed you to make me your mistress. What else does she need to know?"

He let her slide slowly back to the floor and pressed his forehead against hers, his breathing a little unsteady. "As if you could have stopped me that first night. I laid you back on that damned table and just took you."

"Oh, Hayden. I didn't try to stop you. I didn't *want* to stop you." Her mouth found his, and she tasted his forbidden, sinful lips. "Please don't make me sit down to dinner with that hateful woman," she said softly, curling her arms around his neck. "I don't care what she thinks of me. I just don't like the way she makes me think of myself."

He slanted his mouth gently back and forth across hers. "All right." He fumbled to undo the tie at the neck of her dress so he could push it down. "But for your sake, not for hers."

Her bared breasts filled his seeking hands, and he smiled against her mouth. "And now, I'm going to tumble my servant right here against this door." He reached down to ruck up the frilled hem of her fine dress. "And as long as I don't consort with you afterward, I have it on the expert opinion of a Devonshire squire's daughter that it is all perfectly acceptable."

Bryony might have escaped dinner, but she still had to pour the tea, since Ann McBride couldn't be trusted not to trip and dump the contents of Laura's delicate china cups down the front of their guests' finery. It was only quick action by Hayden that had saved Sir D'Arcy from getting a bowl of soup in his lap at dinner, for Hayden had refused to allow Bryony to wait on them at the table. He was unhappy enough that she'd insisted on cooking the dinner herself.

But pouring tea was a genteel occupation. Bryony had been well tutored by her Aunt Eunice, and performed the office with a skill that raised Lady Priscilla's eyebrows, although she still refused to utter one syllable to Captain St. John's convict mistress. Neither she nor her daughter even said thank you when Bryony handed them their cups.

Bryony would have left the room immediately afterward, but Hayden snagged her arm and pulled her down beside him on the settee, beneath Lady Priscilla's affronted gaze.

She sat there, feeling stiff, feeling branded as a whore by her presence in this house, by the delicate muslin dress she wore, courtesy of the man beside her . . . the man whose use of her body earlier that evening she could still feel as a slight but pleasant soreness between her legs.

Lady Priscilla lifted her teacup, flashed Hayden her most brilliant smile, and said, "It's a pity about Thornton, don't you agree?"

Hayden fixed his uninvited guest with a level stare. "What about Major Thornton?"

"Why, he's to be court-martialed. Didn't you know? The fool actually *married* that woman of his—she was off the *Earl Cornwallis*, I believe, wasn't she?—and had the affrontery to attempt to take her into society." She took a sip of her tea, then rested the cup carefully back in her saucer before adding, "He'll be cashiered, of course."

Beside her, Bryony felt Hayden stiffen. Lady Priscilla turned her gaze on Laura's harp and sighed, as if in sympathy over the passing of its former owner.

"What a pity you don't have a pianoforte, Captain St. John. Then my dear Amanda here could play for us. It's always so pleasant to have a bit of music in the evening, don't you agree?"

"Of course. What an excellent idea," said Hayden, a wicked smile spreading over his face. "Mrs. Wentworth here shall play the harp for us. Won't you, Mrs. Wentworth?"

It wasn't really a request. He was already raising her with a firm hand beneath her elbow. She tried to demure, but he pushed her down in the chair beside the harp and, under the guise of taking the cover off the instrument, leaned over to say under his breath, "Play, damn it, before I strangle the bitch and end up on manslaughter charges myself."

Her eyes flew to his. They sparkled with amusement and something more. Something that filled her with a warm, happy glow. Something that enabled her to play for him, and to make it through what was left of that hideous evening.

Sir D'Arcy Baxter spent the next morning with Hayden, looking at his breeding stock and talking about sheep and wool and the new lamb crop. Then he announced that Lady Priscilla was anxious to spend the evening with friends in Green Hills and very sensibly bore his scandalized wife and daughter off as soon as possible after the midday meal.

"Will he ever visit you again?" Bryony asked when Hayden strolled back onto the veranda after seeing the small party off.

"Baxter? Of course. Although he'll make sure he

comes alone next time. There's a lot I don't like about
the man, but I'll say this for him: *he* couldn't give a damn
about my domestic living arrangements. God knows
they're common enough in this colony."

"So it's only the ladies who object to being asked to
consort with a man's convict mistress?"

"Yes, I suppose so. Although even Baxter might complain if a man started taking his mistress around in public
with him."

He would have gone into the house, but she stopped
him. "Like the officer who is to be court-martialed for
marrying a convict woman?"

He swung slowly back around. "Yes. What's your
point, Bryony?"

"I just want to know where I stand. Some of the subtle-
ties of this colonial code of conduct escape me."

"Like hell." He walked up to her. "Nothing escapes
you, Bryony."

She sucked in a deep breath. "And what about the children of these *irregular unions*?"

"They're usually acknowledged by the father. Why?"

When she didn't say anything, his hands fell on her
shoulders and he backed her up against the side of the
house until she could feel the rough, sandstone bricks
digging into her shoulder blades. "Why? What are you
trying to tell me?"

"The men in the yard are staring."

He cast a quick look over his shoulder to see that it
was true, and dragged her through the French doors into
the dining room. "Tell me."

"Do I really need to?"

He released her abruptly and took a step back, his
breath expelling as sharply as if she'd hit him. He
searched her face, but she couldn't begin to guess what
he was thinking.

Then he said, "I thought from something you said the
other night that you'd be pleased."

Unconsciously, she pressed her hands to her belly. "I

am. Or at least, I was. Until yesterday. I knew I wanted another child—wanted your child. But I don't think I'd stopped to consider what it would mean."

She turned away from him. "We're so isolated here. It's just you and me and Simon. And Ann and Gideon and the men, of course. But there's been no one to look askance at me, no one to condemn us. No one to make me feel like a whore carrying a man's bastard child. Which is what I am."

"Don't say that." He seized her arm and swung her back around. It was only then that he saw the tears she'd been trying to hide. The blazing anger died out of his face. "Oh, hell . . . Don't cry, sweetheart." He pulled her into the protective circle of his arms. "Don't cry. I'll take care of you, Bryony. You know that. I'll always take care of you, and our child."

She knew he meant it, but although she was relieved to hear it, it wasn't enough.

She wanted him to tell her she was the most important thing in his life, and that he would never, ever leave her or send her away. She wanted him to tell her he loved her as desperately, as hopelessly, as eternally as she loved him. But she knew it would never happen.

She was his convict mistress, and that was all she ever would be.

That night it started to rain.

All night the rain pounded on the shingled roof. A howling wind whipped about the house and found its way around windows and under doors.

The rain continued for days. The dry, parched ground was so hard and sunbaked it couldn't seem to absorb the steady downpour fast enough. Water ran off the surrounding hillsides in ever-widening rivulets.

The Hawkesbury River rose, and rose, and rose.

Bryony walked out onto the veranda and stood clutching her cloak against the cold wind, watching the river rush past, incredibly wide and deep and treacherously fast.

"Louisa told me the river could get so high it'd reach halfway to the house. I didn't believe her."

Hayden paused beside her. He buttoned up his great-coat and pulled on a pair of gloves. "No one does, until they actually see it in flood. It's only thanks to Louisa and Will Carver that I built the house this high. I originally wanted to put it there." He pointed to a spot now under some five feet of water.

She glanced up at him, and her heart filled with her love for him. He looked so tall and strong, standing beside her. Yet suddenly she felt an unexpected and totally inexplicable frisson of fear run through her. "I wish . . . I wish you wouldn't go out in this."

He pulled her roughly into his arms. "I'll be all right," he said, pressing his lips to her hair. "But there are a lot of families whose houses are under water, and they didn't all have the sense to get out of them while they still could."

She nodded. "I'll have blankets and plenty of hot water ready."

But in the end she couldn't seem to let him go. He finally had to put her bodily away from him before he could leave.

The woman clung to the roof of the hut with one claw-like, cold-numbed hand, and tried desperately to clutch two small, shivering children to her with her free arm.

Hayden maneuvered his boat as close to the woman as he could, then called out, "Hand me the children!" His shout was barely audible above the roar of the flood-waters and the howl of the wind.

"I can't!" the woman wailed, rain streaming down her white face. "I can't!"

"You must."

Her eyes widened with terror. "But if I let go of the

roof to try to hand one of them to you, I'll drop the other child and slide right off myself!"

"She's probably right," said Gideon, doing his best to keep the boat close in the swirling, rushing waters. "She musta been hanging' on there fer hours."

"Bloody hell," cursed Hayden under his breath. To the woman he called, "All right. Hold steady, and I'll climb up and get you."

Gideon's head swung around, and he stared at him in dismay. "Cap'n! You ain't goin' up there yerself?"

"Well, what the hell else can I do?" he said, tearing off first his greatcoat, then his boots. "Leave them up there to drown?"

"But ... The whole hut's liable to give way any minute now!"

As if to underscore his point, the structure beside them shuddered violently.

"Just hold the boat as steady as you can and be ready to grab the children and the woman as I hand them to you."

The hut swayed alarmingly as it took his weight. He edged along the peak of the roof on his hands and knees. He realized he was sweating, in spite of the cold wind and driving rain. The wet shingles were treacherously slippery underfoot, and he decided that if he ever got his hands on the man who'd built this damned hut so close to the river, he'd drown the bloody bastard himself.

It seemed to take forever to reach the woman, and longer to make it back to Gideon with the first child. He had just taken the second child from its mother when he heard Gideon call, *"Look out!"*

He turned. He had a brief, sickening glimpse of the trunk of a giant red gum hurtling toward him through the swirling, raging floodwaters. Then the tree crashed into the hut, and the entire structure flew apart beneath him. He pitched headlong into the swirling river.

He tried to roll, curling his body to protect both his own head and the boy he held from the debris. But it was a purely instinctive movement, because all he could seem to think about at that moment was Bryony.

And how the hell he was going to take care of her and their unborn child if he were dead.

CHAPTER
TWENTY-FOUR

"You stubborn, thickheaded, bloody fool."

The words, uttered on a broken, husky sob, penetrated his consciousness as a gentle hand placed a cool cloth on his forehead.

"I'd kill you myself if you weren't already half dead."

Hayden felt his lips twitch appreciatively, but a savage, angry pain pounded his head, and he wasn't ready to open his eyes yet.

"It's no thanks to you you're not dead, you pigheaded—" She paused, as if searching for the ultimate insult, but she couldn't seem to find it.

"If you're so bloody mad at me, Bryony, why are you crying?" His voice surprised him. It sounded weak and fluttery, like the wings of a dying moth.

He opened his eyes to see her beautiful face, swollen and wet with tears, bending over him. She didn't answer him. Just sobbed again and shook her head.

He reached up to wipe the tears from her cheeks, but his arm was as weak and shaky as his voice. She captured his hand in hers and cradled it against her as if she held something precious. He tried to sit up and take her in his arms, but a tide of sick blackness threatened to swamp him, and he eased back down again.

"What happened to me, anyway?" he asked when he could catch his breath. "My head hurts like hell. All I can remember is seeing this bloody big red gum barreling down at me."

"Gideon said the hut broke up under the impact of the

tree and one of the slabs must have hit you on the back of the head."

"The child?"

"He's all right. You managed to hold on to him until Gideon could get you in the boat. Both children are asleep in front of the fire in the parlor."

"And the woman?"

Bryony shook her head.

"Christ." He squeezed his eyes shut, seeing once more a white face and dark, terrified eyes. "I'd like to throttle her husband."

"You can't. He's already dead. One of the little boys told me they had an older sister. She slipped off the roof before you came, and the father tried to go after her."

"Christ," he said again, then opened his eyes to stare up at her. "Bryony . . ."

"Hush." She took the cloth and rinsed it in fresh water. "You shouldn't try to talk so much."

He smelled lavender and valerian, and thought dreamily that it was probably from her garden. "I want you to marry me, Bryony."

Her hands stilled at their task. She sat for a moment, barely breathing. Then she gave him a wobbly smile. "That board must have hit you harder than we thought." She reached out briskly to replace the cloth.

He caught her hand before she could pull it away. "I mean it, Bryony. It occurred to me today that if anything ever happens to me, you'll be sent right back to the Factory. Our child would be taken away from you when he turned three and sent to the Orphan Asylum. I can't let that happen."

She had a curious, frozen expression on her face. He'd expected her to be overjoyed. All women wanted to be married, didn't they? Especially if they were already carrying a man's child. So why was she looking at him like that?

She twisted her hand from his weakened grasp and stood up. "Go to sleep, Hayden."

And so, because his head hurt so badly when he tried to figure it all out, he did.

Bryony sat before the fire and watched a tiny finger of yellow and blue flame curl around a blackening log on the hearth. Outside, the wind howled and the rain poured.

"Bryony?"

She glanced toward the bed. His dark, handsome head had turned slightly against Laura's fine white pillowcase. He was staring at her with unsmiling eyes.

"How do you feel?" she asked in a forced, light voice. "I have some soup here I've been keeping warm, if you're hungry. And some—"

"Bryony, come here."

She stayed where she was.

"Damn it, Bryony, if you don't come here, I'm going to get up and come over there, and since my head hurts like hell, I can promise you I won't be in a very good mood by the time I get there."

She got up, but she paused to ladle some soup into a bowl and carried it with her to the bed.

"Put the bowl on the table and sit down here."

She gripped the bowl between tense hands. "You should eat."

"I will. Just put the bowl on the table and sit down."

"I hate it when you order me around like that. It makes me feel like a—"

"A servant? I want to make you my wife, Bryony."

She set the soup down, but continued to stand beside the bed. "No," she said, shaking her head. "You don't want to make me your wife; you want to protect your child's future."

"It's the same thing."

"It isn't."

He captured one of her hands, a look that was more puzzlement than anger in his face. "What are you trying to tell me, Bryony? That you don't want to marry me?"

No, she wasn't trying to tell him that. She was asking

for something. She was asking him to tell her he wanted to marry her because *he wanted to marry her*. She wanted him to tell her he loved her. She wanted him to tell her . . .

Oh, foolish, foolish woman, she scolded herself. But it didn't stop her from trying again. "You can't marry a convict. You'd be ruined."

"Like that officer Lady Priscilla was telling us about?" He shook his head. "I've sold out, remember?"

"Maybe you can't be court-martialed, but you can still be ostracized."

"It doesn't matter, Bryony. Not compared to what's at stake here. Your future, the future of our children."

It wasn't exactly what she wanted to hear.

He pulled her down on the bed beside him. "As a convict, you'll need to apply to the Colonial Secretary for permission to marry, but in this case it'll just be a formality. And then, as my wife, you'll be able to get a ticket-of-leave. That means that even if something happens to me, Bryony, you would still be allowed to live here with the children. You'd be safe, Bryony, and so would they."

She lay down beside him and hid her face in the curve of his shoulder, so he wouldn't see her expression. A ticket-of-leave. Next to a pardon, it was every convict's dream, for it gave the holder the right to live and work where she wanted, until her sentence expired and she was given her certificate of freedom. Except for the ever present danger of losing the ticket as a result of misconduct, it was almost like being set free.

Bryony swallowed the lump that had suddenly arisen in her throat. A ticket-of-leave, marriage to the man she loved and the father of her unborn child—how could she be so greedy as to want more? How could she be so greedy as to want his love, too?

"I would be telling you a lie if I said we won't be ostracized." He ran his lean, hard fingers through her hair. "You especially. The military men and settlers who came here free are very proud and exclusive. It doesn't matter how educated or wellborn a man was before he was transported, or how much money he makes after he's emancipated, he'll always be a convict as far as the exclusivists are concerned, and they'll never have anything to do with him. Oh, they might do business with him, or even take their wives to him for treatment as in the case of Dr. William Redfern, but they wouldn't dream of inviting someone like Simeon Lord or Andrew Thompson into their house for dinner."

He laughed softly. "It's a bit of a farce, isn't it? Lady Priscilla would let William Redfern deliver one of her children, but she wouldn't sit down with him for a cup of tea."

"Yet you forced her to drink tea with me. She'll never forgive you for that."

"Probably not. Bryony . . ." He tucked his fingers under her chin so he could lift her head and look into her face. "I expected this to make you happy. I thought it was something you'd want."

She reached up to brush a stray lock of hair from his forehead, letting her gaze roam freely over his dark, handsome face, sharpened now with confusion. Her love for him welled up within her until it was like an ache. He talked of marriage, but he had said nothing of love because he had none to give her. Laura had been his love, and he had buried her.

He was Laura's husband. Bryony knew that even if he married her, he would still be Laura's husband, always. He would never really be hers.

But he cared for her, she reminded herself. Cared for her enough to brave social ostracism by marrying her in order to keep her and her child safe.

His eyes narrowed. "Is it because of what happened before, with Oliver? I'll be a good husband to you, Bryony, I promise you that. I—"

She pressed one finger against his lips. "No," she said. "I know you're nothing like Oliver." She lifted her finger and replaced it with her mouth, kissing him hard. Then she raised her head so she could stare earnestly down at him. "I want to marry you, Hayden."

She watched a slow smile warm his face. "Good," he said simply, and she wanted to laugh at the sheer male arrogance of it. "It'll take awhile to clean up the mess left by this flood, but as soon as it's possible, we'll take the sloop into Sydney and make the necessary arrangements."

He tightened his arms around her to pull her down to him for a long, lingering kiss. "I can't promise I won't still try to order you around," he said a moment later.

"I wouldn't believe you even if you did," she said with a gurgle of laughter that was smothered as he gently claimed her lips again.

"No, Simon, you can't get down," Bryony told the kicking, wiggling, squirming baby in her arms. "You'll get in the sailors' way."

"Give him to Ann," said Hayden, coming to stand behind her at the rail.

Bryony glanced toward Ann McBride, who was running from one side of the sloop to the other in an attempt to see everything there was to see as they sailed through the Heads into Port Jackson. She was giggling and exclaiming like a child herself, her red hair flying out behind her. "I'm afraid she might drop him overboard."

Hayden laughed. "You're probably right—if she didn't fall overboard with him. Now that he's weaned, you should have left him home with her. After all, we're coming here to get married."

Bryony leaned back against Hayden's chest and felt his arms go around her, hugging her close. The wind whipped her hair about her head, and the cold stung her cheeks; but the sun was out, and the sea and sky both sparkled with a clean, inimitable light that was pure Australia.

She couldn't help but contrast today with the last time

she'd sailed into Sydney Cove, less than a year ago. It had been cold that day, too, but dark and raining. Low, threatening clouds had obscured the surrounding rolling hills, turning the bay to a harsh gray and robbing it of much of its beauty. She had felt so alone that day; alone and terrified, facing an uncertain, bleak future and clutching a dying baby in her desperate arms.

She blinked back the tears that suddenly stung her eyes. Dear little Philip, hers for such a short time. She rubbed her cheek against Simon's chubby, rosy face and breathed deeply of his baby-sweet smell. She would never want to erase the memory of her own lost darling, but Simon did help ease the pain that remembering Philip or Madeline always brought with it.

Life goes on, she thought, looking out over the vibrant, sunlit hills, bursting forth with fresh greenery in the wake of the rains that had brought new life to the colony even as the flood had taken lives away. Life goes on. Even when you don't think it can, even when you're not sure you want it to, it goes on.

She shifted Simon to her hip, her hand lingering as it often did on her belly. She held a new life within her. A new child. It could never replace those she'd had taken from her. But, like Simon, this new child would help to ease the pain left by the loss of her other children. And one day soon, Bryony had decided, she was going to talk to Hayden about trying to have Madeline brought out to New South Wales. She didn't know what she could do if Uncle Edward refused to send her, but she had to try. She'd been tempted to ask Hayden about it, before, but as his mistress she'd always hesitated. Now she would be his wife. Even if he didn't love her, she would still be his wife.

A seagull floated by, just off the railing. Simon reached for it and chattered angry nonsense when he failed to grab it. "Here," said Hayden, lifting the squirming mass of arms and legs from her. "Let's go watch the sailors and give Bryony a rest, shall we?"

He walked away toward where Gideon stood at the front of the sloop. She watched the sun glint on his dark, handsome head as he held his son balanced easily on his strong arm, and she loved him so much in that moment that it hurt. He was such a wonderful man. He desired her and he cared for her, even if he could never love her. She was so lucky, so very lucky.

Then the scene darkened as a cloud passed in front of the sun. It was just a small, puffy white cloud, one of several floating high in the sky. But it was enough to take the warm sparkle out of the day and send a chill up Bryony's spine.

Perhaps it was because too many awful things had happened to her in her life, but she suddenly found herself afraid. Afraid this newfound happiness wouldn't last, afraid something would happen to snatch it from her.

The sun was out again in a moment, as bright as ever. But Bryony stood beside the railing, watched the cottages and storehouses of Sydney Town come into view, and felt cold.

She sat in a chair beside the hearth, sewing a cap for the new baby and admiring the way the golden firelight played over the high cheekbones of Hayden's face.

They were in the private parlor of the Three Jolly Fishermen. Through the casement window, the sun glinted low over the bay. Nothing in the room had changed. Only they were different.

"I made an appointment to see the Colonial Secretary in the morning," Hayden said, leaning back in his chair and stretching his long legs out in front of him.

"I could simply have submitted the petitions, but I thought it would be better to meet with him personally. As it is, it will probably be awhile before the approval comes through. You should have time to have a wedding dress made."

"I don't need a new dress." She set another stitch in the cap she was making. "I have so many new dresses."

His eyes crinkled with amusement. "Nonsense. Every woman should have a new dress for her wedding." Then his gaze narrowed and moved restlessly over her, as if he knew there was something wrong but couldn't quite pin down what it was. "Bryony, you do want this, don't you? You don't seem very happy."

She laid aside her sewing and went to kneel at his feet so she could gather his hands up into hers. "I am happy, Hayden, for myself. It's only . . . I can't help but realize that as wonderful as it is for me, this marriage is a disaster for you."

His strong hands grasped her shoulders and pulled her up onto his lap. "Don't say that, damn it. Don't even think it. I'd call a man out for saying less, and I sure as hell am not going to listen to it from you."

Bryony laughed softly and put her arms around his neck. "What are you going to do, Hayden? Challenge me to a duel for insulting your wife?"

"If I have to."

"Ha!" She relaxed against him. "Then, I would get the choice of weapons, wouldn't I?"

"Now, that might be interesting," he said, but as she chose that exact moment to reach up and nibble at his ear, his voice had a slight break in it.

She smiled against the warm skin of his neck. "I can think of several possibilities." She let her hand trail lightly down his shirtfront.

He grabbed her hand just as she reached the top of his breeches. "You abandoned woman." He carried her hand to his mouth and placed a kiss in her palm. "I think I'm going to enjoy being married to you." She curled her hand so that she could run her fingers along the fullness of his lower lip, and he groaned.

"Enough." He stood up and set her away from him. "Or I'll be late for dinner."

"Dinner?" She went still, all the playfulness draining out of her.

"I've been invited to dinner at Government House."

He watched her carefully, his brows drawing together in a thin frown. "Under the circumstances I didn't think it would be politic to refuse."

She turned away so that he wouldn't see her reaction betrayed on her face. But he obviously knew anyway, because he came up behind her to wrap his arms around her and pull her back against the comforting warmth of his body. "I'm sorry, Bryony."

Because of course she hadn't been invited. Even if she'd already been his wife, she still wouldn't have been invited.

A woman like her would never be invited to Government House.

CHAPTER
TWENTY-FIVE

The candles on the altar flickered and then flared, casting long, cold shadows over the low-ceiling and whitewashed walls of the church. The morning was dull and overcast, the windows of the church so small and high-set that little daylight penetrated the gloomy interior. A stale, musty smell of disuse hung oppressive and unwelcoming in the chill air. Bryony, clad in a new blue silk gown embroidered over with tiny pink rosebuds, paused beside her husband-to-be and shivered.

She leaned toward him and whispered, "This place reminds me of a prison."

Hayden slipped his arm around her waist and ducked his head until his mouth was so close his warm breath tickled her ear. "It *is* a prison. Every Sunday, the government convicts are herded in here to have their souls saved—whether they want them saved or not."

"A-hem."

Standing on the platform before them, regally outfitted in full canonicals, the Reverend Richards cleared his throat and glared at them. He was a tall, thin man with a long, pointed nose and a pinched, disapproving expression. It might have been habitual, but Bryony suspected his acerbic mannerisms reflected his opinion of the ceremony he was about to perform.

Hayden removed his arm from her waist and tried to look solemn. The reverend opened his prayer book, cleared his throat again, and began to read.

"Dearly beloved, we are gathered together here in the sight of God and in the face of this congregation . . ."

Bryony cast an involuntary glance at the dark, empty rows of pews behind them. The only other people in the church were Ann McBride and Gideon Shanaghan, pressed into service as witnesses. Dr. William Redfern, who had planned to attend, had been called away at the last minute to deliver a baby up at the Female Factory.

Her stomach knotted with distress as Bryony brought her gaze back to the man beside her. The absence of Hayden St. John's friends and peers spoke more clearly than anything else could have about society's opinion of this marriage. But if Hayden was regretting the noble impulse that had led him to brave social ostracism by marrying his pregnant convict mistress, it was not apparent. He seemed utterly relaxed, standing tall and handsome in formal morning dress.

As if sensing her troubled gaze upon him, Hayden turned his head slightly and smiled reassuringly down at her.

"Matrimony . . . is an honorable estate, not by any to be taken in hand lightly," she heard the reverend say, and she realized he was looking straight at Hayden. "Or wantonly," he added significantly, "to satisfy men's carnal lusts and appetites."

Hayden frowned. Bryony had to bite her lip to keep from smiling.

"Matrimony," continued the reverend, the word rolling off his tongue like an ominous clap of thunder, "was ordained for the procreation of children." Again he paused, this time focusing his malevolent gaze upon Bryony's belly. The folds of her high-waisted gown hid the soft swell of the growing babe, but Bryony felt herself flush anyway. Beside her, Hayden stiffened.

"Secondly," said the reverend, "it was ordained for a remedy against sin and to avoid fornication; that such persons as have not the gift of continency might marry and keep themselves undefiled . . ."

Hayden's head reared back, and when Reverend
Richards paused again to cast the groom a censorious
frown, the groom glared back at him with such lethal
menace that the minister seemed almost to shrink before
Bryony's eyes. The hand holding the open prayer book
shook noticeably, and he continued in a rush.

"I require and charge you both, that if either of you
know any impediment, why ye may not be lawfully
joined together in matrimony, ye do now confess it. For
be ye well assured, that so many as are coupled together
otherwise than God's Word doth allow are not joined
together by God; neither is their matrimony lawful."

Again he stopped, and not even Hayden's cold stare
could compel him to continue before a decent interval
had elapsed. However incidental this part of the marriage
ceremony might be elsewhere, in New South Wales
it was not passed over lightly. With so many soldiers
and convicts leaving wives or husbands behind in Britain, bigamy was almost as common in the colony as
fornication.

The reverend waited what he evidently deemed a suitable length of time to prick their consciences. When both
continued to merely watch him expectantly, he turned to
Hayden.

"Wilt thou have this woman to be thy wedded wife, to
live together after God's ordinance in the holy estate of
matrimony? Wilt thou love her, comfort her, honor, and
keep her in sickness and in health; and, forsaking all
others, keep thee only unto her, so long as ye both shall
live?"

Hayden's gaze settled on her. One corner of his mouth
quirked up in an odd smile. He sucked in a deep breath
that lifted his broad chest noticeably, and said, "I will."
His voice rang out loud and strong in the prisonlike
church.

When it was Bryony's turn, the surge of joy that
welled up from within her seemed to clog her throat. Her
response was little more than a hoarse whisper.

"Who giveth this woman to be married to this man?"

There was an awkward pause. With commendable quick thinking, Gideon scrambled out of his seat, seized Bryony's hand, and offered it to the minister. Frowning disdainfully at the Irishman's convict garb, Reverend Richards took Bryony's hand and passed her quickly on to Hayden. "Repeat after me."

Hayden's hand closed over hers in a warm, protective grip. "I, Hayden Seymour St. John," he said, his eyes roaming over her in a slow, almost sensual caress. "Take thee, Bryony Peyton Wentworth, to be my wedded wife, to have and to hold from this day forward, for better for worse, for richer for poorer, in sickness and in health, to love and to cherish, till death do us part; and thereto I plight thee my troth."

Solemnly, reverently, Bryony repeated the same words.

The minister held out his prayer book expectantly. Hayden reached into the pocket of his waistcoat and brought out a small gold band set with a line of exquisitely tiny pearls, which he laid upon the open book for the reverend to consecrate. Reverend Richards reached to pick up the ring and hand it back to Hayden. But before his fingers closed on the symbolic band, the prayer book tipped violently to one side. The ring slid across the worn page, and tumbled to the floor to roll to a stop at Hayden's feet.

"Lord amercy," shrieked Ann McBride from her pew. "The ring! He's dropped the ring. Heaven preserve us, it's a sign. A bad sign."

Hayden bent gracefully and picked up the ring from the floor. As calmly as if nothing had happened, he reached for Bryony's left wrist, gently lifted her hand and, his gaze riveted to hers, solemnly said, "With this ring I thee wed, and with my body I thee worship, and with all my worldly goods I thee endow, in the name of the Father . . ." His gaze dropped to her hand as, slowly, exquisitely, he slipped the ring over the tip of her first finger. "And of the Son . . ." He touched the ring to the second finger. "And of the Holy Ghost." His grip on her wrist tightening, he slid the ring home, then raised his eyes to hers again and whispered, "Amen."

The moment stretched out and became something they shared, something precious and memorable. Bryony was barely aware of the minister's voice, droning on in the background. It seemed as if every sense in her body was tuned only to the man who stood beside her, holding her hand in both of his, his thumb playing idly with the ring he had just slipped over her finger.

Then she heard the minister say, ". . . I pronounce that they be man and wife together, in the name of the Father, and of the Son, and of the Holy Ghost. Amen."

She saw Hayden smile. It was a glorious smile of satisfaction and joy and promised passion, that started in the sparkling depths of his crystal-blue eyes, creased his lean, tanned cheeks, and parted his sensual lips in a delighted laugh.

And took her breath away.

A fire crackled on the hearth of the private parlor. Bryony sat in one of the high-backed chairs, her head turned slightly to one side, her eyes closed, as if she were asleep. The firelight mingled with the light from the candles in the nearby wall sconces to cast a golden glow across her smooth cheeks.

He'd been called out to attend to an unexpected business problem that couldn't wait, and it had taken longer than he'd expected. Carefully, so as not to disturb her, Hayden held the handle and eased the door shut behind him. She didn't move. He leaned back against the panel, folded his arms over his chest, and looked at his wife.

She still wore the blue gown she'd had made for their wedding. It was cut high at the waist, with a scooped bodice that showed off her long, graceful neck and beautiful collarbones, and just a hint of the swell of her fine breasts. Her flame-shot hair was pulled up into a prim and proper chignon at the top of her head, the way she had worn it that morning when she stood beside him in the church. But some stray tendrils had loosened and now lay softly against her cheek.

He remembered another evening, less than a year ago, when he had walked into this same parlor and found her asleep in front of the fire, her beautiful breasts bare, her hair curling in wild abandon about her face.

He wanted to see her that way again.

Reaching behind him, he turned the key in the lock. At the sound her lashes fluttered. She opened her eyes and saw him standing there. A slow, welcoming smile curved her lips in a way that brought a tightening to his loins.

"You were a long time."

"I didn't want to be."

He realized a book lay open on her lap. She closed it and set it to one side. "Come," she said.

He didn't move. "Take down your hair."

She looked at him across the length of the room. Wordlessly she lifted her hands, her elbows held wide, and one by one pulled out the pins that held her chignon.

Her rich, flame-shot hair tumbled down about her shoulders, gleaming chestnut and gold in the mingling candlelight and firelight. She shook her head to loosen the heavy fall, sending it swirling about her shoulders. He felt the predictable, warm throbbing begin low in his belly. It was all he could do to stay where he was, his shoulders pressed against the door, watching her.

"Now your dress," he said, his voice low. "Take off your dress."

Her eyes widened slightly, but she reached back to untie the tapes that held the dress at the neck, then at the waist. Her gaze still fastened on his face, she slowly pushed one sleeve down over her bare arm, then the next. Rolling her hips to one side, she eased the silk dress from beneath her and let it fall in a shimmering blue cascade to the floor.

Besides her shoes and stockings, she now wore only a thin petticoat and a fine batiste chemise held at the neck with a blue satin ribbon.

"Your chemise. Open it."

She untied the ribbon and peeled back the edges of her chemise, baring her beautiful breasts to the gentle firelight and his eyes.

He sucked in his breath in a soft hissing sound between his teeth.

She leaned back in the chair and gave him a sultry smile. "Did you want me to take off anything else?"

"Not yet." He pushed away from the door and walked toward her, taking off his hat and coat as he walked. He tossed them on the table by the window. "Not yet." Reaching up, he loosened his cravat and started on the buttons of his waistcoat.

She watched him come at her, her beautiful brown eyes wide and shining, her lips parted with a gentle smile of expectation. And it occurred to him that she was the most relaxed, openly sensual woman he had ever known. From the day she had first given herself to him, she had never been shy or hesitant with him. She wanted him with the same hot, unquenchable urgency that he wanted her, and she was never ashamed to show it. It seemed impossible to believe she was now his wife.

He tugged off his cravat and waistcoat, then opened the top button of his shirt as he knelt on the floor between her legs. He laid his hands on her knees and ran his fingers slowly, enticingly, up the outside of her thighs, over her hips, over the soft swell of his baby in her belly. He stopped with his palms resting on her ribs, his thumbs curling up to lie in the valley between her breasts.

She sucked in a quickly drawn breath. Her gaze held his fast. He could see the desire in the depths of her eyes, feel her body tremble beneath his touch, as if her breasts ached for his hands to close over them.

"I remember the first time I walked into this room and found you asleep beside the fire." He brushed his thumbs, ever so gently, against the sides of her breasts. She quivered.

"You looked like this. Your hair wild, all over your face, glowing like a sunset in the light of the fire. Your shift was open, your breasts bare. God, how I wanted you."

Her lips parted soundlessly.

"I wanted to put my hands on your breasts. Like this." He slid his palms up over her breasts, his fingers spread wide.

She was breathing hard and fast. He could feel her breasts rising and falling beneath his hands. Her eyes had taken on that glowing, heated look that always made him think of bed.

"I wanted to lay you down in front of the fire and take you, right then and there."

"I know," she whispered.

He smiled. "How did you know?"

She reached up and ran a finger across his cheekbone. "I could see it in your face. No, it's true," she said with a laugh as he shook his head in disbelief. "You get this look in your eyes. Sort of heavy-lidded and sleepy, yet somehow intense at the same time. And the rest of your face looks sharper, harder. Except for your mouth . . ." Her finger trailed down his cheek. "Your mouth gets full. Soft." She rubbed her finger across his lower lip. "Kissable. Like it is now."

He ran his tongue around the tip of her finger. "Kiss me now," he whispered, his hands leaving her breasts to slide around her back and ease her into his arms.

She brought her other hand up to cradle his face between her two palms. Leaning forward, she tipped her head to one side and brushed his lips, ever so lightly, with hers.

He went utterly still, waiting.

She drew her head back, but only enough so she could look into his eyes. Her face was solemn, her dark eyes glistening with emotion.

"I love you, Hayden."

It was so unexpected, he jerked. He opened his mouth, but she slipped the fingers of one hand across his lips, stopping whatever he was about to say. Which was a good thing, because he didn't know what to say.

To his surprise, a wry smile twisted her lips. "Don't look so scared, Hayden. You don't need to say anything. It's only that I've loved you for so long, and it's been so difficult, holding it inside. Before it would have been wrong to say it. But now . . . It's good for a woman to love her husband, isn't it?"

The shadow of a worried frown hovered between her brows. He pressed a kiss there. "You did promise to love and cherish me, remember?" he said, striving for a light tone. But the words were unfortunate, because they reminded him that he had repeated the same vow. Only, when he'd said it, he'd thought of loving her the way he loved her in bed every night with his body.

What he saw shining in her face now was more than that.

Her hands moved behind his head, drawing him forward to her until her lips hovered just beside his. "Kiss me," she whispered.

Her voice was low and husky beckoning him, seducing him. His lips parted, closed over hers. She gave a little mew and pressed against him. She wrapped her arms around his neck, her knees hugging his hips, her breasts flattening against his chest. He could feel her nipples through the fine linen of his shirt. He ran his hands down her sides, over her hips, up again, holding her to him as he slanted his mouth back and forth across hers.

The kiss grew more urgent. Roughened. His tongue slipped between her lips, took her mouth. He couldn't get enough of her. He was devouring her with his mouth, and still it wasn't enough.

He pulled away from her just long enough to snatch her chemise over her head so that he touched only bare skin as his hands coursed over her back, her shoulders, her arms, her breasts. She was his now. Not just his convict mistress, but his wife. His.

She would bear this child of his that she carried in her womb. And in the years to come he would plant more children within her. Sons, who would grow up strong, strong enough to carve their homes out of this great wilderness. And daughters. Daughters who would grow up beautiful and strong, too. Like their mother.

He gripped her hips tightly, holding her snug against him as he turned with her, lifting her away from the chair, easing her down before the hearth.

The gentle light from the fire turned the smooth skin of her bare arms and breasts a warm gold. She lay sprawled on her back, looking up at him with that tender, passionate smile he knew so well. He leaned over her, and she reached up to tug at his shirt. "Take it off," she said, her voice raw with need.

He sat back on his haunches, pulled the shirt from his breeches, and yanked it over his head without bothering to undo more than the top few buttons. He lowered his hands to his breeches, conscious of her watching him as he opened the flap. Easing back, he pulled off his boots and stockings, then shoved the breeches down over his hips, peeling them off. She never stopped looking at him.

"You're beautiful," she whispered, splaying her hands against his naked chest when he leaned over her. "You're so beautiful that sometimes just looking at you takes my breath away."

He laughed. "Men aren't beautiful."

She stared up at him with wide, serious eyes. "You are."

He smoothed her wildly curling hair away from her high forehead, and kissed her there. "*You're* beautiful," he said, propping himself up on one elbow. He trailed the back of his hand down her cheek and the side of her neck, down between her breasts, to lay his palm on her belly.

She moved to spread her hands self-consciously over her gently rounded stomach. "I'm getting fat."

He grinned down at her and pushed her hands away so he could flick open the buttons at the waist of her petticoat. "You're going to get even fatter still."

She lifted her buttocks as he slid her petticoat down over her thighs, his hands gliding softly over her bare skin.

"You don't mind?" she asked. There was an anxious note in her voice that surprised him.

He looked up from easing her stockings and slippers off her feet. "I think you're beautiful, Bryony," he said again. "You'll always be beautiful to me."

"Even like this? Growing big with child?"

"Especially like this."

He knelt between her legs and lay forward, half on her, so that his head just hovered over her breast, his warm, moist breath washing over her nipple.

His tongue flicked out, wetting her flesh. She jerked and made a soft, sighing sound. He laughed with satisfaction and lowered his lips to her breast, drawing her nipple into his mouth, sucking long and deep. Her shoulders arched off the floor as he brought his hand up to knead her other breast.

He was swollen hard with his desire for her, but he forced himself to take it easy. He must have made love to this woman several hundred times in the months since she'd become his mistress. But this was different. This was the first time they would come together as man and wife.

So he made love to her slowly, exquisitely, touching her everywhere, luxuriating in the feel, the smell, the taste of her, discovering anew this woman who was now his wife. He nibbled on her earlobe. Nuzzled her neck. Pressed his lips to the pulse that beat beneath her strong wrist. And when she was ready, almost begging for it, he slipped his hands beneath her bottom so he could lift her up to him as his tongue and lips did all the things he knew she loved best.

She plunged her fingers through his hair, holding him to her, her hips bucking up as she arched her back. He loved the noises she made. Breathy, erotic noises, her voice throbbing with pleasure and delight. Then his fingers replaced his tongue, parting her, plunging inside her, as he slid his body up to lay half on her, half beside her. He wanted to see her face as, her eyes closed, her head tipped back, he took her to that unfathomable point where tension and desire peak in an almost painful intensity, before exploding in waves of ecstasy and shattering fulfillment.

A knot of tenderness swelled within his chest as he watched her lips part, her body convulse with pleasure. Then she collapsed back, her eyes still closed, and he buried his face in her hair, breathed deeply of her sweet woman's scent.

"Hayden," she said as his mouth left hers to kiss her eyelids, her cheekbones, the tip of her nose. He eased himself inside her, holding himself up on his forearms so he could watch her expression as he filled her. Her face was suffused with tenderness. Passion. Love. The thought of it made him tremble, humbled him, made him want to give her something in return.

So he gave her his body. She wrapped her legs around his waist and dug her fingers into the muscles of his back and screamed as the deep, delicious tremors shuddered through her. It was all he could do to keep from exploding inside her, but somehow he controlled himself, giving her pleasure until finally, unable to hold back any longer, straining, desperate for release, he exploded inside her. He drove into her one last time, holding himself braced above her, his head thrown back, his eyes squeezed shut, his lips curled back over his teeth as his entire body convulsed.

He felt her hands on his sweat-slicked back. Opening

his eyes, he dropped his chin and looked at her. She was smiling, but her lips were trembling and her eyes were shining with what looked very much like tears.

He bent his head and brushed her mouth with his, lightly, tenderly. "What's wrong?" he asked, lifting his head so he could look at her again. "Why are you crying?"

She shook her head, smiling through her tears, and wrapped her arms around him, hugging him close. "I'm just happy, Hayden, that's all. I'm just so very happy."

He eased himself onto his side, his body still joined to hers, cradling her tightly against him. She turned into him, burying her face in his shoulder. With an oddly trembling hand, he reached up to run his fingers through her hair, smoothing the tangles, stroking her, comforting her.

He held her until their breathing eased and his heart stopped thundering. But a strange sense of awe lingered still, and he realized suddenly what it was.

Peace. And happiness.

"Bryony?" he said softly.

"Yes?" she murmured, her face still half buried in the curve of his neck.

"I'm glad you love me."

CHAPTER
TWENTY-SIX

They lingered in Sydney for several weeks. Hayden had a number of business interests that he'd had to neglect during the long, busy days of autumn and early winter at Jindabyne. He was out every day, talking to other settlers about bloodlines and wool prices, and to other shipowners about tariffs and import restrictions. Bryony visited the Government Store and ordered supplies for the homestead. And, at Hayden's insistence, she had some more new dresses made.

"But I have my wedding dress," she'd told him when he brought the subject up. "I don't need any new dresses."

At the time he'd been sitting on a low stool before the fire in their bedchamber at the inn while she moved quietly about the room, setting it to rights. Reaching out, he grabbed her hand and pulled her toward him until she was nestled between his spread thighs. "You will," he said with a grin, running his hand over her growing belly.

So she asked the seamstress who had made her wedding gown to visit her at the Three Jolly Fisherman once more. She visited the store again to inspect bolts of muslin and serge. And she suffered through the endless measurements, fittings, and comments about her *interesting situation.*

"I'm making the hem extra deep here in front," said the thin, gray-haired seamstress, kneeling at Bryony's feet with a mouthful of pins. "You'll probably need to let it down a bit when the babe starts showin'." She thrust another pin through the material. "And I've put some extra tucks in up at the top. Like as not, you'll need to let it out some there, too."

Bryony ran her hand down over her hip, smoothing the simple muslin she had chosen. In the past she had always felt uneasy, almost shamed every time Hayden bought her clothes. She'd expected it to be different now. Now that she was no longer his mistress, but his wife.

Yet the uneasiness remained, and she suspected it was more than a simple lingering of old, outdated attitudes. She was Hayden's wife. He had stood before God and the Reverend Richards and married her. She took his body into hers every night, and every day she grew bigger with his child. And yet . . .

And yet, in some elusive way, he was not hers. She hadn't even managed to talk to him about arranging to have Madeline brought out from Cornwall. Every time she thought about trying to bring the subject up, she found herself shying away from it, unwilling to be seen as making demands on him. Seeing herself as not in any position to make demands on him.

A shout from the street in front of the inn interrupted her thoughts. "Bryony!" Gideon's excited voice drifted up from somewhere out of sight below the window. "Bryony, come quick. It's here. It's here!"

Heedless of the scattering pins and the clucking seamstress, Bryony crossed to the front of the bedroom and threw open the casement window. "Gideon?" She leaned out to find the Irishman hopping impatiently from one foot to the other in the street below. He had one elbow cocked skyward, his hand clapping his cabbage-palm hat to his head to keep it from falling as he craned his neck to look up at her. The winter sunlight shone on a face so flooded with joy that Bryony laughed at the sight of him.

"What are you talking about?" she called. "What's here?"

"The *Lady Laura*. She's back! The Cap'n sent me to get you. He's down by the waterfront already."

"The *Laura*?" Bryony leaned out farther, straining to see the distant, sunstruck bay, where some half-dozen ships bobbed at anchor. She could just make out the wind-filled white sails of a merchantman, lifting and falling with the swell of the waves as it headed toward the cove. "Are you certain that's her?"

"Aye. She was seen sailin' through the Heads. She musta made grand time to get here so soon."

Bryony's gaze dropped to the Irishman's excited face. "And Mary and the boys? Are they on it?"

"I don't know yet. But my Mary, she'll be the first one off that ship, if she can be. Do come quick, Bryony. They'll be anchorin' in the cove any minute now."

"You go ahead," said Bryony, reaching for the tapes that held her new gown in the back. "I need to get out of this dress first. Tell the Captain I'll be down as soon as I can."

"I will," called Gideon over his shoulder.

He was already running toward the cove.

Some twenty minutes later Bryony joined the laughing, shouting crowds hurrying down to the sun-soaked docks. Gulls wheeled, screeching, overhead. A tow-headed, barefoot boy wearing nothing but a pair of cut-down overalls dashed past her, shouting, "Ship's in! It's the *Laura*."

She could see it now, already riding at anchor. Not a fat, old-fashioned Indiaman, but a sleek, well-built craft designed as much for speed as for carrying capacity. Its copper-clad hull rocked gently in the dancing, azure-blue waters of the cove, setting the three towering masts above to swinging lazily back and forth against the cloudless sky.

Bryony's gaze scanned the crowd, taking only an instant to search out the tall, lean figure of her husband. He stood some distance away, near the edge of the cobbled quay. He was talking to a man with a salt-stiffened gray beard and the spraddle-legged stance of a seaman. But at the sight of her, he nodded to the man beside him and came toward her.

A warm smile curled the edges of his lips and brought a gleam to his eyes as he wove his way through the knots of gawkers that clustered near the shoreline. "Have you seen her?" he asked as he came up beside her.

"The *Laura*?" Bryony returned his smile, her heart filling with love for him, as it always did, each time she saw him. "Yes, she's lovely."

He laughed. "No, I didn't mean the ship." He took Bryony's hand and drew her to where Gideon stood at the water's edge. "Come see."

Gideon had his hand up, shading his eyes from the glare off the water as he watched the *Laura*'s long boat being loaded. He suddenly let out a joyful whoop and tore off his cabbage palm hat to toss it high in the air. "They're here!" He flung both his arms around Bryony and whirled her around in a circle until she felt giddy. "They're here."

He released her to leap onto the dock and do a little jig that brought him so close to the edge, Bryony was afraid for a minute he was going to tumble into the bay. "There's my Mary. And the two boys, both of them." His voice broke with emotion, and he went still again, staring off across the water. "Ah, Bryony. Will you just look at the size of them?"

The salty sea breeze tugged at Bryony's hair, sending a loose strand flying across her face. She reached up to tuck it behind her ear and sucked in a quick, deep breath as her gaze riveted on the boat being slowly rowed toward the dock.

The laughter and shouting of the crowd seemed to retreat into the distance, along with the cries of the gulls and the splash of the oars from the boat.

A stout, pleasant-looking woman with plaits wrapped around her plump, smiling face sat in the center of the boat. She was flanked by two boys with freckles and ears that stuck out from their heads like flags from a flagpole on a windy day. Both boys were smiling and waving like their mother. But on her lap, Mary Shanaghan held a little girl. A little girl with guinea-gold hair who wasn't waving at all.

"Madeline," Bryony whispered. She reached out almost blindly, and found herself clutching the lapels of Hayden's coat. Her startled gaze flew to his warm, smiling eyes. "God, Hayden," she said, her voice little more than a husky whisper. "You sent for Madeline."

"Yes," he said simply, sliding his hands around her waist to steady her.

She pressed her cheek against his broad chest and hugged him to her. "Why didn't you tell me?"

Hayden laughed. "I had the devil of a time keeping it to myself. But I couldn't be sure your uncle would let her come, and I didn't want to get your hopes up only to have you disappointed if the *Laura* came back without her."

Her face still buried against his chest, Bryony shook her head back and forth. "Uncle Edward never really wanted to take Madeline. He only did it out of a sense of duty, because there was no other option. I'm sure he jumped at the chance to rid himself of my daughter. But . . ." She tilted back her head and searched his face. "You must have sent for her last spring, before I—before we—" She swallowed hard. "Why did you do it?"

He cupped her cheek with his lean, strong hand. "To make you happy, Bryony. I've always wanted to make you happy."

Her love for him was so great, it seemed to choke her. "You have made me happy."

He didn't say anything. But she saw something leap in his eyes, something warm and tender. Then he looked away and nodded toward the approaching boat. "They're almost ready to land."

Bryony whirled around, picked up the long skirt of her dress with both hands, and ran. *"Madeline,"* she called, over and over again as she flew down the dock. She stumbled over an uneven plank on the rough decking, but her gaze never wavered from that stiff little figure in the boat. "Madeline!" she cried. "Oh, dear Lord, Madeline."

She ran out of dock. She stood on the end of the pier, trembling, anxious, watching as the child she'd feared she'd never see again was slowly rowed toward her. Tears of joy rolled down her cheeks unchecked as she waved her arms wildly back and forth above her head in greeting.

Then her arms fell slowly back to her sides, and her breath came whistling from between her lips as the joyous smile faded from her face. For Madeline sat unmoving on Mary Shanaghan's lap, staring at her without any emotion on her face. No emotion at all.

The boat knocked against the side of the dock and a seaman jumped out. Bryony stood where she was, a painful swirl of feelings raging within her as she watched a sailor lift the solemn-faced little girl from the boat and set her on the dock.

Bryony knelt down on the weathered planks, her heart in her throat, her hungry gaze roaming ravenously over the child who walked up and planted herself in front of her mother.

This was not, she realized with a swift pang, the Madeline she'd held, cherished, in her memory. Gone was the winsome, laughing toddler who had played in the foaming surf of Cadgwith Cove. Gone, too, was the thin, forlorn three-year-old who'd clung so desperately to her mother in the prison in Penzance.

The Madeline standing so rigid and wary on the Sydney docks was older, older by far more than the year and a half that had passed since Bryony had last seen her. Her face was painfully serious, not the face of a child at all. There was an air of cold aloofness about her that was terrible to see in one so young.

She cocked her head to one side and regarded Bryony appraisingly. "Mrs. Shanaghan tells me that you're my mother."

It was all Bryony could do to hold her hands clenched

into fists at her sides, when she wanted so desperately to clutch this unhappy, beloved child to her breast. But she knew from the stiff, unwelcoming slant of Madeline's shoulders that to give way to that impulse now would be a terrible mistake.

So she smiled a tremulous smile, which was all she could manage. "Yes, Madeline. I am your mother."

The fierce expression did not alter. "Mrs. Shanaghan says that some mean people took you away from me, and that you didn't want to leave me because you love me very much."

Bryony's face crumpled. Her trembling hands reached out for her little girl, stopping just short of touching her. "Oh, I do, Madeline. I love you so very much. And I've missed you! I can't tell you how much I've missed you."

The child's eyes narrowed with a suspicion and anger that deepened the anguish within Bryony in a way she hadn't thought possible. "Then, why didn't you come back for me? I waited and waited, but you never came."

How could she explain? Bryony thought desperately. How could she possibly explain to this determinedly tough little stranger, with her adult-size hurt and her child's naive vision of the world as someplace where things like ability didn't figure, only *want* and *will*.

Bryony swallowed hard, and even then her voice cracked when she answered. "I wanted to come. Truly I did. But I couldn't, sweetheart. They wouldn't let me." Unable to hold herself back any longer, Bryony reached out and let her fingers gently stroke the fine, golden hair that tumbled over Madeline's shoulders.

The child jerked back, away from Bryony's touch. "I don't believe you," she shouted. She was shivering now with barely suppressed emotion, her hands curling into two fists at her sides. "If you had wanted to come, you would have."

"Madeline, no—"

Bryony would have reached for her again, but Hayden's hands closed in a gentle warning on her shoulders, stopping her. She could feel him behind her, warm and comforting. But inside . . . Inside, some very important part of her felt as if it were dying.

Slowly, shakily, Bryony rose to her feet. Hayden's strong arm came around her waist, silently supporting her. She thought if it weren't for him, she might have collapsed.

"Mrs. Shanaghan says I have to go with you." Madeline's chin quivered, but her eyes were painfully dry as she stared up at Bryony. "Only, I don't want to. I want to go with her and Patrick and Sean."

A pain that was like nothing she'd ever known pierced Bryony, striking her to her core. She could not breathe. She had known pain before; the devastating, blinding, smashing pain of loss. But not this. Not this *hurt*. It was too much. Too much pain, coming on top of the rapturous, unexpected joy that had thrilled through her just a few minutes before.

She glanced wildly to where Gideon knelt on the dock, one arm wrapped around each small son, his eyes squeezed shut in joyful thanksgiving. Over his head her pain-filled eyes met the troubled gaze of Mary Shanaghan, and held it.

"Sure then, Madeline," said Mary Shanaghan soothingly. "Didn't I say we'd all be goin' to Jindabyne together?"

"I don't want to go with her at all! Never!" wailed Madeline. Whirling about, she flung herself against Mary Shanaghan's apron.

Before Bryony could stop it, a low, keening moan escaped from her lips. Hayden pulled her back against the solid line of his body and pressed a kiss on the top of her head.

"She'll come around, Bryony," he said, his voice oddly strained. "It's going to take time, but it will happen. You must believe that."

She turned within his arms and buried her tear-streaked face against his chest. "What have I done to her? What have I done?"

They went back to Jindabyne two days later.

All the way up the coast and into the mouth of the river, Gideon Shanaghan's two boys scampered about the sloop, dodged busy seamen, and exclaimed excitedly each time they spied a stray kangaroo, or whenever a great, noisy flock of cockatoos took to the sky.

But Madeline stood quiet and aloof beside the railing, her sturdy little body stiff and still as she gazed out over the long, golden beaches and exotic, olive-green stands of eucalypti slowly slipping past. Bryony tried to talk to her about New South Wales, about the homestead on the Hawkesbury that was now their home. Madeline listened to her with wide, blank eyes, and said nothing.

It was a solemn homecoming.

Bryony stood on the veranda, watching Madeline and the two Shanaghan boys play chase around the men's huts.

It was only at moments like this, when Madeline was with the Shanaghans, that the child seemed to relax. For an all-too-brief instant, the hard, protective shell she wrapped around herself would crack, and Bryony would catch distant, tantalizing glimpses of the child Madeline once had been.

Madeline laughed as Patrick tagged her, and a fierce, howling kind of loneliness suddenly caught at Bryony, shocking her, shaming her. It was wrong, this desperate longing that sometimes came over her. She should have been content with what she had—her daughter once more beside her, a home, a husband she loved with an intensity that transcended life itself.

She sucked in a deep breath and forced herself to look back on the blackest days of her despair, when she'd been bereft of everything a human being stood to lose.

She knew how lucky she was now. But that unfilled need within her remained, desperate and frightening.

A spur rasped across the stone flagging of the veranda, and Hayden's arm came around her waist, pulling her up against the warm, hard line of his body. She clutched at his arm, holding onto him, wanting him, wanting him to want her and love her the way she loved him.

"She seems happy," he said, nodding to where Madeline stood with her arms braced against a slab hut, her face buried in the crook of her elbow as she chanted: *four, five, six—*

"When she's not with me, yes." Bryony leaned against him with a sigh.

There was a brief pause. Then he said, "Bryony—"

"I know," she said quickly. "I know it's only been a few weeks. It's just that I . . ." She found she had to swallow hard before she could continue. "I'm so terribly afraid she's never going to forgive me. That I'm never going to get back what she and I had before."

Nine, ten. Ready or not, here I come.

Together they watched the children run, laughing, toward the far end of the yard. "I think maybe part of the problem is me," he said thoughtfully.

She twisted her head so she could look up at him. His brows were drawn together, his eyes dark and serious with concern for her. She suddenly felt ashamed of herself. Ashamed of that earlier rush of loneliness and fear that seemed now more like a weak indulgence in self-pity than anything else. "What do you mean?" she asked him, staring up at his lean, handsome face.

His eyes narrowed, his attention still focused on the distant children. "I think she resents me. Resents me being with you." He rubbed his hand down Bryony's hip, then back up in a lazy caress. "Has Madeline ever said anything to you about her father?"

Bryony thought about it. "No."

"Don't you find that strange?"

A cold wind, blowing up from the icy regions of the

south hit them with a blast of damp, frigid air. "She knows he's dead," Bryony said.

"Yes. But they told her you were dead, remember? You turned out to be alive. Maybe she expected to find Oliver here, too. Maybe she's angry because I'm here instead."

"But Oliver is dead. You're my husband now."

Hayden's hand slid around to come to rest against the swell of her belly. "She's not even five yet, Bryony. It's a lot to ask her to try to understand how we all fit together. You, Oliver, me, her, Simon, the baby you're carrying."

Bryony pressed both her palms against Hayden's strong, tanned hand. He brought his other arm up and hugged her against him. She felt him kiss her hair, just above her ear, and her love for him swelled within her. Not hot and urgent and desperate, the way it usually was; but gentle and comforting, warm and calming.

Warm enough to thaw the chill of loneliness in her soul. And calming enough to soothe the fear in her heart.

For a while.

July turned into August, and an unusually bitter cold settled on the Hawkesbury. Rain fell incessantly. The men cursed the clouds and worried about the crops. The women sighed and tried to dry the washing in front of fires that burned sluggishly on their hearths.

And Hayden ordered the station's bricklayer to build an indoor oven for Bryony.

It was midway through the morning, while he was in the kitchen checking on the progress of the construction, that Madeline confronted him.

"What are you building?" she asked. She came no closer than the open doorway. Her voice was hostile rather than curious, and when he turned to look at her, he saw undisguised animosity spill across her face before she shut it off, hiding behind that blank stare that so worried her mother.

The winter light was flat, the air damp and filled with

the pungent scent of wood smoke. She was wearing sturdy leather boots and a thick red wool cloak that flapped in the cold breeze. But the pinched, miserable look about her face had nothing to do with the cold. Her hair fluttered loose about her shoulders, fine silken hair the color of a gold guinea. Oliver's hair had been like that, Bryony had told him. But the child's eyes were a deep, earthy brown, and her long, graceful neck and strong jaw were all Bryony.

He felt a tug of compassion for this forlorn, lost child. Compassion, and something else. Something that owed its existence to the way he felt about her mother. He nodded to the bricklayer, and walked toward her.

"It's an oven," he said, pausing in the doorway. She retreated a few steps, out into the yard, then stood her ground. "Your mama wants a proper oven, so she can bake real bread and cakes and pies. Do you like pies?"

She didn't answer him, just stared at him with those wide, disturbing brown eyes. After a moment she jerked her chin at the brick building behind him and said, "Why is the kitchen out here, instead of in the house where it belongs?"

Hayden propped his foot up on the section of log that served as a rough stool. "Two reasons, really. First of all, it gets so hot around here in the summer, you wouldn't want anything adding to the heat in the house. And then we need to worry about things catching fire. It's much safer to keep the kitchen away from the main house."

She turned half away from him, and he thought she was going to leave without saying anything more. Then she spun back around and pinned him with a fierce frown. "Mama told me she has your baby in her tummy."

He was so surprised his foot slipped off the stool. He straightened up and returned her intense regard. "Yes, she does."

"My mama's other baby had the same papa I did. His name was Philip."

"That's right." Hayden was beginning to feel dangerously out of his depth. He glanced toward the house. Bryony was nowhere in sight.

"He died," said Madeline.

Hayden wasn't sure if she was referring to the baby, or her father. "Yes, he did," he answered noncommittally. "I'm sorry."

"I remember my papa. He used to read me stories and take me with him when he went down to the village."

"He sounds like a nice father." It didn't square with what Bryony had told him about Oliver Wentworth, but perhaps it was better that Madeline remember him as she wished he'd been, rather than as he was.

There was a sudden explosion of fury and movement as Madeline hurled herself against him. She caught him off guard, her tight little fists flailing against the hard ridges of his stomach as she screamed at him over and over again, "I don't want you for my papa. I want my own papa back."

He tried to put his arms around her thin, trembling shoulders, to comfort her. She reared back, unwilling to let him touch her.

She was breathing hard and fast. The cold wind caught her red cloak and billowed it out behind her. She snatched at it, hugged it close. They stared at each other for a frozen moment. Then she sucked in a deep breath and said, "I wish you were dead instead." Her voice ended on a strangled sob. She whirled around, heading for the house.

The French doors from the dining room opened, and Bryony stepped out onto the veranda, holding Simon by the hand. At the sight of her mother, Madeline's step faltered for only an instant before veering off toward the hut Hayden had given to the Shanaghans.

Even across the span of the muddy yard, Hayden could see the hurt that crumpled Bryony's face as she watched Madeline change direction and run away from her. She watched the child until Madeline had disappeared into the hut, the door banging shut behind her.

Bryony's gaze swung back to him. He saw her breasts heave as she sucked in a deep breath. Hot anger swept through him, seeing her suffer, guessing at how much more she suffered than she let him see. But it was a directionless rage, for what he felt toward Madeline was a kind of helpless, gut-wrenching compassion that left no room for anger.

She turned away from him and stooped to sweep Simon up into her arms. He watched her hug his child close, watched her struggle to hide her pain. And he knew that he would never tell her about those furious words of hatred Madeline had just hurled at him. Or about the deep, disturbing trauma they hinted at.

Time. He kept telling Bryony the child needed time. Time to grow accustomed, time to heal.

Only there were some things no amount of time could heal. And he was suddenly very much afraid that maybe this was one of them.

It was a week later when the stranger rode into the yard.

The day was unusually fine, the air cold but clear, the sky a deep, cobalt-blue. Hayden was working with some of the men, rebuilding a section of fence down by the barn. Bryony, Mary Shanaghan, and Ann McBride had loaded all the children and an enormous pile of laundry into the cart and disappeared toward the river.

Hayden paused, his elbows resting on the top rail of the fence, and watched the rider rein in and take stock of his surroundings.

He was a gentleman, of average height and build, mounted on a showy chestnut. His bottle-green coat was of an inimitable cut that could only have come from one of the best tailors in London. His cravat was meticulously tied, his gleaming Hessians sported white tops and tassels. Except for the mud that splattered the chestnut's legs clear up to its flanks, he might have been a Town Beau, out for a trot in Hyde Park.

A cold wind flattened Hayden's shirt against his

sweaty body. He climbed through the rails of the fence and strolled toward the stranger. "May I help you?"

The man's head swung around. He was young, Hayden noticed, probably in his mid-twenties. A handsome man, with delicately chiseled features and a head of guinea-colored curls.

"I'm looking for Hayden St. John." The voice was cultured, educated. A gentleman's voice, with the vaguest hint of a Cornish burr.

Hayden came to a halt some ten feet from the horseman and stood with his legs spread wide, his hands on his hips as he eyed the man before him. His gaze settled on those guinea-gold curls, and a strange tremor of disquiet shimmied through him.

"I am St. John."

The man's eyes widened in a quickly hidden start of surprise. The work in the paddock was dirty, and Hayden had long since tossed aside his coat and neck cloth. The quality of his waistcoat, shirt and breeches might be finer than the rough convict garb of his men, but there was a smear of mud across his chest, and a rent in his sleeve that Bryony would need to mend.

Bryony . . .

The stranger swung down out of the saddle. The two men stared at each other across the space of ten feet that separated them. From somewhere on the hill above the homestead, a kookaburra laughed, its call long and guttural and oddly mocking.

"My name is Wentworth," said the stranger. "Oliver Wentworth. I understand my wife is here."

CHAPTER
TWENTY-SEVEN

The laundry cart bumped and swayed over the rough, grassy track that led from the river up to the house. Bryony splayed her feet wide, trying to keep her balance on the hard board seat and still stop Simon from climbing out of her arms. The sun was out, bright but distant, leaving the air crisp and fresh enough to bring a healthy red glow to the children's cheeks.

"You're supposed to miss the ruts in the road, Mama," said Patrick Shanaghan after a particularly rough jolt knocked his hat flying. "Not aim for them."

His mother, holding the reins in her broad, capable hands, snorted. " 'Tes no road, this, Patrick me lad. This, 'tes nothin' but a *collection* of ruts." Bryony heard Madeline giggle, and turned her head in time to catch the child's smile.

Bryony smiled herself. A rare glow of peace and happiness seeped through her. Tipping back her head, she watched a band of thin white clouds scuttle across the sparkling sky above. There was something both timeless and extraordinarily soothing about moments such as these, she thought. Women working together while their children laughed and played. The sweet, heart-lifting chirping of birds filling the high branches of the trees. The deep, swift rush of a rain-swollen river curling around the bottom of the hill.

"Looks like the Captain's got a visitor," said Ann McBride, raising an arm to shade her face against the glare of the sun.

Bryony's head snapped around, but she caught only a quick glimpse of a man swinging down from a horse before the cart moved behind the store, hiding the lower end of the yard from sight. "Oh no," she murmured, one hand flying up in a probably futile attempt to shove her hair back up under her cap. *Visitors.* And here she was wearing her old gray work dress and servant's cap.

They pulled up in the sun beside the barn, and Bryony handed Simon to Ann McBride. "I wish there was some way I could get to the house without being seen," she whispered to Mary as she hopped off the cart.

Mary eyed Bryony's water-stained gown and grinned. "Sure then, you look more like a scullery maid than the master's wife." She nodded toward the yard. "And och, that's a fine gentleman what's come callin'."

Bryony started to laugh. Then her gaze fell on the two men facing each other in the yard, and the laughter died on her lips.

Hayden stood with his legs braced in that way he had, his hands on his lean hips, his fingers toying with the hilt of the knife he wore strapped to his thigh. His back was to her. She could not see his face.

Beside him, the other man looked slight. He wore a well-cut coat and a fashionable, curly brimmed beaver pulled down low on his forehead. He was turned half away from her, but there was something familiar about the way he held his head, about the way he moved . . .

Bryony's heart began to beat in slow, heavy lurches. "Mary," she said in a quick low voice to the other woman. "Mary, get Madeline away from here. Get her away from here fast, and keep her away."

Mary Shanaghan gave Bryony a puzzled look, but moved quickly to do as she'd asked.

Bryony walked toward the middle of the yard, her fingers entwined before her, her limbs moving stiffly, as if she were old, or ill. The stranger turned. Sunlight flashed on gold curls, limned a face so classically perfect in its features that a woman might stop in the street, just to look at him.

"Oliver..."

It was only a whisper, more like a startled exhalation of breath. She stumbled to a halt, unable to think, unable even to breathe. A cool wind whipped at the hem of her skirt and rustled the eucalyptus trees on the hill behind the house. The air was heavy with the smell of lemon gums and newly sown fields—the smells of Australia. She stared at the man who in another time, another place, had been her husband. Who was still, God help her, her husband. And all she could think was: *It's not possible. It cannot be.*

Oliver. Oliver was *alive*. God in heaven, she hadn't killed him. And if she hadn't killed him, then that meant she was a free woman.

Grateful, heart-lifting joy flooded through her, followed swiftly by a dismay so deep and terrifying she thought she might die from it. Her gaze flew to Hayden. She felt as if something slammed into her stomach, almost doubling her over in physical agony as she realized that she could lose him. He was her husband, she carried his unborn child within her, but she could lose him. Because her husband, her *other* husband, was alive. *God*, she whispered. *Oh, God. No.*

"Bryony?" Oliver stepped toward her. He had a worried look on his face, as if he were not quite sure how she would react to seeing him.

She stared at his once-familiar features, and felt ... nothing. "Oliver." She tried to smile at him, but couldn't. "Oliver, you're alive."

He laughed. "Is that the way you greet a husband you haven't seen in two years?" He pulled her into his arms and brought his mouth down on hers in a wet, intimate kiss.

She pressed her hands against his chest and wrenched her head away. "Oliver, please." She stared at him. "How can this be? Where have you been?"

He let go and stepped back. "Where have I been?" he

repeated, his brows drawing together in the beginnings of a frown.

She glanced quickly at Hayden and found him regarding her with an intense, questioning look. He pulled a cheroot from his waistcoat pocket and stuck it between his teeth. "As I understand it," Hayden said, all his attention seemingly focused on lighting his cigar, "Bryony was transported for killing her husband." He exhaled a cloud of white smoke before lifting his cold blue eyes to Oliver's face. "So why aren't you dead?"

"I practically was, thanks to my lovely wife here." The words were said with a lopsided, seemingly humorous smile, but Bryony felt herself blanch. She'd forgotten how casually cruel Oliver could be. "The crew of a French ship hovering off the coast happened to spot me just about the time I thought I couldn't hold on any longer. They pulled me out."

"You've been in France?" she asked. "As a prisoner?"

Oliver returned her intense stare. "There is a war on, remember?"

Bryony felt a lump rise in her throat. She could always tell when Oliver was lying. No, not always, she reminded herself, not at first. But it hadn't taken her long to learn the little signs that gave him away. The almost imperceptible, nervous tug at his lips. The way he made it a point to stare straight into her eyes, as if daring her to disbelieve him. She supposed it was one of the reasons why he'd lost so much money in gaming halls over the years. That classically beautiful face was simply too easy to read.

"When did they let you go, Oliver?" Bryony asked quietly.

He thrust his jaw forward, his voice rising with the threat of righteous indignation that was his usual response whenever she questioned him. "What the hell difference does that make?"

"It makes a big difference, when you disappear for two years and I'm transported for killing you."

He sighed. "Bryony, I came as soon as I could. By the time I got back to Cornwall, you had already been deported. It wasn't as easy as you might think to have your conviction officially overturned, or to secure all the paperwork I needed to guarantee your release."

"You have it, of course," Hayden said.

She saw Oliver's gaze flicker from her to Hayden, then back again. "Of course."

Her release. A thrill of excitement shot through Bryony. Freedom. Not just a ticket-of-leave, with all its restrictions and the ever present danger of accidental forfeiture, but real freedom. She was almost afraid to believe it.

Oliver reached inside his coat and produced several sheets of parchment, folded together. "I assure you, everything is in order." He held the papers out, not to her, but to Hayden. "So it looks as if you'll be needing to get yourself a new servant," he added as Hayden leafed through the documents. "And a new whore."

Hayden's head snapped back. Bryony saw his eyes narrow dangerously. Quietly, carefully, he folded her papers and slipped them into his pocket.

"You think I don't know what you've been doing to her?" Oliver sneered, his nostrils quivering with disdain, with disgust. "I might have been in this godforsaken colony only a few days, but it's long enough to have heard what goes on here." He seized Bryony's arm, his gaze raking her, his face darkening with rage as he focused on her swollen belly. "Look at you," he spat at her in disgust. "He didn't just crawl between your legs. He planted his bastard on you!"

"Let her go." Cold and deadly as a saber slash, Hayden's voice sliced through Oliver's ugly torrent of words. "Shut your filthy mouth and take your hands off her."

Oliver threw back his head, his lip curling. "She's my *wife*, damn you. If I want to, I can bloody well *beat her*, and you—"

Hayden's fist caught Oliver just under the chin, lifting him up and sending him spilling backward onto the cobbles.

"She might have been your wife in the past, you bastard. But she isn't anymore. She's mine now. And if you ever lay a hand on her again, I swear to God, I'll kill you."

Oliver sat up. His fingers splayed against his chin, he opened and closed his jaw a few times, then reached to pick up the beaver hat that had landed beside him. Only then did he tip back his head and look up at the man who loomed over him.

"Her conviction has been overturned," said Oliver, enunciating the words carefully, as if he thought Hayden might not have understood clearly. "Whether you like it or not, she is not your servant anymore."

"My servant?" Hayden repeated incredulously. "She hasn't been my servant for months. *She's my wife.*"

"Wife?" Oliver gave a sudden, harsh laugh, his gaze flicking back to Bryony. "You didn't waste any time, did you, Madame Widow?"

Oh, yes, she had forgotten how mean Oliver could be.

"Only, you're not a widow, *Mrs. Wentworth.*" He settled his hat on his head. "You're married to *me.*" He stood up, his gaze raking the yard. "Where is Madeline? Get her."

For the first time Bryony noticed the men who stood, silent and watchful, outside their huts, down by the barns, in the door of the stables. Ann McBride was on the veranda, Simon still clutched in her arms. Only Mary Shanaghan and Madeline seemed to have disappeared.

Oliver brought his gaze back to her. There was a tight, unpleasant set to his lips that Bryony had never seen there before, and she thought that in some way the last two years had changed him, changed him a great deal. "Did you hear me, damn it? I said get her. We're leaving." He reached to seize Bryony's arm.

He never touched her. Hayden's fists closed around the

lapels of Oliver's impeccably tailored bottle-green coat and yanked the younger man almost off his feet.

"I told you to keep your hands off her." Hayden's voice was low and frighteningly even, and there was a gleam in his eyes that Bryony had never seen before.

This is a man who can kill, she thought. Who *has* killed.

"Now, I'm going to let go of you, and you're going to get back on that horse of yours and ride out of here. Is that understood?"

One thing Oliver had never been, was a coward. Hayden might be larger and stronger and infinitely more skilled in the art of fighting, whether formal or dirty. But Oliver refused to cringe. He met the wintry frost of Hayden's eyes, and said, "I'll leave."

Hayden's fists opened. He took a step backward.

With fastidious care, Oliver shook out his coat and straightened his neck cloth. "I'll leave," he said again. He seized the chestnut's reins and swung up into the saddle. "But I'm only going as far as Green Hills. I'll be back. With a magistrate and troops, if necessary." He wrenched the chestnut's head around but paused a moment to look at Bryony over his shoulder. "You and Madeline are returning to Cornwall with me, Bryony. Willingly or not." Then he dug his heels into the chestnut's ribs and cantered away.

It was cold in the house, cold and quiet. The feeble warmth of the winter sunlight hadn't penetrated the thick walls. Hayden hunkered down before the fireplace in their bedroom, using an iron poker to stir the coals left from that morning. Bryony stood some distance away, staring blankly at the far wall and hugging herself. Except for one hand that kept running up and down, up and down her opposite arm, she was motionless.

He glanced at her again. She hadn't moved, hadn't looked at him, hadn't said a word. "Say something, damn it."

It came out louder and harsher than he'd intended. Her hand stopped its restless journey. She glanced at him, then away. *Why?* he wanted to shout. Why wouldn't she look at him? She couldn't possibly be wondering what *he* wanted, could she?

"What are we going to do?" she asked quietly.

He laid the poker on the hearth and reached for a fistful of kindling. His heart was wedged up somewhere near his throat, but he had to ask, had to know where he really stood with her. "That depends largely on what you want, doesn't it?"

"Hayden."

He heard the hurt in her voice, and was ashamed to discover he was glad of it. He remembered a night, long ago, when he had stood on the edge of his veranda, admiring the curve of her cheek bathed in the glow of moonlight and wanting so very much to take her into his arms and into his bed. *Did you love him very much?* he had asked. *I loved him,* she'd answered. The memory of it was like something twisting in his vitals. Something sharp and painful.

He threw the kindling into the fireplace and watched it burst suddenly into flame. There was obviously more heat left in the coals than he had thought. He hefted a small log and balanced it with one hand, his gaze swiveling back to the woman standing as if she were frozen in the middle of the room. He had to ask, had to know. "I thought you might be glad to see him."

"I am glad to see he is still alive." She took off her old cap and dropped it on a nearby chest. "I'm glad that I will no longer have to carry the burden of thinking I killed him." She raked her fingers through her hair. "But that doesn't mean I'm glad to see him."

Hayden tossed the log on the fire, sending a shower of sparks shooting up the chimney. "Is there a difference?"

He saw her eyes narrow in a quick, almost angry frown. "What are you asking me? If I am happy at the thought of him coming here to take me away?"

"Yes. That's what I'm asking." He braced his hands on his knees and looked at her. Dread surged through him, pounded through him, making his chest ache and almost robbing him of breath, but he had to say it. "You're free, Bryony. Free to leave here. Free to go back to Cornwall the way you've always wanted. You don't need me."

He watched her lips part, then close again as she swallowed. For a long moment they simply stared at each other. "Should that change things?"

"Doesn't it?"

An eternity passed while he waited for her answer. Her brows drew together, and he saw her chest rise on a quickly indrawn breath. "For me, or for you?"

"For Christ's sake!" He pushed to his feet and faced her with his arms hanging loose at his sides. *"For you."*

She shook her head once, an odd smile playing at the edges of her lips. "Hayden, what I want hasn't changed." She walked right up to him until she was close enough to lay her hands high on his chest and stare deep into his eyes. *"I love you.* I want to be your wife. I want to stay here and help you make a home in this wild, wonderful place. A home for you and me and Simon and Madeline and this baby, and for all the other babies we talked about having."

Her hands slipped down to grip his upper arms. She tilted her head to one side and searched his face intently, her eyes dark with something he thought might be fear. "That's what I want, Hayden." She swallowed, her gaze still fixed to his face. "Now, you tell me what you want."

He dipped his head until his mouth brushed hers, his lips open, trembling. Then he rested his forehead against hers and squeezed his eyes shut. "How can you not know what I want?" His voice was hoarse, strained. He speared his fingers through her hair, rubbed his thumbs across her cheeks. "How can you not know?"

She searched his face. He saw a glimmer of wetness on her lashes and realized it was tears. "We talk a lot, you and I," she said softly. "But there have always been some things we've never talked about. Some things we are always very careful not to talk about." A band of color stained her wide, high cheekbones, and her gaze dropped.

He molded his hands to the back of her head, shifting his thumbs beneath her chin to lift her head so that she stared into his eyes again. Their faces were only inches apart. Their warm breath mingled. "Bryony . . ."

She waited, utterly still, for what he was going to say.

"*I love you*, Bryony. I know I should have said it before, but you must believe me now when I tell you I've never loved any woman the way I love you. No, listen," he said quickly when she made a small, startled movement of denial. "I know you're thinking about Laura, but don't. I loved Laura, but there was always something missing between us, something missing from my life when I was with her. Whereas with you . . ." He tightened his fist in her hair, his gaze intent on her face as he searched for the right words to say. "With you, nothing is missing. But if I lose you . . ." His voice broke. He rubbed his thumb back and forth across her lower lip, but he still couldn't bring himself to finish the thought. Finally he drew in a deep, shaky breath and said, "I can't lose you, Bryony. Whatever I have to do, I'm not letting Oliver Wentworth or anyone else take you away from me."

She buried her face in his shoulder, her hands gripping his waist so tightly she shuddered. "God help us, Hayden . . . Can Oliver do it? Can he force me to go back to him?"

"If we hadn't married, probably." He stroked his hands up and down her back, feeling her flesh warm and solid beneath his touch. "As it is . . . I'm not so sure."

"But our marriage isn't legal," she whispered, her face still buried in his shirt. "It's . . ." He heard the horror in her voice. "It's bigamous."

He shook his head. "No, I don't think so." Wrapping

his hands around her arms, he drew her back so he could look down into her face. "Oliver was declared dead, Bryony. That must make a difference."

Her eyes were huge, full of fear and love and consternation. He wondered how he could ever have doubted her, how he could ever have questioned what she wanted.

"And if it doesn't make a difference?" she asked.

He almost said, *Then I'll kill the bastard myself,* but he didn't. Instead he pulled her into his arms again, so she wouldn't see his face. "We'll fight this, Bryony. I'm not letting him take you."

She laid her cheek against his breast. "What I don't understand is why he even wants me. It's not like Oliver to take back a wife that other men have . . . touched. Let alone come all the way out here to New South Wales himself to get me. How could he even *afford* it?"

Hayden rested his chin on the top of her head. "He didn't look like a man on the verge of being imprisoned for debt, did he? I wonder what he's really been up to the last two years?"

Bryony tilted back her head to look up at him. "What do you mean?"

"I mean, I don't think he was picked up by a French naval ship. Smugglers would be more likely. And if he did fall in with smugglers, it would explain both what he's been doing for the last two years, and why he's suddenly in funds again, wouldn't it?"

"Yes, it would. But it doesn't explain why he wants me back."

"I think there's only one way we're going to find out the truth about that," said Hayden, setting his jaw.

A shade of anxiety passed across her face. "What are you going to do?"

"Tomorrow morning, I am going into town to have a talk with Mr. Oliver Wentworth. I'll get the answers out of him. Whether he wants to give them to me or not."

* * *

Quincy slipped the bit into the mare's mouth, then glanced at Bryony over the horse's back as he led the reins through the check rings. "You sure the Cap'n knows you're goin' into Green Hills?"

Bryony kept her gaze firmly fixed on her own hands as she eased her gloves over her fingers. "Of course he does. Do you think I would be going if he did not?"

"Yes."

She met Quincy's knowing brown eyes and let out a puff of breath. "All right. He doesn't know. He's planning to go into Green Hills himself in the morning."

"And yer goin' in this afternoon instead, because yer afraid if he gets his hands on that husband of yers again, he'll kill him."

Bryony nodded. "Maybe if I can see Oliver this afternoon—talk to him calmly, explain things—he'll agree to leave us alone." She threw an anxious glance toward the river, where Hayden had taken some of the men to move stock away from the low ground. A wild, ugly storm had been hovering over the mountains for days now, and Hayden was worried about a flash flood.

"Hurry, Quincy. Someone might come by and see us and mention it to the Captain."

Quincy checked the harness. "It'll probably be dark before we get back. You do know that, don't you?" He turned to squint up at the distant cloud-shrouded peaks. "And if that storm decides to move down the valley—"

"*Quincy.*"

"All right, all right," he muttered. "I'm ready."

Perched high beside the riverbank, the Buckingham Arms Hotel in Green Hills was a pitiful, single-story colonial structure with an awkward-looking veranda tacked on across the front.

Oliver stood gazing out the narrow, double glass doors that opened from his room directly onto the veranda. Just a few steps beyond the hotel, the rough track of red mud that passed as a street ended. A jumble of gray, weathered wood formed a crude combination ramp and steps that led down the steep bank to the jetty and the river.

Oliver's nostrils quivered with distaste. An untidy wilderness, this, he thought, staring out beyond the struggling, primitive village to the coarse fields and rough bushland beyond. Winter lay heavy and wet upon the land, yet everything still seemed desiccated and half dead, as if the scorching, merciless sun that beat down on this continent for so many months of the year had seared the freshness, the very life out of everything. He thought of the neat streetscapes and achingly green fields of Britain, and an impatience swept over him, an impatience to have done with this business and be gone from here.

A cart pulled by a matched pair of high-stepping grays turned down the street, drawing his attention. On the wooden seat beside a slim, dark-haired youth sat a woman. Her gown and spencer were surprisingly fashionable, and cut from what looked like an expensive blue serge. Nice, full breasts swelled noticeably above a high waist. Oliver smiled. He'd always had an eye for good horseflesh and a fine woman.

Then the woman's head swiveled around, her gaze raking the facade of the inn as the cart pulled up across the street, and Oliver Wentworth recognized his wife.

He really hadn't believed it yesterday when that man, St. John, claimed he had married her. Tumbled her and impregnated her, maybe. But married her? Oliver hadn't thought it likely.

On the off chance it was true, though, he had gone to the trouble last night of hunting up a half-dead, half-drunk lawyer who had been transported for embezzlement. Oliver had not liked what the old sot had to say.

It turned out that if Bryony had indeed remarried, then it would not be the simple matter of bigamy Oliver had at first assumed it would be. It seemed it made a difference that Bryony's first husband had been declared dead. The old fool had been too fuddled to be certain which of the two men Bryony would be considered legally married to, but he thought if the marriage had indeed taken place, then Oliver's position would be questionable, to say the least.

Now, as he watched the landlord usher Bryony into the room and shut the door behind her, Oliver felt a surge of uncertainty that bordered on alarm.

Her gown was definitely new, and probably devilishly expensive in this farflung corner of the world. She wore her heavy auburn hair twisted up into a neat coil at the top of her head and covered with a smart hat. She didn't look like a convict, or even a servant. She looked like a wealthy man's wife.

It was a complication he hadn't counted on. There were not many men who would be willing to take back a wife who had been through the kind of handling Bryony had undoubtedly been subjected to these last two years, no matter how great the inducements. Oliver had expected her to be duly appreciative and grateful, humble even. He hadn't expected her not to need or want him anymore.

He searched her face and found it at once familiar and yet . . . different. She'd always been a handsome girl, attractive enough to have made him fall in love with her even if she hadn't brought Cadgwith Cove House and its valuable acres to their marriage. But there was a new look of wisdom, a hint of great sufferings borne and overcome about her lovely brown eyes, a more pronounced strength about her mouth and chin.

"Oliver," she said. She was watching him warily, he realized, and he cursed himself for a clumsy fool. He'd obviously frightened her yesterday, and he warned himself to be more careful. She'd always been an independent-thinking woman, difficult to manage. He couldn't afford to turn her against him.

He held out both hands and gave her his most

charming smile. "Bryony." After a minute's hesitation, she came to him, placing her hands in his. He was wise enough not to press for anything more. He simply squeezed her hands, then let her go. "Would you like something to drink?" he asked, turning away.

"No, thank you." She pulled off her gloves in quick, jerky motions. "But please, go ahead if you'd like."

"If you don't mind." He picked up a decanter of Madeira. The distant sound of men's voices and laughter carried from the public rooms down the hall. But except for the liquid swirl of the wine filling the glass, the private parlor was uncomfortably silent. He glanced up and found her watching him. "I am glad you came," he said, picking up his glass. "I wanted to talk to you alone, but I wasn't quite certain how to arrange it."

She gripped her hands together before her and said, "Oliver, I have come to tell you that I do not wish to be your wife anymore."

For a moment he froze, his wine raised halfway to his lips. He forced himself to take a sip and swallow.

"I am grateful that you came out here to find me, that you did everything that was necessary to free me. But too many things have happened, Oliver. Too many things have changed. I cannot go back."

He set his glass down on the table with a snap, feeling a rush of annoyance that he had to fight to keep from coming out as raw fury. "I realize it has been a shock for you, Bryony, thinking I'm dead all these months, only to discover I'm alive. But with time, especially once we get back to Britain, you'll—"

She shook her head. "Oliver, I am not going back. Don't you understand? I've made a new life for myself here. The person I was before . . . she doesn't exist anymore."

He sucked in a deep breath, trying to calm himself, trying to get a grip on the situation. "You're still angry with me." He turned toward the window, his fingers playing nervously with the chain of his fob. "About Flory Dickens. I can explain—"

"Can you? Why don't you try explaining instead why you stayed with those smugglers for so long?"

He swung back around in surprise. "Smugglers? Who said anything about smugglers?"

"What did you expect me to think? That you were picked up by a French naval ship that just happened to take advantage of a dark, moonless night to slip into Cadgwith Cove and have a look around?"

Her nostrils fairly flared with her scorn. Christ. She had always been a bit of a shrew, but the past two years had definitely not improved her. "So what would you have had me do?" he asked sardonically. "Drown, rather than consort with such an unsavory group of rescuers?"

"You didn't need to stay with them!"

"Oh, I didn't, did I?" He took an angry step toward her. "Well, let me tell you, smuggling has become a damned lucrative business since Napoleon imposed his so-called blockade. You know the kind of debt I was in."

"I *didn't* know. But I certainly found out, didn't I? Did it never occur to you to wonder about what was happening to your family while you were off in France recouping your fortunes?"

He pursed his lips and blew out his breath in a long sigh. "I had no way of knowing you had been charged with my death, Bryony."

"You bloody well knew you had left nothing but debts behind you! Cadgwith Cove House was seized and sold before I was even brought to trial."

When had she started swearing like that? He couldn't remember ever having heard Bryony say anything more violent than "heavens." "It probably would have been seized anyway." He raised his glass and downed its contents with one flick of his wrist. "If I hadn't gone over that cliff, like as not I'd have ended up in debtors' prison. I was all rolled up, Bryony. At a standstill. All to pieces.

Besides," he added, reaching to pour himself another drink, "I knew that with me out of the way, your Uncle Edward would take care of you."

"Uncle Edward? My Uncle Edward hasn't talked to me since I ran away to marry you. The only time I saw him was the day he came to the prison to take Madeline from me."

He didn't like to think about her and Madeline in prison. But there was no reason for her to look at him as if it were all his fault, because it wasn't. She was always trying to make him feel guilty for things that weren't his fault. He felt a spurt of self-righteous anger, and slammed the decanter back down. "I didn't know you were being transported, damn it, so don't make it sound as if I should have done something to stop it."

She looked at him with a queer expression on her face. "I was eight months pregnant with your child when I was put on the *Indispensable*, Oliver."

He stared at her and swallowed hard, unable to speak.

"It was a boy, Oliver. You had a son. I named him Philip, after your father. He had dark hair, like me, but the most laughing gray eyes you'd ever want to see. He was such a sweet baby, even though he was never really well, even though he lived only . . ." Her voice cracked, and she had to suck in a shuddering breath before she could continue. "Even though he lived only five months. How much thought did you give to him, Oliver? How much thought did you give to any of us, while you were running your French brandy and tumbling your French whores?"

"Bryony . . . I'm sorry. But it wasn't my fault."

He would have taken her in his arms, but she wrenched away from him. "Whose fault was it, then? *Whose?*"

"Well, it was your fault, for starters, damn it! You're the one who knocked me off that bloody cliff. All right! Maybe I should have made more of an effort to find out what was happening to you. Maybe I should have come back sooner. But did you ever ask yourself why I didn't?

You've always been so bloody quick to criticize me as a husband. Did you ever stop to think about what kind of a wife you make? Look at you," he said, his eyes sweeping over her. "I came rushing out here, expecting to save you from some kind of hell. Well, you don't look like you've been in hell, Bryony. You don't look like you've had such a bad time of it at all."

"I have been through the worst kind of hell."

"What?" he jeered. "Are you trying to tell me you haven't enjoyed being Hayden St. John's whore?"

Her head jerked as if he'd slapped her. "Hayden St. John is my husband."

"No." He seized her by the shoulders. "He is not your husband, damn it. I am."

He saw the fear and anger in her eyes and cursed himself for being so quick-tempered. "Oh Jesus, Bryony, I'm sorry." He tried again to pull her into his arms. "You don't know how it has torn me up inside, thinking about what you've been through these last two years. I know you think I'm a selfish, heedless bastard, but I . . . I love you so much. I know we fight, and you make me as mad as hell at you, and sometimes I don't even want to be around you. But I *love* you, Bryony. You're all I have. I'm nothing without you; you know that. You're more to me than just my wife. I can't lose you and survive it. I can't. And I am so afraid I have lost you."

She held herself aloof, but he saw a worried frown line form between her brows. "Oliver, please try to understand. Whatever we once had, it is gone. You—" She broke off, her head turning toward the street.

Oliver heard it, too. The quick *thump-thump* of small feet pounding across the veranda. A young man's harassed voice, calling, "Come back here, you little—"

The outside door burst open, and Madeline hurtled into the room. She was wearing a pale blue muslin gown covered with a pinafore that once might have been white but was now dirty and crumpled and decorated with what looked suspiciously like hay.

The dark youth hard on her heels stopped short at the threshold. "I'm that sorry, Bryony. She musta hid herself in the back of the cart before we left Jindabyne and waited till my back was turned to climb out. I didn't see her till she was already on the veranda."

"It's all right, Quincy," Bryony said, her worried gaze on the child. "Leave her."

The youth cast Bryony a sharp look, then left.

Madeline stood stiffly just inside the door, her chest heaving, her eyes narrowing as she stared at Oliver. "Is it true? Are you my papa?"

Oliver raised his brows in mock astonishment. "Can this be Madeline?" He walked over and squatted beside the child to bring himself down to her level. "Why, you've grown so big." He cupped her square chin with his palm. "And so pretty."

In his experience no female from two to ninety-two could resist a compliment and an admiring smile. Madeline giggled. But the delight faded quickly from her face, and she threw an angry, accusatory glare at her mother. "They told me my mama killed you."

He heard Bryony gasp. "Well, now," he said slowly, feeling his way carefully. "Your mama did hurt me pretty badly. So badly, in fact, that it was a while before I was well enough to come after you. But I am here now."

Oliver caught her just in time to keep her from flinging her dirty arms around his neck and ruining his new coat. "You won't go away and leave us again, will you, Papa? Say you'll never leave us again."

"I'll never go away and leave you again, darling." Over the little girl's head, his eyes sought Bryony's. "You are my daughter." The words might have been said to Madeline, but they were really directed at the child's mother. "No one has the right to take you away from me. You and I are going home, to Cornwall."

Oliver watched the color drain from Bryony's cheeks as the full meaning of his words hit her. Whatever the legalities of Bryony's marriage or remarriage, Oliver was still Madeline's father and, as her father, his authority remained absolute. If he wanted to take the child back to Cornwall with him, then there was nothing Bryony could do to stop him. Bryony would either have to come, too, or lose her daughter forever.

The last two years might have changed Bryony, but Oliver knew nothing could ever have changed Bryony that much. It didn't matter how much she might imagine herself in love with Hayden St. John. She would never allow Madeline to be taken from her again.

He almost laughed out loud. He had won. And he hadn't even needed to tell her about Uncle Edward's money.

CHAPTER
TWENTY-EIGHT

Bryony turned to Madeline. "Wait outside on the veranda, please."

"But—"

"Just do as you are told," said Bryony sharply, far more sharply than she'd meant to.

The child dragged reluctantly to the door. She depressed the latch slowly, then paused to throw a dirty look at her mother over her shoulder before she slipped outside.

Bryony spun around to face Oliver. "Why did you do that?"

He picked up his empty glass and carried it back to the tray. "Do what?"

"Promise to take her home, to stay with her. You know it is not going to happen."

"But it is going to happen." He picked up the Madeira and eased out the stopper. "You can stay here with your new husband if you like. But Madeline is going back to Cornwall with me."

A fierce pain stabbed Bryony's chest, a pain she recognized as bone-chilling, mind-numbing fear. "But . . . why?"

"Why?" He sloshed more wine into his glass. "Madeline is my daughter." He picked up the glass and pivoted around to face her. "My only surviving child. Of course I want to keep her with me."

Hatred welled up within Bryony, so raw and murderous that it almost choked her. "Don't bother." She slashed the air in front of her with her hand, as if to wipe away his words. "You forget, Oliver, I know you. I still remember the time you told me that while you *liked* Madeline well enough, your affection for her was what you called a vague, general thing. It didn't specifically require her constant presence."

He sipped his wine slowly. "Did I say that?"

"Yes!"

"Perhaps I've changed."

"You've changed, all right. But not in that way." She looked at him through narrowed eyes. "Why do you want me back so badly? What could possibly be so important to you that you would use the threat of taking Madeline away from me to get it?"

He drained his glass and turned away to refill it. "You mistake, my dear. It is Madeline I want, not you. I am simply generous enough to tell you that you can come along, too, if you like."

An ugly, pounding silence descended on the room. "It's money, isn't it?" said Bryony.

He paused in the act of pouring himself another drink, the decanter suspended in the air.

"My God," she cried. "I was right! It is money. But what—how—"

He laughed softly and set the wine aside. "All right." He turned around to face her, the glass cradled in his palm. "I'll tell you. Why not? It's Uncle Edward."

Bryony frowned. "Uncle Edward?"

"He's dead. In a house fire, in London. Along with his dearly beloved wife, Eunice, and his only son and heir." Oliver leaned back against the table. "Quite tragic."

Bryony stared at him. "Richard, as well?" She had never been close to her cousin, but the idea of him dead was unsettling. She shook her head, confused. "What do you think, then? That Uncle Edward left all his money to me? That's ridiculous. He said I was dead to him."

"And so you were." Oliver took a slow sip of his wine. "It is Madeline who inherited everything."

Bryony gaped at him, too stunned for a moment even to react. "So that's why you want her—why you pretended to want me? For the *money*?"

"Crudely put, but essentially accurate."

"Take it."

He straightened up, the smile wiped off his lips. *"What?"*

"You heard me. Take the money. You can have it. Just go away and leave us in peace."

His lips curled back in a parody of a smile. "Very generous of you, my dear. Unfortunately, the money is not yours to give. It is Madeline's."

Bryony felt as if something were squeezing her chest, making it increasingly difficult for her to draw breath. "I will not let you take her," she said in a low, fierce voice.

"I am afraid you don't have much of a choice. You can come back to Cornwall with us. Or you can stay here with your new husband . . . and say good-bye to the child forever."

Neither of them heard the door to the veranda quietly open, or saw Madeline standing, wide-eyed, in the narrow gap, watching them.

Bryony stared at Oliver as if she were seeing him—really seeing him—for the first time. "I can't believe I was ever such a fool as to imagine myself in love with you," she said, her chin held high, every muscle in her body tight with revulsion. "I would rather go back to being a *convict* than ever be your wife again."

She saw his arm raise, and drew back. But she wasn't fast enough. His hand caught her high on her cheekbone.

The boy slouched on the cart seat, his cabbage palm hat pulled low over his face.

"Quincy." Hayden's voice was pitched low, but it was only about three feet away from the boy's ear. Quincy's head shot up. His startled brown eyes met Hayden's narrow, angry ones, and he gulped.

"I ought to peel the hide off your back for this stunt," Hayden said, steadying his big bay gelding beside the cart. "Except I know you were only doing what she asked you to do. Where is she?"

Quincy jerked his head toward the hotel. "With that husband of hers. She had some idea that maybe she could talk him into just goin' away and leavin' her alone."

A sudden cry brought both men around. A small, golden-haired girl erupted out of one of the hotel rooms. She sped across the veranda and leapt down into the muddy street, narrowly missing being crushed beneath the trampling hooves of a wagon team that shied at the sight of her.

"Madeline!"

Hayden heard Bryony's scream even as he spurred his horse down the street. He scooped the kicking, crying child up into his arms, then rode back to the cart and dumped her in Quincy's lap. "Here, hold on to her."

He wheeled his horse around to find Bryony standing at the edge of the veranda, staring at him. She had her hands twisted together in her skirt, hugging her pregnant belly. A haunted look shadowed her eyes. He was mad as hell at her for coming into town like this, and he didn't doubt for a minute that his fury showed on his face. But nothing, not even Madeline's brush with the wagon, could explain that expression of shock and torment.

He swung out of the saddle and looped his reins several times around the veranda post. His spurs rasped against the stone as he stepped up onto the flagging. When he approached her, Bryony quickly turned her face to one side, as if she were afraid to meet his eyes, or as if—

His hand shot out, gripping her chin and jerking her head around. Her left cheek was swollen and already beginning to discolor.

He clamped his jaws together. "Wentworth did this to

you? Did he?" Hayden demanded again, harshly, when she refused to answer.

"Kindly remove your hands from my wife," said Wentworth.

Hayden turned slowly to find the younger man lounging against the open door, an ivory-handled malacca cane sliding back and forth between his long, slim fingers. Hayden's hand closed over Bryony's arm, moving her behind him. "I thought we went through all this yesterday," he said.

"That was yesterday. Today the lady has changed her mind."

Hayden swung back around, his angry gaze raking Bryony's pale, beautiful face. "Tell me he's lying."

The eyes she lifted to him were full of pain and longing. Hayden felt a cold ball of fear settle in his stomach. "He . . ." She swallowed hard. "If I don't go with him, he'll take Madeline away from me."

Hayden filled his lungs, then expelled all the air in one, sharp word. *"Why?"*

She pushed a stray lock of hair out of her face with a shaky hand. "Uncle Edward is dead. He left all of his money to Madeline."

Hayden speared Wentworth with a contemptuous stare. "You would take a child away from her mother for *money?*"

Wentworth's hands stopped their repetitive journey up and down his cane. "Madeline is my daughter, too. Remember?"

Hayden had to tighten his own hands into fists to keep from wrapping them around the bastard's neck. "All right, what's your price?"

Wentworth raised his eyebrows as if insulted. "I beg your pardon?"

"You know what I mean. I'll buy you off. How much will it take?"

A mocking smile curved the other man's lips. "More than you have."

The two men's gazes caught, and held.

Hayden glanced at Bryony. "Take Madeline and wait for me inside the hotel. I won't—" He saw Bryony's eyes widen, her lips part in alarm, and whirled around just in time to see Wentworth, his fist gripping the handle of a long, deadly dagger Hayden realized must have been concealed in the shaft of the cane, lunge at him.

Hayden fell back, grabbing Wentworth's coat and letting the momentum of the other man's own attack carry him up and over in a throw that sent him somersaulting down the embankment, toward the river.

Tearing off his coat and tossing it to one side, Hayden plunged down the steep hill after him. Wentworth must have lost his knife somewhere in the long grass of the riverbank. He came up from a crouch to smash his fist into Hayden's face.

Hayden's head snapped back. He staggered, then bent forward and plowed into Wentworth's stomach, carrying him backward and down into the river. The two men rolled together, over and over, through the shallow water.

A rumble, oddly reminiscent of a mighty drumroll, vibrated the air and shook the earth beneath them. Hayden saw Wentworth's head jerk around to stare up the valley, but it was still a moment or two before Hayden realized what the sound was.

And then he knew. It was the thunderous roar of a wall of water, sweeping down the river from somewhere high in the mountains.

The floodwaters crashed down the valley, thick with silt, choked with debris. Giant, uprooted trees, piles of branches and trash, dead cattle and sheep were caught up in a raging mass that surged down the river, obliterating everything in its path.

Standing on the veranda, Bryony watched, horror-stricken, as the foam-flecked brown hand of death swooped down on the two men, now locked together and rolling over and over in the shallows of the river beside the jetty.

"Hayden!"

She ran to the edge of the steep embankment, then stopped, helpless, the cold air sawing in and out of her lungs, her hands cupping her unborn child.

Both men seemed to become aware of the danger at the same time. Breaking apart, they scrambled up the steep, grassy slopes of the bank. Hayden had almost reached the top when Oliver's feet shot out from under him. He went down hard, sliding on his stomach back toward the water as he desperately clutched at clumps of weeds and brush, trying to stop himself.

She saw Hayden hesitate, then turn back. "Here, take my hand," he called, his arm outstretched as he slipped back down toward the fallen man.

"Go to hell," Oliver spat. Ignoring Hayden's hand, he staggered up onto his feet, only to go down again.

"Don't be a fool," said Hayden, glancing up river. "There is no time. Take my hand."

The river bore down on them with ferocious speed. Bryony's mouth opened in a wail of terror and despair as the rushing water slammed into the gray, worn planks of the jetty, then crashed over it, obliterating it. With a fearsome, tearing crack, the entire structure exploded as if it had been struck by an artillery shell. Broken timbers rained down from the sky, to be swept up and carried along with the raging torrent.

Where the two men had been there was now only boiling brown water.

"Hayden." Bryony's scream echoed back at her from across the raging brown river. Her legs buckled beneath her, and she sank to her knees in the grass. She felt the warmth of the sun shining down on her bowed shoulders, heard the clear, sweet song of some bird, calling in the distance.

She was only vaguely aware of Quincy beside her,

Madeline clutching at his neck. Suddenly Quincy flung out an arm and shouted, "There he is!"

Hope seized Bryony, squeezed her chest, stopping her breath. Several of the pilings from the jetty and the steps still stood, thrusting up like monoliths from out of the swirling water. And clinging to one of them, his dark hair plastered against his head, was Hayden.

She realized there were other people milling about. There were shouts of "Get a rope!" and "Here, tie that end to the post." A loop went sailing through the air. She saw Hayden's hand snake out, catch it. But the water was still rising fast, the current swift and deadly.

She saw him let go of the piling, and held her breath as the rope stretched taut. The water caught at him, tried to tear him away. He slipped and slid, working his way up the steep, submerged bank, only to lose his footing completely and crash back into the water. The swirling cauldron closed over his head, and Bryony screamed.

"No!" She lunged forward, but Quincy snagged her arm, holding her fast. She saw Hayden stagger up onto his feet again, saw that he had somehow managed to tie the rope around his waist. She felt a great ache in her chest and realized she'd forgotten to breathe. She sucked in a deep draft of air, unable to hope, unable not to hope . . .

"Aw, hell," Quincy whispered.

Bryony realized he was staring upriver. She tore her gaze from Hayden's slow but steady passage back toward the shore long enough to cast one swift glance toward the mountains.

And saw another, deadly surge of floodwaters crashing down on them.

"God, no!" she screamed.

The second wall of water hit when Hayden was still only halfway up the bank. She saw him stumble to his knees. Hands reached out to haul in the rope, to grab him.

Somehow he managed to stagger back up onto his feet and splash to the edges of the swirling, sucking morass.

"Hayden." Bryony surged forward to throw her arms around him. She felt cold water seep into her shoes, soak her skirt to the knees. "Oh, thank God," she whispered, over and over again. She cradled his wet cheeks between her trembling hands, kissed his eyes, his mouth.

Then a sudden, hideous thought struck her. She whirled back toward the river, but saw only heaving, white-crested waves sweeping on down the river and out of sight.

Oliver had disappeared.

She refused to believe he was dead.

Once before Bryony had thought Oliver lost to a watery grave, and yet he had somehow managed to survive. This time she would not believe he was dead until she saw his body.

The floodwaters surged for three days, rising over the high banks of the river, spreading out over farmlands and settlements, carrying away livestock and buildings and the odd, unlucky colonist. But by the fourth day, the worst had passed.

From Barrenjoey to the Long Reef, the beaches were strewn with the flotsam of the attempts of transplanted Englishmen and women to build themselves a new life on the banks of a river they had not yet come to understand. Dead pigs and cattle, bedsteads and smashed window frames, lay entangled with piles of hay and sodden corn and twisted, muddied lengths of wool and muslin. In places the debris was piled so high one couldn't even see the sand, and the poor and the dispossessed came from miles around to search through it and salvage what they could.

Thus it was that they found the body of the man with the guinea-gold hair, the man whose wife had refused to believe he was dead until she had seen his body. They wrapped him in a muddy tarp and carried him back up the river to her, so that she might bury him in the small cemetery high on the hill above Hayden St. John's house.

Next to the grave of Hayden St. John's first wife, Laura.

EPILOGUE

March, 1811

The wind danced slow and easy through the dry leaves of the gum trees down by the river. It was a temperate wind, swinging up from the south. A wind that whispered of soft rains and shortening days and the bonfires of autumn to come.

Bryony set aside her trowel and rose to her feet. Sighing with contentment, she lifted her face to the breeze and let it cool her damp forehead and cheeks. The summer had been hot and long, but the harvest had been good. Life had been good.

A gurgle of laughter at her feet made her look down and smile. Miss Sophie St. John, a year old now and already steady on her feet, toddled over to where her half brother and half sister sat in the newly turned earth of the garden bed.

"Want a mud pie?" Madeline offered, holding out a tin plate heaped high with a squishy brown concoction.

"Mud," repeated Sophie, reaching out with one chubby fist.

Madeline's head fell back, a delighted smile creasing her cheeks. "She said 'mud.' Did you hear her, Mama? She said mud!"

Bryony stared at her daughter, feeling anew the sheer delight of having Madeline beside her. Never again, she swore, would she take the simple things in life for granted. All were too precious. And far too easily lost.

Madeline's smile was as bright as the summer sun. There had been a time, especially in the dark weeks after Oliver's death, when Bryony had feared the child might never recover from what she had been through. But that blank look she had worn in the first months after her arrival in New South Wales had eventually faded, to be replaced by the ready laughter and hushed wonder of the child Bryony remembered from the days at Cadgwith Cove.

"Mud," said Sophie again, or what sounded like mud.

Bryony started. "Oh, my goodness—"

She made a grab for the baby, but Sophie was too quick. Her hand closed over Madeline's proffered mud pie and brought up a fistful to smear it liberally over her cheeks and mouth.

Bryony scooped the baby up in her arms. "We don't eat the mud pies, darling," chuckled Bryony, using the edge of her apron in an attempt to wipe off the worst of the muck. "Nor do we wear them."

Simon's gleeful laughter floated up, to be carried along with Madeline's giggles toward the house. The sound of hammering filled the air, blending with the children's laughter and the bleating of the sheep on the hillside and the raucous cawing of the flock of cockatoos passing overhead. The homestead had acquired a second story the previous winter, and now Hayden had decided to add a northern wing. The new brick walls were already higher than Simon's head.

One of the hammers stopped swinging, and a man came out onto the veranda. A tall man with broad shoulders, lean hips, and long legs. Bryony smiled, a glow of happiness and love warming her heart at the sight of her husband. She had married him all over again, just to be sure he really *was* her husband.

She watched him step down onto the garden path. Hot, golden sunlight glanced along his sharp, high cheekbones. Gravel crunched beneath his boot heels as he strolled toward them. His deep blue eyes narrowed with silent amusement when he caught sight of Sophie's face.

"What's this?" he asked, reaching out with his thumb to swipe at some of the mud Bryony had missed. "You look like a beggar brat."

"What's a beggar?" asked Simon, squinting up at his father.

"A beggar is someone who is poor and has no money," answered Bryony.

"We're not beggars, are we?" asked Madeline. She stood up and dusted her seat with hands that were dirtier than her dress. "Quincy says I'm a rich woman—richer even than Papa." She stared up Hayden. "Is it true, Papa? Am I rich?"

Hayden's amused gaze caught Bryony's and held it. "Rich?" He grinned. "You're not just rich. You're very rich." He reached down to swing Madeline—grubby hands and dirty dress and all—up into his arms. "Do you remember Peyton Hall?"

Madeline wrapped her arms around Hayden's neck and hugged him close. "No," she said. But Bryony saw the shadows that darkened her brown eyes and the barely perceptible tightening of her mouth, and knew the child remembered something.

"Well, it's a great big house that belongs to you now. In a place called Cornwall. You were born in Cornwall, you know. One of these days we'll go there for a visit and see it."

"Really?" breathed Simon, his emerald-green eyes growing round with the wonder of it. "Will we go on the *Laura*?"

"Yes." Hayden glanced thoughtfully at Bryony. "When your mother is ready."

Bryony shifted Sophie to her hip and swiveled to look down at the river. It was low now, and sluggish after the dry months of summer. She remembered that afternoon, long ago, when the sun had shown golden and hot, and the water had flowed placid and peaceful, and Louisa had told her of the floods that could swell the river until it reached halfway up to the house.

"There's Sean!" shouted Simon, surging to his feet and pointing toward the yard. "Come on, Madeline." Hand in hand they ran, leaving Sophie to fuss and wriggle until Bryony put her down. The baby tottered off toward the shovels and plates abandoned by her siblings, and happily plopped down on her bottom in the dirt. Bryony watched the child warily, but she didn't seem inclined to repeat her mud-eating experiment.

Hayden came up behind her, his arm slipping around her waist to draw her back against the long, hard line of his body. They held each other in silence for a time, her hands wrapped around his strong arm, her head tipped back against his shoulder. She felt the solid heat of his palm lying against her waist, heard the gentle swish of the river sliding past, flowing slowly but inevitably toward the sea. A deep, quiet sense of peace filled her. "I remember reading something one time . . . something that compared fate to a current, sweeping us all on to our destinies."

He ran his hands in a slow caress up her sides, turning her in his arms to face him. "Is that what you believe?" he asked, his eyes narrowing as he studied her expression.

She considered a moment, then shook her head. "No." She touched the tips of her fingers to his tanned cheek, marveling again at the simple things in life. Such as the laugh of a child. The beauty of a heat-hazed afternoon. The love of a good man. The simple things that made life worthwhile. "I think fate is more like a tide. Something that ebbs and flows. Something we can miss or catch. Something that can save us." She paused. "Or destroy us."

The freshening breeze brought her the heavy scent of freshly cut hay and the warm, musky smell of turned earth. A sudden gust caught at her hair, blew it across her face. Hayden snagged his fingers in the loose strands, drawing them back behind her head. "You saved me," he said in a soft, throaty voice. His thumb rubbed back and forth across the angle of her cheekbone. "With your courage, and your strength, and your love. I'm glad . . ."

His voice trailed off as he swiveled his head to stare out over the silver band of the river winding down through the valley. A lone sulfur-crested cockatoo lifted from a nearby red gum, its heavy wings beating the sultry air and flashing like white sails against the hot blue sky.

"Why are you glad, Hayden?" she asked gently.

He brought his gaze back to hers. She saw the love that shone in the depths of his blue eyes and the contentment that lifted the corners of his mouth into a teasing smile. "I'm glad fate brought you to me."

She laughed, and he caught her laugh with his kiss.

HISTORICAL
NOTE

Until the late eighteenth century, Britain transported its convicted felons to the colonies of the New World. When the American Revolution eliminated that convenient outlet, British jails soon became so overcrowded that the government decided to establish a new colony, a penal colony, at a place called Botany Bay.

Botany Bay had been explored in 1770 by Captain James Cook during his famous voyage, but when the First Fleet arrived there in 1788, they decided it was not a suitable site for a colony and moved their settlement some miles up the coast to a small cove in Port Jackson that they named Sydney. Although the first settlement in what was known at the time as New South Wales was actually at Sydney, the name "Botany Bay" continued to be applied, which is why Bryony's lawyer told her she was likely to be transported to Botany Bay, when her actual destination was Sydney.

When Captain Matthew Flinders circumnavigated the southern continent in 1803, he referred to it as "terra australis." After that the name "Australia" gradually came into usage, particularly after the arrival of Governor Macquarie in 1810. Thus it is not a complete anachronism to have Bryony occasionally use the term in 1808–9. Besides, "the wide New South Wales sky" just doesn't sound right.

Because this is a novel rather than a history, I have allowed myself some laxity in geography and chronology. There was no homestead called Jindabyne, set high on its

hill overlooking the Hawkesbury River, although a town
of that name can be found in the Blue Mountains. No
ship carrying a cargo of women prisoners arrived in New
South Wales in September 1808, so I have sent Bryony
on the *Indispensable*, which did make several such trips
around the turn of the century.

The history of the colony in the years 1808–9 was a
turbulent one. In January 1808, the New South Wales
Corps revolted against the then Governor William Bligh
(yes, the same Captain Bligh who suffered through the
mutiny on the *Bounty*) in a sordid but colorful incident
known as the Rum Rebellion. The political events that
followed were highly involved and beyond the scope of
this tale, so I have simplified them. The heinous Foveaux
was indeed acting governor when Bryony first arrived at
the colony in 1808, although he was not in residence at
Government House at that time. Because of the rebellion,
some important figures from the early years of the colony
were actually absent at this time, but I have taken the lib-
erty of keeping them there.

Several scenes in this story were inspired by events
that actually occurred. There were two floods on the
Hawkesbury in 1809, one in May, the second in August.
The destruction and loss of life were severe. The tale of
the sentry given eight hundred lashes for falling asleep
is real, as is the story about the officer court-martialed
for marrying his convict mistress. Other incidents, such
as the sad tale of the bark-covered graves, the lost
child found clutching a bouquet of wildflowers, and
Bryony's brush with the dogs, were inspired by events
that took place in other parts of Australia, in other times.
Because the Aboriginal peoples who originally inhabited
the Hawkesbury died out so early, little is known of their
language, which is why the Aboriginal people in this tale
speak with a distinct South Australian accent.

The arrival of the new governor, Macquarie, in January 1810 brought many changes in New South Wales. He
improved the roads, embarked on an ambitious building

program (with the aid of a talented transported architect named Greenway), and eliminated rum as the colony's unique form of currency. Highly disturbed by the state of moral laxity in which he found the colony, he published proclamations in the newspapers against the pernicious local practice of "living in sin" and encouraged (vigorously) those involved in "irregular unions" to regularize them. Thus, the former Major George Johnston, who had taken the convict woman Hetty Abrahams as his mistress when they met on the *First Fleet*, finally married her in 1814—after more than half-a-dozen children and some twenty-five years of living together.

Governor Macquarie also went out of his way to encourage the "emancipists," as the ex-convicts were called, much to the fury of the so-called "exclusives," who were free of the criminal taint and therefore considered themselves superior. The new governor even went so far as to invite ex-convicts to dinner at Government House. One can imagine that Bryony St. John was one of them.